Burnt Umber

Burnt Umber

A Novel
By

Sheldon Greene

Leapfrog Press
Wellfleet, Massachusetts

Published in 2001 in the United States by
The Leapfrog Press
P.O. Box 1495 95 Commercial Street
Wellfleet, MA 02667-1495, USA
www.leapfrogpress.com

Distributed in the United States by
Consortium Book Sales and Distribution
St. Paul, Minnesota 55114

First Edition

The characters and events in this book are fictitious.
Any similarity to actual persons, living or dead,
is coincidental and not intended by the author.

Library of Congress Cataloging-in-Publication Data

Greene, Sheldon.
    Burnt umber : a novel / by Sheldon Greene.—1st ed.
      p. cm.
    ISBN 0-9679520-1-8
      1. Americans—France—Fiction. 2. Marc, Franz, 1880-1916—
Notebooks, sketchbooks, etc.—Fiction. 3. World War, 1914-1918—
Fiction. 4. World War, 1939-1945—Fiction. 5. Berkeley (Calif.)—
Fiction. 6. Paris (France)—Fiction. 7. Sculptors—Fiction. 8. Paint-
ers—Fiction. I. Title.

    PS3557.R3875 B87 2001
    813'.54—dc21

                                                    00-065542

            10 9 8 7 6 5 4 3 2 1

            Printed in Canada

To Judy and Talia

Author's Note

Franz Marc was born in Munich, Germany in 1880. Along with his more famous friend, the painter Kandinsky, he founded *Der Blaue Reiter* (The Blue Rider) group. Like their contemporaries, Nietzche, Wagner, Jung, and Freud, the two artists were striving to destroy the conventions of the past and invent new ways of perceiving the  world for the Twentieth Century. Paul Klee later joined the group.

Marc used elegantly drawn animals as abstract symbols set in brilliant color fields and planes suggesting landscapes. As the First World War approached, the content of his work became more ominous and explosive. He joined the Kaiser's army believing that the ensuing apocalypse would give birth to a new world order. Better known in Europe than the United States, his work can be found in virtually every major museum collection in the world.

 American print maker and sculptor Harold Paris, the artistic source of Harry Baer, served in Europe in World War II. After the war he studied and worked in New York, Paris, Madrid, and Munich. Most of his creative output was produced in the San Francisco Bay area. He taught art at the University of California, Berkeley campus during the Viet Nam era. Paris worked in many materials exploiting their unique qualities, including clay, bronze, plexi-glass, vacuum formed vinyl, silicon gel, hand made paper, and video. He constructed room-sized sculptures which could be entered and experienced, and life-sized ceramic walls from which ambiguous forms emerged. His work is abstract yet suggestive, always inviting dialogue with the viewer. The Holocaust and Viet Nam were recurring thematic sources. A *Time Magazine* reviewer wrote of his silicon soft souls in 1972: "Memory and touch, a poignant archeology of the self: at its best, Paris's work is pure magic." Paris's works are in many major museum collections.

Burnt Umber

1

Harry Baer, 1945, Europe

January 1, 1945 – Near St. Vith, France

The vaulted roof of the basement might have been Roman by its shape and the look of the long thin bricks. A dusty spear of light from a single broken ground level window gave the chamber no further definition—it might have had no walls at all. Harry dropped to the damp stone floor, propped his carbine against a trunk and slumped forward, wrapping his cold arms around his legs below the knee. His eyelids, heavy as lead, kept falling shut and he fell into that numb state between sleep and waking only to start at the shock of a shell exploding nearby and the percussive vibration as the building absorbed it.

He had been without sleep for two wearing days and nights that had mutilated time, anesthetized fear, washed out every emotion save the will to get through it. Red and Jonas were dead, both shot in the back as they had run from a sudden German tank and infantry assault. Their crude talk, their tense bickering would have been welcome now. All he had between him and three German tanks were 42 bullets, two ruined stories of an abandoned farm house and eventual darkness that might enable him to cross the flat fields of stubble to where, he hoped, his company had redeployed. For now he could rest and hope that a shell didn't bring the roof down on him or that the Germans didn't decide to take the farmhouse before dark.

Harry stretched, felt the aching weariness in his arms and realized that he hadn't eaten since morning. He tore open a ration, a block resembling chocolate, took a listless bite, chewed and let his eyes probe the twilight focussing at random on objects cast off by the family. There was a high wheeled baby carriage, dusty and neglected; a floor lamp with a moldy silk shade; and stacks of French magazines. He imagined a woman, overweight, bending down to pick up an infant; a farmer wearing a clean blue work shirt, sitting comfortably in the canopy of light from the lamp reading about his favorite soccer team.

Harry leaned back and the hasp on the trunk cut into his back. He turned to examine the lock. The hasp sprung open at his touch and he raised the lid. Something ephemeral escaped with the smell of mildew and flew around him like an agitated bat. The inside of the trunk might have been an old room, abandoned, shut off in an unused part of a house. Floral wallpaper stained brown, foxed with mildew, faded pink roses, forget-me-nots and violets in a spiral. It was empty or nearly so, except for a few ironic mementos of another war. A pair of blue woolen pants with a red stripe on the side lay under a moldy leather belt with a brass buckle, a German black leather helmet with a brass spike, now more green than golden, and a notebook, bound in brown cracked leather.

He picked the notebook up as he might handle a dead butterfly and opened the cover. It was an artist's sketch book. Another shell exploded near the house, but he ignored it as he focused on an elegant gestural drawing of a capering horse. He turned the pages, studying the crabbed precise writing; German, it seemed. The sound of gunfire became more distant.

Absorbed in the images, Harry forgot his fatigue. The lines were beautiful, sure and yet spontaneous. They called to mind master drawings he had seen in the Cleveland Museum of Art. A drawing of a dead horse held his eye. With few lines, the artist had caught the pain and the fear. With each new image the artist seemed to be striving for a reduction of detail, seeking to capture just the essence of the subject. Stressing one or more traits—line, shadow, muscle, texture, motion—the later drawings were abstract and spare as Chinese calligraphy.

The last page had nothing but an inadvertent shadowy

thumb print, little more than dirt on clean paper and a brown stain that might have been blood. He looked around realizing that it had grown almost too dark to see the images. Harry closed the notebook and put it in his pack. The firing was now even more remote. It was time to leave.

2

Franz Marc, Munich, 1909

"And so, I've been reading Rilke, soaking him up like a, like a blotter soaks up ink," Franz said between heavy breaths as he pedalled up the slope. He was sweating in his new English tweed suit and wished that they had taken the train.

"That's good."

"Do you know him?"

"I met him once, twice maybe," Kandinsky grunted and began to pedal standing up. He was blinking from sweat that had run into his eyes.

"His work I mean."

"It's good. What I've read of it."

The bicycle pedals resisted as they climbed the rise, gaining on a farm wagon half full of hay. A young girl smiled and waved from the back of the wagon. Her legs were trailing over the edge and her braided hair was the color of the hay. She was no more than fifteen Franz supposed as he tried to capture the essence of her simple spirit and etch it on a note pad in his mind. The fact that he would never see her unaffected beauty again made him a little sad. Sight of the black chevron wings of a predatory bird wheeling and soaring on the wind above his head dispelled the feeling and replaced it with envy of the freedom and perspective of flight. Finally he wondered whether the simple delight of the farm girl and the soaring of the bird were, at some abstract level, the same. He made another mental note and resolved to paint the nexus of simplicity and freedom.

Franz's front tire wobbled. Gravel crackled and spun away from its pressure and the tread made a pattern in the dust that reminded him of a design he'd seen on the edge of a plate, not long before. His heart was thumping in his throat when he finally reached the crest and the sweat was running down his chest and his sides under his arms. He would need a good wash when they arrived.

"Look at that cloud!"

"Which one, the sky is full of them. Too full. Not enough contrast." Kandinsky was thinking of a painting by Holzel which might have been done on this very crest, a landscape with heavy lumbering clouds weighing heavily on the patch-work of fields interspersed with dark stands of woodland.

"That one up there just above the lone tree, beyond the meadow."

"I see it. What about it."

"It has a wonderful shape. Do you mind if we stop a minute? I'm a bit winded from the climb."

"We'll be late. Holzel is expecting us for lunch." The trouble with Franz, Kandinsky thought, was his perpetual distraction. Not that he didn't focus, often with brilliant insights, but his mind had the pattern of a fly: aimless.

"I was ready on time. You were half an hour late." Franz was already skidding to a stop and lunging off the bicycle and easing it to the uncut grass of the berm.

Kandinsky looked impatient but stopped beside him still astride the bicycle. "I'm glad I brought a poncho. It feels like rain."

"I suppose Holzel will want us to stay the night. He is fond of you."

"And you."

"Here let me read you this and then we can get started again."

"Read me what?"

"From Rilke. We can't be more than a few kilometers from Dachau, after all."

"We could save the reading for later, Franz. I'm sure Holzel will appreciate your insights."

"But you should hear this now. It's so appropriate." The

wind brought them the distant carousel sound of a train whistle, and a bird perched on the branch of an oak seemed to answer with its own song.

Kandinski sighed, pulled at the seat of his pants while Franz fumbled in the deep pocket of his jacket and produced a thin book bound in off-white paper. A restless finger probed for the page he'd marked with a dog-ear and, clearing his throat, he read, "We transform these Things; they aren't real, they are only reflections upon the polished surface of our being." Franz looked up from the book seeking his new friend's reaction. Kandinski nodded encouragement and Franz ranged down the page searching for the next passage. "I will go to watch the animals, and let something of their composure slowly glide into my limbs; will see my own existence deep in their eyes, "

"Shall we go on?" Kandinski was already perched on the top of his right pedal and his rear tire sprayed gravel as the bicycle began to move.

"Rilke looks inside and turns things inside out."

"Save it for Holzel, Franz," said Kandinsky over his shoulder.

March 9, 1911 – Wedding Day,

Franz perceived his wedding through the distorted lens of a high fever. Colors were brighter or out of place. The rosette behind the pulpit bled fractured hues of rose, gold, deep blues; through veins of swirling dust into the indigo twilight of the church. The church, smelled of limestone and incense and roses. It was cool as a grotto but he was smothering. His stiff collar was strangling him, his dove grey vest constricting his chest. Even his shoes, rented with the formal clothes, were vises. The creased face of the minister, propped on his vestments, was porcelain. Only the eyes seemed to live and these were lit with judgmental, cold fire that contradicted the benign smile fixed on his thin lips. The sacred words that would bind them might have been in another tongue, and yet the sound was full of meaning; profound, yet unexplainable.

He couldn't see her face, only her spectral profile behind the veil adorned with small pearls. He wasn't sure who she really was under the layers of social propriety and form. An aspiration, perhaps, wrapped in silk and yellowed lace even down to the wrist, an idea of purity or was it concupiscence, or were they incompatible? Only her long fingers, clutching the black leather hymnal, were exposed carnal flesh.

The gold ring on a crimson velvet cushion was offered by a boy, her nephew, a Gainsborough in blue velvet, his head cast of plaster and painted in the Renaissance style. Franz's hand shook as he picked it up and managed to guide it on to her own trembling finger in a ritual of possession and penetration and the perpetual renewal of life.

She looked at him for the first time. Her dark blue eyes were glistening with feeling-was it fear or hope? He couldn't tell.

Throughout the reception Franz was feverish, giddy, self-conscious, awkward, spilling a glass of champagne on the parquet floor, taking a plate of cakes offered by his mother but too nervous to eat more than a forkful. He accepted the good wishes with distraction, the kind words, the searching mocking looks, Kandinski's refracted gaze that told him he had made a mistake, more good wishes, the ceremonial waltz, two dolls spinning on top of a music box, the polite distant embraces and, finally fleeting impressions across the window of a speeding train.

Wedding Night

The furniture of their spacious hotel room smelled of recent polish and showed the wear of countless occupants. How many had spent their wedding night in the room before? Franz wondered. He paced off the dimensions and stopped to glance through the gauze curtains that rippled vertically over the full length windows at the faint warm glow of other windows across the street. Now that the ceremony and reception was behind him, he was more self-possessed but still agitated with the thought that he was trapped in this room and would never escape.

He turned and looked at Antonia, his wife of a few hours, seated erect in an ornate chair. Her silk chiffon dress was simple, dove grey, trimmed in darker grey-blue silk ribbon, with round dark blue buttons shaped like roses. Her rich auburn hair was piled high on her head although a few strands had escaped and stood out over her ears. Antonia had beautiful skin, the texture of the open petal of a rose, like the roses on the brown marble top of the tea table, roses, which shaded from pink to almost peach and gave off an intense scent of lemon and spice. He studied the delicate shading of her cheek, so curiously pigmented with pale sunlight and wheat. Around the soft lines of her jaw was a faint down, like a peach. Her lips were a perfect bow, and her eyes, narrow, were almost as grey-blue as the ribbon of her dress.

Her legs were pressed together at the knees and formed a precise right angle to the floor. Grey shoes and a few inches of stocking, fine black silk, could just be seen below the fluted skirt. Franz's eye drifted from the floor to the table top. A half-finished bottle of champagne leaned on the silver edge of the ice bucket and the tall flutes had remnants of a toast. A half-eaten orange, the peel scattered around it on a blue and white china plate separated the flutes.

Antonia turned toward him with a slight frown. "Why are you pacing so, Franz. You're like a lion at the zoo." Her tone was accepting, but chiding, and the words probed and demanded like the pointed finger of a teacher. She would be his teacher, she thought, helping him to channel his expansive, random creativity as water could be made to flow from a mountain torrent through a bathroom faucet. Under his commonplace black suit, behind his slightly skewed cravat was a spoiled, undisciplined, pampered little boy who could be alternately charming, original or outrageously inappropriate. And that side of Franz fascinated her, just as she had been transfixed by her first sight of the constrained restless energy of the Bengal tiger in his cage at the Vienna Zoo. She would help him advance himself as an artist, help him with acceptance, so that one day his works would hang in the finest Viennese parlors and he would chide starchy and pretentious society with his audacious style. And they would have children, three or four, and a house in the country where they would play lawn tennis and the children would ride a pony. And the best German and Austrian minds of the day would visit and make conversation over tea in the afternoon and brandy in the long summer evenings.

"It's only that I am exhausted from the day," he finally replied in a weary half audible voice.

She looked at him and thought, it is I who should be exhausted and yet I am calm. Calm, yet apprehensive and a little choked with anticipation of the night. All those stories from Sophie, her only married friend. Antonia wanted it to be different, didn't want to be passive, just to let him have his way with her. She imagined Emma Bovary—she had just finished reading the book. It was more than a woman's duty, more than just a way of bringing children into the world. What about the Song of Songs after all? She would bring herself to him, open slowly but rapturously like a rose unfolding its petals. But who could say what she would feel. Sophie had reluctantly admitted that on her wedding night she'd been frozen like a closed vice. What would he think if she felt the same? her artist, her Bohemian who had, no doubt been with Gypsies and prostitutes. How would she compare?

Franz twisted the brass handle on the window, it released and swung open, letting in air that was both bracing and pungent with coal smoke.

"Please, close it, Franz. You know I can't stand a draft. I've told you so." She drew her shoulders together and shivered.

"Yes, yes, I had forgotten. But it's stifling."

"Hardly. I don't know how we will find a middle ground. I like a cozy room with a good fire while you seem content with no heat."

"I like fresh air. I smother without it."

"If that is our only disagreement we'll find a way. Two down quilts on the bed, perhaps."

"Yes, of course. Two feather beds," he answered, his voice flat and unconvincing, imagining himself sinking down into a deep bed, drowning in feathers, not even hearing Antonia's hum of acknowledgement if not assent. He turned from the window to see her head dip toward an open magazine.

He stood for a moment in front of the window, feeling shut off from the outside, from the world. His collar was choking him. A pillow was over his face pressing down and he couldn't breathe. His face felt hot, full of blood. "If you don't mind, darling, I will go out for a few moments to smoke a cigar. I've been dying for one. I know how you hate the smoke." He reached inside his coat pocket and found his wallet. "I'll just go down to the lobby. They must have a good selection in the buffet."

He walked toward the door almost on tiptoe, as if he were afraid of disturbing a sleeper, feeling like he was swimming through molasses, struggling to reach undefined safety.

June 9, 1911 – Eisenbahn

The boulevard in front of the hotel was choked with cabs, a cacophony of hoof and wheel sounds, the clatter of metal on cobbles, the squeal and whine of trolleys giving off a pale golden electric glow behind steamed windows and showering blue sparks.

Oscillating between oppressive guilt and hysterical elation, his lungs burning from acrid coal smoke, Franz ran through the surging crowd toward the railroad station. A thief chased by a policeman would have the same mixture of fright and relief, Franz imagined, as he dodged or jostled startled couples on their way to early supper before the opera. Every strained gesture and rigid line in his face expressed his torment and fixation. With this act he had broken with reality, at least the gloss of reality beyond which few people probed, except perhaps the thief, the murderer, the lunatic, the visionary, and he was none of those.

No, he was someone with the will and the courage to break with convention. Antonia would survive abandonment and humiliation, and she was better off without him, he rationalized. She had no idea of the rip tides that surged beneath his abstracted surface.

He arrived at the ticket window breathless and shaking, looking around him, sure that someone he knew would see him and ask questions that he couldn't explain, except to someone who was like him. These were the people he would seek out when he got to Paris. People like Rilke, for one.

He looked around furtively while the ticket seller counted the money for the fare. The clerk looked up with a nod and fingered his persimmon mustache. He was done with Franz. Franz meant no more to him than a hand taking a ticket.

Franz read the ticket to confirm that it was "Paris, First Class." It had taken nearly all of his money but he needed the comfort of the First Class compartment. Any more agitation and he might throw himself from the train into the darkness. But just the thought of suicide dispelled the impulse. He would never kill himself, not while life held the promise of temptation and surprise and the satisfaction of creation.

August 14, 1911 – Correspondence,

Dear Franz:

It has taken much time and pain, and a subordination of pride to write to you. And even now I do so as much out of the deep sense of duty and propriety that was imparted to me by my family as out of love for you. Yes, love still resides uncomfortably in a corner of my heart, hard as it is to confess it to myself, let alone to you, after what you have done. It embarrasses me to confess that love for you remains, like a once welcome guest who has stayed too long. Your cruelty, selfishness, is unspeakable. Yet, as a Christian and a wife, your wife, I can and must find in my heart the seed of forgiveness and hope that it will sprout on the soil of your creativity, and renew the relationship which brought us to the pulpit as bride and groom.

Yes, even after your outrageous and cowardly departure, without even a hint or an apology, I can still bring myself to accept you as a husband and, to my own utter surprise, feel that we have a future together, that we can find common experience, can raise children, can live a normal life. I await your letter, your explanation, and will answer with forgiveness. I have not shared this with my father. If he saw you, I suspect that his first move would be to the stables to find a horsewhip.

On the same subject, I took the liberty of visiting, on more than one occasion, with your mother and once with your father, who has always seemed to spend all of his waking hours in his office at the bank. Needless to say your

mother is distraught, humiliated, vexed by your behavior. As for your father, I got no sense of his feelings, other than a permanent flush around his Franz Josef mutton chops and his apparent agitation at having dropped a bit of cherry confiture on his cravat. He gave me the impression that he has a curtain rod for a spine and a railroad time table in place of a mind, but I confess I've never cared for him. Perhaps he . . . no point in getting into that. In contrast your mother is so gentle and kind and rather fragile. She insists that as a child you showed no sign of lunacy or even wild impetuosity. You were, in her eyes, a model child: polite, dutiful; considerate of your older sister, prior to her unfortunate illness and death from which your mother has apparently never recovered. You were always creative, she insists. She has a bursting folio of your sketches and watercolors, all dated from the age of four and on to the Gymnasium. Many of the drawings are quite lovely, especially the animals and flowers. She also showed me your beetle collection, all neatly categorized and mounted. You were quite fastidious. You might have been a biologist, like your mother's brother, Ernst. What happened to you? Were your collars too tight? metaphorically speaking. Your mother thinks that you began to manifest "odd behavior" after your sister's funeral. She told me that you ran off during the burial service and hid behind some crypt in a corner of the cemetery. Did you blame yourself for her death? Your mother believes that it was your father's insistence that you and your sister sleep with the window open in all weather, not that the air outside the window was particularly salubrious. Perhaps you harbor a deep grudge against your father for giving you too much Bible and too little affection. Your mother more than made up for it, I suspect. Please return to your senses soon.
Antonia

September 3, 1911

Dear Antonia:

Everything that you say is true and deserved, even the horsewhip. I deserve to be punished, do not deserve your forgiveness although I appreciate it. I could not bear to write after my flight. But, although I am ashamed, you must know that I don't regret what I did. I am sorry, but not regretful, if you understand the difference. You see, you married two men, not one. One was raised as you were, in duty and propriety and politeness. The other is full of barely controllable longings for self-expression, comprehension of a chaotic world, and the personal need to understand, see the inner soul of the world and life and somehow express it as an artist. That would make little sense to your father who gets knowledge from the black ink of a newspaper, and I doubt even that you could accept it in your spirit although I know you would try.

Otherwise, why would you even have wanted to be my wife, knowing that I am consumed by the desire to express the universality of experience in my work. You would have been better off with a lawyer, like my own father, who would have taken you to the opera where you would have captured the attention of all the men. You could spend your time raising money for abandoned Serbian orphans, serving tea at a literary afternoon, getting on in a conventional world. While I, in contrast, am no more than a shadow in that world.

Enough of that. I should tell you something of my present life. As the companion that you still hope to be you will be interested. I have a respectable room in a good house, not far from the Luxembourg. It is on the second floor and looks out over roofs and chimneys and other windows where I see frames of other lives. My landlady is a sweet old posie of dried lavender whose only son was killed in the Franco-Prussian war. She has taken me on as a substitute, and I must confess that I am both put off by the intrusion, and shamelessly appreciative of the attention which includes fresh croissants and cafe au lait in a bowl, with jam made by a sister in Langedoque-an older sister no less. In return, I do little errands for her, the post office, the repair of a chair leg. I hope you are not jealous, thinking that we two could have, can have, this life as well and more. I understand that, but the difference is that Mme. Cozet makes no other demands on me and I am free, utterly free.

How do I spend this freedom? Some of the time with other artists, recognized and would be. We talk, we criticize each other's work. There are many galleries and exhibits here, as you might imagine. I have been celibate, living like a priest. In that regard I have remained faithful to our marriage, if only in that. I have also spent time drawing in the studio of a well recognized artist, though one who is controversial and not accepted by the so called art establishment which for me is the best credential he could have. I am working, 12, often 16 hours a day, drawing, painting, thinking, reading, absorbing, throwing things away, looking for the new.

If you will be patient, perhaps we can make a life together. Just saying that is cruel of me, cruel to tantalize you with a promise that may never be fulfilled. If not, take your father's advice and find yourself a lawyer. I will give you an annulment if you want it.

Fondly,

Franz

September 14, 1911

Dear Franz:

I was both pained and heartened by your response. Having brought myself to take the initiative, I was prepared for everything you said. After all, having heard nothing from you, anything was, is an improvement. Believe me, I have not kept my despair to myself or let the bright hope of our marriage degrade like a moldy piece of wedding cake. I have spoken freely with my closest friends and confidants, some of whom are married, and I am sorry to say, for them, that their lives and those of their husbands are increasingly separate, especially when children enter the house.

Do women give most of their energy to their children, and men to their careers and, ultimately, to their carousing colleagues or mistresses? I don't know. I hoped that with you it would be different, but you have your own devils it would seem.

Now to the point. My Great Uncle Gustav, the one

you will recall with the eye patch, has a small, well situated farm near Lenggreis that he has agreed to let me-let us-have, as a kind of sanitorium, as he puts it, "to cure our marriage." I visited it twice as a child. It's simple, even rustic, with a lovely view of meadows, forests and distant hills. The house is small, but there is a shed with a good stove where you could have a studio. Yes, the light is good, and we could even expand the windows, although you will have to wear more than one layer of wool in the winter. The area is exposed and subject to winds, but you have never minded the cold. Think about it and let me hear from you.

I am well. My father's sight is failing, which makes him understandably more irascible. He no longer wants to horsewhip you. He is more inclined to dismiss you as a childish, worthless eccentric. I do not totally share his opinion.
Your wife,
Antonia

February 12, 1912

Dear Antonia:

I expect to arrive in Lenggreis by way of Munich within two weeks. I appreciate all that you have done and admire your patience and commitment to our marriage. I hope to be worthy of your trust. Will there be horses?
Franz

June 7, 1912 – A Visitor

"It's very nice here, Franz, very," Kandinsky looked up at the cobwebbed crossbeam and pulled at his beard, searching for the right word. "Peaceful," he said with finality.

The shed had been converted to a studio. A window added on the north side gave a view of rolling green pasture and, beyond, a meeting of fir trees, their mantle somber dark green, almost black against the bright green of the young grass. The top of the half door was open to the gravel path that meandered toward the back of the two story stucco farm house.

Kandinsky walked to the door and gazed toward the house, focusing on the naive mural of an exuberant milk maid painted on the wall of the house just under the eaves.

"Yes it is," Franz muttered after a lapse in which he daubed a few strokes of burnt umber onto a corner of the canvas.

"Antonia is easy to be with, different than I had expected."

"In what way?" Franz stepped back from the canvas bumping the corner of the heavy work bench and gazed thoughtfully at his nearly finished painting.

"Oh, I imagined her to be stiff as a starched shirt front, if you want to know the truth. I couldn't understand why you wanted to marry her in the first place."

"Obviously I saw something beneath the surface that escaped you." Franz turned his head momentarily toward Kandinsky with a disapproving squint, then returned to his exploration of the canvas.

"Well, that is your focus in life, to see beneath the surface."

"And don't you?"

"I don't know," Kandinsky replied, seriously engaged by the question. "I sometimes just want to paint. Start with a line, then another line, see what happens, *reductio ad absurdum,* but not quite that far."

Franz was too absorbed in his exploration of his painting to digest Kandinsky's observation. As he waited for the rejoinder, Kandinsky pulled a cigarette out of the pocket of his jacket, found a box of matches on the work table and lit up. He inhaled, held it in his lungs, then let it slowly out of his nostrils.

His voice hoarse from the smoke, he said, "What do you think Polux the dog sees when he looks at that painting of yours?" Hearing his name, the dog, a German Shepherd, lifted his massive head then dropped it again on his heavy paws.

"Lines and colors." Kandinsky answered his own question and turned his head to look obliquely at the painting. "Does it look to him like a house or a horse or a hill or a sunset or just an object that he can't sort out, something that is neither hostile nor edible." The dog got up slowly on his forelegs, stretched, yawned, and sniffed at the wind coming through the door.

"Should we leave it all up to the viewer then?" Franz surfaced from the depth of his contemplation.

"Obviously, we select the gross image that the viewer sees, but what he focuses on, or makes of it, is up to him."

Franz walked in a circle, turning first toward Kandinsky, then looking at the painting, wondering what his friend thought, wondering in fact what he thought. He was as yet too close to the almost completed work to judge it fairly. Only after leaving it for a few months could he come back and see a work with any detachment, almost as if it had been painted by a stranger. For now he saw horses in primary colors, unmistakable horses that weren't horses at all, at least not to him.

"That is elegant, Franz, quite elegant."

"What is?"

"This line, here," he said pointing to the back of a red horse. "This is a single stroke from here to here?"

"Yes, I wanted to catch spontaneity, power, grace, the essence of the movement of a horse. Of course, I've spent days drawing the horses out there in the pasture, in my sketchbook, to get it right."

"You've got it, I'll give you that much," Kandinsky said, feeling sincere admiration tainted with envy.

June 12, 1912 – Franz and Antonia In The Kitchen

Antonia: What are you working on Franz? You don't talk to me about your work so much as you used to."

Franz: I don't want to bore you with it.

A: But you talk with Kandinsky continuously, about your plans for the journal, your ambitions.

F: Well.

A: Do you mean to exclude me or don't you think me worthy of your high minded goals.

F: It's not a question of exclusion. It's a lack of patience, a sense that the ideas are too abstruse, perhaps nonsensical, indigestible.

A: You think me too shallow.

F: Not at all

A: Stupid then.

F: Hardly.

A: What then. I am your wife.

F: Are there no borders, between a man and wife, then?

A: The tips of our fingers, our lips are our borders.

F: What do you want to know?

A: Share with me, whether or not I understand, bring me into it a little. That's not much to ask. You are so withdrawn sometimes, so preoccupied, as if I'm not even in the room with you.

F: Forgive me.

A: I have forgiven you. Many times.

F: I am struggling with a new order of reality. Not new really, rather something older than knowledge, something pretermitted. I'm looking behind the cultural archetypes, looking under the primal relationships, seeking the golden mean, the counterpart of mathematical absolutes, a new language for art, to spill into all phases of knowledge, to reinterpret reality for the next century. That's one of the objectives of our publication.

A: Rather presumptuous isn't it?

F: Now you see why I have been reluctant to talk about it. I too have my doubts, but that doesn't keep me from my struggle. This is an extraordinary time to be living. The old world that has dominated European culture, since Rome, is collapsing. Consider the aristocracy, blind, stupid, insipid, selfish, bent on their own destruction, as Durkheim has pointed out, and the bourgeois, equally selfish, their lives dominated by appearance, possession, eating the abject poor who comprise most of humanity, at every meal, werewolves, predators. Against this place the efflorescence of science, observing, categorizing, theorizing, abstracting. A chaotic and contradictory web of concepts, facts, processes. Consider its practical applications and their consequences on life; fertilizer, the dynamo, electricity, telegraph, the railroad, the internal combustion engine, anesthetic, structural steel. We want to create some order out of it, to find motive sources, tidal rhythms, harmonies and disjunctions.

A: And the end of all this?

F: Not an end. A beginning. A new way of thinking, a new world order based upon humanistic principals which the arts will help to define. A new mode of thought to animate humanity at all of its levels of interaction.

A: You and Kandinsky want to bring this about?

F: Yes. We'll do our share, we'll try. Along with the others. Weininger, Freud, Semmelweis, Schnitzler, Wagner, others. Yes we'll try to do our small share.

A: Are you hungry? Franz. You haven't eaten all day. Gerta has brought us some fresh sausage and she's made a hot potato salad.

F: Did she remember to add the pickles?

July 3, 1912 – Blau Reiter

A fire in the hearth and the spirit lamp suspended over the heavy wooden table gave the low ceilinged kitchen the look of a stage. The wind moved the lamp, the tines of the fire swayed, and shadows danced across the wall. The long exposed wooden pendulum of the ancient clock made a brittle sound of breaking kindling. Outside the deep set windows, the wind sighed, a hunting owl called to its mate, and the neighbor's watchdog barked to amuse himself.

Antonia was sitting in the upright wooden arm chair beside the fire knitting the sleeve of a black wool sweater. Franz and Kandinsky were hunched over the rough pine table like conspirators, a half empty bottle of Mosel wine, the remains of a loaf of coarse rye bread, and a wedge of Ementaler cheese between them. They had been sitting there for hours, sometimes talking in gusts, then falling silent for a time, chewing and digesting what the other had said, reorganizing thoughts, often sketching with a single pencil, taking turns on a drawing, a game of sorts in which each was limited to a single line, to be added anywhere.

"You've spoiled it!" Kandinsky slammed his hand down on the table and the dog, sleeping on a rug by the fire, raised his head with a start.

"Spoiled what?"

"Now boys, don't fight," said Antonia, without looking up

from her knitting.

"My vision."

"And what precisely was your vision?"

"It was just emerging," said Kandinsky.

"Well, maybe it wasn't meant to be just yet."

Kandinsky seized the paper, crumpled it into a ball and tossed it into the fire. It crackled, burned a brighter orange than the wood, but soon turned brown and dissolved to ribbons of ash.

"So much for your vision."

"But didn't you see it escaping from the drawing? The Blue Rider?"

"You mean your lonely knight riding on my blue horse."

"That's what we should call it, the Blue Rider."

"You're back on the journal again? Kandinsky, you should have been a missionary. Think of it, you could have converted the entire continent of Africa. They would have done it just to shut you up."

"Well, if I'm not welcome." He began to pout.

"It's not that at all. You are quite refreshing but you are as persistent as a fly on a cow's eyelid."

"Ah the bucolic metaphors. You've been too long in the country. You will rusticate," Kandinsky intoned with pontifical weight.

"Look, it's not a bad name. Just give me a little time. You make me feel like a mouse crossing a railroad track."

"We'll use my painting on the cover. The folk idiom, the importance of primal values, the masculine as a concept, the allusion to the past, deference to the masters, the archetype as symbol, as abstraction, the lonely courageous struggle of creative expression. It's all there."

Franz watched his friend expound and mused that he could light up the room with self infatuation. "You see, Kandinsky, I didn't spoil your vision after all. What more is there to do? You've summed it up."

"Don't trivialize it with humor, Franz, I'm very serious."

"There's nothing trivial about humor. It can get to the root of things. You have seen collections of the sayings of your Russian peasants. They exceed De Rochefoucauld in irony, to my way of thinking."

"When did you read De Rochefoucauld?"

"In Paris."

"What do you think, are you in with me or not?"

"I've come to resist going to Munich since living here. All the noise, the frenetic pace of the traffic, the bad air." Franz picked up the pencil and began to twirl it between his fingers just as he was toying with Kandinsky. In fact he liked the idea of the journal as a focus for their ideas but he was loath to even suggest to Antonia that they pick up and move. Besides, he had no money of his own.

Antonia got up, put her knitting on the seat of the chair, turned with a peremptory glance toward the table and said, "Good night, gentlemen." She nodded to each of them, patted Franz on the top of his head and left the room.

"Goodnight," said Kandinsky without looking at her. "What's become of that refined sense of Christian duty, Franz?"

"Don't vulgarize my motives."

"Come Franz you're too young to turn into a tree fungus. Next thing, you'll take to painting bland landscapes for haberdasher's sitting rooms, pastoral scenes with shepherds."

"Do shut up!" Franz's voice quivered and he felt the blood rush to his head.

"I've touched a raw nerve." Kandinsky sat back in his chair with a look of triumph. "Just think of the excitement, Franz. You can always come back here when you need a good night's sleep and the smell of fresh cow dung as a tonic."

"You're disgusting." Franz said, not willing to admit to him that he was right. He had gotten what he'd had wanted out of the farm; a chance to develop ideas tentatively formed in Paris, to explore pastoral images as a metaphor and to make amends to Antonia, who was paying for it all. But Munich remained the center of everything that interested him, and sooner or later he had to be there.

"We are all of us disgusting, to the rest of the world. That's why we do what we do." Kandinsky said this almost to himself as he got up and went to the buffet to drink the last of the cognac he had brought with him as a gift.

October 23, 1912 – Munich

Concentration brings insight, Franz wrote on the first page of his sketchbook. If he could only focus his observation like a telescope drawing in a distant star and expanding it, seeing what with the ordinary naked eye could not be seen. He envied the arc lamp for its ability to magnify a blinding point of light and throw it far across a darkened place to illuminate a singer on a stage and focus the consciousness of a diverse audience and turn it into a single collective observer.

Now and then he felt it. His concentration would intensify with such strength that the object, be it stone or tree, lichen or bee, woman drawing water or combing her hair, or dying light against an old stone wall, would bloom and expand as if in response to his attention and share with him something of its essence.

In these rare moments he felt himself possessed by powers both foreign and familiar, as if something in his mind bonded to another object as magnets cling.

Sometimes, these illuminations found their way into his work, to be discovered, or just observed with no idea how or why the colors and lines came to be arranged in just this way. The insight usually passed as quickly as a spark escaping from a dancing tine of flame. Sometimes the vision wouldn't go away. Possessing his thoughts, it pushed mundane functions aside, returning again and again as if his mind was a vessel filled to the brim with it.

Never before had it come to him in the form of a woman. He first saw her at the opera at a table in the buffet with an acquaintance whose name he could not recall, another artist, perhaps one he had met in Paris.

Her hair was black with oriental silky highlights and body. The shape of her eyes also had the memory of the east, as did her features, delicate, regular as if carved and polished by an artist who had sought to endow his work with sensitivity and elegance. And yet her eyes were blue as iris, and her skin except for a blush at the high peak of the cheek, was creamy white. Her eyes wandered from the man across from her and met Franz's awestruck gaze in unspoken acknowledgment, then passed back to her companion.

November 14, 1912 – Marguerite

Her first name, he soon found out, was Marguerite. An acquaintance, Von Reiman, knew her. She was a friend of Von Reiman's sister. They had gone to school together in Geneva. Marguerite was staying in Munich for a time, with an aunt. Not really an aunt, more a close friend of her father who was, or had been, a high ranking officer in the Swiss army. Yes, she was interested in meeting him. She had asked about him on the way back to their seats, in fact.

"She observed your interest, and was flattered," said Von Reiman. "She is an acute observer. Nothing gets by her, of that I warn you, Franz."

"Why a warning?"

"See for yourself." And that was all he would say beyond the address of her aunt who was not an aunt.

That same day he sent red roses with his card. His behavior surprised him and he found himself looking over his own shoulder. After all he was a married man and sending roses to a woman who he had seen for ten minutes in a buffet was the ostentatious gesture of a gigolo, if not a romantic buffoon, and he was neither. But while he ridiculed himself, he revelled in his flamboyance and he welcomed this romantic facet of himself as he might greet a fascinating acquaintance.

The address, it turned out, was on the edge of town, beyond the trolley line. A two story house behind an ornamental iron gate with *Jugendstil* references, set in a well designed, if young, geometric garden, it was a recent design of beige stucco, self-consciously devoid of ornament, the work of an innovative architect.

Marguerite met him at the door, although the maid was there as well, standing just behind her. He took it to be both a bold democratic statement and a token of her interest in him. The sight of her turned his bones into rubber and quickened his breath. She was a vision. Her dress was champagne silk, cut at the top to a bold V. Her black hair was loose, parted at the center and hanging down her back like a school girl. Her cheeks were glowing and her lips were naturally red.

"Thank you for the roses," she said, and for the first time he heard her soft and golden voice. She led him on an invisible leash to an enclosed porch on the back of the house, with windows on three sides and a double door into the garden. A gravel path bordered by low box hedges led to a circular pond on which floated the green discs of water lilies. The room had a tile floor and the furniture was light rattan with comfortable floral cushions.

"Please sit down Herr Marc. Elke will bring coffee, or would you prefer tea?"

He sat forward on the edge of his seat and faced her feeling the blood rush to his cheeks, not sure what to do with his hands. He had lost his speech. She watched him with bemused attention.

"I am interested in your Almanac, Herr Marc," referring to the artistic journal that he and Kandinsky were publishing. "I read the first issue." Her German was perfect, he observed, but there was a slight accent that might have been French or English.

He managed a strangled, "Thank you."

"You flatter me with your attention."

"I can't help myself." My God, how could he have said that?

"Is it your usual way of behaving? If so it must often take you to the edge of danger." She sat down across from him her legs together and at an angle to her torso showing him the slender flank of her thigh through the thin fluted cloth of her dress. She reached in front of her for a cigarette. Her movements as she struck a match and inhaled, narrowing her eyes were confident and casual.

"Yes . . . no. I have been known to act on impulse, but I am usually more methodical, deliberate, except for my painting. I let myself go when I paint." Was she toying with him? He couldn't be sure. How much did she know about him? he wondered.

"Are you in the habit of sending roses to strangers you encounter in restaurants?"

"I swear to you, it is the first time."

"Not even to your wife." The word smarted like a playful slap carrying an undercurrent of reproof. So she knew, not that he intended to hide it from her.

"I must confess to you, not even to my wife. If that tells you something about my feelings then, now, at this moment, so be it. I didn't come to play games."

"You do come right to the point, Herr Marc. Don't you run the risk of taking some of the excitement out of it?" She looked at him speculatively from behind the curling scrim of the smoke.

"Not at all, Fraulein Alpen."

"Call me Marguerite. We've already passed the point of formality." She leaned back on one elbow in a way that made him feel she was already taking him for granted.

"Very well, Marguerite," he added, testing the word, "this is nothing I've ever done before. It is new to me, totally new, and I confess, I hadn't any idea what I would do or say, except to admit that I had to see you."

"Indeed. Would you have serenaded me at my window like a troubadour, written love poems?"

"Don't mock me. I'm quite vulnerable. I can't control my feelings for you. It's agonizing and exquisite."

"I'm glad."

"Glad for what?" Franz recalled his first experience with the fencing master at the gymnasium.

"Glad for you. What you are feeling doesn't happen every day in life."

"For that thought alone I am thankful."

"Why?"

"I would not have wanted to think that anyone else in the world could affect me this way."

"Thank you."

The coffee and cake came

"I hope it will not be lost."

Marguerite didn't respond. She sat up and looked from Elke to the tray. Her next words were, "Linzer torte! You will love this, Franz." She ground out her cigarette and her face took on the look of a child of eight who had seen her birthday cake for the first time. "Now confess your heart's desire,

cream, sugar, a large portion. Don't hold back!" she said play-
fully, turning her eyes up to look at him.

Franz wasn't sure how to answer. Was she speaking in
riddles? "Uh, cream no sugar," he finally said and the look
she gave him made him feel as though she had just read the
most sensitive page in his diary.

May 10, 1913 – Nude

Again and again, Franz came back to the house in the garden. Marguerite refused to see him anywhere else. She was
working, writing, poetry, a novel, her journal, an article on
Jugendstil, and there was no time for distractions. Cafes were
"empty," the conversation "self conscious and hollow," the
smoke gave her a headache. As for restaurants, the food was
too heavy—she preferred yoghurt, whole grained bread, fresh
fruit. She was a vegetarian.

He was free to accompany her on her daily walks, long
walks on country lanes to small villages. Or they might even
bicycle longer distances, to the Wansee. She rose every day at
dawn and worked for several hours while her mind was fresh.
No, she wouldn't share even a page of her work with him,
not just yet. It was personal, too personal. She had no intention of publishing anything but the articles, perhaps the novel,
but she suspected that no one would want it. It was too un-
orthodox.

Given her magnetic beauty and social ease, Franz couldn't
understand her penchant for solitude. She confessed to having
many acquiantences but only one true confidential friend,
Carolyn Von Reiman. Carolyn was in Greece, working on an
archeological excavation. When Carolyn was in Switzerland,
the two of them lived together, outside Zurich, in a modest farm
house only ten minutes walk from a village with a marvelous
bakery.

No, she didn't mind being alone when Carolyn was away.
They led unconventional lives, she admitted, but these were
times for experimentation in all things, were they not?

Franz was perplexed and frustrated. She was engaging, open.
But there were spaces in her mind that were emphatically

closed to him. Any time he turned the conversation toward intimacy, other than verbal expression of feelings, toward passion, other than for ideas or for life itself, she parried with the elegant motion of a master fencer, yet in a way that left an opening for another probe. She was by turns oblique and confidential, brusque and seductive, charming and aloof, teasing and mocking. Franz felt like the blindfolded child in the game who, having been spun around by his playmates, must stumble in the dark as they elude him.

"What do you want of me, Franz?" Marguerite asked him as they rested on the edge of a field. Marguerite was leaning against the trunk of a gnarled oak tree, her upthrust knees making a tent of her long black skirt. She was wearing a balkan peasant blouse embroidered with intricate geometric patterns in red blue and gold. A wide brimmed straw hat with a red band lay beside her. Her eyes were focused on a farmer guiding a plow behind a shaggy white horse, cutting deep rolling furrows in the moist earth. A chewed stem of grass dangled from her lip and she was idly twirling a buttercup between her thumb and finger.

"That should be clear by now, Marguerite."

"Nothing is clear between us, or between anyone for that matter."

"Certainly true in your case."

"You think me an enigma, then?" She turned toward him and waved away a fly that was hovering near her nose.

"You confound me."

"Without intention. I am just being me."

"I can't disagree."

"If you are seeking to possess me..."

"Not possess. Love you in all of its dimensions and depths."

"That could be dangerous."

"I'll risk it."

"I won't." She flung that back at him with an insouciant pout.

"Will you, will you at least let me capture what I can of you in a painting?"

"If you don't take too much."

The plowman began to sing. A lark offered a counterpoint.

A sudden wind feathered the edge of her hair and chilled the sweat on Franz's back.

"You agree then?"

"Why shouldn't I?"

"Will you permit me to set the pose and costume?"

"Should I?"

"Will you let me paint you nude?"

"Would you like to begin your studies now?" She said unbuttoning the top button of her blouse.

"Do you dare?" Franz looked askance at the farmer just turning toward them.

"Do you dare me?" She unbuttoned the second and the third, exposing the lace top of her chemise and the swelling of her breasts.

Embarrassed by what was happening to him, Franz got up, turned and strode away to the music of her mocking laughter.

May 18, 1913 – Portrait of M.

Marguerite posed for Franz, not at his studio, rather at her aunt's home, in the sun room, while her aunt was away. She sat in a rattan chair with her legs crossed and her chin propped in the palm of her hand, her long hair streaming down her back and forming a cowl about her shoulders, just touching the nipples of her bare breasts. The light, fresh and bright in the morning, bleached at mid-day and waning pallid in the late afternoon, worked its evanescent wash of tone and texture, pattern and shadow on the soft contours of her skin. Franz stroked with his eyes, every crevasse, every broad sloping field, every flank, ridge, peak, and valley.

He would leave off in the evening when the light gave out, covering the painting and making her swear an oath not to peek. She would see him to the door wrapped in a silk lavender robe, and he would stumble down the gravel path, lightheaded, exhausted, his muscles stiff, as if he had climbed the Jungfrau.

The whole, from sketch to completion, took no more than three days. His hand seemed to work with a mind of its own.

Every stroke was sure, without forethought, directed by some primitive impulse, beneath words.

"Now you can look," he finally said, late in the afternoon of the third day. She rose from the chair with no attempt to cover herself and drifted like the gauze scarf of a dancer to the other side of the canvas. He watched her face turn from expectation to question.

"Where am I?" she finally asked.

"You are the golden mountain." He had painted a landscape, a golden peak rising all alone from a plain, cutting an orange sky, and in the foreground, a single peaceful blue deer, grazing near a tree with orange leaves.

The rhythmic scale of her laughter ascended, danced around the room. Surprise, bemused satisfaction, crossed her face. She looked at Franz with nodding respect, or so he thought, (it could as well have been ironic mockery).

"What do you think?" he asked.

"Think? This is not to think."

"What do you feel then?"

"Pleased, happy." She returned to her chair and carelessly slipped into her robe, then flipped a card of her hair out of the collar. "Franz, you are a brilliant idiot."

Franz smiled at that, recognizing that for him there was no contradiction in the terms.

"What will you do with it?"

"It will go into the *Blaue Reiter* exhibit, here. Then I think even travel to Berlin. You will be exposed to the world Marguerite, exposed for what you are. Will it embarrass you much?"

"I think I can endure the notoriety, Franz."

June 10, 1913 – Ainmuller Str. 13, Schwabing

"You just missed Schonberg!" said Kandinsky. "You might have passed him on the street." Brush in one hand, palette in the other he was standing in front of a canvas full of soft blurry streaks suggesting a rider on horseback riding down a slope.

Kandinsky looked like he'd been blown about by a storm, as did the room. His dark bramble of hair was chaos, his spade of a beard, twisted, and his glasses were smudged with paint as were his hands. He looked furious, distracted, yet focused.

There were unfinished canvasses everywhere, stacked against each other. The great table in the center of the room on which he mixed his paints and wrote was scattered with used paint rags, spilled colors, partially read newspapers, a huge white coffee cup half full, a plate with a half eaten sandwich, and a spray of galley proofs that, Franz suspected, was the impending issue of *Blau Reiter Almanac*. Everything seemed half complete and abandoned for the time being as his restless mind leaped like a mountain goat from point to point.

"How is Schonberg?" Franz took it all in, assessed the painting, silently comparing it to his own work for influences. Kandinsky was a sponge, absorbing everything creative within his range.

"He has a cold. Can't seem to shake it. And what about you? Still smitten? Yes, I can see it. You've been neglecting our work, you know, leaving everything to me."

"You love to be the center of things, it suits you." Franz would not be manipulated. Kandinsky was always goading him to do what he, Kandinsky, thought important. Still he had to acknowledge that but for the goading he would be back on the farm painting in relative obscurity. "All the same, I do apologize," he added.

"Apologize? Franz? that rings like a bell without a clapper. No matter. The proofs of the Almanac are there on the table."

"I see them. I'm sure you're pleased to see the work in print at last." Kandinsky's entire play was there, to the exclusion of several other pieces by Scheffler and Endell, both bumped to the next issue whenever it would appear.

"*Der Gelbe Klange*?" Kandinsky looked as if he'd forgotten about it. "I'd rather see it performed."

"But they are doing it?" The Munich Artist's Theater had planned a production.

"I don't know. It's, as always, a matter of money. How are you coming with your set designs for Tempest?"

"All in good time."

"It's a great opportunity, after all, something altogether new, a real syntheses of all the arts. It will be an historic performance."

"I know, I know." Franz was in fact grateful for Kandinsky's influence, and enthusiastic over the project. The theater was remarkable, with its deep stage and innovative lighting system. There was nothing like it in the world.

"Then why are you diddling away your time, mooning over that which is unattainable, or should I say, impenetrable? Sit down, sit down or have you just dropped in for a moment."

"I've just painted her," Franz said, taking a seat in the heavy black oak knight's chair in front of the table. Kandinsky glanced at the painting, put the brush and palette down without looking, took out a silver cigarette case, found and lit a long Russian cigarette and inhaled so deeply that Franz imagined the smoke coming out of his ears. He slouched into the chair on the other side of the table and assumed a casual Faustian pose.

"She let you do something then. You're happy with the result?"

"Very."

"Take what you can in this world. Old Serbian proverb." Kandinsky's eye turned toward the newspaper which, Franz saw, carried a description of the latest Serbian aggrandizement against Albania.

"So it would seem." In truth Franz hadn't been paying much attention to the Balkans except to appreciate the fact that their music, dance and textiles were still in touch with their pre-Christian roots.

"They're all idiots." Kandinsky declaimed with a smoke polluted voice and a dismissive wave of his hand. "The Serbs, the Albanians, the Montenegrans, Bosnians, all of them. And the region is like a whirlpool that sucks everything to the bottom. They'll all drown."

"Where's your Pan Slav loyalty, Kandinsky? "

"Somewhere in my art, just where it should be, not coming out of the barrel of a Mauser."

"Pity the statesman and soldier who have no other way to express their creativity."

"Is war creative, then?"

"Of course, in a way that mixing paint or making an omelette is creative. Something new always comes out of it, and something else gets covered up or changed."

"Or broken. Don't tell me that you actually believe that Austria was wise to stick her nose in?"

"I have no love for that decadent empire, but I believe that Germany would, and even Austria might, calm the Balkans down." Franz pulled these thoughts slowly out of his head like laundry squeezed through a wringer. "They're none of them any better than the filthy Turks. And they'll never stop fighting till someone puts a boot to their collective backside." They weren't worth the trouble, not when there was so much poverty at home to be reckoned with.

"I suppose Germanic order and all that will bring civilization and enlightenment to the region."

"Do you deny it? And does it help if your Czar jumps in under the guise of helping his little Slav brothers? All he manages is to pour gunpowder on the fire."

"Well, I'm here in Munich, am I not? That says something about my Pan Slav identity." Kandinsky reached out and picked up a white trouser button. He took it between thumb and forefinger, flipped it and let it drop with a light tapping sound on the golden oak surface of the table.

"Lose something?"

"No, I found it. In a puddle in front of the house. Listen to it. You can hear its voice. It tells a story. Its function, the loss of the function, its existence for its own sake, the shape, even something of the poor fellow who lost it."

Franz picked it up and put it to his ear with a smile. "Since you're here and I'm here, you might offer me a drink. I'm exhausted. Where's Gretchen, where's Frau Kandinsky? The place is a mess."

"She left me."

"Who, the maid?"

"My wife, Ania." Kandinsky looked abused, offended.

"Left? Why didn't you say so?"

"What am I to do, put a note on the door? Have it painted on the window in gold?" This with sudden wind. "After nineteen years," he continued, more subdued. "And she took the maid with her. Imagine."

"I might have expected as much. She was starved for affection. You treated her abominably so much of the time."

"I did not. And you should talk. Franz, the model German husband. God you're disagreeable today, for one mooning about swaddled in mucid adolescent love. Or maybe you're just frustrated."

"I'm disagreeable? A polite word hasn't escaped your lips. You're a veritable bear, a hungry Russian bear! I'm surprised you're not wearing that moth eaten fur coat."

"Pity there are no bears left in Germany. All killed dead. Except for the zoo, of course. The last time I wore it, a jaeger took a shot at me." Kandinsky took off his spectacles and began to clean the lenses with a turpentine soaked rag. "Come on, Franz, let's go get something to eat and drink. Drown our mutual frustration and celebrate our good fortune. I'll even pay. And we'll bring along the proofs. They're due back at the printer's tomorrow." Kandinsky was already up, stalking around his lair, a deep crease on his brow, trying to remember where he'd abandoned his hat.

Correspondence

December 14, 1913

Dear Franz:

Tired of waiting in rustication for your return, I decided to go to Vienna, where I might find solace in friends and family, since you provide neither. I have appreciated your dutiful letters and am glad that your paintings and the Almanac have inspired the attention, albeit controversial, which you sought. Everyone is entitled to some part of their wishes in life. Mine appear to be a marriage to a brilliant artist, who darts in and out of my life like a hummingbird, drinking a little of my nectar only to pass on to the next flower with no promise of return. I know now that for all of my pretensions of wanting something more than the platitudes and complacencies of my family, I should have taken my father's advise and found someone like him. A boring, conventional life would have been more than I have. A widow has more social latitude than I have in society. My friends all pity me, I see it in their faces. As if my rejection and isolation were not hard enough to bear, rumors have reached me that you have taken up with a woman of great beauty, eccentric charm and every bit as mad as you. The shame and degradation you bring down upon me. And not even a child to console me.

I have also heard that Kandinsky, that overblown genius, is now without a wife, she having returned to her family to pursue a divorce. The poor tom cat has no window to climb into any more, but will no doubt find another to leave him a saucer of milk after his nocturnal adventures.

I never thought I would come to this but it might be best if you didn't return to me. That way at least I will not have my frayed hopes renewed only to be torn again. The cloth of our marriage is no longer whole, it has been patched too often to cover both of us. Go your way.
Your no longer devoted wife
Antonia

January 10, 1914

Dear Antonia:

Your letter makes me overflow with remorse. I have been wretched to you, I know, but I must be true to myself, and that requires me to do my work where I can. For now it is here in Munich that I have gained some recognition for my work and my ideas. Only in Munich, the present art capital of the world in terms of innovation, would it have been possible. Do you think that in stodgy Vienna they would pay any more attention to my work than they would to a street artist who draws a flamenco dancer with pastel chalk on a sidewalk?

If you are neglected it is not out of indifference or malice or a cold heart. I care for you and would like to have children with you, one day, when it is possible. As for now I must seize the moment and make the best of it. Recognition does not always come with merit.

As for the woman you allude to, she is no woman, but a siren, or similar supernatural force that drives men insane with desire, turns them into animals. Yes, I confess desire, a passion that I hope will, now that it has broken out of its religious bonds of guilt and inhibition, manifest itself in a more fully satisfying relationship with you.

Abandon me if you must, but better than that, be patient as Odysseus's wife was patient, until I return from my adventures.

Affectionately,

Franz

(Third draft. First two destroyed.)

Franz jammed his thumb trying to retrieve the letter as it slid from his grasp into the post box. Once out of his hands, he was resigned to it, convincing himself that it could do no more harm and might even provide Antonia with some solace. And within another ten minutes, it had dropped out of his thoughts like water though a sieve.

3

Franz: The Great War

February 21, 1914 – A Broken Mirror

The mirror broke while Franz was shaving. He knocked it off the marble top of the washstand with his elbow. It shattered with a sharp musical sound into piercing beams of moonlight much like the French painter, Delaunay's, broken planes, and much like Europe's shattering peace, he concluded. He finished shaving by touch, washed in the basin, and cleaned his strait razor, all the while contemplating the random fragments of the mirror giving back a nose and a piece of cheek, a single eye. His visit to Paris came to mind and the long conversations with Delaunay over the theory of his work. It was so different from Kandinsky's approach. At the moment he felt a part of something momentous, not a spectator but a player in a grand, panoramic opera.

Franz went back to the nearly completed painting, eager to immerse himself in the process. He had to confess that there was some of Delaunay in it. The planes of color, rose and fell like shafts and beams. The orange of fire, displaced the blue and green pointed abstracted mountains and trees. In the center were three animals, one grazing, another no more than an outline, resting. The third, a bull, was dominant, its horned head rose belligerent and ominous. The same bull's horns had adorned the helmets of his ancestors, when they went to war.

He worked for hours, oblivious to the muffled sounds of the street and the shifting fading shadows, concentrating on the tension between the forces of harmony and strife that struggled for dominance in the painting.

Kandinsky came into the room with the stealth of a cat, doing his best to avoid the squeaking floor boards. He didn't like to be disturbed when he was working and, feeling magnanimous that morning, extended the same courtesy to Franz. He eased himself into the arm chair and watched Franz's brush strokes as one violinist might study the fingering of a competitor.

Franz turned and groped for his cigarettes and saw Kandinsky who responded with a sly look and a nod of approval.

"How long have you been sitting there?" Franz tried to cover his irritation.

"I arrived last night. Didn't you notice me sleeping in the chair? Or were you still in the thrall of Marguerite's spell."

"Oh, don't start with Marguerite! It's none of your business. Why do you keep on about it, you of all people."

"It seems I've touched a nerve."

"Touched it? You never let go!"

"It's only as a friend. She's turned you into one of your animals with her power."

"What if she has. You see for yourself," he said gesturing toward the canvas. "If anything, she has opened me up. Look at the clash and synthesis of colors, the dynamic tension in the composition. Quite frankly, this painting reveals its undercurrent of meaning as much as anything I've done."

"Yes, it's good work. As good as you are capable of, but you still flirt with, rather than commit to abstraction."

"So? The fact that these forms are recognizable as objects doesn't make them any less universal or detract from their symbolic meaning. One can get so esoteric, so obscure that only the artist knows what he's communicating."

"And you think that I've reached that pinnacle of obscurity do you?" Franz planted his brush in a jar of turpentine.

"Not at all." His tone was bland.

"Everyone must find their own place and manner of expression," Franz blustered. He observed Kandinsky shaking his head and said in a subdued tone. "And in any event none of this has anything to do with my obsession with Marguerite Alpen."

"Perhaps not. Perhaps I'm merely jealous of the time you spend with her." Kandinsky saw the shards of mirror, picked one up, looked into it, turned it this way and that.

Franz came around the table and touched Kandinsky's shoulder. "We are two blind fish, Kandinsky."

"Yes, well, I thought we might have supper." Kandinsky was still holding the shard, not sure what to do with it, looking suddenly uncomfortable.

Franz looked back at the painting with a strange detachment and satisfaction. It was his creation; every stroke, every intuitive decision. The inner light, the colors which gave back more than they absorbed, the symbolic message, the frozen tension; all were unique. And yet the work was not only his for he felt himself to be the medium for some universal enduring truth. Marguerite was also the medium. The spell ridiculed by Kandinsky was the emanation of a primordial feminine force.

"Well Franz? My belly calls."

"Why not. I've worked enough for one day." Franz shed his blue smock and dropped it on the corner of his work table. They started toward the door. "Someday I will paint you, Kandinsky."

"And what animal will I be?"

"The fox. Have you ever noticed your resemblance to the fox, the shape of your mind?"

"Franz, you are a prince's fool."

"Call me what you will, Kandinsky. If I had barged in on you like that you would have thrown me head first through the window."

April 6, 1914 – Marguerite Revealed

Franz: "Tell me more about yourself."

Marguerite: "There is nothing to tell. What you see is what I am to you."

F: "I know that. What are you to others?"

M: "A friend, a daughter, a cousin, a patron, a student, a stranger."

F: "Yes, a stranger, that above all."

M: "Not to the clear sighted."

F: "You suggest that I can't see?"

M: "Oh, you, Franz, see everything, the inner reality, the absolute truth."

F: "You mock me."

M: "Tease, not mock."

F: "I am so frustrated."

M: "Because I deny you physical access."

F: "Of course."

M: "But Franz, you are a saint, it is the City of God you seek in your work, in your life, not Sodom."

F: "Sodom, why Sodom?"

M: "The place where all gratification is sensual. You wouldn't be happy there."

F: "And you, Marguerite, would you be happy?"

M: "We are not discussing me."

F: "I thought we were."

M: "You think too much."

F: "Do you like me?"

M: "What a silly question. Would I spend time with you if you bored or offended me? That much you know about me. Come Franz, do you want an affectionate *Billet Doux*? A lock of my hair. You already have the portrait."

F: "You deflate and disarm me."

M: "All the better between friends. My father, you know is a military man, as is my brother."

F: "You never told me that."

M: "You never asked."

F: "Tell me about him, about your family."

M: "Do you want to paint him too? What would he be, a wolf perhaps, chasing an innocent doe through the forest?"

F: "If he had the soul of a wolf."

M: "Not that I could see. He was my toy soldier when I was a child, a little girl. He brought me sweets, took me to the zoo."

F: "Was he kind?"

M: "He was a man in a very neat uniform with brass buttons and gold braid, and a lot of shiny medals although he never went to war. The Swiss, you know, are not overly fond of war. It is wasteful and destructive of the national wealth. He let me play with his medals, put them on and parade around the house with my brother. He let me shine the brass of his sword hilt. Later, he let me trim his beard. It was very precise, shaped like an arrow head. Now you know everything about me and my father."

F: "Is he still alive?"

M: "No. He had an unfortunate accident. His horse missed a jump. They both went down. My father broke his neck. They had to shoot the horse. It was a beautiful horse."

F: "What about your mother?"

M: "What about her? You want to paint her too? She would have been a flower in your painting. Although you don't seem to paint flowers, Franz. Why not?"

F: "What sort of a flower would she have been?"

M: "A gardenia, I think, pale, creamy, delicate, fragile, easily bruised, fragrant."

F: "Beautiful, like you."

M: "I do look like her. But I am not so fragile."

F: "Were they happy, your parents?"

M: "They were very proper. But there was another woman in my father's life. Someone very unlike my mother and very unlike him for that matter. Perhaps she brought something out in him that my mother couldn't reach. Love is mysterious, chemical, don't you think? Take your infatuation with me, Franz. Is it only the way I look or is there something indefinable?"

F: "And what about you, Marguerite, have you ever been smitten with love?"

M: "Franz, my pet, use your keen imagination. I live with a school friend, Carolyn Von Reiman, who by the way should be returning to Munich this week. Do you not suspect that this is more than convenience?"

F: "Well, I never really gave it. . . ."

M: "Surely, you have a familiarity with Greek mythology, Franz."

F: "It's a rather broad topic."

M: "You have read the poetry of Sappho?"

F: "Then you and she are more than good companions?"

M: "Yes Franz, does that shock you? You have turned bright red."

F: "Well . . . I . . . it takes me by surprise, that's all."

M: "That's all?"

F: "I . . . I'm jealous, I suppose. Jealous and disappointed. Deeply so."

M: "I love her, Franz. I love her as you love me."

F: "How stupid of me not to have understood."

M: "Blindness is an affliction of the perception, not the mind."

F: "Yes, an artist who is blind. That's a nice metaphor."

M: "Blind people sometimes have inner sight, Franz. You have inner sight. But it doesn't always match reality, as the world perceives it."

F: "So there's no hope."

M: "Hope has nothing at all do with it."

F: "It's hopeless."

M: "Franz, you look so very sad. Come, kiss me. Let me console you. Not on the cheek on the lips, like this. I don't love you but I'm quite fond of you. That's better. Now touch my breasts. Let's see what happens. Heaven has twelve gates. There, you're not so sad anymore. Now. . . ."

June 11, 1914 – Three Comrades

Franz couldn't tell what Carolyn Von Reiman thought of him: she presented so many confusing and contradictory faces. She was, he concluded, a woman who liked to entertain herself at the expense of others, one who might have become a great actress, given her capacity to mimic, mock, emote, put on and take off personality traits. But for his obdurate fixation with Marguerite, he would have spurned Carolyn after the first encounter. But there was no seeing Marguerite without Carolyn. Rather than stay with her brother, Carolyn had moved in with Marguerite. Marguerite's aunt was on an extended tour of North America and was expecting to spend as much as a year in Santa Fe.

Ever the observer, Franz studied every nuance of the relationship of Mag and Car, as they called each other.

"Der Franz is staring again, Mag. Please make him stop!"

Carolyn raised both hands and rippled her fingers in mock subservience.

"Stop staring, Franz." Marguerite said with conspicuous disinterest.

They were sitting in the sun room in the late afternoon, just finished with tea. There was nothing formal, no special conversation; it was as if they were brothers and sisters who had spent their lives together. Mag was reading something on aesthetics; Car was making notes in her black leather bound notebook while Franz was sketching. Carolyn was of middle height, wide-hipped, thick-skinned, the kind of woman Renoir liked to paint, Franz thought. She had broad cheeks, full flaring unshaped lips, narrow dark blue eyes and thick hair the color of ripe wheat. She was dressed in a full fluted skirt—pale blue-gray—and a white wide necked peasant blouse that fell to the cleavage of her ample breasts.

"I'm not staring. I'm sketching Carolyn."

"Did I give Franz permission to sketch me, Mag?"

"Stop speaking to me indirectly, Carolyn. If you have anything to say, say it to me. I'm not a child."

"Franz says he's not a child, Mag. What do you think? Is your Franzl a child?"

Marguerite's only reaction was to shift her expressionless eyes up for a moment.

"Mag won't intercede, Franz. Very well. You may capture my soul with your pencil. But don't leave the house with it."

"What nonsense, Car. It's not even funny," said Marguerite, her tone gently admonishing. Then to Franz without looking up but sounding confidential, "She resents our friendship, Franz. She says you are my love slave. What do you think of that?"

"Your Franzl is turning red, Mag. Has he choked on his strudel? Or have you choked on it?" Carolyn stifled a laugh.

"I think, Carolyn, you feel excluded," said Franz barely masking his distaste.

"Or your Franzl feels excluded."

Marguerite closed her book and put it down. She looked from at each of them in turn, her face shifting from mild disgust to bemusement. "I'm a little tired. I think I'll take a nap.

Who wants to come along?"

Carolyn and Franz looked at each other not sure what the other would say or do if they agreed. While they were hesitating, Marguerite got up, ran her hand down the side of her white skirt, and walked toward the hall. "Come along, both of you," she said like a mother admonishing her naughty children.

Carolyn got up looking both wild and gleeful, but Franz imagined an undercurrent of contempt in her darting gaze. She seemed to know what was coming. He followed Carolyn watching the shift of her hips and thinking of a horse walking slowly. He found himself both dreading and looking forward to what might happen upstairs. Marguerite had, since that first kiss, managed to draw the life out of him again and again in ways that might, in other years, have made him ashamed. She was so fierce, so free of convention, and now she meant to tie him in some way to Carolyn, to bind the three of them in some warped intimacy. She intended this, he was sure, knowing what would give Carolyn satisfaction and pleasure. He followed her up the stairs wondering how many times Carolyn had been with a man and in what way.

He entered the bedroom as Marguerite was already drawing the heavy drapes. The room was furnished with golden *Biedermeyer* covered with mauve and deep green. One wall was hung with six African masks. In the corner was a carved wood screen that he took to be Indonesian. Carolyn had gone to her own room. Franz shifted self consciously from one foot to the other and waited for instructions.

"Do help me undress, Franz." He moved closer to her, undid the button at the top of her skirt and she let it drop around her feet. Her fragrance, musk, made him light headed. With her back to him she slowly unbuttoned her blouse. The rhythm of her steady breathing invaded him. A light silk petticoat dropped to the floor and, still standing, she bent to unroll her white silk stockings. Doing so she brushed against him. His heart rushed and his bones turned to putty.

"What are you waiting for, Franz? Do you think I invited you up here just to undo my buttons?"

"What? . . ."

"Undress."

He was standing in nothing but his underdrawers when Carolyn appeared at the door wearing men's grey silk pajamas. Marguerite, wearing only loose white silk panties and a white silk camisole, faced her and they exchanged smiles: Carolyn's hysterical, Marguerite's understanding and benign. Marguerite removed her camisole and Franz's cheeks began to burn as he watched her brown nipples rise.

"Franz, reach into my closet and bring me the negligee hanging on the door." She was so calm, so casual. He recognized the garment, pale rose silk with a low collar of lace exuding her fragrance. He offered it to her but she waived it away with her hand.

"That's for you, Franz. Put it on. We're the same height. Since it's open it won't impede your freedom, not in the slightest."

"I . . . I don't understand," Franz said feeling the blood rush to his head.

"Of course you do. From now until supper, Carolyn will be Franz, I will be Carolyn and you will be Marguerite. We'll have a little play. Carolyn loves fantasies and so do I. You'll see, Franz. You'll love it too. If it isn't the best time of your life, you can just go back to being Franz." Her eyes leveled a challenge within a sardonic mask. "Now put this on and get in bed. It will be tight, the three of us, but all the better. You, Marguerite, will be in the middle."

Feeling both shame and a rippling thrill, Franz/Marguerite let his underpants drop to the floor and slipped into the silk robe as the other two watched.

August 23, 1914 – Fatherland

"I love this time of day," Franz said looking across the gravel at the nimbus of color; merging clouds of blue campanula, yellow lacy yarrow and lady's mantle, spiking clusters of blue delphinium and coronas of lupin, mats of green of differing texture, hue, and shape. "It's like a feverish dream, these pulsating, concentrated colors."

"Neither day nor night, the hour of ambiguity," said Marguerite looking meaningfully at Franz. They were seated across from each other at a small white iron table under a pergola roofed with a net of pink tea roses. On the table was a half full bottle of *Ruedesheimer*, two pale green stemmed wine glasses and a wedge of Ementhaler cheese, Marguerite's favorite. Franz was dropping crumbs to an insistent starling.

"Ambiguity. Your time of day, Marguerite."

"Franz, when will you stop searching for absolutes? It's a vain, medieval, waste of time."

"Oh yes, it's not right for these practical times."

"You could say that war is a practical solution." Marguerite shifted and crossed her legs.

"A release of pent up tension, like the explosion of gunpowder in a confined space." Franz felt the blood rush to his head. He took a deep breath to calm himself and pulled his shoulders back to ease the tension. What would she say when he told her. Would she be sad, remorseful?

"Or an orgasm. Oh, aren't we cerebral. Car should be here. She loves word play." Marguerite looked toward the house.

"And every other game. Where is she?"

"The University. A meeting with fellow archaeologists."

"Curious, these archaeologists, sifting through the rubble of forgotten battles for the things left behind when the people fled or were killed."

"Will archaeologists one day excavate Berlin?"

"Not if I can help it."

"What will you do, Franz, paint it?"

"I enlisted." His tone was matter of fact, fatalistic.

"You're joking." Her head moved toward him with a look of concentration as if she hadn't understood.

"No," Franz replied, doing his best to mask the quick beat of his heart.

"Why?" The word was a sustained rising and falling tone, a chant of incredulity. "What possible purpose could you have? You are crazy, self-destructive." Marguerite looked offended, hurt by him. "War is the antithesis of what you stand for as an artist."

"In a way it is exactly what I stand for."

"How possibly could it?"

"Never mind that."

"It's not, not because of me. It couldn't be. You're above behaving like the hero in a cheap romance." Her voice grew sharp, admonishing and she had the look of denial.

"Thank you very much for your confidence." Franz leaned back in his chair, relieved to have gotten it out and pleased at her reaction. She cared. That assumption brought with it a wrenching regret. Given time he might have won her, he thought for an instant and immediately denied it. Marguerite was a narcotic. Enlistment was a cure.

"It is because of me."

"No."

"I see it written on your face."

"You misread me."

Marguerite looked as if something was hurting inside her. She poured some wine, lifted the glass, forgot to drink.

"Don't tell me you'll be sorry to see me go, or that you'll miss me." He hoped that she would.

"Yes, to both questions. Franz, I have grown," she paused, searching for the right words, "I am fond of you, even attached to you. But taking up my father's vocation won't increase my affection."

"I hadn't thought that it would."

"Why did you do it?"

"You wouldn't understand. I'm sure you would ridicule my reasons."

"Because they are not real, not valid!" She was urgent, truly distraught.

"If I thought for a moment, Marguerite, that you and I could share a life, could go off to a farmhouse, I to paint, you to your writing. If I thought that we could love as man and woman love. . . ." He stopped, his voice thick.

"I *love* Caroline."

"That fact is worse than any wound I might suffer in the war."

"I'm sorry."

"If there were any way I could get you to change."

"Leaving for the war would not be one."

"I should go." He got up to leave. She took his arm and held him back, drew him toward her and kissed him with soft moist lips. For a moment he was aware of nothing but her touch. He pulled away wanting to hold on to her but knowing it was futile, aware that she would only rebuff and dismiss him.

"Wait, Franz," she said urgently.

"Kandinsky's right, you are a siren," he said and walked away, conscious of the impression of her lips on his.

Marguerite let her head drop to her arm and listened to the receding crackling of his tread on the gravel path. She would miss his attention, his stimulation, his dog-like adoration, but she was relieved to see him go. It would be just Mag and Car again. Men could be such fools.

February 6, 1915 – Consecration

Franz's unit arrived by train at eight in the morning at a town in Belgium near the border. As he climbed down from the car, he could see no visible sign of damage. The town must have been given up without a fight.

Although it had been only six months since his enlistment, Franz had the feeling that he'd been a soldier for years. The routine, monotony, regimentation, and discipline were, in a way, a purge for Franz; a curb on his restless, impulsive nature. Being in the army was like being a child again. He made no decisions of his own. Everything was determined according to schedules and procedures. It was also like choosing a vocation in the church. The rules were immutable, the lines of authority perfectly defined. The life was austere. Again and again it made him think back on the rigidities of his youth, the silent prayer before meals, the finger nail inspections, the ritual polishing of shoes on Saturday, the Thursday night Bible reading, the suppression of spontaneity. As a child he had rebelled in every possible way, defying the rules obliquely, reveling in every victory.

In contrast, as a recruit he found himself to be acquiescent, passive, except for ironic observations shared with Fritz Biebelmeyer. The mindless humiliations of a soldier in the Kaiser's army were visited on a mannequin who resembled Franz. Franz, perched on his own shoulder, observed with clinical detachment his response to boots that rubbed his feet raw; long, hot marches carrying sixty kilos; five hours sleep followed by a cold shower with laundry soap; and toilets arranged in a row like seats at the Opera.

He marched in file with men dressed in grey tunics, each carrying identical packs containing exactly the same necessities, the same rifles carried the same way, their hob nailed soles striking the cobbles with martial rhythm. Franz's baritone merged into a deep hoarse collective male organ sound, *"Lieb vaterland, magst ruhig sein. . . ."* Despite all the regimentation, he felt as free as he had ever been in his life. Merged in a collective body, committed to perform a common function, mutually supportive as an ideal society should be, he was no longer burdened by perplexing choice and responsibility. The smell of sweat and oiled leather was strangely comforting. Marguerite was far away, as was Kandinsky. They couldn't tug insistently at his sleeve in different directions.

As a youth he had considered a vocation in the church. He recalled the thin silver hair and pale, transparent skin of Father Hauser; the pale light in his eyes as he interpreted some passage of the New Testament. Franz had seen and in his own way absorbed that mystical aura of faith. Now he had that vocation and purpose.

They had descended to the platform from the coaches of a long train, spilling onto the narrow space and forming into ranks on barked commands. The coaches were marked with their destinations and the numbers of the units and decorated with sprigs of evergreen. Far down the platform, cavalry horses, nervous from the long confinement, were being led clattering down a ramp from wood-sided carriages. In front, nearer the hissing and clanging locomotive, open cars were being emptied of wood crates of ammunition and food by weary looking Belgian prisoners overseen by indifferent looking *Landsturm* in dark blue tunics with red collars.

It was Sunday morning. Franz was still stiff from having spent the night in a cramped 3rd class coach, sleeping sitting up wedged between two of his comrades. They had eaten a hurried breakfast—bread, sausage and coffee—passed around at the station and were marching to church, a sacrosanct initiation in the ritual of war. A paradox that the minions of the Prince of Peace should bless the warriors, he mused. But it had always been this way, men going off on campaigns to take lives and destroy property. Out of the ruin and chaos came order and civilization, the lesson of Roman history. The great *Pax Romana* fused with iron and discipline.

Except for the endless rows of supply wagons filling the ample town square, the stacked rifles, cars, trucks, ordinance, and soldiers, the town was going about its Sunday business, he saw. Shops were opening, there was a crowd of women outside a bakery—he could smell the fresh bread. A man in a green apron was washing the window of a cafe. The occupation seemed benign on the surface.

The church was brick with two spires and a sharply pitched slate roof. The interior was neo-gothic under a soaring pitched ceiling crossed by wooden beams. A large stained glass rosette window was suspended above the altar and chancel like a many colored imploding flower. Light, muted and enriched, was trapped in its web. Windows on the side aisles were opaque, filling the church with white light. Given its relative simplicity it was, he assumed, a church meant to express the values of the Enlightenment.

Franz's company was the last to enter. Except for a smattering of civilians in black, everyone wore a uniform of the German army. A group of sisters, their heads covered, looked fresh and starched as clean sheets. Officers in tight tunics with double rows of brass buttons were sitting in a block in front

The organ resounded with, *A Mighty Fortress Is Our God*. The notes shot from the pipes and exploded against the ceiling. The chaplain officiated in a military tunic. He spoke of their mission, of the preservation of the Germanic people, of the higher goal of bringing a lasting peace to a tortured and fragmented Europe, of the need to defend the Fatherland decisively to put an end to the conflicts that had seized and ravaged Europe so often. German order, German justice, German respect for law, subservience to higher authority, German industry, German enlightenment, were values worthy of sacrifice and propagation. Seven hundred varied voices filled the space with *Deutschland Uber Alles*, the national hymn.

As the anthem reached a climax, Franz's eyes filled with tears. He longed for a purer more just world and longed equally to belong to it, to have a role in creating it. His voice joined with others, blended in the same words, the same notes, the same spirit. It was a moment of completion in which he felt suddenly one with a great human destiny. The echoes died and, on command, the units rose and filed out row by row.

Beside him, Fritz Biebelmeyer muttered under his breath, "Shit."

March 11, 1915 – Till

A slanting rain, hard and cold as hail, dropped from heavy bruised clouds. The road was slippery. Teams of six dray horses struggled to pull the loaded ammunition wagons through mud up to the axles, and the outriders were spattered head to foot. Sounds of battle, the first Franz had heard, came from a distant forest, low rising rumbles, an ominous sound like rolling kettle drums. The sound and its meaning sent a thrill of fear through him. His comrades were stolid as they slogged along the side of the road flanking the endless chain of supply wagons headed for the front. Fritz, his comrade on the left, reached into his pocket for a chunk of bread and began to chew slowly. "If I liked swimming I'd have joined the Navy," he slurred through a full mouth. He was a broad chested, bandy legged man. Still in his twenties, his face was already tracked with fine red veins. He was from East Prussia and had a pointed Slavic nose, a receding chin, and narrow bleached blue eyes. A long blond walrus mustache covered his upper lip.

"Turn your collar up," said Franz.

"What and collect rain water down my back and into my boots? Thanks for nothing."

They passed a staff car that had slid off the roadway. Three officers with identical pointed waxed mustaches, peaked hats and long ankle length coats were watching impatiently as a group of soldiers, showered by spraying mud from the spinning wheels, tried to push and heave it out of a ditch.

Horst Baum, one of their squad, began to sing. He had a fine baritone voice and usually started the songs. The others followed, slowly at first, but the spirit was contagious and soon they were all singing full-throated and defiant, merging the rhythm of the martial song with the pace of the march.

Franz was miserable, but somehow content with his misery. The cold, the damp feet, the burning blisters on his soles where his boots chafed, the cramped muscles in his shoulders and back from the heavy pack and rifle were to him, a ritual fulfillment of an atavistic Teutonic fate. As he slipped and slogged along Franz imagined Siegfried bravely approaching the cave of the giant and heard a fragment of the magic fire music. He smelled the smoke curling out of the chimney of a farm house beside the road and wondered what it would be like to be simple, uneducated, even illiterate, to be bound to the rhythm of the seasons, the crops, the animals, to have no sensitivity to, or part in, the tidal changes taking place in the world.

Two farm horses, one black the other sorrel, stood in a pasture under the branches of a tree, their heads down, looking forlorn in the rain. Did they envy their cousins in harness pulling a load of heavy artillery shells toward the front? Each shell could destroy a house, kill half a dozen people and the horses were delivering them to their, as yet unassigned, destination. He wished at the moment that he could stop, take out his sketchbook and capture the enduring mood of the troops, the muscular struggle of the team. He would do it from memory later when they put up their canvas tent for the night.

He looked sidelong at Fritz, his comrade, a man who in normal times he would never have met. They had been together since the training camp, their cots had been next to each other. Franz loved the working man anonymously but he was not the kind of cerebral socialist who hung around in working class bars trying to be something he wasn't. Yet he and Fritz had become friends. Fritz was muttering to himself. He liked to talk and was glib and amusing. Self-educated, mostly from anarchist newspapers and pamphlets, Fritz was earthy, vulgar and irreverent, often making his comrades laugh with his pranks and jokes. And he was sly, avoiding blame with his quick tongue. Franz's private name for him was *Till Eulenspiegel*, the peasant clown of German folklore, but he hadn't mentioned it.

"What are you mumbling, Fritz?"

"I was imagining that ammunition wagon there, the one marked 14-7, was filled with beer barrels. What a war that would be. Franz, what do you think, everything has numbers on it, we are so organized. Do you think the artillery shells are marked as well? This one for the 5th Parisian sewer cleaners battalion, that one for the general staff of the fifth army?"

"I'm told the artillerymen write messages on them just to kill time," Franz said.

"Even time gets killed in the war."

Franz slipped and went down on one knee in the mud. Fritz and Horst grabbed him under the arms and hoisted him to his feet. His hands were covered with mud.

"Step smartly now!" barked Corporal Fromm, a tall, stoop-shouldered man with a gaunt long-jawed face, a bank clerk from Wiesbaden.

"Thank you for the advice," muttered Fritz and Franz had to laugh.

July 18, 1915 – Hospital

The town was little more than a double row of houses and shops flanking an arching stone bridge over a shallow roiling stream: a bakery, a cafe, a post office, and a church, its spire perched on a square bell tower watched over the crossing. The boots and shod hoofs of the advancing German army echoed with the reprise of scraping sandals of Roman legions, the heavy footfalls of armored knights on their war horses and the cleated boots of combatants of the Thirty Years War, drowning out the quiet commerce of traders and farmers and the grinding of their high wheeled carts on the stone surface. All had made their mark on the stone, had passed over this bridge—or one like it—stopping to drink or wash in the clear spring fed stream before disappearing through the far notch

between the hills. Most, thought Franz, had come with purpose which, to the leaders if not the conscripts, had made
sense and seemed worth the risk of life and fortune. Every
mission had been blest by one church or another. The face of
the bridge was like a lithographic stone, each new impression obliterating the one before.

The valley was narrow, the forested hills rose steeply, leaving barely enough room for narrow fields set off from the
road by low, grey, mossy stone walls. Their company was
camped for the night in a field nearest the village. Double
rows of tents were staked in the mud. At one end horses had
been tethered; at the other, smoke was curling from the bean
shooter, the tall chimney of the cook wagon. The smell of the
cooking pea soup blended with the smoke from the chimney.
Sentries in long coats walked the perimeter. Soldiers idled in
groups, smoking, talking quietly. Several men were washing
underdrawers and socks on the river bank. The constant rush
and susuration of the river over grey stones contrasted with
the sporadic distant drumming of the French artillery.

Franz crossed the bridge slowly, stopping to look at the
play of silver and gold on the water, the trembling leaves over-
hanging the banks, the twisted roots of trees exposed by late
winter flood. Below the surface of the water he saw the languid fluid movements of a fish. He took out his notebook
and sketched the shadows and light, the trees and branches.
A lumbering red-faced man in baggy blue work clothes clutching a loaf of bread stopped to see what he was doing, then
passed on without a word.

The smell of fresh bread made him aware of his hunger
and he went to the bakery and bought a roll. The hollow-
cheeked young woman who took his money avoided his eyes
as she counted out his change.

An ambulance was parked in front of the church. Wounded
soldiers lying on stretchers were being carried up the twelve
worn stone steps to the gothic arch of the doorway. A doctor
in a white coat asked Franz to give a hand. He walked to the
back of the ambulance and was repelled by the astringent
smell. An orderly passed the handles of a stretcher to him
and he backed away as the man holding the other end climbed

down the ambulance steps to the ground. The wounded man was covered by a maroon blanket, his head swathed in thick bandages down to his nostrils. Blood had seeped through the bandages and made a fresh red to rust stain where his ear was or had been. Franz felt pity for the man, wondered if he would recover and was seized with dread.

The church, he saw, had become a hospital. Most of the pews had been removed and stacked against the walls leaving an open stone floor covered with straw pallets in rows, carefully laid out with regulated thoroughness, leaving just enough room between them to walk and bend. At the far end, the altar had been converted to an operating space separated from the makeshift ward by white curtains concealing the operation and yet, implying a hidden function, a shadow play, its meaning suggested but unrevealed. Over the screened area a long cross was suspended by wires from the high ceiling. It hovered in space pointing toward the function below, its arms outstretched in a gesture of benediction, embrace, or hopelessness. Light from the clear round window behind it gave the cross an aura defining its dark silhouette. Within the compass of the cross men lay in silent shock, sedated or dying.

He carried the stretcher down the center aisle toward a beckoning doctor, lifted it to an examining table where, he knew, a decision would be made to try to save or let die. Triage, they called it. The doctor was all in white: a white cap covered his head, white gloves stained with blood covered his hands. His eyes were concentrated, intense, the grey-blue of surgical steel, reduced behind round steel rimmed lenses. Attentive nurses in white aprons over grey dresses, their hair covered like nuns listened watched, and responded to his muttered commands. Overcome with a wave of nausea, Franz turned away as the doctor began to cut away the bandages. The astringent carbolic smell, the cloying ether fumes, a memory of incense combined to make him light-headed and he hurried down the aisle before the angel of death could take note of him. Bright sunlight coming through the door made him squint and he looked up toward the filtered colors of a rosette.

His eyes turned inward, focused on the layers of observation, seeking the shape of the invisible reality of the field hospital, Franz walked toward the camp. He found his comrade, Fritz, behind their tent, sitting on a stump, plucking the white feathers out of a plump hen.

"How's that for luck, Franz. This hen volunteered to make us a dinner. No pea soup tonight, huh?"

"Volunteered?"

"Ran up to me and dropped dead at my feet."

"You know the punishment for looting. If Corporal Baum sees you, you'll pay for your bite of chicken."

"The corporal gets his choice, half a breast."

"Already agreed?"

"You bet. He's not such a bad guy, Corporal Baum, even if he is regular army."

"Can I help?"

"Make a little fire and find something for a spit so we can do a nice even roast, and cadge a little paprika from the cook."

"What do you think this is, the Hotel Excelsior? Paprika!"

"He's got a stash of it. He's Hungarian."

September 23, 1915 – Recent Battle

The fields around the village bore the raw wounds of recent fighting. The dead had already been buried, some just where they had fallen. By the side of the road, Franz saw a fresh mound of earth marked by a board on which was written in black script, "Klaus Scharm no. 1463 142d reg. Died for Kaiser and Country." Beyond the road was a farmhouse, its roof a charred skeleton of burned timbers; beside it the remains of a French gun emplacement, the gun, a howitzer, sleeping on its side. The bare field between the house and the road was pocked where shells had fallen. The verge of the road was littered with the detritus of battle; bloody fragments of uniforms; bright brass shell and bullet casings; a rifle, its stock broken. A white horse lay on its side, just beginning to give off the putrid smell of decay from spilled entrails and torn flesh. Franz turned to study the head eyes clouded, mouth open, black lips drawn back in a frozen scream, yellow teeth clenched and bared.

They came into the cobbled square of a village. The buildings were pitted by bullets and shell fragments, windows were broken and there were jagged holes in many walls including the grey stone church. A detachment of Uhlans were just dismounting from tall black horses, steaming flanks shining with sweat, metal shoes ringing against the cobbles. The high black leather boots, tall hats, wood lances were ceremonial, anachronistic relics of earlier wars, Franco-Prussian or even Napoleonic, Franz mused. They might have been ghosts of dead warrior ancestors, symbolizing the continuity of warfare like the myths of long dead Teutonic knights riding out of the mist. A strain of Tannhauser ran through his head What could they do with their lances against armor, or machine guns, he wondered?

Late afternoon. A penumbra of sun was hidden behind an unbroken pallid sky. The air was still but brittle and chilling. The column came to a welcome stop. For a change they were to camp inside a building, the church. Most of the long peaked windows were out but jagged pieces of glass remained. A part of the roof had fallen and the debris, fragments of timber, slate, brick and mortar from the walls were strewn everywhere. Another unit, Landsturm by the look of their dark blue tunics, was already settled in. Pews were hung or stacked with drying underwear, tunics, packs, stacked rifles, ammunition pouches. It was a telegraph unit, Franz saw. Wires ran from tables up and out the windows. The wood boxes transporting the equipment were stacked in front of a life-sized grey stone Pieta.

Franz settled down on a pew beside Fritz. They lit cigarettes. Fritz allowed that the only good that had come of the war so far was to turn every church into a hostel. He found a hymnal, riffled through the pages, tore out twenty and put them in his pocket.

"That's pretty low, even for an anarchist," said Franz shaking his head.

"Which is better, Franz, from a Christian point of view, to kill a fellow Christian in battle or to use a few pages of his prayer book to wipe your ass?"

"I must yield to your logic, Fritz."

"I'm going to send a telegram," Fritz said and he got up and slid down the pew to the aisle and walked to the front of the church. The equipment was sounding a high nervous pulse and the operator was bent over the table transposing the sounds on a white lined pad with a short pencil. When the instrument fell silent, the operator looked up at Fritz with fatigued condescension. He had a deeply creased forehead and thinning hair.

"How about a message to Berlin for a can of sardines?" said Fritz with mock authority.

The operator took his measure. "To your pregnant wife, no doubt, or maybe it's your dying mother."

"How did you guess?"

"You are only the twenty-fourth soldier to ask in the last two days."

"So can you do it?"

"Even General von Moltke can't do it."

"How about the Kaiser?"

"Not even him."

"Ah well, what kind of place have we come to."

"You can see for yourself."

Fritz walked about, chatting with the Landsturmers, trading a cigarette for a swig of schnapps and eventually strolled back to where Franz was sitting. He had left the pew and was stretched out on the stone floor his back against the wall, sketching the dead horse they had passed on the edge of town. His arm was resting on a *blindganger*, an unexploded artillery shell. Fritz slid to the floor beside him and watched.

"A dead horse! Of all the things you've seen. Why that?"

"It sums it all up, don't you agree?" Franz answered without looking up, his hand still moving quickly on the drawing.

"What are you going to do with all those drawings in that notebook, give them to your friends after the war?"

"Maybe. If there is an after."

"Think you'll die? That's a bad attitude, Franz. You got to keep your head. Bullets look for the soldiers marked for death, you know."

"Just superstition, and you an anarchist."

"Don't you want to live?"

"I want to live but I don't mind dying. It's the ultimate adventure, the end of all suffering, all fear, the beginning of perfect peace."

"What a load of horse shit. Hit yourself in the head with a rock because it feels good to stop. Franz, you know what I think?"

"What do you think, Fritz?"

"You're too sensitive. You think too much."

"Is that so." Franz was still drawing.

"You miss the point of life. A good sausage, a good beer and a good fuck is what it's all about."

"There, its finished. What do you think?"

"I think it's a dead horse."

April 6, 1916 – In The Earth

It was spring. Warm rain, a welcome change from the freezing torrents of March, had turned the bottom of the trenches to a fecal muck that both looked and smelled like a cesspool. The dugout Franz shared with ten of his comrades was, by comparison, comfortable. Roofed and walled by logs covered with earth, the walls lined with narrow sleeping shelves, the space was both drafty from the single doorway blocked by a canvas curtain, and rank and stifling with the smell of sweat and unwashed clothing. Despite their efforts to keep it livable, it was filthy. The floor was packed dirt; sand and soil seeped between the logs of the low ceiling as shells exploded and formed a film in the coffee or on the soup. Fritz called it "French pepper" and claimed it improved the flavor. Franz named it *gout de terre,* taste of the earth. Fleas lived in every straw mattress and lice passed from man to man. Rats stole food. Even so, a kerosene lamp suspended over the rough plank table gave enough light for reading, letter writing, and card playing, and there was an arm chair with a pillow made of a threadbare Turkish rug covering the broken woven seat. It was all that home stood for; shelter, respite, companionship, food; yet disrupted by the constant threat of death.

The trench was narrow but deep enough to stand up. Rough slabs of wood kept the earth in place. Sandbags and a bramble bush of twisted barbed wire rose above the surface of the ground. Franz called it the crown of thorns. To the left of the opening of their bunker was an emplacement that housed a Maxim machine gun and upright binoculars with mirrors so that an observer could safely look over the rim of the trench at the French lines barely 100 meters away.

It was a rare moment of calm. Franz and Fritz were sitting at the table, finishing their hot meal of boiled mutton, potatoes, rice.

"Did you hear 14 Company lost its peashooter last night?" asked Fritz, as he mopped the bottom of his tin plate with a clod of bread

"No," said Franz.

"Direct hit from a French growler. The commissary has a new recipe for the pea soup: add bones from the cook."

"Funny."

"You can't let it get you down, all this dying. You can't get like Hasse, a living corpse."

"You can't close your eyes, either." Franz shoved the plate aside and scratched a pattern of flea bites on his chest. He wrinkled his nose at the fetid smell of his unwashed body.

"You, Franz, told me a while back that it was all part of making that new world."

"I believed that."

"You don't now?"

"It's easy to say in the abstract, Fritz. Until you see somebody who has just shared his last cigarette with you chopped up in front of you, and pieces of his brains or his guts are all over your tunic. Still, we're all going to die. Why not for a purpose."

"Call this a purpose? It's all for the rich."

"Maybe. I'm not so sure as I once was."

"Shut the fuck up, I'm trying to sleep," came a muffled whine from one of the bunks.

In a lower tone Fritz continued, "I read a book about Napoleon a couple of years ago. He had the same idea. United Europe. No more wars. But all the frog and snail eaters got was a military burial. You know that's why the French are so short?"

"Are they short?"

"Yeah. You've seen them coming at you."

"I wasn't thinking about their height."

"You aren't curious?"

" So why?"

"Because all the big ones got killed fighting with Napoleon. I read it in a book."

June 24, 1916 – Attack

The barrage began exactly at ten o'clock. The bright orange flashes spread like spilled wine then paled an instant before the sharp concentrated explosion that sent the shell rattling on its whining track toward the German positions. Franz hunched down as the shrill sound grew louder and flinched as the expanding impact deafened him. The ground shuddered under his feet before earth and metal slivers rained down on the trench nicking wood and slicing through the cloth of his uniform. The same again and again and again, each shell causing the same tension, the same fear, the same anticipation, until his mind sandbagged it out but never completely.

All of the French batteries were firing and the reports and explosions overlapped, merged, were continuous. Shells sometimes landed near enough to cave the trench in, collapse a bunker, or exploded right over the trench sending weapons and men flying in pieces of bloody flesh and shattered bone. The men remained in place crouched, plastered against the wall of the trench, hoping that their new steel helmets would deflect the fragments, hoping that the shells didn't have their name on them, would fall short, pass over, not explode. Franz waited, almost eager to know what his last feeling or thought would be if his body were blown apart, wondering where his spirit would go if anywhere, wishing that it would be over!

Precisely twenty minutes later, the barrage stopped. As the echo died, the vacuum of silence was like a breath of ether. His nerves froze and he was aware of a flutter in his heart. Sometimes the barrage presaged an attack. Would it be this time? he wondered, feeling a taught wire in his body slowly release.

Captain Sharnhorst had both eyes pressed against the binoculars, turning them slowly to scan the French line for a sign of movement. Nothing moving. Five minutes passed, minutes that seemed like half an hour. Tension pulsed along the trench.

Franz watched the Captain turn away for a moment, wipe his forehead with the back of his leather glove, turn back, stiffen and recoil. "The French are coming over!" he shouted. An orderly immediately ran to the field telephone station and the alarm passed up and down the trench in shouts. Within a minute men, some half dressed, spilled out of their bunkers and took their places, bayonets glistening darkly in the moonlight.

The spool in Franz's gut wound his nerves taut and he rested the Mauser on the cradle notched between two sandbags and looked down the sight. They were coming, not rushing as a flood but cautiously, rising, rushing and falling, hoping to gain ground in safety before the running assault on the German salient. How many waves would there be? How many times would the German machine guns cut them down before they were repulsed?

He heard the rifle bolts sliding smoothly and snapping bullets in place. Nearby, Manke was running the belt that fed the bullets into the Maxim machine gun over his bandaged palm to reduce the possibility of a jam. The French were back on their feet and running now. The Captain would give the command when he could see the red of their pants in the moonlight. Franz reached back and opened his cartridge case and felt around for the clips. Ten seconds could make a difference. They were an undulating moving wall. He felt the force of their will pushing the air ahead of them.

"Fire!"

The four Maxims began their rhythmic stutter up and down the line, slowly rotating in an elliptical pattern of overlapping fields of fire. The German Mausers sounded like spattering oil. Franz leveled his weapon, focused on the moving shadows and began to fire, over and over again, stopping only to snap a new clip into the breach. The shadows spun, leaped, stumbled, staggered forward, fell, arms flew up, but others kept coming. His head was full of a pulsating steady roar, the sound of a great cataract of water at spring flood. A grenade exploded in front of him shattering a sand bag and blinding him with sand and earth. He stopped and wiped his eyes. When they had cleared he saw that the machine gun on his right had jammed and Manke was fussing with the breach to clear it. The Maxim flew into the air and Manke spun around and fell. The gun landed on top of him. Down the line the French had breached the barbed wire and were spilling and tumbling into the gap firing at random, falling as German bullets found them at close range. He fired reflexively at the men leaping into the trench until they stopped coming. The rest of the line had held and the French were apparently falling back.

The firing slowed like the end of a sudden spring shower and finally stopped. Bayonet thrust before him, he and the others cautiously approached the tangle of fallen Frenchmen. The first, a stain of blood spreading over the side of his blue tunic, looked up at him, his eyes wide.

"Don't be afraid," said Franz in French. It was the first time he had looked into the face of a French soldier. The man was young. "Can you walk?"

"I think so. I'll try."

Franz reached down and helped the soldier to his feet.

"The dressing station is just down there. Where are you from?"

Franz asked as if he had just encountered him in the compartment of a train. He felt no animosity, felt nothing at all. His legs felt like they were made of lead, his hands were trembling. He wanted to sit down in the comfort of his dugout, drink some coffee. Where was Fritz? he suddenly asked himself. The man beside him, leaning on his arm, answered the question but Franz had already forgotten he had even asked it.

July 8, 1916 – Conversation

It should have been an ordinary summer day. True, it was hot and damp and the sun's fingers burned. The heavy steel which deflected shell fragments also fried the brains. Franz rubbed the sweat out of his eyes and wondered what the knights encased in heavy amour head to foot had felt like on a day like this. It was an ordinary day for the trenches, a day when nothing happened. Men, their bare backs exposed to the sun, were drying out clothes, stretching them on the rear lip of the trench. Others were strip-cleaning their weapons, or changing the straw in the mattresses. The mail had just been distributed and letters were being read and read again.

Franz and Fritz were on duty, watching the thin line of barbed wire across the wasteland, bored but relieved that nothing was going on. Between their trench and the French salient was, to Franz, a landscape abstracted by war. What had once been open meadow shaded by random beech and oak was now a matrix of pits and shattered columns. The trees, their branches amputated by shell fragments to the length of outstretched arms, had been sculpted into rustic crucifixes or cenotaphs. True, there was grass, and here and there a flower, a recollection or a portent, well fertilized with blood, growing between water filled pocks. The field was littered with broken rifles, cartridge cases, helmets with holes through them, boots, one with a bone and rotting flesh sticking out of it. At least there were no corpses. Each side under the pass of a white flag removed their own wounded and dead after the firing.

The German salient was as close to the French as anywhere in the sector. At the closest point flag poles faced each other with the regimental colors, red and black for the Germans, blue and gold for the French.

Franz felt something against his leg and turned to see Geistle, a small collie, nudging his leg with her long nose. He reached into his pocket, found a crust of bread and fed it to her. More than a mascot, Geistle was trained to locate the severely wounded after an engagement. For that reason at least, everyone, even the soldiers who had no love for dogs, treated her to sausage, hoping that she would recognize them and bark to summon the medics. He rubbed her head, ruffled her ears. She looked up, made contact with her gentle brown eyes. Her head turned toward something only she could hear and she made her way down the twisting bed of the trench

sniffing the ground and looking up hopefully at other soldiers as she went.

A rifle crackled from the other side and Franz looked up
to see if the limp pennant hanging from its staff trembled.
On days like this sharpshooters honed their skills by shred-
ding the other side's pennant. Buchmann, a lanky farm boy
from Schleswig-Holstein, had just come out of the bunker
cursing, having as usual, hit his head on the low lintel. Fritz
saw him. "The frogs are out of bed and looking for something to do, Buchmann. Raise the target. We'll see if they got
any better than last time."

"Not my job to make them better."

"C'mon, Buchmann. You got nothing better to do."

Buchman scratched a flea bite, looked around, saw the
broom and the old helmet on the ground. He put the helmet
on the broom, raised it above the level of the barb wire and
bobbed it up and down. Within a few seconds bullets whirred
over the top of the trench, missing the helmet.

Fritz laughed cupped his hands to his mouth and shouted,
"You frogs couldn't hit a barn with an ammo wagon."

"Stick your head up Fritzie and we'll air out your brains if
you have any." The words were distant, in an Alsatian dialect,
but understandable.

"The frog knows my name," said Fritz.

"You and the other ten million Fritzs."

"I know that, Buchmann. Buchmann thinks I'm stupid,"
he added, turning to Franz. "Give them a second chance,
Buchmann." Again, the helmet went up and the shots were
wide.

"Must be the crooked barrels on your guns," Fritz shouted.

No response from the French for about five minutes, until
a blue cloth forage cap was raised over the French barbed
wire and shifted back and forth. Franz looked down the line
at Visser, the sharpshooter on duty. He was steadying his rifle,
his cheek was stroking the gun. He squeezed the trigger and
the hat spun around on the first shot. Half a dozen
soldiers,watching, cheered.

"There you go Pierre, come over and we'll show you how!"
Fritz shouted.

August 13, 1916 – The Milk Cow

"Do you hear what I hear, Franz?"

"Sounds like a cow."

"Even a city boy like me knows a cow, and that's a cow. An unhappy cow by the sound of it."

"Must have gotten out of its pasture and wandered out there."

It was early dawn and the horizon was beginning to glow with pale grey light. The mist lay heavy on the ground, a swirl-ing, eddying grey skin that covered the debris of war and al-most made Franz forget the wasted ground that lay between the serpentine trenches of the two armies. They had both been up on watch all night, with still two hours to go before relief. Franz was groggy, his eyelids were heavy, his limbs felt like they were hung with weights. It was more than just the fa-tigue and monotony of the night on duty. The war seemed to be dragging him into the ground like so many of his fallen comrades. The night before he had started awake from a re-current dream in a sweating panic, still feeling the rotten bony hands grasping at his legs, dragging him into the stinking muddy bottom of a shell crater.

Sometime, he wasn't sure when, the belief that the war would unify and harmonize Europe had become absurd and meaningless against the tens of thousands of lives destroyed, wasted in a single, futile, frontal attack. His sense of high and transcendent purpose had faded like newsprint left in the sun. It had become a curious, dangerous custom observed by tribesmen in a nameless land. The attacks came at any time, always preceded by an endless deafening, nerve-rending downpour of metal. They seemed to take turns, the French and the Germans. It was a ritual, with no more purpose than to see how many shells might be exploded, how many bullets ejected from rifles and machine guns and with what toll on the adversary. Somewhere in headquarters, fastidious records were being kept by shipping clerks in uniform. How many times had he and his comrades run madly and fearfully into the cacophonous hail of bullets and rain of shrapnel only to return exhausted, limp, with but half the men who had left the trench. He had lost count. In fact he hadn't counted. Each time, he was convinced, would be his last and he was always surprised to find himself tumbling behind the earth and wood walls of the German trench, nearly hysterical with release.

If he had learned anything from the experience, it was to savor the small favors of life: the taste of a cigarette, hot coffee, a cold shower, the smell of soap, a change of socks, the bacon rind taste of bean soup, sight of the orange ball of sun flattening on a distant ridge and its fevered wake of retreating light. He missed the singing of birds, the scent of a rose.

Franz shifted his rifle to his left shoulder and muttered, "How long do you think it will last, that unfortunate cow?"

"Why? You think the frogs will shoot it for target practice. No. Too many farmers in the trench."

"What about our boys?"

"Same thing. Who can say? The cow might make a truce between us. Maybe end the war altogether. The generals bent down by all their medals for bravery and cunning will sit down at a long polished table with pens and red wax seals and sign the treaty of Olga."

"Nice thought, Fritz."

"So when will it end, Franz?"

"When we are all dead."

"No sooner than that?"

"Every war ends, sooner or later." Franz fished for a cigarette. The pack was empty. He crumpled it and tossed it over the lip of the trench.

"Who do you think will shoot first?"

"Whoever is the biggest fool."

The cow kept up a steady miserable lowing, reminding Franz of the imperatives of men in pain left behind, perforated sounds that only ended when the hope had spilled out with their blood, merging with the lingering cordite fumes and sucking mud. Often, men risked their own lives to bring a comrade back. Sometimes, it couldn't be done and there was only the sound, the guilt, and relief that it was someone else.

The waxing opaline light exposed the cow, midway between the lines, black and white, head down, a lead rope caught in a tangle of barbed wire. Franz knew the cow, he had painted one like it before the war. The painting had symbolised a simpler world threatened by change with unpredictable results. The cow, a simple animal, a passive food-giver, represented in part an agrarian way of life based on the land, and here it was before him, an emissary from that plane of life, a sacrifice to institutionalized slaughter. Liberating the cow, his cow, suddenly became the imperative of his day.

"I'm going to see the duty officer, Fritz. You hold off the French till I get back." It was a standing joke between them.

"*Javohl.*"

Captain Schwam had only been with the company three weeks, replacing Herbst who had lost his left arm to a French mortar shell. Schwam was a puffy pudding of a man with a gurgling voice and a habit of punctuating every sentence with several "ahhs." He greeted Franz with a scowl and a yawn that expired foul breath.

"What's up?"

"A cow, sir, caught between the lines."

"So?"

"I would like permission to free it, under a white flag of course."

Schwam took his measure with a weary contemptuous gaze. There was nothing in the rules of war about cows, nothing that he could recall in the army code. "Look, aahh. . . ."

"Marc, sir."

"I don't have the authority to send a delegation out under a white flag. That's within the authority of the regimental staff."

"It's not a truce sir, it's more like recovering wounded men."

"You a farmer, Marc?"

"No sir, a painter."

"House painter?"

"Pictures, sir. I thought Vogel could go with me. He's a farmer. He would know how to handle it. The men could use some fresh milk in their morning coffee sir. It would be good for morale."

"Which one's Vogel."

"A little cross-eyed sir. Hair like thatch."

"Oh, him. If you must. Nothing to be signed of course. Nothing in the reports needed, not for a cow."

He found Vogel, poured a cup of cold water on his head—he was a sound sleeper. Vogel was ready to kill him until he heard about the cow. They found a bucket and the white flag on its telescopic pole and raised it high enough to be clearly seen by the French. It took the French ten minutes to respond with the same signal. With an expectant nod, Franz and Vogel, unarmed except for the white flag and bucket, stepped cautiously over the barbed wire rim and began to walk toward the French lines, skirting shell holes, trying not to see the rotting flesh and shattered bone fragments. Across the field they saw two red and blue clad French soldiers carrying a similar white flag. One returned to the trench and seemed to call for something. Franz smiled to himself as he saw a bucket handed up to him and the man trotted forward and soon caught up with his comrade.

Sure enough the cow was caught by a lead rope in a tangle of barbed wire and its udder was full. Its head down, eyes rolling and wide, bellowing repeatedly, the cow tugged and tugged at the rope, and Franz observed, due to the internal law of ropes, the harder the cow pulled, the more the rope clung to its tangle of barbed wire. Without a word, Vogel bent with the bucket and began massaging the cow's teat with a regular motion and the milk began to squirt into the bottom of the bucket. Bending lower, he opened his mouth and sent a stream inside, completing the motion with a satisfying, "Mmmm, makes me think I'm home. Want some?"

The French soldiers came up and looked at them with uncertain smiles. They introduced themselves and stood facing each other, not sure whether it would be correct to shake hands. One of them was a corporal, a tall, long faced man with a dominant nose. The other was slight, with a weathered face and small dark feral eyes.

"Save some for them, Vogel, or there'll be war," said Franz, and Vogel, still on his knees backed away with a gesture to the smaller man, who moved in and resumed the milking.

Franz turned to the rope and, while the tall Frenchman

held the halter, he managed to wrest it from the grip of the rusted barbed wire. The two of them held the animal, no longer moaning, while the milking continued. Franz breathed in the smell of the cow, thought for a moment of the farm at Lenggreis, looked the Frenchman in eye and searched for something to say.

"I guess we both had the same idea," Franz said.

The man's expression brightened as he recognized Franz's fluent French. "After all, it's just a poor innocent beast. It's the least we could do. What did you say your name was?"

"Franz Marc."

"You're not the painter are you?"

"Why yes," he said, pleased to have been recognized.

"I saw your work exhibited in Paris, before the War. I liked it very much. Are you done, Rouselet? Why not leave a little for the poor farmer's children." The four men looked at each other with unspoken satisfaction. They looked at the cow reluctant to let go of the moment. Then, as if by signal, Franz looped the rope end into the halter so that the cow would not trip on it and opened his hand. The cow turned and lumbered away from them, showing them bony haunches and a switching tail.

The Frenchman watched it, then turned toward Franz and said, "At least we've accomplished something here."

Franz extended his hand and the man took it. The two men squeezed firmly, held on to the amity, then released. Franz turned back toward the fluttering red and black pennant, still feeling the calloused contact of the man's hand. He and Vogel returned to cheers from their comrades. It was the only moment of war in which he felt human.

4

Harry, 1945, Post-War Years

October 13, 1945 – City of the Dead

The guards had left in trucks, without ceremony, abandoning the fastidious records of food consumed, daily caloric intake per inmate, admissions and deaths by coded causes, even the no longer sacred flag found floating in the latrine by the first Americans to drive through the open gates. The survivors had been moved to other camps. The mounds of rotting skin-covered skeletons had already been buried by subdued nauseated civilians from nearby towns brought to the camp at gun point. A double electrified barbed wire fence interspersed by guard towers separated the compound from the surrounding pine woods which could be seen across a cleared firing range.

Inside the fence were long rows of uniform barracks, geometric, functional, a work of art, he concluded, designed to create the illusion of life, but committed to the death of every human who could not produce for the siege state more than the cost of feeding and maintaining them. Everything was there to sustain the process: large pots to cook soup, boards to remove bread from the oven, mounds of clothing sorted by category, piles of suitcases. There was even a tidy hospital with sterilized nickel-plated instruments, bandages, splints, and pharmacy bottles with simple remedies. Some buildings housed workshops to make and repair clothing and shoes, and restore military salvage. Others contained showers to cleanse the inmate of all pain and desire and rid a continent of those judged to be unworthy of life. Furnaces with tall chimneys reduced the organic evidence to bone meal, transient flame, heat, and effulgent black greasy smoke.

Harry wandered freely through the barracks and ware-houses, traversing paths strewn with pale cinders that might have been bone. Entering a dim warehouse, he came on piles of unsorted clothing reaching to the rafters. Vanity and confidence spilled from the suitcases in no more order than the human contents of the boxcars that brought them. Business suits, white linen underwear consoled by a pink silk slip, the armless sleeve of a shirt reaching out for help, a baby's calico bib, embroidered with a smiling brown bear, resting on top of a ruffled blouse. Each item held some sense of the person who had once worn it to the cinema or in the garden or in the leather swivel chair of a bank manager; a favorite scent, the smell of pipe tobacco, or sweat. The wings of dusty moths beat against his heart as, like a voyeur, he wandered through the abandoned derelict bedrooms and kitchens of the missing, nearly smothered by the residue of motion, affection, ambition, resignation. There were no voices, yet he heard sounds, many languages, but no single word, and when he reached down to feel some object, formless hands reached toward him.

He looked at his watch and saw that two hours had passed and it struck him that he had slipped through the pulse of seconds to a space where time had no meaning. Harry picked up objects at random; a fragment of an official document; part of a stamp, the extended wing of a stylized eagle, still visible; a piece of rough gray cloth; a yellow button; a clod of clay like earth; a splinter of wood; a fragment of what might have been a poem and, finally, a handful of ashes interlaced with fragments of bone. He put them all in an outside pocket of his pack, wedging them around the artist's sketchbook that he had found in the trunk.

November 2, 1945 – An Affair

Off limits for service men, the district was a warren of darkly shining cobbled alleys always damp and smelling of sewer gas. Recessed doors opened into narrow, dim hallways tainted with the odor of rat droppings and cooked cabbage.

Low-ceilinged worker's bars with yellow walls and stained wooden tables exuded the stench of stale beer and cheap tobacco. Boozy whores with strawberry colored hair slouched over their drinks; ran hands with painted nails along their thin flanks. Here moneychangers, smugglers, black marketeers, passport sellers traded openly as bought police turned a blind eye.

What took Harry there in his drab civilian clothes he couldn't say, beyond the fact that he wanted to sleep with a woman. He knew it was unsafe, especially for drunken American soldiers who were often mugged and robbed. But he was never drunk and always watchful. He had picked up some German and was good with accents, so if he spoke only a minimum of words he could be taken for a displaced person.

He didn't look German, and even now, as he sat at the bar drinking a stein of *fass bier*, he imagined that he was, to these lowlifes, the last remaining Jew, the one that got away, hidden in a barn only to surface and remind them that even in this insane task, they had failed. He saw it in the pig's eyes of one square-jawed hollow-cheeked brute, saw it in the hard set of his mouth, the bruising look of hate. He met the look with his own contemptuous challenge. Harry was ready, even eager to give one of these mustered out Jew-killers a beating, feel his knuckles mash a nose even if it meant that he would be battered in return.

Since witnessing Auschwitz he had wanted to spill the blood of one of the many who had shed their uniform but not their character. And here was one. But the man lowered his eyes and turned his back, perhaps aware at some level that only fighting Jews had survived.

Harry swilled his beer and looked around for another to taunt but no one else would meet his gaze except for a woman sitting over coffee at a table in the corner. Her eyes, heavy with mascara, passed on an invitation. Her short black skirt and black stockings, the blood red of her lipstick, advertised her calling. She was slight, anemic-looking, and might have been no more than sixteen with barely a cleft between her breasts, a button of a nose, pouting lips and the round dark brown eyes of an abused dog. She gestured with her chin, leaned back in her chair, raised her pelvis and stretched her legs toward him.

He sat down across from her and saw at once by the lines around her eyes that she was older than she seemed, although it might have been the effect of hardship. She nodded with encouragement, fished in her small black purse for an American cigarette. He lit it for her and, her elbow on the table, the cigarette held erect, she sized him up through the languid curling smoke.

"American?"

He nodded. Hearing this she relaxed her pose and behind her painted mask he caught a glimpse of childish satisfaction. And that was the start of it. The first time he paid with New Marks. Later, he gave her nylon stockings, cigarettes, Nescafe, even shampoo, all impossible to come by in occupied Germany.

Her name was Anna Kraus. Her mother was a seamstress. Nazis had beaten her father, a Communist, to death. Her brother, Egon, was a prisoner of the Russians, so they thought. She was learning English and spoke it well. She was also learning to type and wanted a job with the American occupation.

She would take him to her room down the dark stale hall from where her mother worked. It was small and always cold, with a single high window with a view of the sky and pictures cut from magazines pinned to the walls. A single lamp with a pink cloth fluted shade gave color to her transparent blue-white skin that seemed never to have been touched by the sun.

She made love in a passive way although she clung to him as if she cared. He liked her, wanted her, but only in bed. She didn't help him sleep, didn't even cheer him up.

December 3, 1945 – Purge

The wheel of suspended stamps imprinted with a stylized open winged eagle clutching a swastika had been replaced by a brass triptych of blurry snapshots of a wife with a chignon hairdo and two wide mouthed teen-aged daughters. Up on the wall, just over the staff psychiatrist's flat domed head, crossed by strands of hair like fence wire, was a rectangular light patch on the stippled gray wall that, Harry was sure, was a ghost image of Adolph Hitler.

Captain Harman slouched forward over a cup of G.I. coffee and looked at Harry with detached, if kindly, curiosity. His wrinkled khaki uniform decorated with a food stain, rather than a campaign ribbon, advertised the fact that he was just another middle aged M.D. psychiatrist from Kansas City reluctantly separated from a career and family by the War.

"You say you've been nervous, unable to concentrate, and not able to sleep."

"Maybe I shouldn't have come."

"No, no."

"I took some sleeping pills, even got drunk."

"And you can't shake it off."

"No. I can't."

"And. . . ."

"And so I came here."

"You were right to come. Anything else troubling you that we should talk about?"

"Well," Harry hesitated unsure whether to mention it. "This might sound goofy but I've got this compulsion to pick things up."

"Souvenirs and the like? German army insignia? Everybody does that."

"Not exactly."

"What then?"

"Scraps of paper, shards of broken glass, mud. Not just mud. Dirt from the battle field, from Auschwitz, some with footprints or what looks like prints . . . fragments of bone." And, of course, the sketchbook. Especially that. But he wasn't going to mention it, not to anyone. It was stored in the bottom of his footlocker.

Captain Harlan looked at him as though Harry were discussing his favorite baseball team and made a few notes with his fountain pen.

"Where do you get the ink?" Harry asked him.

The question took the psychiatrist by surprise for an instant, then he said, "Oh the pen, you mean? Uncle Sam provides it. Why? Do you need some?"

"No, no, I was just curious."

"So, Harry, tell me what exactly do you do with it? The mud and other stuff?"

"Well, I've been sending it home, mostly."

"To whom?"

"My aunt." Captain Harman made another note.

"What do you want her to do with it?"

"Save it for me. She has this shop, not really a shop, more like a junk store; three floors, dark, piled with stuff they bought at estate sales and flea markets. They cull through the stuff, sometimes they find valuable things, and the rest they sell to people who collect odd things or who can't afford new furniture."

"You're not sending it back so that she can sell it?"

"No. It's mostly worthless. Just to save it for me."

"What will you do with it?"

"I don't know exactly. I'm sort of an artist. Maybe I'll make something."

"What kind of people are in that sort of business? Used furniture, antiques."

"People who save the ribbons and wrapping paper on presents, the rubber bands around the newspaper, last week's magazines, jars, worn out socks. . . ."

"What about you, Harry? Are you a saver?"

Harry chewed on the question. The wooden seat was suddenly uncomfortable. "I've never thought much about it."

"Do you feel like talking about yourself? Your home, your family?"

"Well. . . ."

"It might help me to help you."

"Where should I begin?"

"Whatever comes to your mind."

So, haltingly, reluctantly Harry began. "I'm from Cleveland. I have an older sister." He stopped and Captain Harmon encouraged him with a slight rise of his head.

"You want more?" Harry joked.

"Whatever you want to tell me. I've got two months before they send me back home to the States."

"I grew up in a railroad apartment on East 81st. I used to

roller skate up and down the hall. My father works for a tailor. He is a presser, a frustrated stand up comedian. My mother sells dresses. Her passion is ballroom dancing. I was a smart kid and they put me in Major Work. Just a few kids with brains, maybe 40 or so out of the whole city. That's where I learned to draw." Harry stopped, already feeling exposed, but wanting to go on.

"What's your family like, Harry? Tell me about them."

Pop

They called him Pop. Nell had started it, and she was the first kid. Harry's father didn't look or act like a Pop. He liked screaming ties, sport jackets with wide shoulders, hats with wide brims, pointy black patent leather shoes, the Cleveland Indians, the Cleveland Barons, Canadian Club with a splash of ginger ale, poker, and an occasional night out at the Roxy with the boys, not to mention the penny arcade across Ninth Street. There was another side of him that loved the Metropolitan Opera on the radio on Saturday. He would take time off work to stand in line for cheap tickets when Heifitz came to town, and a reproduction of Van Gogh's *Irises* hung over the sofa. He loved Van Gogh even though he was nuts. Is this a Pop? Who's to say what makes a Pop.

Harry's dad was many things. In the back room of Rozensweig's Tailor Shop, on 105th Street, next to Perko's Delicatessen, in the yellow sweaty light, his thin body glistening, the steam from the pressing iron rising around him, a dark strand of receding hair plastered on the high dome of his creased forehead, his round eyes locked on the wide lips of the machine which opened and closed hissing like a dragon, Pop looked like a tired, knotted toiler using up, little by little, his vitality, his time, his chance to be something. Ten hours a day he did a slow motion step dance for 85 cents an hour and all the cold water you could drink because he sweated two gallons a day. Sweating was healthy and he claimed that he never had to piss, which wasn't true, but he liked to exaggerate, put a crease in an old pair of patched and baggy pants and make them think that they were new again. Harry couldn't understand how he could stand in one place six days a week, because a day was like a year to him.

"You see, Harry," he explained, in his funny sing-song drawl, "being a presser is like Heifetz playing the violin. Remember how he was when we saw him at Severance Hall? He plays a tune over and over till he don't have to think about it. He just turns it on like a phonograph and it goes."

"So what do you think about?"

"Everything and nothing. What I would do if Roosevelt were here bending over the pressing machine and I was in the White House. What if the Indians win the Pennant? I stand here but my mind wanders and I get ideas."

"Like what?"

"Well, I got to put the pants down on the presser one leg at a time, isn't that right?" Pop showed him how, laying the blue serge pant leg on the white cloth of the presser and smoothing it with his hand all in one dexterous motion. "Everything in life is one leg at a time, remember that Harry. You try jumping off a table into your pants and you'll land on your ass."

"That's not funny."

"That's philosophy, Harry." He lowered the upper lip of the presser and it ate the pant leg, hissing with satisfaction.

"What else do you think about?"

"Mostly the routines, Harry, that's what really makes me happy, to think up some new and fresh story or even a joke. Not the stale stuff, but something taken out of life that's going to make people laugh. Not because they think they should or because the schmuck next to them is laughing but because it's really funny. You know the difference, Harry, between the real thing, and *bubkas*? Sure you do, you're my son, my *boychik*, right?"

"Right."

Pop reached down and covered Harry's head with the blessing of his sweaty palm.

Mother

Mother spent about everything she could on clothes. After all, she worked downtown at the May Company on the

Public Square, in Lady's Ready-To-Wear and she got a discount. Pop liked to say, it's a good thing she didn't work for an undertaker, which always made her frown. Mother didn't like it when he made fun of her—she was proud.

"You've got to put on a bright face, make a good impression, no matter what," she would say. "Even if you're poor, you can wear smart clothes. And if you buy well you'll never look out of place. But never be a slave to fashion," she would add. She was.

Mother spent a long time fixing herself in the morning before work, while Nell was fixing her lunch and Harry's too: hard boiled eggs and thickly buttered bread, always a carrot for the eyes and fresh fruit for the skin and to keep you regular. Harry always ate the fruit on the way to school. He had to take the Hough Avenue trolley bus and transfer to the 105th Street car to get to the Major Work classes. Mother liked regularity in everything although she wasn't very steady herself, except in fixing herself up in the mirror, with all sorts of pencils and make up and powders and perfumes. She could have, should have, opened a cosmetic store, what with all those perfume samples. No matter how often she flirted with exotic and sensual scents in her obsessive search for just the right fragrance for each occasion, she remained faithful to Evening in Paris, which came trapped like a genie in a mysterious deep indigo blue bottle. Pop called it whore's bath. Mother always glared. Her glare and glower would turn a gardenia brown. "Paris never smelled like that," he liked to add, to provoke her. How would he know what Paris smelled like? He'd never even been to Columbus, the state capital.

Mother knew about Paris, in her heart at least. She was a dancer, not a floozy; a polite, genteel ballroom dancer who swirled under the revolving mirrored globe that sent snow wheeling around the walls and made Harry dizzy if he watched it too long. Mother had long slender legs, legs that seemed to go up to her breasts, and when Pop spun her around, her loose white skirt flared out like a pinwheel. Then she would freeze just on a beat like a ballet dancer on a music box, her arm over her head touching Pop's hand and the skirt would cling high before it fell, showing the dark brown band of her nylon stockings and even the strips of her garters. That fascinated Harry. He would watch transfixed as they circled and spun like tops waiting for the time that the skirt would stay so high before it slid down that he would, for an instant, see the creamy white skin of mother's thigh.

Harry thought that mother looked like a calla lily in her white dress, especially when she wore gold dancing shoes. He had been fascinated with the connection between calla lilies and women since the time he had pulled one out of a flower arrangement at the foot of the Corinthian bronze casket of his great uncle, Nate 'Bookie' Gelb. Fortunately for Harry, Uncle Nate's business partner, Itzik Barinsky, appreciated irreverence in a kid and laughed it off commenting, "The little *gonif* would steal the pennies off a dead man's eyes." Mother was mortified. Pop was amused. Only four at the time, Harry just wanted his mother to have one.

Harry was always embarrassing his mother. You'd think she had never been a child, never had to pee, or never dropped the second melting scoop of Pierre's French Vanilla ice cream in her lap, or never had a cold and let the snot run down her upper lip only to lick it off, or never farted in the Astor Theater in front of Clark Gable, or smelled like a goat from playing tag, or tripped over a garbage can lid and scraped a hole in her new pants, or whined because she was bored, or cried because she was tired, or shouted ecstatically, or came home with a bloody nose, or got a note from her teacher because she was wising off in class, or came to the table with dirty hands, or dropped a slab of bread slathered with butter and Welsh's grape jelly face down on the linoleum then stepped in it and walked all over the carpet. What did she want from a kid, perfection?

August 17, 1939 – Puberty Rites

After years of amateur nights, Pop finally made it—a two-night run at the Conneaut Lakeside Family Resort. Not exactly the big time yet, but you never know, a beginning even at this age. After all, Moses or somebody was pretty old when he—so it wasn't Moses. The point is, Pop got a real booking, a chance to make people laugh, strangers yet, and it wasn't amateur night. And he took Harry with him, to have a shill, he said. Not knowing what he'd have to do, Harry went, excited all the same. He wasn't much for shuffleboard and had never learned to swim, and horses were for cops, or junk men, or cowboys. He thought it would be boring like a family get-together.

There were girls everywhere he looked: waitresses, bursting out of flamingo skin tight uniforms, housekeepers earning money for college, high school girls hauled along by their families to watch the little ones while mom and dad, anointed with oil, fried in the sun like sea elephants. Most of them, Harry saw, did the same things they did at home every Saturday night. They hunched over card tables playing Mah Jong or Seven Card Draw and Spit-In-The-Ocean, grumbling over a bad hand, stopping only to gorge themselves on Salisbury steak and mashed potatoes with over-cooked carrots.

Pop was sweating in his rented white dinner jacket. The satin of the shawl collar shone like a mirror in the acid glare of the spotlight that pinned him flat against the curtain like a trapped and skewered beetle. "Pardon me sir," he asked in his best Irish brogue, "is that the sun or the moon? I donno, I don't live in this neighborhood." A moment of suspense before the laughter broke over him like a cooling wind and he smiled with a show of malice in his eyes, for humor was anger turned inside out, he liked to say. From the wings, Harry looked on, smelling the perfume and powder presence of the leggy dancing girls in their fish net stockings that went up to their waists. The laughter shattered Harry's tension for he wanted Pop to make it big or even little, just to make it, to be fulfilled. For everyone should live out at least one of their dreams, at least one, and this was his, to be recognized by some stranger who would walk up to him out of the blue, adulation and respect on his face and say, "You're Berney Baer, the comic!" not the presser or even the sometimes bit player at the Cleveland Playhouse. Pop got laughs that night, more than one resounding laugh, sustained like moving spring thunder, and he was happy and hopeful that it was finally the start.

Harry, too, had his start, the focus for his constant hard-on that popped up on its own, both swelling his pride and humiliating him in his awkward pimply beginning. It was everpresent as he sat in class, watched the swish of pleated skirts over swelling thighs, saw his sister quick step from the bathroom to her own room in a damp towel, even as he labored over a math problem. It uncoiled like a lazy snake rubbing itself on his underwear making him shudder with chills and tingling flu-like ache, demanding always to be fondled and caressed, love-starved and never satisfied in its onanistic bliss.

And then it found the obsession of its life, on the edge of the lapping algid lake, found her as she stepped out of a rowboat wearing a short white fluted tennis dress which floated up her satin, creamy, rounded thigh toward a smallish waist. She climbed to the dock and stood straight showing him high apple-hard breasts that dented with aching suggestion a loose white blouse. She turned toward him and, hooded with light brown billowing hair, he saw a pointed broad cheeked face with smiling flaring lips, the upper arching to show even teeth gently thrusting forward, a short broad bridged nose, angled oriental eyes of jade, and small gull wings for brows.

His pecker rose smoothly to its full height and struggled to break out of the flyless bathing briefs. Before he could turn it had trembled, and throbbed and erupted its smooth and sticky passion and he was forced to turn and flee like a humiliated child who couldn't yet control his bladder, dodging the crowd of suited swimmers on their towels. But in his flight there was exultation and the brio of a brimming heart.

First Impression

As he soon found out, her name was Sandy. She wasn't the stuck-up kind, she wasn't a prick teaser, she didn't return his ardent gaze with a stare that would freeze fire, she didn't look right through him as so many did. They danced and she let him get up close and feel through the thin slinky layers of her clothes his uncoiled spring. And she wasn't put off or scared, or if she was, she didn't show it.

She liked him, he could tell. They walked down to the dock and watched the tremulous reflection of lights from the summer houses strung around the shore and she let his timid, tentative fingers explore her public parts; her moist palm, the tight responsive grip of her hand, the soft buffered edge of her hip, and the billowing cloud like-hair that seemed as fine as spider's work. She sucked the strength out of his muscles, stiffened his joints, and he ached with the arthritis of desire.

Harry tried to be smart, tried to be modest, tried to be funny. Sandy, in her dusty voice, told him not too much. Only that she had no boy friend, lived in Shaker Heights, liked to swim, played the clarinet, had really nice parents, an obnoxious hateful little brother, and hoped to be a baby doctor.

They played ping-pong and she beat him. He had never played. She had a table in her home. He splashed her with a skipping oar as he rowed a yellow boat around the lake. She took it well and even splashed him back. He dunked her as they swam; she came up spouting water, hair streaming down her face and laughed as small fish nibbled at her toes. They lay together on the beaten grass in the sticky heat under the pulsing sun, their naked thighs and shoulder's touching. Later in the twilight, hand in hand, they walked a path shaded by elms to a meadow framed by a white rail fence where wild flowers grew and watched three horses, black and white, caper, dance, and toss their heads. They exchanged phone numbers and longing looks full of promise darkened by the shallow loss, for being young they took it lightly if intensely.

They talked on the phone, once, twice, but she sounded distant and aloof. Shaker Heights was hard to get to from East 81st Street just off Euclid Avenue. The telephone didn't smell of fresh-washed hair or sun tan lotion, it smelled of Bakelite. He never saw her but she never left him either. That was all, a first impression as he later liked to think, and like an etching first to print, Sandy remained for him an image, sharp, clear, and deeper than the rest.

May 14, 1942 – Expelled

Mr. Randle, the Vice Principal, reminded Harry of Humpty Dumpty. His chest seemed concave and his pants came up to the top of his paunch. On top of everything he had an irritating whiny voice that filtered his hostility the way a patched screen door blocked a hot summer wind. And there were soup stains on his yellow red and green tie.

If he wasn't in the process of suspending Harry in his senior year at Glenville High for who knows how long, Harry would have felt sorry for him. Still living with his mother, so the story went, at 47 and he'd probably never been under a woman's skirt in his whole life. Not that Harry knew any more than what he'd seen of his sister through the keyhole of the bathroom door.

"You know why you're here, Harry," he said picking up half of an egg salad sandwich from the waxed paper wrapping and taking a bite. Harry studied the colors and textures, the red line of tomato, the oozing yellow and white paste.

"I got the letter."

"So what do you have to say for yourself?"

"What can I say. I didn't mean any harm. I was just doodling in study hall. I was going to erase it. How was I to know Miss Cathcart would come into the room in the middle of the period."

"You call that doodling? That was a very good likeness of Miss Fink, in her underwear."

"I can't help it if it was a good likeness."

"It was obscene, humiliating and insulting. Not to mention the lewd pictures of the two boys leering at her with. . . with erections sticking up." He waved his egg salad sandwich before taking another bite.

The smell of the sandwich was making Harry salivate. He had left home without his lunch and had just a nickel in his pocket. He squirmed in his seat and wondered if he would have time to buy a Hershey bar before his next class. He looked up and realized that Mr. Randle was waiting for him to say something. "Well you have to admit she's a great looking—"

Mr. Randle slapped his lips together with disapproval or maybe it had something to do with the egg salad, Harry wasn't sure. "Would it surprise you, Harry, if I told you she's become an object of ridicule and she's applying for a transfer?"

"I didn't mean to hurt her. I thought maybe she'd be flattered."

"You have a lot to learn about people, Harry."

"I always thought that the models for the great nude paintings that I've seen at the Art Museum would be flattered." Harry pulled a pencil out of his pocket and began to roll it between his fingers.

"So now you are comparing yourself to Rembrandt?"

"No, Rembrandt didn't paint nudes."

"I appreciate the art history lesson, Harry."

"I was just making a joke, Mr. Randle."

"This is no time for a joke." Mr. Randle deepened the creases in his forehead as he said, "Mr. Ogden is of a mind to expel you for the rest of the semester, which means you get incompletes in all your courses and you have to repeat them all."

Harry shook his head; his cheeks grew hot. This wasn't fair. "Just for a blackboard sketch with only one month to go, Mr. Randle? You didn't kick out Billy Blickstein for breaking Eddie Longinotti's nose, or Andy Twitchell for smoking in the teacher's lounge."

"That's the way it is." He shrugged his shoulders.

"Couldn't I just tell her I'm sorry in a letter? Maybe give her some flowers?" Mr. Randle seemed to weigh the suggestion as he took another bite of his sandwich. A gobbet of egg salad separated and dropped to his desk. Harry watched and the pencil began to move by itself on the cover of his American History notebook.

"Harry, one thing you might learn from this," said Mr. Randle, his voice muted by egg salad, "is what's done can't be undone. What is done, cannot be undone," he declaimed like God revealing a commandment to Moses.

"You're right, Mr. Randle. I hope it's a lesson I carry with me all my life."

"What are you doing now? Here let me have a look at that." Harry passed him his spiral notebook with the pencil sketch on the front and watched Mr. Randle's expression change from a frown to one of bemused approval. He handed it back marked with an egg salad fingerprint. "You did that sketch of me without even looking at the paper. Remarkable."

"My eye was looking and telling my hand what to do."

Mr. Randle put the half eaten sandwich back in the waxed

paper and wiped his lips with a square crinkly paper napkin all the while looking at Harry like a tailor who couldn't decide how high the waistline should rise above the crotch.

"Harry, did your father ever tell you what the Czar used to do to some revolutionaries?"

"Not that I remember, Mr. Randle. My father isn't much of a revolutionary, he's more like a presser."

"Well they would line them up in front of the firing squad and shoot over their heads, then send them to Siberia in exile."

"That was very generous of the Czar."

"Well, Harry, you're in luck. Here read this. You've won a reprieve." Mr. Randle handed him a letter.

"Holy shit! Sorry. But this is great! Who would of thought." It was from the Cleveland Museum of Art. He had won first prize in the High School student art competition. A ceremony was to be held in the Mayor's office in a month.

"There are conditions, and watch your mouth."

"Sorry, Mr. Randle, I got carried away."

"We at Glenville High are happy for you too, Harry. If you can just get hold of yourself, focus on what you have to do, not just what you feel like doing."

"Just what my mother says, Mr. Randle."

"Harry, there's a condition."

"Whatever."

"Drawings of every member of the faculty, from the neck up, and no funny stuff. For the faculty lounge."

"What do you want? Da Vinci, Goya, any style you like."

"No Picasso."

"So what does that mean? Am I still expelled or what?"

"We thought it would be difficult to kick the best young artist in Cleveland out of school. But let it be a warning to you, Harry. No more funny business!"

Harry got up, turned to leave, and then said, "Mr. Randle, if you're not going to eat that half a sandwich, I forgot my lunch, and all I've got in my pocket is a nickel."

"Never let it be said that I didn't go to the aid of a starving artist." Mr. Randle reached into a paper lunch bag and handed him a second sandwich neatly wrapped in waxed paper closed by two rubber bands. "Harry, you should go far in the world. Would you like a banana?"

"Only if you've got an extra."

December 21, 1943 – Farewell Party

Mother had ordered all of Harry's favorite food—even the metallic bronze smoked white fish. You need a can opener to eat them, Pop liked to say, which always got a smile even if you'd heard it twenty times. Of course, there was lox sliced so thin it looked like tulip petals; cream cheese, milk turned to clay; and bagels covered with charred onion flakes—Pop told the one about the guy who stacked five of them on his you-know-what. Mother even cooked pigs in a blanket; gray fluted cabbage-wrapped meatballs floating in tomato sauce. Aunt Selma brought her cheesecake, tall with a brown crust and the taste of sour cream and brown sugar.

Lots of ration coupons went into that feed but after all, when would they see him again? Basic training over, he was on his way to where? Who could say? A military secret, "even the walls have ears" as the poster said. But the Baers and the Goldenbergs were all patriots with little flags in the windows and War Bonds in the safe deposit box or under Aunt Selma's slips in the dresser.

They were all there. They never missed a chance to get together, steaming up the windows, filling the apartment with the pungent smell of honest sweat, perfume, cigar smoke, noise, loud voices. You had to talk loud to be heard over the other loud talkers and the intermittent clanking of the radiators. Uncle Nate, with his jowls and triple chin, short of breath; Uncle Julie, with his apple red pointed cheeks and shoulders that bulged—he wore his sweaters tight to show them off. The family's teamster, he drove a meat truck. Mother, elegant in a trim red dress of crepe silk that made a little dip at the cleft between her breasts, which floated when she bent over the table. Aunt Gwen, the family poet, wrote and sang a song about the war. And Pop, doing what he could to cover up the fear, so many died, you read it every day, his *boychik*, the only one who had a future, a chance to be someone, so smart, so quick, a real Sargent; John Singer, not the three stripe kind.

Uncle Julie promised to send salami if he could, the army food was lousy so he'd heard. Harry's sister, Nell, had knitted him a sweater, khaki too, to match his clothes. "A sweater you need even you should go to the desert, you never been, it's cold at night," said Uncle Hersh, who'd never been. A cigarette lighter he even got, although as yet he didn't smoke, and a Kodak Brownie for London or Paris when he got there. Also a new safety razor and a pen so he should write home all the time.

Wet kisses on the face and lips and hugs to break the ribs or smother him. Mother too held on longer than she should until he pulled away. She told him with her eyes that she loved him even after all the dirty tricks and fights.

Nell told him how they had both changed. Now they were friends, would one day bring their kids to the beach and watch them play and think about their own simpler time.

Watch out for the Nazis, they don't like Jews, Pop told him, trying to make light of it. And mother said, "Inspect yourself for lice and other things. Stay warm and get your sleep."

He looked back and they were waving from the window.

December 20, 1945 – Captain Ramsey's Diagnosis

Harry Baer is suffering from traumatic stress syndrome aggravated by his service during the Battle of the Bulge in which his unit was decimated and was overrun by the German Army twice. Harry was trapped behind enemy lines for five days. It was immediately brought on by exposure to Auschwitz concentration camp. His unit was the first to liberate it. It is possible that the fact that the victims are Jewish may have triggered a survivor guilt reaction. He masks his deeper anxieties around low self-esteem related to a withholding, self-involved mother, with a flip, brassy, somewhat grandiose facade. He is highly intelligent, and very charming. He has pronounced narcissistic personality traits. The anxiety related symptoms should dissipate over time or may be expiated through his art. (My wife will love the picture he drew of me.)

June 17, 1946 – Demobilized

"Harry," said his mother, stiffly standing over him, "get your feet off the coffee table." It was still new, deep polished mahogany with a fluted rim, part of a suite of pretentious front room furniture bought with some of the proceeds of Pop's life insurance policy.

"Don't talk to me that way, Mom, I'm not a kid any more." He used "Mom" when he wanted to provoke her. "Mom" made her feel too used up. He had to admit she looked good. In her mid-forties, she had the legs and the firm stomach of a woman in her late twenties owing to the rigors of ballroom dancing. Now that Bernie was gone she was spending even more evenings at the ballroom and was flirting with the notion of giving up her job at May Company and teaching dancing. Harry's feet remained on the coffee table.

"You're a man. You've been to the war." Mother adjusted the wide belt of her navy blue suit. "You're back in one piece, thank God. And you've been sitting for three months now. Eating and sleeping, listening to the ball game, drawing pictures, sitting in the park feeding the pigeons, like a bum." She dropped down, lifted her foot, bent it back at the knee and ran her right hand up the seam of her nylon stocking.

"I'm trying."

"Look Harry, don't think I was fooled by that business about the discharge." Her stern look gave way to a conspiratorial smile. "You never were crazy and the war didn't change you. But I've got to hand it to you. You came home ahead of lots of them. Sam Mandelbaum is still stuck in Germany. But you, you're here, and the world is your oyster."

"I didn't pull anything funny. I just couldn't sleep."

"You've made up for it since you came home."

He looked back at the open page of Proust. Why provoke her. "You'll be late for work," he muttered without looking up.

"So, what are you going to do with yourself, you could go to Western Reserve. I've read about the G.I. bill."

"You'll miss your bus."

"You could sell something, sell cars, or appliances. I could get you in to see the manager of the major appliance department at May's. They make one percent commission. It adds up. You've got a way with words."

"Thanks. I'll think about it."

"Good. I'll talk to him tomorrow."

"Don't bother."

"Why not?"

"I'm not interested."

"What are you interested in?"

"Art."

"Art?"

Harry put the book down and looked up. "I think I want to be an artist."

"That's nice." Mother was looking around the room for her purse. "You want to take some classes?"

"Yes."

"Where, the Art Institute?"

"I'm going back to Europe. Paris."

"You don't even speak French." Her response was automatic; as if he had told her he was going down to buy cigarettes.

"I'll learn." He was surprised. He had expected a reaction. Maybe she didn't believe him. Maybe she would be glad to get rid of him. Then her fancy boy wouldn't have to face his dirty looks at the door.

"Well, it's your life, Harry. I've done whatever I could to give you good values. I hope you'll tell your aunt what to do with all that trash you sent home before you go."

"She should keep it for me. I'll tell her myself."

"Harry."

"Yes, mother?" She turned toward him with a sudden look of mild affection darkened by concern that she might miss her street car.

"Whatever you do, you know I love you."

"I know that, mother."

She bent over him and kissed his forehead, a feather touch out of concern for her lipstick. As she opened the door she said, "The shopping list is on the kitchen table, Harry. Be sure the butcher gives you center cut chops."

June 19, 1946 – Dinette

The dinette set was wedged like a foot in a shoe in the corner of the kitchen. Nell sat across from him in her usual chair, a smudge on the yellow wallpaper with its ascending green and pink tea rose vines marked the way she leaned back after eating. Bernie's chair was empty, but Harry could see him hunched over his food laughing about something he'd just read in the paper, tightening his jaw when something in Variety made him envious—he had subscribed but, except for the want ads, had never seen his name in print. The table and chair had a maple look and were clumsy colonial with heavy lathe turned legs that tripped you if you got too close, which was impossible not to do in the tight space. Harry inhaled the familiar Maxwell House fragrance and watched as the bubbling and rattling percolator ejaculated its contents into the glass dome. The kitchen was, as always, neat and orderly. Everything was in its place; the knives in their wooden block always arranged small to large, and the dishes always in the same place behind the glass doors so that a blind person could have cooked a meal.

Nell's anarchistic red hair, loose for a change, ranged over her strong shoulders, contrasting with the emerald green blouse and the lighter green of her close-set eyes. All the lemons she had rubbed on her face hadn't faded one freckle on her round thick-skinned cheeks, he thought. The braces had helped her teeth, although she still had a closed smile to conceal them.

They were different now, friends, no longer rivals for the extra blintz; fond and admiring and bound together in their common, but different, love for Bernie.

"Don't pay attention to mother," said Nell making her spoon do a somersault on the tabletop. "Pop would have approved of your plan."

"It's as much his as mine. Who knows where he would have been if he'd gone for it instead of spending his life behind a pressing machine."

"Maybe you and me wouldn't have been here talking over his memory if he had."

"Or maybe we'd have been sitting by a window of a house overlooking one of the Shaker Lakes."

Nell twirled her spoon to see which way it would point when it stopped and wished she could be like Harry, have the courage to pick up and do something crazy, but it just wasn't in her. She thought about his infrequent letters from Europe—she had kept them. She would have accepted the danger to see London and Paris. Would she ever get closer to Europe in her life than seeing it in a movie? Would she ever do anything spontaneous and more reckless than splurging on a hot fudge sundae?

"So what do you think, Nellie? Am I nuts, not that I give a fuck, sorry." It was hard to shake the Army out of his life. He was still shining his shoes and folding his underwear according to the Army regulations.

"So why did you ask, then?" she said, looking hurt.

"I want your blessing, in Pop's name." He got up to pour them each a cup of coffee. She looked at hers and said, "I can't take it this hot or strong. Put some water in it, please."

He took the cup to the sink and turned the faucet on after spilling some of the coffee to make room. The porcelain of the sink was worn in places from incessant scrubbing and the brass was showing through the chrome plate of the faucet. Mother always kept things too clean. No wonder she was badgering Aunt Gwen to throw away the mud he'd sent back from Germany. He brought the cup back to the table and spilled a little more as he set it down.

"You got used to such strong coffee." Nell had the cup suspended between her hands, both elbows on the table.

"We had to stay awake. Sometimes we had guard duty all night."

"I like my job," she volunteered as she had before. She was working as a secretary in a law office.

"Still no guys in your life?"

"You ask that every day, Harry."

"There'll soon be a better choice now that the War's over."

"Yeah, I guess."

"Did she mourn him?"

"Mother? In her way. She didn't cry or wear black except

for the funeral. She said black didn't become her."

"It's a dumb custom anyhow."

"She talked a lot about him. Nice things: the dancing, the laughs, things that happened when we were kids, Cedar Point, family parties. I guess you could call it mourning."

"Is she serious about that dancing teacher?"

Nell's face became a mask of disgust. "I hope not. She doesn't tell me how she feels. You'd think she would. Her only daughter."

Harry looked into his coffee cup and imagined Pop melting onto the floor of the pressing room, little more than a puddle. A massive heart attack, they said, coronary something or other. Quick, merciful, like a bullet in the head—he'd seen men go that way. No pain on the face, not even surprise. No chance for regrets of all the things he hadn't done. What were his last thoughts? The spotlight? The laughter fading? Or was it two little children one on each knee competing for his attention, the girl playing with his hair, the boy trying to take his reading glasses off of his nose.

"You think Pop would approve, Nell?"

"He'd have given you his last paycheck." She nodded her head again and again.

October 4, 1946 – Crossing

Harry sailed to Europe on Noah's Ark, or so he called it. There were two or more of each nationality on the crew, including a dusting of Germans, who, he surmised by their still short hair, were fresh out of the Navy. He would hear them speaking together in soft tones and imagine that, even now, they were planning some crack-brained takeover of the ship's commissary, if nothing else. His cabin, at the water line, had four bunks and a Lilliputian sink. He shared the space with three men, all veterans returning to Europe for something they couldn't put their hands on back home. He called them Hemingway, Faulkner, and Einstein and they seemed to like it, for they saw themselves as heirs to an earlier generation of Americans who had sacrificed their youth and innocence to atavistic European nationalism.

They sat around the smoky, throbbing tourist class lounge, their backs turned on the rolling gray passage, drinking Beck's beer for ten cents a glass, playing penny-ante poker, reminiscing about the War, and fantasizing about the future. The War was their bond, the War and what it had done to them. Beyond that they were as different as California artichokes and Georgia peaches.

Faulkner, whose name was Sam Throckmorton, 'hailed' from Bidwell Georgia. A gaunt, haunted, hollow-cheeked, son of a high school English teacher, Sam had won a national poetry prize for teen-agers: $100 and a trip to Washington.

Hemingway was really Craig Smith. The fourth of five children, he grew up on an Idaho potato farm. With his ample black hair, strong brow, square jaw and tapered frame he might have been a lady killer. But Craig was self-effacing and shy and the bold overtures of more than one of the women passengers were met with no more than a diffident smile and an awkward exchange of platitudes. His ambition was to become the Knut Hamsun of his generation. He was going back to Europe to distance himself from the world of his upbringing and to bring rural Idaho into "cold clear focus." That and because he could "stretch the buck a lot further than back home."

Rudy Schwengen was Einstein. From Chicago, he was the only son of a theoretical physicist and a scholar whose special field was Eighteenth Century English poetry. The others kidded him about his head of "pubic hair gone wild." Rudy hoped to enroll at the Sorbonne—his mother had friends there— and "take some courses, maybe play some chess."

They were damaged and derailed like the Europe they were going back to. Each of them had fought, been deafened and showered by debris from exploding shells, walked for days in sodden boots, waded waist deep in cold rivers, pissed in their helmets in a fox hole, searched their hair for lice, witnessed sudden death and mutilating wounds, and had come through physically unscarred. Craig had been at Remagen. Sam rode in the first landing craft to hit the Anzio beachhead. Rudy's jeep had been blown off the road by a land mine, killing the other two. Luckily, he had been hurled into a rain sodden potato field with no more than a separated shoulder. All of them woke, heart racing from bad dreams.

What they might become didn't yet matter. For now it was enough to have lived without a future and survived. They never talked of marriage, a steady job, a career. It was too soon for them even to imagine a life that might cross a decade in a more or less straight line.

Over the seven days passage, these four, so different from each other, yet joined by their separation from the younger passengers whose only contact with the war had been the headlines, Life Magazine, and Edward R. Murrow, resolved to share a place to live in Paris and divide chores as they had learned in the Army. This much of the future was secure.

October 26, 1946 – Paris

They found an apartment at the foot of a hill adorned with the white croziers of the *Sacre Coeur*. The village feeling of the narrow tumbling lanes contrasted with the tawdry nightlife that thrived in the orbit of the historic if faded Moulin Rouge. An attic, the space had awkward corners and sloping walls defined by a mansard roof cut by several floor to ceiling windows. They slept two to a room, took turns shopping, cooking, cleaning, and soon became habitues of the corner cafe with its maroon glazed front and zinc bar.

The first few months were spent this way; learning haphazard French, exploring the recovering city by day, drinking nights in jazz clubs, sleeping mornings. Though it was winter, with its depressing gray sky, bone chilling cold and biting rains, the unheated apartment was luxurious compared to memories of billets in half wrecked buildings or long nights spent facing horizontal driving snow. Even the ancient boiler that produced a little hot water and the hole-in-the-floor toilet were conveniences to men who had gotten used to dropping their pants in freezing weather.

The women in their lives were prostitutes, and there were more than enough, the war had seen to that. Their dollars bought them all the sex they wanted and little more.

Harry spent his days wandering around the City absorbing

details. He spent hours in the labyrinthine antique markets, studying everything he could, picking things up, turning them in his hand, as if by contact he could absorb their essence. Some things he bought for centimes, carted them back to the apartment and piled them in a corner of his room: old magazines, match boxes, buttons, a hook to lace up boots. He spent hours each day at the Louvre and other museums, returning again and again to a painting or sculpture to study it from a different point of view. Like the process of painting itself, each observation layered on the last offered a new and deeper insight.

The wildly expressionistic, tortured paintings of Soutine and Roualt were a revelation. Here was reality dissolved by madness, not broken into planes or lines, but impulsively applied with vital colors, not gaudy like the Fauvists, but deep and irrational. One painting was of a putrid side of beef hanging on a hook, and he saw in it a profound visual evocation of sacrifice. He even tried to find Soutine—someone told him that he had survived the war in Paris. He had the fanciful notion that Soutine might take a liking to him and talk with him, even give him lessons. Too late. Soutine had checked out in 1944. But there were those who had known him and Harry brashly sought them out and asked them random questions, which they answered with varying degrees of Parisian patience. He was after all, an ex-GI, and they owed him something.

June 8, 1947 – The Sketchbook Identified

One day in June he had two encounters, the kind that leave a permanent imprint on life. Harry had gone to the Luxembourg Garden. It was the kind of day that made Parisians forget the winter's gloom and chill. Linden trees were in fresh leaf offering still unwelcome dappled shade, gravel paths were freshly raked and golden, folding chairs wore new coats of glossy deep green paint, borders and circles were newly planted with geometric patterns. Red spears of salvia, orange and ruby marigolds nurtured in greenhouses were complemented by the bright floral patterns of the spring fashions. Children prodded freshly dusted sailboats on the circular pond as pensioners stretched their legs and soaked up the sun's new warmth.

On the way back toward the Seine he stopped at a gallery showing the recent drawings of Max Beckmann. In the back room his eyes were caught by a painting of horses grazing on a background of elliptical and triangular planes. The horses were elegant in their grace and simplicity; the background was almost abstract but unmistakably a simplified landscape. The colors were bright but muted umber, yellow, green, brown and black. It came to him that this could well be the artist of his found sketchbook and he had the feeling of having discovered that he had the winning number in a lottery. Harry went closer and saw the name; Franz Marc. He had never heard of him, which wasn't surprising since Harry had never taken a formal course in art history and simply followed his eyes and senses to educate himself.

Near the painting was a catalogue in French. He understood enough to learn that Marc was a colleague of Kandinsky and a co-founder of an influential journal called *Der Blaue Reiter*. As he had suspected, the sketch book, found in the trunk, might be the work of an important European painter. For a moment he felt guilt at having taken it, but he dismissed the reaction. Whoever had left it for years in a mildewed trunk with old military uniforms had little appreciation of its worth. Probably some French soldier had picked it up on the battlefield along with the German helmet.

He was still absorbed by the painting when a voice startled him. He turned to see a young woman plainly dressed in a black skirt and white blouse. She was almost his height but thin. Her dark brown hair was long and fell straight to her shoulders. She had a long angular face, a sharp nose with a Parisian bump, and wide inquisitive brown eyes shot with amber. She spoke again in quick cadenced Parisian French and he stammered a response aware that she would immediately know that he was American.

She switched to well pronounced if simple English. "You know Marc's work?"

"I . . . I've seen it before, but this is the first time I really appreciated it for what it is."

It was obvious that Harry wasn't a buyer and he was flattered that she stayed with him, chatting easily about Marc, Kandinsky, Klee, and others who had shown in the *Blaue Reiter* exhibitions. He had heard of the other two, had even seen their work in the museum, but Marc was obscure.

"He died in the Great War," she explained. "The others went on to have long careers."

"If he'd lived in Rembrandt's time it wouldn't have mattered," Harry said, pleased with the idea. "Everybody died young."

"What about you? How long will it take you to make it?"

"Make it in what?"

"You must be an artist," she said with bemused conviction.

"Do I look like one?"

"I saw the ink on your hands." She looked smug. Then she volunteered her name, Aurora Romboise, and offered her hand like a man. She had a strong grip.

They went on chatting easily. She was friendly without being flirtatious or coy, nice looking but not stunning, and obviously interested in him.

He hung around until the gallery closed and offered to buy her coffee at a nearby cafe. They sat at a marble topped table just inside the partly opened art nouveau doors. Above the high dark wood wainscot were faded posters in the Toulouse Lautrec style. Smoke and a *charivari* of sound filled the room. She lit a Galoise and squinted at him through the scrim of blue smoke. He liked the way she sat: self assured, at ease with herself, open. She asked a lot of questions, personal questions, in a direct way that made him wonder if she might be Jewish, not that it made any difference to him. She loved America, identified with its openness and informality. The gallery belonged to her aunt, who knew everyone in the art scene. Aurora had no artistic talent herself, but she loved art. She was studying French literature at the University.

He walked her to the Metro entrance, an art nouveau opening that resembled the veins of a leaf. He was gawking at it when she said, "You have a special affinity for Art Nouveau?"

"It's so different from the New York subway."

"But you have buildings taller than the Eiffel Tower."

5

Harry; 1947, The Formative Years

July 20, 1947 – Street Smart

Sam, Craig, and Harry were on their way home about two in the morning, more than a little drunk. Sam had just finished a short story, Craig was struggling with the outline of his first novel and needed some relief, while Harry had completed the plate for the first three of what he hoped would be a series of abstract Goyesque etchings based on the War. The night was damp, chilly, moonless. A recent rain had glazed the pavement and the pale yellow light from street lamps ran like spilled watercolor.

They were swaggering and stumbling down the middle of a cobbled street singing fragments of songs. A black and white cat observed them from a stoop and turned its head away as they passed. Only one window was lit on the whole block. Lit windows spoke to Harry at an abstract, yet palpable, level revealing in their forms, fragments of decor and gesture, patterns of emotion, aspiration, anguish, complacency, constrained violence. Harry saw a bent silhouette through the opaque curtain, some insomniac student at work on a dissertation, he imagined, and he sensed the aura of a struggle to make something original out of other people's words and associations.

The sound of a scuffle, an animal cry, made Craig look toward the dark mouth of an alley. "What was that?"

"Just cats," said Sam.

"It's a woman." Craig ran toward the angry, anguished cry of indignation and pain, and the other two followed. In the deep shadow they saw a man bent over a slender woman doubled up on the ground. He was beating her on the side of her head with one fist and pulling at her purse with the other hand.

Craig kicked the assailant in the side of the head as he might have kicked a football. The man splayed on the ground his hands behind him on the cobbles and Harry, Craig, and Sam gathered in a tight knot around him. He looked from one to the other like a cornered animal, his face pinched and mean. He scrambled to his feet, reached into his pocket and withdrew a switchblade knife. A six inch blade snapped out and he thrust it menacingly at each of them. Alert, heart pumping fast, Harry watched the man's face and the hand that held the knife and listened to his harsh breathing. Behind them, the woman got to her feet, staggered, then ran toward the street.

The man tried to break away from them and chase her but Sam blocked his way and he thrust at Sam with the stiletto. Sam tried to dodge but Harry was in his way and the blade tore through Sam's shirt and cut into his side. He bellowed in pain and anger, reached out for the man's wrist and grappled it. Craig spun behind the man and chopped the back of his neck with the hard edge of his hand. He stiffened, exhaled a gasp. The knife dropped from his hand and rang on the cobbles and he slowly slumped forward to the ground. They gathered around him, silent and solemn except for their heavy breathing. His legs convulsed and were still.

Sam was holding his side, feeling the warm blood seep through his fingers and wincing from the burning pain.

"You broke his neck," said Harry, his voice muted and matter of fact.

"No." Sam protested.

Harry bent over and felt for a pulse. "He's dead," Harry looked at Craig for confirmation. "Let's go." Three windows were lit. Someone must have called the police, Harry thought and he envisioned, jail, a trial, even prison.

"Are you hurt bad, Sam, can you run?" Craig asked.

"I'm OK."

"Then let's get the fuck out of here before it's too late," and they ran down the alley to the next street, emerged, and walked with studied nonchalance toward their building.

In the safety of the apartment, they sat down around the table and passed the bottle of cognac, stunned and hurt by circumstances that had been flung at them like a sharp stone spun out of the tread of a tire of a passing car.

Craig noticed the stain of blood on Sam's shirt, "Christ you're still bleeding!"

Sam looked at him as if he'd forgotten about it. They helped him take off his shirt. The flesh below his rib cage was broken by two clean incisions, each welling blood. Harry cleaned the wounds with hydrogen peroxide and bandaged them just as he'd done in the War.

"I hope the knife was as clean as it was sharp," he said inspecting his work. "When did you have your last tetanus shot?"

"Within a year."

"He might have killed you if you hadn't dodged."

"I thought we were done with that." Sam looked from Harry to Craig, who nodded. "What do you think was going on, a robbery?" Sam poured himself more cognac drank it off and grimaced.

"Just a pimp and his tart," said Harry.

"He never expected what he got. The goddamn fool wasn't smart enough to know when to run." Sam stared at Craig seeking confirmation.

"Yeah, I really feel sorry for the bastard."

"The world's a better place," said Harry.

"All the same, I didn't come here for this." Sam poured another drink.

"It could have happened in the States."

"You all right now?" Craig seemed to come out of his thoughts.

"Yes."

"Better take a couple of aspirin and go to bed, Sam."

"Hmm."

"What a way to end a night."

"Who would have thought. . . ."

"Think it'll be in the paper?"

"I doubt it. Just another low life," said Sam.

"All the same, there's probably somebody waiting for him."

"Maybe."

With that uncomfortable thought they fell silent. "Strange thing is you might have met the bastard in a bar, shot pool with him and come away thinking he wasn't so bad," Harry said.

"The same goes with the Germans."

"Yes, I've thought that many times. Is it any easier to kill a stranger?" asked Craig. He had thought that killing with its nauseating guilt and remorse was behind him. He had acted without time to reflect, as they had been trained to do—the reflex of a junkyard dog.

"It shouldn't be."

"You didn't mean to kill him, Craig."

"I knew what I was doing, Sam. I knew just where to hit him."

"Let's go to bed." Harry got up. As he walked to his room he weighed the contrast between his deep horror at the death camps and the fact hat he didn't feel any shred of sympathy for the pimp. He undressed and wondered if some piece of what made him human had been destroyed in the War. As if to comfort himself, he unwrapped the sketchbook he had found in the trunk and looked idly through it, studying the clean sure lines of the horses and the sorrowful, reflective dog. He returned it to the bottom of his suitcase and began to sketch a new image for his war etchings, amorphous gargoyle shapes wrestling in the mud.

July 21, 1947 – Festering

"What happened last night?" Rudy asked each one of them, but they avoided the question, why involve him? All they would say was that a drunk had attacked Sam with a knife. They went on with their lives but a miasma of apprehension hung over them as they ate the fresh baguette and drank *cafe au lait*. Harry went back to the atelier looking forward to starting work on the second plate of his war etchings.

Craig went around looking solemn, thoughtful. He asked

Sam how he felt, but said nothing about the night before. He spent the day in his room. Judging by the rhythmic click of his portable Smith Corona, he was making progress. Sam bought a paper and looked through it for a report of the death. A train accident outside Lyon in which 26 passengers were injured and an outbreak of hepatitis in Marseille were all he found.

Despite Harry's daily inspection and dressing the wound began to swell, redden, and fester. On the third day when the edges began to turn white, Harry told Sam he'd better see a doctor. The concierge, a shapeless woman with wispy grey hair who always wore the same black dress, sent him to an old doctor on the next street who turned out to have a gynecological practice. No matter, he knew an infection when he saw one, he said as he prescribed sulfa drugs and warm compresses saturated with some purple pills he fished out of a drawer. He also identified the injury as a knife wound and made out a report which would be given to the police.

That night Sam told Harry about the police report.

"There's no way they could tie this wound to the pimp." Harry said. "Do you know how many people get cut with knives every night in this town?"

"I suppose you're right." Sam pulled a folded piece of paper out of his pocket and gave it to Harry—a poem he had written about a man's thoughts as he watches a stranger collapse and die at a bus stop. "What do you think?"

"I'm no judge but I think it's good. What are you going to do with it?"

"Just put it with the others."

"Why don't you try to get it published?"

"Maybe someday. I'm not ready yet. I'm waiting till I've got fifty I'm not ashamed of." Sam's long face took on a look of vulnerability and uncertainty.

Harry knew the feeling, one that always came when he exposed his work to another's judgment. Yet Harry had no reservations about his own talent. Whatever he did seemed good enough to show others, even now. "You're good, Sam. Don't keep it to yourself. Get it out there."

"Harry, we're all of us just beginning. We've got time."

"No we don't," said Harry with conviction as he took his rumpled brown corduroy jacket off the coat hook and left. He was meeting Aurora for dinner.

Aurora-alpha

Harry sat in the roaring isolation of the metro car gazing abstractly at faces, figures, forms and colors. He watched the momentary pulse of light flash across the windows and alter the hues of faces, clothes, the ribbon of advertisements. He studied the way people sat, whether slumped or erect, and how they held their heads, the shape of their mouths, looking for clues to their personality or state of mind. And he thought about Aurora. It felt right walking beside her on the crowded sidewalk. Not that she turned men's heads, but she carried herself with such assurance. Also, he liked that she always turned to look at him when she talked even when they were walking. She always watched him.

He found her at a table in the art nouveau cafe she favored, an empty espresso cup in front of her on the marble table, a still burning cigarette on the black ashtray. She was reading *Le Monde*. She sensed him even before she looked up, a welcoming smile on her face. He met her gaze and smiled in return, feeling pleased with the prospect of spending an evening with an appealing French woman who shared his interest in art and appeared also to be attracted to him. She looked smart, his mother would have said. The cardinal red beret on her smooth brown hair complimented the short darker red jacket that flared at the waist, and her tight black skirt showed off the long flank of her leg. She had already paid for the coffee, he saw—the white chit was torn.

As they walked in the indigo twilight toward the restaurant her hand touched his, he reached for it and they wove their fingers together, each accepting the small commitment to intimacy. The bistro was a narrow place with beige walls and faded velvet banquettes with mirrors above them. The place smelled of a rich veal stock and pate. Harry liked the smell; it was foreign, European. There were even white tablecloths. "A real splurge", he told her but she didn't know the word.

The place was full, more than a few men were wearing ties, and there were only two dogs, a Pomeranian sitting on a woman's lap and a brown and white spotted retriever lying at its master's feet looking attentively at every pair of legs that passed his quivering nose. Harry watched the waiter step adroitly over the large paws as he served a plate of *tete de veau*.

"Two things I'll never get used to," he said.

She was sipping her wine, an actual bottle with a vintage, a St. Emilion, 1945, too young, but not much had been produced during the War and the pre-war vintages were beyond his reach. Still, it wasn't the usual house wine in a carafe.

"What's that, Harry?"

"I'll never get used to bringing dogs into restaurants, and the fact that you French will eat anything."

"The French take their dogs everywhere."

"Why?"

"Custom. Sometimes on rainy days they do smell like sheep, I must say."

"So do some of the people."

"During the war, people couldn't bathe as much. There wasn't much of anything in the City." Her voice chilled and her eyes grew distant.

"Yeah, I was here too, you know." They looked at each other and exchanged an unspoken solemn question. Harry wanted to ask her about the War, how it had affected her, but this wasn't the right time.

"Oh, I wanted to tell you. My aunt sold the Franz Marc, to a Swiss collector, the Baron something von somebody."

"I'll miss it." He thought of his sketch book, thought about telling her. No one knew about it, and until he decided to sell it, if ever, no one would. There was something magical about it. One of his war buddies had carried a rabbit's foot all through the war thinking that it would protect him from harm. Another had a St. Anthony medal. The sketchbook was like a philosopher's stone, it gave off creative energy or so he let himself think. "That painting gave off something, it spoke to me," he said, sharing his thoughts. He picked up a piece of baguette and took a bite.

"Every great painting or sculpture does. The sum is always

greater than its parts." Aurora began to speak with intensity about Vermeer and Rodin and De Vinci, showing intimate familiarity with specific works Harry had seen in the Louvre. At a loss for words she reverted to French. He listened, understanding only part of what she said, watching the way her lips moved, one side of her mouth raised more than the other, and the way her eyes widened as she spoke about something she particularly liked. She stopped, a little breathless as if she'd been running and shared a look of self-deprecation.

"That was great. You should be a professor."

"One day, perhaps." She pushed her hair back from her cheek and searched for something else to say. "Have you ever thought of sculpture, Harry? Your work would adapt well."

"What makes you think so?" Harry was flattered that she had gone from the Masters to her impressions of his work.

"I have a feeling, from the way you worked those etchings." She liked them and had shown them to her aunt. "My aunt knows a place where you could work, I asked her. The owner is a sculptor with a large atelier. A well recognized man. He needs some money. You could pay him some rent and he'd teach you the basics."

Harry thought of the mud collected in Germany. He should write home. He had gotten three long letters from his sister, a note from his mother, but had confined his own correspondence to a few post cards. He had never thought of himself as a sculptor, but the idea appealed to him. He needed another artist to critique his work. He had thought about enrolling in some classes, but he preferred studying the work of the Masters at the museums. Before beginning his war etchings he had spent days in front of Durer, Rembrandt, and Goya etchings, studying the lines, absorbing their techniques with his eyes .

"So, does it interest you?" she asked leaning toward him.

"Yes, thanks," he answered and saw that Aurora was pleased with herself.

November 18, 1947 – Night Music

Since the death of the pimp, the camaraderie of the apartment had weakened. There were no more long carousing nights. Sam and Craig, tied by assault and injury, drew closer. Both crafting words, they spent their hours alone, one with a typewriter, the other with a fountain pen, or drinking coffee together at the corner cafe. Rudy, they hardly saw. Between the library, lectures, and hours at a chess club, he came and went like afternoon shadows.

Harry imagined that they were envious of him, because his prints had already been hung in a small gallery, on the recommendation of Aurora's aunt. One had been bought, and he had a small group of admirers, friends of Aurora. He even had a girlfriend, while they, due to reticence, taciturnity, whatever, had nothing more than the fragmented world of their imagination and an occasional whore. Little suggestions that he should do more of the work around the place, some cooking, shopping, he magnified in his head and concluded that they were picking on him, not being fair, finding fault. For he was sure in his own mind that he did as much as anyone.

He was simply better off. Luck of course had helped, but he had done his part. He had reached out and embraced the city, absorbed it, until he felt himself becoming Parisian, in manners, colloquialisms, gestures. Not that he wasn't still Harry, the comedian's son, but Harry was metamorphosing into something more, something different. In contrast, Sam and Craig seemed to watch through the window while Paris undressed and brushed its teeth.

Harry had come to Paris haunted and empty. Already, he was happy, with his work, his friends. He had almost put the War behind him, not out of him, but it was no longer troubling him. It was like malaria, controlled, and every day he exorcised it in his art. His French was developing, not just the words but the pronunciation sometimes won praise from Aurora's friends who were accustomed to Americans whose speech was like "bent fenders." He absorbed ideas as quickly as images, could turn them around, make them his own, and despite a total lack of formal education, an indifference to the printed word, he could hold his own in the extended animated witty conversations of Aurora's literate friends. Now he considered them his friends, for despite the fact that he was an American, he had the impression that they respected him as a singular talent, possibly a genius. Harry wanted to set the world on fire and, with the breaks, knew he could.

Aurora. At first she was just a season ticket. Fun to be with, she gave more than she got and seemed content with his company. He wasn't infatuated—the sight of her didn't give him a hard-on, although he liked the way she looked. He didn't even care if he slept with her because he was afraid his lack of passion would show and she would lose respect for him. Once they danced close and he waited for a sign, a stirring, apprehensive that Aurora was expecting a bone in her crotch and wondering why not. Sometimes it came, but slowly. It was strange, almost as if there was another Harry driving that part of him.

He would analyze it on the Metro. What was it about Aurora that inhibited or maybe intimidated him? Not that he was a priapist, but he was easily aroused. Was it that she was too forward in showing her affection? Or maybe she was too self-possessed, requiring nothing of him as a man and in fact giving to him everything that he had attained in Paris. Everything. Without her friends and contacts he would have been no closer to his goals than his buddies.

Was he intimidated and diminished because he was an outsider while this was where she belonged? She was born to France, while he was, in a way, putting on a mask and a costume, playing a part, one that was either shallow or false, no matter how well he played it. He still wasn't on the same plane with her and never could be, not here. Sometimes, despite all of his confidence, he couldn't help feeling a little like the haunted Africans he saw shambling about the streets. Whatever it was, very soon he would have to sleep with her. He couldn't go on just being her protégé.

Even so, they floated on in easy companionship, living on the surface of the days, drinking from the top of the bottle. Although he wasn't even aware of it, Harry didn't know much more about Aurora than what he saw and received from her. He didn't ask probing personal questions, and her focus was on ideas, happenings, her research, and meeting Harry's needs as she saw them. In all the months they spent together, he never got beyond the public rooms of her life.

And then, one day, she told him she was staying at her aunt's apartment and invited him to dinner. Aunt Natale was away for the weekend, visiting her sister, Aurora's mother, at Epernay. He accepted, knowing that he would either spend the night or she would feel hurt, rejected, and end up distancing herself from him. He owed her this at least for all she had done.

Harry had been to the apartment once before and liked it. A roomy space in an old building, it had high ornate plaster ceilings, brass wall fixtures shaped like swans that had been converted from gas to electricity, inlaid parquet floors, fine rugs, and best of all, some wonderful paintings—a Duchamp; a Picasso, a woman from the Blue Period; and a Matisse, a seated woman in a mostly red studio. Just to be in the same room with them, not in a museum but a private room, sitting, drinking, eating, made him feel like a battery being charged. Other than the paintings, the place was casually furnished; French country chairs in graceful light wood next to a faded *Louis Quinz* armchair all salvaged from flea markets and antique stores by her aunt who delighted in discovering an overlooked and unidentified treasure.

Aurora was a good cook when she turned her mind to it, a natural cook, who sliced, chopped, added spices without resort to a recipe, all the while talking, sipping wine, laughing. She made *poularde au Champagne*, a specialty of her region, with a green salad and some *chevre* and fresh pears. They drank the rest of the champagne and went on to a chardonnay from her uncle's vineyard. There was an apple tart to finish off and her aunt's best cognac.

They sat at the small table, dressed with white linen, now cluttered with fragments of crust, an eroded disk of chevre, and white china demi-tasse with a dark dross in the bottom. They had moved the table in front of two French windows. The night was clear, there was a moon and the roofs and chimneys across the street made a broken pattern across the lighter sky. Candles in low baroque silver holders—the only interior light—colored Aurora warm and golden.

"Well?" She looked over the peak of her prayerful hands, a self-satisfied smile curling her lips.

"You passed cooking," he said. "But I have to tell you, it doesn't take much to do better than my mother. Even Sam is better."

"Small praise," she said with a slight, disapproving turn of her head. "You cook the next time."

"I cook American, you wouldn't like it."

"I like America."

"You like ketchup?"

"What is it?"

One ceremony had passed. The next, he knew, was inevitable and he still had his doubts but not about Aurora. She wanted to be with him tonight. It made him feel self-satisfied, in control. How to get on with it? Should he move to the sofa? It was too uncomfortable. Stretch out on the floor? Too obvious.

"Have you ever seen Aunt Natale's bedroom?"

"No, she never invited me."

"There's a lovely Cezanne drawing. And the bed is exceptional, a temple of love."

"What about cleaning up?"

"Leave it for Blanche. She'll come tomorrow morning. She'll even bring fresh croissants. We won't have to go out."

"What makes you think I'll stay the night?"

She gazed at him with momentary doubt, but the expression soon shifted to curious irony. "You'll stay, Harry, your manhood is on the line."

"If you put it that way." This would never happen back home, unless he'd stumbled onto a nymphomaniac, and he would have known that the first night. French women didn't dance around the fire once they knew what they wanted. She got up, took him by the hand and coerced him gently.

She was right about the Cezanne. It was a jewel, a little still life, a basket of oranges on a table, full of light. The bed was ornate gilt and white and had a classical love scene painted on the headboard, a satyr with an erection that you could hang laundry on, and a voluptuous nude at his feet with an expectant concupiscent smile on her face.

"What do you think?"

"Hey, it's intimidating. Don't expect anything like that."

"I wasn't." Her voice grew tender.

"What do you expect?" She was silent. She looked at him, suddenly solemn and began to open the pearl buttons of her white silk blouse.

Harry drew close and kissed her softly on the lips. He ran his hand gently down her back to her skirt and felt the slippery silk under it. He lifted her skirt and ran his hand up the silk of her stocking to the smooth skin of her slender thigh. She was already moist. The other Harry began to stir. It would be good. She would be pleased.

Without removing his hand, he asked, "This isn't the first time?"

"Do you want it to be?"

"No, I hope it's not."

"Then it isn't."

January 6, 1948
Aurora—The Room at the Top of the Tower

Aurora loved Harry, she wanted to marry him, help with his career. She understood him, or thought she did. He was self-centered, as were many artists according to her Aunt Natale, who should know. A brilliant child, Harry, the one who liked to perform and be admired. An exotic with his American-Jewish ways, so alien to hers. Together they could bridge two worlds, hers and his. Although Harry didn't understand it, possibly never would, Aurora's tie to him and his to her, was a mutation of the War.

Typical of Harry, he had never asked her how she had passed the occupation, and she was relieved that he hadn't for she couldn't begin to tell him, not yet at least, the wounds were still bleeding. Her deepest, most intense feelings, shame and rage, were unshared with anyone and the metaphor of her life, as she defined it, was the keep, a wall and then another wall and finally a tower into which the occupant might retreat and be safe from harm. Beyond the inner wall spread the ceremony and commonplace of every day living, informal yet as ordered as a table set for dinner. Inside the inner wall she kept treasures, loathing, secrets, rituals known only to her.

From all outward appearances no one but her mother would guess the degrees of her privacy. She was friendly if reserved, she laughed, but not hysterically, she felt compassion, but without tears, she had close friends, but gave more than she took. A Catholic by birth, she never sought a priest's counsel, never confessed, kept her shame to herself, ritualized it.

As a child she had ingested the tales of the knights, of their search for pure love. Aurora was fascinated by the formalism of Medieval France in which everyone had their proscribed station and role. The residue of this structure she recognized in small town life: tradesmen, craftsmen, farmers, bureaucrats, symbiotic and static in a comforting way.

She had read and written her first essay on Froissard's *Chronicles of Fourteenth Century Europe* at seventeen and she knew even then that it would be her life's work. During the long gray years of the occupation, Froissard was her refuge, and when circumstance took her to Paris to live with her Aunt, access to the National Library archives gave her an early start on her doctoral thesis and the eventual recognition that she hoped to earn with the publication of *Dance of Death*.

What she couldn't give to herself, a wild spontaneous enthusiasm for the moment she admired in Harry, and for that matter, in Americans generally. She thought of Harry as personifying the American character: confident, brash, informal, childish, and powerful in a youthful innocent way, decent in a simple way that ignored ambiguity. The fact that Harry was a Jew, but not much of one, also served her need to punish Christian Europe for its violations and febrile acquiescence to Nazi rule, and what it had done to her.

If the source of her rage and shame had been a German rather than a Frenchman, even a stranger rather than someone she had passed many times in the street, she might never have succumbed to her attraction to Harry. The fact that it had been a Frenchman and one who had actually worn a crucifix around his neck—she could still feel it cold as a knife against her breast—made her reject France as a sanctuary and idealize another place. Harry was the stranger-knight who could take her to that far away land.

With patience and planning, she set out to capture him long before the night they first slept together. Aurora didn't have much confidence in herself as a seducer, she didn't like the way she looked, her legs were too thin, her body too angular and bony, her breasts too small, her face too long. She was hard on herself, especially since that night in the holding cell. It didn't surprise her at all that Harry didn't seem attracted to her sexually. Had she been a man she would have been attracted to someone more vivacious, more sensual. Not that she was cold or frigid, although she had to struggle to overcome those early feelings of revulsion, those psychic scars. To her shame, her sensuality always won out even as it had then.

As for Harry, even if he didn't love her, he needed her. Her disciplined mind would be a lens to focus his random brilliance. It was good that night in Aunt Natale's seraglio. Harry had proven himself to be a worthy lover and she had at length lost herself in the exquisite undulating waves that broke within her. In the morning, in the bright intrusive sunlight, he was still Harry, rumpled and puffy, looking across the pillowed landscape at her with what, she hoped, was a new tenderness.

February 14, 1948 – Czampolski

The studio was a long dark loft over a former livery stable, wood from the rough floor boards to the aged cross beams of the pitched roof. Large windows at both ends and two dirty skylights provided a mote-filled twilight. The dead air was a catalogue of everything that had existed in the space: harness oil and hay, unwashed clothes, coffee grounds, ageless dust and hot metal. The casting furnace made of clay brick squatted at one end as well as stacked ingots of bronze and what looked like a large tea cup suspended on a heavy metal frame. Just under the two skylights were platforms with skeletal frames covered with a skin of molded clay, evolving spectral human figures. Several large work tables were littered with tools, large basins and other utensils that were, at this point, entirely foreign to Harry. The whole scene called to mind the

Sorcerer's Apprentice sequence of Fantasia.

Kazimir Czampolski reminded Harry of Rodin's sculpture of Anatole France, a wide-shouldered brooding Zeus. His wild white hair touched his shoulders; his face was thick skinned and folded, his Neanderthal brow, sprouting with eyebrows as anarchistic as his hair. A pipe was clenched in his teeth, and his rough voice testified to the years his vocal chords had been abused with smoke. He had been in France for at least twenty years but his French was still so heavily Polish that Harry could barely understand him.

For all of his fierce appearance he was a gentle, quiet man, dedicated to his work, not caring whether any one bought it, so long as he had enough money for bread, cheese, wine, fruit, coffee and the materials he used to create. His life was austere, monastic. A narrow bed, more an army cot, a table, a stuffed arm chair, some cooking utensils, a few hundred books, a radio, a phonograph, were all he possessed. He worked to the accompaniment of Rachmoninoff, Chopin, or Brahms. His figures were romantic but semi-abstract, linear, Medieval or African. Critics likened him to Giacometti, but Czampolski was more introspective, contemplative, even solemn.

Although Czampolski needed the money, he was not open to taking Harry in until he had seen enough of his drawings and the war etchings to be convinced that his would-be student would not waste his time. The artist studied each image silently, while Harry walked around the studio looking at the bronze and wood sculptures of thin, spiritual people; the tools; pictures torn from art magazines tacked to the wall of the work of other artists, Moore and Epstein, interspersed with Czampolski's own charcoal sketches.

Harry wasn't at all apprehensive or unsure. Everyone told him that his own work was good and he could see by the look of Czampolski's images that their approaches were compatible. Czampolski finally looked up at Harry with a nod and a slight sign of approval, even admiration.

"Where did you study?" he asked as he closed the folio.

"The museums."

"With whom."

"Whomever I liked."

Czampolski gave a gentle laugh. "Good. You have promise."

"When can I start?"

"Put on that old coat over there. It's messy work."

"Now?"

"Tomorrow you may be dead."

So he began that very hour to confront and explore the
unrealized potential of a lump of damp, pliant, clay. It was
Harry's first experience with clay since kindergarten. Eventually he shaped a figure no more than a foot high, building
it on a wire frame. It was abstract but recognizable as a human shape, a three dimensional representation of a figure in
one of his etchings. He had just begun and already liked the
medium. It was soft, impressionable, pliable, forgiving, and
the surfaces could be infinitely modeled.

Next to him, Czampolski was shaping, with his fingers and
palm, a life sized Christ crucified, a form that, though only
half finished, already revealed both suffering and transcendence. He worked silently, stopping occasionally to take a sip
of wine, or put a record on.

Harry had sketched for a day with charcoal to arrive at a
form and proportion that he could live with. His work with
the wire frame and the clay took another three days. The whole
time, Czampolski never even looked at it.

When Harry finally had gone as far as he could with it, he
asked Czampolski for an opinion. The man was on his knees
at the time, modeling the feet of Christ. He looked up as
though he had forgotten that Harry was there. Without a
word, he went to the table, studied the model silently, turned
it around several times, then smashed it with his fist.

"Shit!" Harry exclaimed. "I worked on that for a week!"
The guy had to be nuts.

"It comes too easy. The next one will be better."

"But you have no right just to destroy my work."

"It was not yet your work. I will know when it is your work."

"But. . . ."

Czampolski approached him and stared into his eyes. "Decide how good you want to be, Harry. How good do you want
to be?"

"As good as it gets, I suppose."

"Well then." He had already gone back to his own work.

Harry struggled with the same concept for three more days, using the same drawings, but building on what he had learned with the first attempt, using a new vocabulary.

When he was satisfied, he again asked Czampolski to look at it, but with the admonition, "If you smash it again, I walk out of here."

Czampolski looked at the work from all sides while Harry waited, this time with apprehension. Finally, the sculptor said, "Better, but its still not your work." Harry reached out to shield the model.

Czampolski said, "It is your turn."

"To what?"

"Destroy it. You have the drawings. It is not good enough. Don't fall in love with everything you do. Destroy it," he repeated with gentle authority.

Reluctantly, Harry used his fist as a mallet and drove it with reluctance into the middle of the figure. He was about to do it a second time when Czampolski seized his wrist. "Leave it!"

"But I've ruined it."

"Look again."

Harry studied the abused model with a different eye.

"I say you should leave it Harry. Begin again with the original concept, of course. But come back to this later. There is no hurry. If you like it, I will teach you to cast with it, just as it is. It will be your first sculpture."

It remained for him, the most important lesson of his creative life.

June 28, 1948 – Epernay

It's never what you thought it would be, Harry mused as he sat in the compartment next to Aurora, across from a mother and her twin sons, all in mouse grey, except for their red caps. The boys, barely school age, squirmed as little as possible, read silently, gazed out the window, occasionally elbowed one another. The mother knitted what looked like a canary yellow muffler and her pale eyes constantly moved from the intersecting needles to her boys. What would it be like to be responsible for two children? he wondered.

He imagined Aurora bending over a crib, a book held carelessly in her left hand, a finger serving as a book mark. If there was a place in his life for children, it was not something he could see happening soon, not at least until he had more than the chump change he was making now from the occasional sale of a print. He had read about the comfortable life of artists like Monet, but in another time, and who knows how many years he had struggled before buying that home in the country. As for Aurora, she would rush off to a lecture on Fourteenth Century poetry, leaving him to make lunch and take the children to school. The children—now there were two. It was just not in the cards, not now, and he hoped her parents didn't get any ideas.

The countryside was torn by the metallic roar and rhythmic clatter of the train. Images of rough fretted fields; plain stucco farmhouses of faded gray, their dull walls splashed with the bright blood of geraniums; hurling thickets of trees; meandering, mirror flat streams with soft green banks; farmers in uniform blue work clothes astride fragile tractors, passed across his field of vision. It was so foreign to his eye and yet he found himself absorbing it like a sponge.

Aurora sat beside him, her head bent into a paperback edition of Camus' *The Plague*. Now and then she touched his hand without looking up from her book, an act of possession or reassurance which he both resented and welcomed. Just the thought of a weekend with her family in Epernay made the muscles in his neck tighten. Aurora and her Paris friends, after all, belonged to an emerging omniculture, while Epernay, he was sure, had to be a French counterpart of a county seat in rural Georgia. Beyond the uncertainty of whether he had anything in common with her family was his vision of a dinner sitting across from the local priest, a pale, constipated relic of the inquisition in a long black cassock, in a room dominated by a crucifix big enough for Harry. Then there was the undercurrent of the visit, a symbolic commitment to Aurora. That had to be the reason she had pushed him so hard. He would feel like a rare butterfly pinned to a paper.

The Romboise family lived in a square two-story stucco house on the outskirts of Eperney. It was separated from the narrow cobbled street by a white fence and a raucous cottage garden in which pale damask roses competed with spiking blue delphiniums, golden columbine, lacy yellow yarrow, brash pink hollyhock, fox glove, sun flower and lavender. Herbs, sage, angelica, catmint and chamomile formed low borders. Standing in front of the shiny, apple-red paneled door, Harry thought again of Monet.

Aurora's mother, Cybelle, put him at ease at once. Her warm smile of welcome and firm handshake drew him toward the doorway. In no time he was at ease, sitting at the country pine kitchen table drinking strong coffee and complementing her on the fresh brioche. As she moved about the kitchen chopping fresh basil, carrots and potatoes for the *blanquette*, she brought Aurora up to date on the news of the family and the neighborhood. He watched Aurora for any sign of reticence or hostility, but saw only the relaxed smile lines of an easy friendship and affection. He was envious of a mother who seemed so casually accepting of a stranger, although he was not exactly someone who had been invited in out of the rain.

The house was comfortably lived in. Bright floral patterns alternated with unfinished country antiques. A corner of the dining room harbored a wall of books. The only paintings were pleasant watercolors of the countryside done by Cybelle, interspersed with blurry photo portraits of relatives in ornate guilt frames. Aurora and her mother chatted casually about Guy, her brother, an aeronautical engineer at Dassault—he had just been promoted—and her younger sister, Claudette, who was studying industrial design in Geneva—she had broken her finger. They took Harry for granted, neither including nor excluding him from the conversation.

Her father, Raymond, taught English at the local school. He came in wearing a rumpled moss colored wool jacket and carrying a worn leather brief case. He was tall; his face was long and deeply wrinkled. Friendly deep-set eyes were keen and observant. He embraced Aurora, kissed his wife on the forehead, and offered Harry a long fingered hand blanched with chalk dust.

They ate supper under a grape arbor in the back garden. Cybelle was a self-styled nutritionist and she had raised all the vegetables and salad greens. After the first bottle of wine, Harry began to feel like he had visited many times before. He finished a second portion of the *blanquette*. How different they were from his family in Cleveland, who would have asked countless embarrassing questions. They didn't demand anything of him. If either of her parents had any curiosity about his relationship with Aurora, they didn't hint at it. He was there, Aurora's friend, a guest to be enjoyed, nothing more. That they were of different generations made no difference. They spoke of Communism in France and in Italy, the Government's policy in Algeria, the latest novels, Camus, Sartre—Raymond had just read *The Reprieve*—and the quality of Raymond's students. All topics were picked at but not exhausted. Harry listened, contributed and watched the indigo wash the garden. Distant birds called to each other. Chekhov came to mind and, forgetting the War, he imagined the tranquil life Aurora must have had growing up in languid security. That night he slept in Guy's room, dodging model airplanes hanging from the ceiling.

The next day they borrowed the low slung black Citroen and toured the district on narrow country roads that followed the contours of small valleys dense with vineyards. Stone houses with pitched slate roofs stood out in clusters against rolling forested hills. Aurora was a cautious driver and they made slow progress behind what seemed like every smoke-belching truck in France, but they were in no hurry. She pointed out a field where Julius Caesar had camped and trained his troops—the stone walls of the castro were still visible. They walked in a field on the edge of the Marne where, in the Fifth Century, the Romans defeated Attila the Hun, and nearby they stopped to read a sign marking a First World War battle. Later they climbed up to a stone chapel on a hill and Harry marveled at the exquisite rosette stained glass windows and the pillars sculpted into saints, amazed that something so elegant could be found at the end of a path on a country lane.

Across the square from the Rhamnose Cathedral they dined on *Jambon de Rhamnose* and *Pied du Cochon*.

"This is like a conversion," Harry confessed.

"You like Cognac?"

"I love it! All of it: this town, this Cathedral, the country-side, the houses, the wine, the history, the patina. Jesus Christ, I never thought I would envy anybody for having been raised anywhere, but to have this as a heritage, a place to come home to and belong to."

"And you like my parents?"

"I have to tell you, Aurora, I was scared. I didn't know what to expect, but they are just great. It's a world apart from how I grew up. That garden. We had a rubber plant in a pot, maybe some daffodils raised in a hot house."

"You didn't have any tie to the soil. You never had to defend your country." Aurora brought her hand to her mouth and her eyes veiled.

"Not since the Red Coats burned the White House."

"You Americans take everything for granted. It's part of your charm."

"What was it like, growing up under the German boot?"

"We tried to stay out of their way." Aurora hesitated, wondering how much she should volunteer and stopped short. There were other things to be said and she didn't want to taint the moment. "It was hard, impossible." Her eyes filled as she felt again the penetrating cold and endless hunger, the constant tension of the prison cell.

"At least your relatives weren't taken off to Germany to die."

"We came close, very close."

"Why, you're not Jewish?"

She took a cigarette out of the blue pack of Gauloise on the table in front of her and lit it, hiding behind the eddying smoke before she answered. "My father was in the underground. Among other things he helped find places in the country for Jews to hide."

"But he got through it without—"

"Not really, no." Her voice thickened and her breathing

quickened. She didn't want to talk about this, not now.

"What happened?"

"The Gestapo took him in for questioning. They tortured him, broke his fingers, burned his eyelids with lit cigarettes. After a week they let him go."

"Why?"

"They couldn't get anything out of him. And . . . my aunt Natale interceded."

"How?"

Aurora looked hesitant, uncomfortable. "I don't know if I should say this but . . . she had some highly placed German friends. Art collectors."

"So your family was on both sides of the street." Harry imagined that he had shared Natale's bed with some Gestapo colonel.

"It was hard not to be. The Nazis and their minions, the French fascists, were ubiquitous."

"Is that how your aunt came by the paintings?"

"What do you mean?"

"Refugees, trying to buy their way out of Europe?"

"I really can't say." Her voice was muted.

"You can't say or you won't say?"

"Haven't I already been candid enough? I didn't have to tell you about my aunt." Her voice was taught and breaking and she turned her head away from him.

"You're right. I'm sorry. It's just the raw Jewish nerve. What I saw."

She turned back and looked at him, an earnest, relieved look. "I should have been more sensitive to your feelings myself. It's, of course, a difference between us, a cultural difference."

They fell silent. Next to them a middle-aged couple were locked in a strident argument over the wife's management of money. Aurora said with a wry smile, "Were your parents that way?"

"You can't live with somebody for twenty years without fighting once in a while."

"My parents don't. Not in public at least."

"Your parents are perfect."

"As close as parents get."

"You're smug."

Aurora moved her shoulder dismissing his words. A bus came into the square. A girl chasing a brown wire-haired dog tripped and fell. Her mother rushed to pick her up. A resounding chime from the Cathedral tower struck three times.

The conversation curdled his new attachment to her district. He didn't belong here, he had to admit. He was an alien, as different as the African busboy who was, at this moment, clearing the plates from their table.

They left the restaurant and walked into the twilight of the cathedral. The high vaults echoed with the organ, a Bach fugue, the notes careening off the surfaces. They stopped at an alcove that held an enameled sculpture of Mary holding an infant Jesus to her breast. Harry took it in, the serene expression on her face, the trusting dependence of the baby.

"I'm pregnant, Harry." Aurora said this almost to herself as if she was afraid to have him hear it. He turned and faced her. Not knowing what to do, he took her hand and tried to feel tenderness, concern, something more than the apprehension of a door slamming shut and trapping him.

"Can't you say something?" His blinded eyes focused on Aurora's face, and he recognized the look of someone who has just been insulted or struck.

"I don't know what to say."

"It's our problem, you know, not just mine."

"I understand that. What do you want to do about it? You don't want to have it, do you? After all you've got school." The climax of the fugue rose and filled the church, a bursting shower of notes fading to silence.

She stared at him, a hard penetrating stare. She had expected tenderness, a certain ambiguous joy; it was after all a life that they had made together. She had been wrong just to drop it, she should have prepared him, but his response was so selfish and cold. Her lips began to tremble, but she didn't want to cry. She turned and quickly walked away. He followed.

"Wait, Aurora!" Without turning she stopped listening for the tone of his next words, more deliberate than the last.

"Forgive me. You took me by surprise. I'm struck dumb."

"I expected something better." She fished in her pocket for a handkerchief and blew her nose.

"Like what? You want to keep the baby? You want marriage?"

"At this moment I really don't know if I'd say yes if you asked me."

Free

Harry wasn't ready for marriage, not even to Aurora. It wasn't in his plan. He wasn't even sure that he loved Aurora, not at least in the way he perceived love. Love was still an obsession, an adolescent infatuation with a nubile teenager in a swinging tennis skirt, and a perpetual hard on. He liked Aurora's company, liked sleeping with her, liked her family, was grateful for everything she had done for him. She had given him access to a life as an artist. Every contact with the art community that mattered had come through Aurora or her aunt. Without her help, he would still be an alien drifter, looking into windows late at night like his friends. He wasn't ready to be a father, to be responsible for a child. His work took up all of his time and energy—there was nothing left.

"What about your doctorate? How could you get on with it with a kid? And how would we live? I don't make *bubkes*."

"What?"

"Peanuts, beans."

"You've got your military money. We can live on that. And my salary from the gallery."

"What about your degree?"

"I could put it off for a few years." She was clasping and unclasping her hands, looking into the window of a shoe store, seeing nothing but her own troubled reflection in the glass.

Harry took her agitation to be uncertainty and regret and assumed that she only needed a little convincing. Aurora was just as committed to her work as he was to his, he was sure. She hadn't expected or wanted this.

"You'd never get back to it. And it means a lot to you. As much as making it as an artist means to me, Aurora. You know it."

"But I want to have children as well."

"This isn't the right time. Not for either of us. Not even for the kid. He'd be hostage to my ambitions and your dreams."

"What do you want me to do?" She turned toward him, her voice rising, her eyes red and welling.

"It's not just me, Aurora."

"What do we do then?"

"What people do. There should be doctors around."

"Yes."

"Have you looked into it?"

"No."

"Will you?"

"What about you?"

"Jesus, Aurora, I'm a foreigner."

As it turned out, Harry found the doctor, the same one who had treated the knife wound. Harry went with her, waited, thumbing through old magazines in the drab outer office until she came out walking stiffly, looking withdrawn and chastened, as if she had been punished. He took her arm, doing his best to take on some of her pain, but she pulled away and walked ahead of him. Again she had been violated, suffered the wound, the humiliation of the invasive bruising cold metal and a life, begun and nurtured in her womb, had ended in the white rubber-sheathed hands of a stranger. Aurora was on fire inside, weak, trembling, angry with herself and Harry. What if she could never have a child again? It sometimes happened.

There was no more talk of marriage, but within two months Aurora moved into Harry's apartment.

April 4, 1950 – Honeymoon

Dear Nell:

     I know I'm a lousy correspondent: about one letter to your four. It's not that I don't think about you a lot. I do. But somehow the days fill up and I never seem to get the time to sit down and write. Maybe it's just because I want it to be something more than a greeting card.

We're here in Barcelona, a kind of deferred honeymoon. Aurora is off to the library at the University for a few hours. Would you believe it, she heard about a manuscript in old French or something that her professor touted her on to and she couldn't resist. That's how it is with both of us, which makes for a good marriage. I wrap myself in my work for hours at a time and she immerses herself in her studies—she's working on her doctoral thesis, as you know.

We've got this great cozy apartment, two rooms, a quaint little bathroom with one of those French hole-in-the floor toilets, a tub for an amputee, a Rube Goldberg copper water heater on the wall, a closet of a kitchen with a double gas ring and a box you put on top of it for an oven; no refrigerator. We buy everything fresh except for things like cheese. It makes a nice distraction The market with its stalls is just a short walk. The best thing about it are the windows cut into the mansard roof with a view that looks across a forest of chimneys to the Eiffel tower. We never would have gotten it without Aurora's aunt's influence. It's one of those cheap gems that gets passed from one friend to another. The owner is an elderly art professor who inherited the place from a rich uncle. Apparently Eric Satie lived here for a few months. There's even some notes scribbled on the wall that are supposed to be his—it has a fair amount of artistic patina.

Right now I'm sitting at a table outside a cafe with a coffee in front of me gazing at the Church of the Holy Family, Gaudi's wildest creation. If you haven't heard of him, he was a local building designer who created spires and ornament that look like melted wax candles or cake decorations. Everything seems blurred and, at the same time, concentrated. He ornamented the surfaces with bits of rubble, fragments of colored tile, leftovers. Makes me think of all that mud and stuff I collected and sent home. It looks like a joke, a child's drawing, a goofy dream, something Walt Disney would animate, something Miro drew, but it's grand and real, a Twentieth Century interpretation of rococo, whatever.

By now you're probably saying, why doesn't Harry get down to his feelings? OK. Aurora and I are happy, which is to say everything and nothing. Happy, what does it mean? Content with our simple, work-centered, impoverished, life. We like each other, complement each other, seldom fight, and when we do it's over little things. She's getting very much like a rose bush with swelling buds. She is swollen, her color is brighter, her emotions are at a higher pitch, tears of joy come quickly and pass like spring showers. We like to talk about the difference between the creativity in making art and making a child. Her function as carrier is passive but dictated by the codes of life, hers and mine. There's so little of outside influences, other than what she puts into her body, that goes into the evolving fetus. Making art is external, a product of hands and mind and feeling, influenced by the way that what we've seen and felt is fused into who we are and expressed in a dialogue with the materials we use. That's a mouthful.

Having a kid in the hamper makes us dream about the future as we sit at our little table at dinner, watching the late light sky over the roofs. Mostly expecting a kid gives us a stake in that future. We wonder what it will be like for the kid, for us, what we can do for our little Rachel or Ariadne or Joshua or Francois and what he or she will become in · tomorrow's world.

You still don't know how I feel. I feel lots of things. I get a little tearful when I think of having a kid. I get scared when I think that I have locked my fortune to Aurora and have closed off other options. I'm grateful for what she and her aunt Natale have done for me. I could never have gotten the recognition and help without it. I like being a part of this different world, meeting people and making friends I never would have met without her. Yes, I'm sure that I love her in a non-possessive way. She and I can be independent and be with each other at the same time. I don't feel confined by her. I like to see her in her work, with no time to make a good meal. It frees me to be who I am: impulsive, spontaneous, free. So now that I've written it down, I'm not sure it's even true, but there had to be some truth to it because I didn't think about it. It just came out of me. And for me, that's where the truth lies, in art and in life.

I hope that mother is well. I got a letter from her a few months ago and wrote back. I guess she told you that.

I'm glad to hear you're engaged. He sound's nice. Maybe you'll come over and see us some time.

Love,
Your brother, Harry

July 20, 1950 – The Group

It was halfway to dawn and they had gone through six bottles of Cote Ventoux, four packs of Gauloise, a stack of records—Billie Holiday, Stan Getz, now Ma Rainey's earth call on the tinny portable phonograph that Aurora had brought from home along with her collection of American jazz. The conversation ebbed and flooded, sometimes staccato and contrapuntal, rarely solo, then as quickly died and they would fall back against the pillows that mostly passed for furniture, take the smoke deep inside them, the smoke and the music, which had the same effect. They talked of writers, Celine and Sartre, capitalism, colonialism, Algeria and Indochina, communism, existentialism, abstraction, Duchamp, Klee, Kandinsky. They criticized the critics—art and literature—picked apart the literary journals, decried the relevance of culture, questioned the government's policies on education, praised a new patisserie, disagreed over the qualities of scotch malt (which was beyond their reach in any event), duck liver, goose fat, the curative properties of herbal remedies, the reliability of the National Railway, the end of the civil war in Greece, the significance of ceremonial military garb and the popularity of soccer as manifestations of tribal revanchist nationalism.

A small group, they were often together, familiar, with no need to impress or posture, comfortable, predictable, accepting, almost an extension of the small town circle that Aurora had known growing up. Mostly they were her milieu of fellow students from the University, people who Harry liked and who respected him. Harry tolerated almost any idea or behavior so long as it came from someone who liked him and his art. Harry, in his way, was as exotic to the French as the Afro-American musicians who played or sang jazz and blues in the smoky left bank clubs.

The seven were sprawled, leaning on elbows or on each other, in a circle around a single thick candle that daubed each of them with pale, changing light. Josette, a French literature student from a village in Normandy was Aurora's closest friend. Lise was writing a dissertation on the American expatriate writers of the 20s. Yet another student, George, an old admirer of Aurora, was a self-styled Bergsonian. Sam, was the only one of Harry's original apartment mates still living in Paris. He was working at American Express and writing a war novel. Hypolite was a painter, Lise's lover.

Harry was using a corner of Aurora's swollen belly as a pillow. She didn't seem to mind and was idly playing with his hair. They had coaxed Sam into reading a passage from his manuscript. He had just finished and they were taking turns praising and criticizing it. "Time we broke up," said Sam having wrung the last ounce of encouragement out of them. "Believe it or not, I've got to work tomorrow."

"Why do we do this?" said Josette, struggling to her feet. "Hypo, can I get a ride?"

"Sure. If you buy some gas." Hypolite had a Simca sedan, the only car. The rest had bicycles or mopeds, except for Sam who had a restored British Army surplus Triumph motorcycle.

Harry got up, turned on the lights, and rummaged for handbags that had been tossed at random around the room.

"Shouldn't I help you clean up?" asked Lise, always solicitous of Aurora.

"Harry will do it tomorrow."

"Yes, don't worry Lise, I've washed more dishes in the last month than in my whole life."

"You're forgetting KP," said Sam.

"Best forgotten. I'll walk you out, Sam." Harry turned the switch to start the hall light timer and descended the steep narrow stairs with Sam. "Heard from Craig?"

"Yes, as a matter of fact. He's enrolling in law school."

"How about that."

"Sure surprised me."

"Coming to my opening?"

"Count on me to wear a black sweater, drink the wine, eat the cheese, smoke up the room, maybe even complement the work."

"Great, I can use a good shill. Don't forget to walk your machine down to the boulevard before you start it."

"It's a lot quieter now. I found a muffler."

July 25, 1950 – Debut

"You should be very pleased, Harry." said Aunt Natale, raising her champagne flute and taking a polite sip. He caught the limpid crystalline reflection of distant light in the glass. She had invited him to lunch—nothing elaborate, just the bistro up the street from her gallery: *Croque Monsieur*, a green salad and a good champagne, a demi bottle, to celebrate last night's successful opening.

"Don't expect any comments in the press, not the first show. What's more important is that six pieces and seven, or was it eight, etchings sold. Of course we priced them well. But that's not critical. I've seen many shows of new artists come and go without a single sale. What is even more important, your largest piece, *Lost Illusion*, sold to a very important collector."

"Eight."

"You counted."

"I've got my memoirs to think about."

"Very droll."

Her posture would make a good form for a sculpture, he thought. She was sitting obliquely on the chair, her legs turned to the left, her torso somewhat to the right, her head to the left, showing the strong cheek line and Voltaire nose. Because their noses weren't their best feature, Parisian women, he observed, made a habit of looking at a man square in the eye. He had just read Cyrano and had been drawing noses.

"The sculpture is very evocative, Harry. The molten surfaces, the suggestion of reality, the ambiguity, the humor, the pathos."

"You see more than I do, Aunt Natale."

"Come now, Harry, modesty doesn't become you."

"Really, I never know what will be in the work until it's done."

"But you must intend something, Harry."

"Not with the sculpture. Not when I start. I just begin working and let the form and theme come out of the clay. I must have told you that before."

"I recall you did, but I was frankly incredulous."

"It's not the same with some of the etchings. I know just what I'm looking for." He put his fork down and looked at her. She was a slightly worn yet elegant woman, Aurora's aunt, in the way that Paris was elegant. The fragrance of rose that she often wore came through the cigarette smoke. In spite of his affection for her he couldn't look at her without imagining how she had acquired the collection of paintings that hung in her apartment and her war time associations. One day he would ask her about the men she had entertained.

"Harry, now that you are becoming someone you've got to look the part. Those," she paused, looking for a polite word, "Mediterranean features set you off. Appearances don't make talent but talent is enhanced by showmanship."

"What do you suggest?"

"Try something dramatic. Perhaps a cape."

The image came to him of Claude Raines in *Phantom of the Opera* or was it *Murders in the Rue Morgue*, rushing about the shadowy streets of Paris cape flying, looking like a bat. As a child he'd loved going to Saturday matinee horror movies at the Astor Theater with his stickball buddies, Ben and Chester, who lived on the same block.

"Harry, you're laughing at something. Share it with me."

"Was I?"

August 2, 1950 – Goya

"It's from the Fondación Goya," said Aurora, handing him the envelope.

"What would they want with me?" He reached out, looked at the envelope, and hefted it in his hand. "Nice paper," he said and put it down on the table.

"Open it, it's not a bill."

"Here. You read Spanish."

She sliced the envelope with a knife and he watched as her swollen face turned from curious concentration to wide-eyed, open-mouthed surprise. "They want you to come to Madrid for three days, all expenses paid."

"To do what?"

"Prepare a show in one of their smaller galleries. Goya's *Disasters of War* and your *Dogs of War*. They want you to select the images and write something to go with the catalogue."

"You're bullshitting me."

"No. See for yourself. You can make it out."

He took the letter and parsed it with blossoming exultation. He had gotten a fair amount of attention for his work, but this was the first time an institution had noticed him. Of course the connection was obvious. The reviewers had all compared his etchings and lithographs to Goya's famous anti-war statements with all their gruesome cynical images. But for the foundation charged with preserving Goya's work and memorabilia to recognize the connection was an honor that even Harry would have thought impossible for at least another 20 years.

"They want me to come down there in two weeks. I can't do that what with you expecting. Can I?" he asked hoping she would willingly give him leave.

"Don't be silly. You'll only be gone a few days. Besides, you're just in the way." Despite the discomfort and preoccupation of pregnancy—Aurora was edemic from head to foot—she plodded steadily on at her typewriter halfway through the first draft of her dissertation, napping, drinking water, and going to the bathroom incessantly.

"But what if something happens and you need me." Harry was trying to be a dutiful husband, but he knew that he had to take this opportunity. After all, that was the deal between them.

"Lise is just a few minutes away. Besides, nothing will happen. The women in my family are the proverbial give birth in the morning, back in the field types." Of course Aurora wanted Harry to stay close to home, but she wouldn't say so and she knew that, presented with a comparable offer, she would have traveled to Madrid even within a week of her appointed date. After all, there were gynecologists in Spain.

"I don't see why I should have to go personally. We can bundle up the lot of the etchings and send them down. I can write something from here. After all they aren't planning the show for another year."

"Just tell them that, Harry. That will be very good for your career. I can't be bothered to make a visit even if you have offered to pay me."

"Franco gives me the creeps, Aurora."

"I'm sure you'll be invited over to his summer house for sherry. This has nothing to do with politics. Who do you think you are, Picasso?" she stabbed him with a critical stare and audibly drew in her breath. His doubt was just a charade; she knew that.

"So you've convinced me."

"Convinced you indeed. You'd have left your mother's deathbed for such a chance, you reprobate."

"Don't be cruel, Aurora. And while we're on the subject, how about ironing my only dress shirt."

"*C'est droll, mon cher.*"

Housed in a mansion in Madrid, the former palace of a Jesuit general, the Fundación was appointed with furnishings, carpets and sculpture of the late Eighteenth Century. There was even a small museum of sacred objects: heavy vestments embroidered with silver thread, crucifixes inlaid with ivory, encrusted with precious stones; censors; a golden chalice; the plunder of the new world during the halcyon days of the Spanish Empire, Harry assumed.

He was given a room on the third floor with a canted open beam ceiling, wide planked wooden floor and dark, heavy furniture. The white walls were hung with a dozen Goya etchings and lithographs, and an elegant, if tortured, crucifix. The private bathroom was not Eighteenth Century but early Twentieth Century with massive porcelain fixtures. In fact the building had always been a hospice for functionaries and visiting notables.

As he wandered the halls, Harry imagined the voices of

militant clerics, plotting the subjugation of Peru or a manual with 100 ways to save the souls of heretics. Despite his fantasies, he was on his guard not to be irreverent or outrageous. Aurora had made him promise to be more European than American, if for no other reason than the advancement of his career. Even Aunt Natale had put in her word of caution with several ornamented stories of promising artists who had ruined their careers by being unremittingly offensive and outrageous.

Unable to control his mental associations, he entered into a dialogue with himself. Where are the dungeons? The instruments of torture? Where do they park the *auto da fe*? And so on. To his patron, the curator, he tried to present the image of a serious, intense artist with unassuming confidence in his creativity and potential genius.

With his hollow cheeks, long face and round opaque eyes, Francisco Huertas y Somez, the curator, looked to Harry like he'd stepped out of an El Greco. Middle aged, he was stooped, pale with wrinkled dry skin and thinning black hair. Somez was conservator of Goya's works on paper, a collection of over 2,000 pieces ranging from every state of every etching to drawings fully realized, sketchbooks, notebooks, not to mention the lithographic experiments. Yet another part of the archive held documents of historical note and even trivia such as bills for supplies and correspondence with his patrons over the terms of the commissioned works.

Harry saw very little of the curator, except for a luncheon the first day at a nearby modest restaurant. They talked technique for most of the meal and Somez gave him what seemed to be a ritual introductory lecture describing the history and development of the collection and the function of the foundation in "fomenting" the study and appreciation of the Master. Finally, over the flan, coffee, cigars and Fundador brandy, the curator loosened up.

"I suppose our invitation surprised you, Senor Baer."

"I was flattered."

Somez seemed to be analyzing his response. "Occasionally, we locate a talent such as yours that is in harmony with Goya, although not often, I can assure you."

It was one of those comments that can't be responded to, and Harry tried to look pleased but humble.

"We sometimes appoint fellows of the Foundation. There is a small stipend. Not much, but helpful to young artists. Would you be interested?"

"Of course. I would be honored."

"We hoped so. In that case, this afternoon my assistant, Pilar Mendoza, will acquaint you with some of the archives, particularly the plates of the *Disasters of War*. I'm sure this will interest you."

"I would like that very much."

After lunch the assistant curator took him to one of the print rooms. It was windowless, dry and cool, to inhibit deterioration of the works on paper stored in stacks of narrow drawers. In contrast to the public areas, this archive was utilitarian, dominated by a large table, a soft overhead light, and an adjustable magnifying lens suspended on an arm.

"Would it interest you to see, side by side, each state of one of the *Disasters of War* etchings?" Senora Mendoza had a beautiful nose, he saw, long, straight, high-bridged, the nose of a Renaissance virgin. Her eyes were round, wide-set and dark brown, so dark that the iris and pupil could not be distinguished. Her skin was pale white, contrasting starkly with straight black hair pulled into a prim bun. She was slender, of average height. Her tight beige skirt constricted her step. She waited, looking at him with a remote, patient expression.

"Very much."

She brought out seven images of people hanging from tree limbs while others stood about indifferently. Handling each piece carefully with cotton gloves, she put them in turn under the magnifying lens, and together they bent over the table as she exposed the subtle differences between the states.

"This one is from the first edition, published in 1863 by the Academy of San Fernando," she said sounding like a docent. "You may be surprised to know that the first publication of this series was a full 43 years after Goya finished the plates." Harry bent over the suspended lens, so close to her head that he could smell the faint herbal fragrance of her hair. She continued, sheet by sheet, showing him the areas in which successive impressions had worn and blurred the fine lines that the artist had etched into the master plate. "Of all his works, these represent the purest etching, the least aquatint, a little dry point, here and here. As you may know Goya used aquatint to great effect in his *Caprichos* series, for example."

Harry let himself be drawn into the image so that he was both standing side by side with the spectators and feeling, in his hands, the movement of Goya's hand as, line by line, he built the images and evoked the dark, cynical despair of the scene. Occasionally, his concentration was broken by her shoulder or arm touching his and by her lilac scent.

"Finally, here we see a sorry example of the 1906 edition, published by the Calcografia Nacional using the original sadly worn plates. There is a regrettable deterioration of the image, no?"

"I don't know. It's just something different with its own appeal, a softer impression, blurred, lacking in some power, but gaining some as well."

"You think so?"

"If you apply modernist values to the impression, Renoir could have done it."

"Interesting." She looked at him taking his measure. "But it's certainly not what the Master intended."

"That's for sure. He worked on hard ground I suppose?"

"Yes, we have his formulae of course. Not to mention the original plates."

"The one's he worked?"

"Yes, 80 of them. Do you want to see them as well?"

"I'd love to." He waited while she went to get a few, remembering the anticipation he felt, standing in line to get into the Saturday matinee to see the latest Roy Rodgers double feature. He was so lucky to be here!

He spent the next two days with Goya and Pilar Mendoza studying the *Disasters of War* and selecting the prints to be shown with his own etchings. They had lunch in the buffet.

She was polite, interested in his approach and technique, curious about his life, especially his war experience and its impact on the work. He gathered that she would be writing the notes for the show. When he tried to move the conversation to her personal life, what she did when she wasn't working, she rebuffed him with an enigmatic smile or a dismissive wave of the hand, a hand that, he saw, had no wedding ring.

He was left to himself at night and found his way to a bar in a vaulted basement with rough pine country furniture, basque cooking, and a Flamenco guitarist. He sampled small plates of fried sardines, shrimp sauteed with garlic, and drank a peppery Spanish white wine that cost him an unbelievable equivalent of eight cents a liter. The tavern and the streets were crowded until two in the morning and he wondered when the Spanish found the time to work, given the three hour afternoon supper break.

The night before he was to return to Paris, he came back to his room early. On impulse, he passed Pilar's office. A wedge of light shone through a crack in the door. He hesitated, and then looked in. She looked up from her writing, her startled expression softening to an embarrassed smile. For the first time her black hair was hanging loose and framed her face, giving her a softer aura.

"It's you," she said. "I've been working on my notes for the exhibit. I was just about to leave." She got up, ran her hand down her skirt and picked up a brown leather purse. "I'm sorry that Senor Huertas y Somez won't be able to say goodbye. He extends his well wishes." He was still standing in the doorway, blocking her path. She came up to him, stopped and looked at him as if she wasn't sure what to do next.

Harry took in her fragrance and wanted to touch her hair to see how soft it was. He moved his head closer to hers and saw that she didn't recoil.

"If you like I'll walk you to your room," she said her voice muted as if she was afraid someone might hear her.

They passed the night watchman in the hall as he was about to turn the key of one of the clocks that measured the frequency of his rounds.

It was a gentle night, humid, but not oppressively so. He opened the door and was met by a soft breeze smelling of diesel exhaust.

"You can come in if you like. I've got a little brandy left and it ought to be finished. I won't take it home with me." He waited, doubting that she would take up the offer. Still, she had offered to come as far as the door.

"No, I don't think so."

Harry encouraged her with a tilt of his head. "Come on. A farewell party."

"Well, only for a few minutes."

Harry bowed and welcomed her with a flourish of his arm.

Once inside, she stood in the middle of the room, looking ill at ease. He gestured toward a chair and she sat on its edge carefully putting her purse down on the floor beside her.

He handed her a glass, touched it with his own. "*Salud.*"

She drank it down, shuddered, and immediately smiled as if the alcohol had already numbed her nerves or anesthetized her reserve.

"Another?"

"No thank you. I should go or I'll miss my bus."

"You could stay the night." She looked at him as though she hadn't understood his words and he added, "There are plenty of bedrooms up and down the hall and they're all open, I've tried the door of one. As far as I can tell I'm the only guest."

"You are the only guest." She repeated his words emphasizing each word as if it had special meaning.

"I like you with your hair down. It's very lovely. It has a luster."

"It's rather limp."

"And your skin is like porcelain. It's almost translucent."

"It's very sensitive to the sun."

"If I were a realist painter, I would want to do your portrait."

"Have you, have you ever done life drawing and the like?"

"Not with models. Just sketches here and there. Impressions.

"Have you ever posed for an artist?"

"Me? No." A flush came to her cheeks and she shook her head.

"Ever wanted to? If you'd been asked?"

"No. No. I'm much too shy."

"They say that still waters run deep."

"What?"

"It's a saying."

"I see."

Harry drew closer, took her hand. She stood up as if on cue and faced him soberly, her breathing short and audible. He kissed her on the lips, softly, but sustained. She met him, at first tentatively, then willingly.

Grass

There was a note on the table, on blue paper, in Aurora's precise linear hand. "The time has finally come. I'll be at St. Agnes Hospital. Don't worry. Lise is with me. Hope your trip was a success. I'll be fine. Love, Aurora"

Harry felt a jolt of foreboding, but dismissed it. Still he should have been there. And all along he had told himself that he would make it in time. Maybe he still would. Childbirth sometimes took half a day, especially the first time, and there was no date on the note. They might have just left. Without changing into fresh clothes or even washing his face he rushed down stairs, found a taxi, and went to the hospital. There was a flower seller on the steps in front of the entrance and he bought ten red roses.

At the front desk, he waited impatiently as the receptionist took her time with three people in front of him, making them wait while she took a personal phone call. His anxiety rose up through him like mercury and he felt like someone running for a departing train.

The receptionist searched for Aurora's name and without looking at him, said, "She's not shown as a patient."

"I know she's here, perhaps she hasn't been admitted yet. I've just come from out of town."

"Was it for an operation?"

"She's having a baby."

She nodded, dialed a number and waited before asking if Aurora Baer had been admitted. She listened, nodded, responded and turned to him. *"Entendez, Monsieur."* She made another call and said to the person answering, "Mister Baer is here." Then she told him that a sister would be down immediately.

"Is anything wrong?" he asked, his anxiety choking him. If she heard the question she avoided it. An old man in a black suit got her attention. Harry tried to smother his growing sense of dread by focusing on the details of the entry, the cracked and worn black and white marble floor, the yellow water stain on the high ceiling, the ornate hanging globes, and the abstract design where the pale green wall met the white ceiling. A child, dressed in a sky blue smock ran a wooden pull toy, a farm wagon, over his foot, and his father, broad and square, offered apologies.

After what seemed like ten minutes, a nun approached the desk. Except for the egg shape of her face, she was a triangle of gray cloth. A large ebony wooden cross dangled and swung as she walked toward him. "You are Mr. Baer?" Her pale gray eyes were placid yet caring. "Follow me please."

Harry had an impulse to turn away and run. "How is my wife?" She didn't respond as she led him into a small room with two chairs. A second nun with a smooth ruddy-cheeked face was holding a sleeping newborn child, swaddled in white cloth. The face of the child was red and solemn and the head was covered with light brown down.

"This is your daughter, Mr. Baer. Therese. Would you like to hold her? Sister Monica will take the flowers." For a moment he couldn't understand the words. He looked at his right hand and realized that he was still clutching the bunch of roses. The fact that the baby already had a name passed over him. He was in awe of the baby, afraid to handle something so small, so tenuous and new to life. He reached out tentatively and she handed the baby to him guiding his hands. He brought it to his cheek, touched the soft downy head aware of sweet powdery, fragrance.

"Is she alright?"

"Yes, a perfect child."

"And Aurora, my wife. Can I see her now?"

"Please, sit down, Mr. Baer." The foreboding again choked him, his head felt congested. Both nurses faced him now, somber yet comforting. Harry knew what they were going to say. The one that had held the baby said, "I'm sorry to tell you that your wife passed on during childbirth."

His eyes filled, his chest turned to stone and a voice told him that it couldn't be true, it couldn't be happening to him.

"How could it?" he managed to say, his voice strangled, his anger kindling. Someone must be to blame. No one died in childbirth any more.

"A blood clot in the heart. Fibrillation. The heart went out of control, then stopped. The doctors did everything they could. The baby, your daughter, was still in the birth canal. It was very quick. They couldn't bring her back. I'm very sorry."

"When?"

"Last night. You can talk to Doctor Roncard when he returns. Can I get you something? Shall I take your daughter? She is such a beautiful child."

"Yes. Please take her." He saw the infant's blurred face through his tears. He handed her back to the sister and turned away, his chest in spasm, his hand covering his eyes. Beyond resentment, he had no feeling for the child. She belonged to someone else. It was a mistake. They had gotten the names wrong. Aurora was upstairs somewhere waiting for him. No. He threw aside the false comfort of denial. No mistake. This was real. His life had overturned. He saw a corridor with numberless doors and a blind wall. Aurora, his lover, his companion, was gone. Images of her bent over the sink, her fine hair fanned on the pillow, the way she held the bowl of morning coffee between her thumb and forefinger, her chiding, encouraging, comforting voice, her impatient sighs, the pencil that she twisted in a coil of her hair, all flashed in his memory and faded leaving a residue of irreversible loss.

One of the sisters touched his shoulder and he turned toward her. "There is a chapel just down the hall, Mr. Baer. There, you will find comfort."

"Thank you. I'll just wait here a minute. I think I need

some fresh air." He cleared his throat and choked back tears.

"The Luxembourg Garden is not very far."

"Yes, I know."

"God will see you through this Mr. Baer. He will give you strength."

The other sister offered him the roses.

"Give them to someone."

"Thank you Mr. Baer, they will be appreciated." The two women turned and left him alone in the room.

The pattern of his life had shattered like a broken window. He walked out of the room and, until he came out of the shadow and antiseptic aura of the hospital into the diffused sunlight, felt the panic of a child separated from his parents, lost in the penny arcade at Euclid Beach. Then his mind cleared, he took a deep breath and set his course for the Luxembourg. Somehow he would sort it out. And yet as he walked among strangers, unseeing, another feeling agitated and weighed on him: the knowledge that as he was indulging his impulse to sleep with Pilar Mendoza, Aurora had given up everything.

September 1, 1950 – Epernay 2

"I always had the feeling that you never loved her, Harry not at least, in the way I imagine a husband should love a woman," Natale said. They were in the garden under the arbor. The house was full of guests, relatives. Most of them Harry had never met and he was feeling like Kafka's principal character in *The Castle*—he had read it on the train. Aurora's Great Aunt Matilde (he thought that was her name) was sitting on a wrought iron bench against the wall of the house cradling and gently rocking a white bundle of cloth at one end of which was a round rosy face, Therese, his daughter, asleep in the arms of a stranger. Therese. He was beginning to like the name.

Natale's tone and expression informed him that she didn't really care how much he had loved Aurora. She might have been telling him about a smudge of jam in the corner of his mouth. Even so, his first impulse was to deny it, but he held back. This was no time for argument and she was his patron. Besides, it was no business of hers. He said nothing, not even with his eyes.

She went on speaking, as much to herself as to him. "Of course, it's not for me to say what marital love should be, since I have never married. But I've seen good marriages; Cybelle and Raymond for example," she added, gesturing with her half full wine glass toward Aurora's mother and father.

The trauma of Aurora's death was etched on their faces in lines and shadows. They were holding hands, Harry saw. Overriding the loss was a palpable bond, a chrysalis woven from the continuous thread of a shared life. It surprised him that two people in their middle age would look, in a way, like father and child or mother and son. To hold hands, Harry assumed, was to offer guidance, protection, and support. He remembered the first time Aurora had taken his hand as they walked toward a cafe and his eyes blurred with tears.

"You and I, Harry, we could never be that close to another person, not as close as they are." Natale broke into his thoughts. He had almost forgotten she was beside him.

"I don't know."

"Oh, Aurora was a good match for you. She was independent, self-sufficient. She didn't suffer from a deficiency; rather she took energy from your creativity. You were like two plants, growing side by side."

"Well. . . ."

"There's so much that you never knew about her."

"How do you know that?"

"I know both of you." She seemed to gauge his doubt then said, "For example, she never told you the extent of encouragement she was getting from her professor, no doubt. He thought that her dissertation would be published."

"She told me that." Natale looked as if she didn't believe him.

Irritated by Natale's dissection of their marriage, he said on impulse, "Why did you have the baby baptized so soon after she was born? It was you wasn't it?" Before she could answer he asked, "And why were you so quick with a name?"

She looked confused. "She had to have a name."

"But not so soon. Not before I got there. After all, she's

my child as well."

"We weren't thinking. It was so sudden, so unexpected, and we couldn't reach you. You were on a train."

"There has to be more to it than that." As the numbness born of the shock had worn off, it came to him that the hurried baptism had been a kind of vaccination, against his influence. "You wanted to be sure that she was raised a Catholic, that was the reason, wasn't it?" People turned to look at him.

"In truth, Harry, what would you do with an infant, given where you are in life, given who and what you are?"

"That's for me to decide."

"I think the whole family must decide, with the child's welfare in mind. Raymond and Cybelle have thought about it. They intend to talk with you tonight, in fact. They are willing to raise Therese. They *want* to raise her."

Raymond drifted toward them. He only glanced at Natale but focused on Harry, a look that seemed to reach out with consolation and inclusion. He put his hand on Harry's shoulder and said, "This is a hard time for all of us."

Harry responded only with a nod, but he was moved by Raymond's gesture.

"We have much to talk about," Raymond said, "when we are alone."

"Yes."

Raymond nodded meaningfully and returned to Cybelle, who was standing alone, lost in some recollection. He touched Cybelle's arm, said something to her. She answered with a thoughtful nod.

"This is hardly the time to mention this, Harry, although perhaps it is." Natale paused until she was sure that she had his attention and interest. "Yesterday I got a call from Milan. They want to do the sculpture show."

Harry did his best to mask his elation. The first thought that came to him was regret that Aurora wasn't here to share it.

February 8, 1951 – Life after Death

Aurora's death left Harry with open wounds that refused to heal. He was full of straw. His remedy for anything that bothered him was to bury his consciousness in his work. He spent long days in the twilight of the studio sketching possible sculptural forms. Czampolski seldom spoke and was the perfect companion, offering silent encouragement by his presence, his nods of approval, and an occasional touch on the arm with his calloused hands.

While Harry drew with charcoal or modeled clay maquettes only to destroy them and begin again, he lost himself and became the line or movement of the hand modeling the clay. Time, as a component of life, abandoned him and he escaped from its measured grasp. He ate very little, slept fitfully and at odd hours like a cat. During that time, he avoided their old friends, spurning invitations with the excuse that he was working toward an exhibition. In fact, he didn't feel like small talk or any talk. He felt awkward, unable to breath in the hothouse humidity of sympathy and was unable to say even one word about his daughter, Therese, already a child of the Church, a stranger to him. Seeing her left him with a wrenching in his chest, a feeling of loss with no compensating gain. She was in Cybele's care and a postman's wife, a new mother, was nursing her.

"Be careful, Harry or you will become like me," Czampolski told him over coffee and fresh baguette.

"And what are you?"

"A calcified heart connected to a pair of gnarled hands. Nothing more."

"If you wanted more out of life than creation, Kazimir, you wouldn't live the life you live."

"I had more once. I lost it and didn't have the resolve to recover it."

"Even so, you seem content enough."

"My life was once like the trunk of a tree. Over the years I worked it with my tools, until there was nothing more than the heart wood."

Harry thanked him for the advice and dismissed it as the maundering of an old man. He was young, resilient, and capable of healing. He would heal; put the past behind him. He had a future and time would once again join him and jolt him. In fact an idea was growing inside him, one that he found intriguing. Sculpture was solid, external. Could it also be spatial? Could he create the soul of a sculpture and surround the observer with it. He wanted to create a sculpture that could be entered, like a subway station, or a crypt. The idea first came to him as he walked into the open mouth of a Metro station and followed strangers looking at their backs as they passively descended like spirits. He would create the appearance of descent into oblivion into the blind cavern of death. He said nothing to Czampolski, nothing to Natale. But he began to draw in earnest.

September 1, 1951 – Natale

"You seem to be coming out of your eclipse, Harry. I'm relieved." Natale, leaned forward, cigarette poised in front of her lips, elbow on the linen tablecloth, waiting for him to give her a light. Her trim shape in the tight black dress, the quick movements of her hand reminded him of Aurora.

"Why?" He dug around in his pocket for a box of matches, found them, lit one and held it out to her.

"I thought I'd lost you." Her voice came through the smoke, husky.

"That implies that I was yours in some way."

"I like to think that you are in a way my Olympia."

"As long as you don't think of me as your *Golem*."

Neither knew what the other was alluding to. Both chose not to show their ignorance by asking the obvious question. But Natale dropped her head and raised her eyebrow acknowledging his riposte. She blew a spume of smoke toward him, looked toward the ceiling and finally said, "It's just that, I never thought you were so deeply involved with poor Aurora to have mourned her so profoundly."

He was about to respond, resenting the implication that the marriage was opportunistic, but he let it pass.

"I shouldn't have said that, I'm sorry."

"Look, it's not the first time you've said it."

"Which doesn't make it right." A string quartet was playing a movement from Schubert's *Trout*. She turned her head toward the music leaving Harry to wonder when she would come to the point. He was fond of Natale, grateful to her, willing to repay her efforts even beyond being a dutiful artist creating objects that she might sell to "serious collectors, there are still many around, not to mention the new money, there is always new money, even during the occupation," her words. He had already completed five good sized pieces and six small ones for the Milan show. She had seen them and was pleased. One, she had already sold to a Marquis de something. He could never remember the names of the patrons for some reason. Now she wanted something more from him. Harry suspected that she wanted to sleep with him. He certainly wasn't going to take the initiative with her. Since Aurora's death he hadn't even thought of being with a woman. His appetite was still muzzled by a vague, yet pressing, guilt translated into the need to keep his life focused on his work and uncluttered by social demands.

"Did you like the food?" She came back from the music. He shrugged. "High praise indeed."

Harry looked across the room at a lively woman. Through dinner he'd been studying the bone structure of her wide cheeked face. Her lips were soft and full and a bit pouty and her eyes had an upward tilt, but from this distance he couldn't quite make out the color except that they were not blue.

"Would you like some cognac?" Natale said with a touch of irritation, aware that Harry's attention was misdirected.

"I don't mind." He turned toward her, propped his chin in the peak of his fingers and offered her a bland smile.

"Harry, do you really mean to build that depressing cavern and install it in the middle of the exhibition?" He had shown her the drawings for "Lethos," his interior sculpture. "It's so different from the thrust of your work."

"An artist has to grow."

"Yes, but you are just beginning. I'd hate to see you self-destruct with something frivolous."

"I appreciate your concern for my future."

"I have no intention of impinging on your artistic freedom." She jammed her cigarette into the ashtray.

"Then don't. What would you have said to Duchamp when he hauled his bicycle into the gallery?" The waiter appeared with the cognac. Harry observed that the waiter's black jacket was turning brown with age. "*Le Chaim,*" he said, and bolted it down feeling the smooth burning descent.

Natale watched him with the critical eye of an adult observing the antics of a spoiled child. She asked for the check. "Harry?" Her tone was uncertain, coy, repentant.

"Yes."

"Will you come back to my apartment? I have something for you."

"What?"

"It's a surprise."

April 11, 1952 – Nell #2

Dear Nell:

Yes, I am coming out of my funk, if that's a proper word to describe a profound loss. I've been trying to express the death of a companion, someone you loved in many ways, even one you only had in your life for a few years. I think Magritte does it well. You've probably never heard of him. He uses dream images, illogical connections. As you may see I've been reading a lot, kind of educating myself, Jung, Sartre, Zen Buddhism, some philosophy, a little Kabbalah, whatever I see in the bookstores that catches my eye, this and that. I'll never be a scholar, I just don't have the discipline to learn a hell of a lot about anything, but I pick things up, throw them into the peasant seven day soup of my consciousness and something surfaces that is eclectic, (how about that word), but sort of mine. Anyhow, the death of a close companion takes not just the person but a big piece of your own life. If life is a little like an elaborate Persian rug, I think Somerset Maughm used that one, a death is a piece of the rug, cut out of the middle. The pattern is forever altered, mutilated. It can never be restored. You've got to create a new pattern. So far I haven't done it.

I'm glad to hear I'm an uncle. The kid is really cute. Looks like Pop. Fantastic, genetics. I suppose it's the scientific explanation of reincarnation. You keep coming back because your genes get passed on.

And as for you, Auntie Nell, your little Catholic niece, Therese, is doing well. She looks like Aurora. They already have a little gold cross dangling around her pudgy neck to ward off the unpronounceable heretic devils. But they tolerate me. That's being hard on them. They like me. I spent a few days with my in-laws last week. Nice folks. They still make me feel like one of the family. And Therese can say 'Papa' and give me a hug and appreciate the presents I brought her. She's a bright, cheerful little pixie with a coy smile and a charming way, and she's very curious. Well, enough of that. Isn't every kid that way?

You asked if I'm a famous artist yet. So what if you haven't seen my name in the New York Times or the Plain Dealer. I've been noted in Paris, Amsterdam, Frankfurt, Zurich, and most recently Milan. Reads like the grand tour, doesn't it? They like me over here. It must be guilt or something, the War. My work doesn't beat them bloody with remembrance. It creeps up the back of their spine and makes them want to wrap their arms tightly about their torso. Hey, that's what a critic said about my latest show in Milan. It was successful! Not only did the cognoscenti (another fifty cent word) like it, but quite a few works were actually sold. Natale's keeping the prices down, so I'm kind of a steal for collectors. Some day, if I live long enough, these pieces will be known as early work showing promise. Or maybe I'll never get any better, but I doubt it. I know I've got it in me. It just keeps coming, I only have to sit down and concentrate, forget anything but what I'm doing and bingo, something happens, sort of like possession by the spirit of some frustrated painter who died before his time.

More about Milan. What really knocked them over was Lethos. Natale was afraid of it, she didn't want me to do it, too much of a departure. It's a kind of room that you walk into down three steps. A room with very little light, and geometric forms inside, abstract, with the focus of the eye drawn toward a fading point of light, sort of oblivion. There were marks, shadows on the forms that might suggest writing, memories, associations, but nothing concrete. And there was a recording of dripping water and other sounds that might have been fragments of human voices as if blown from far away by the wind, disembodied fragments. I confess to you that when it was complete, I spent time in it and found myself weeping. And when I left I somehow felt renewed. I was returning to this world from the world of shadows. One critic from the Corregio Del Serra went nuts over it. He said I had taken sculpture to a new "plane of expression." He even did an interview which I think was broadcast on RIA, Italian radio. He asked me where the concept came from. I told him "burial chambers," Etruscan and others. But that was a little white lie, as mother used to say. The idea came from my remembrance of the time somebody left a refrigerator carton in the back yard when we were kids. And we made it into a spooky cave. That and the scary ride at Euclid Beach, the one where you ride around in the dark and the monsters jump up at you. I couldn't tell him that.

Natale was ecstatic. She told me over champagne that I have accomplished in five years what it takes most artists twenty, which made me feel pretty good.

I'm sorry to hear Mother has arthritis and isn't able to dance anymore. She cared so much about her appearance, I can't imagine her living with lumpy joints. Yes I do write to her and she writes back, even almost telling me I made a good choice for my life's work, now that I've got some recognition. I sent her a check for $50 for her birthday. I hope she got herself something nice.

Love,

Harry (your brother the artist)

September 19, 1953 – An Invitation

A long, intense day, nine hours of concentrated work, with barely a nibble on some baguette, some overripe brie, a shriveled apple. Harry was in the studio with Caz but he was alone; fixated on a painfully congealing image: the blurred form of a woman seen through a floating cloth. He had before him an amorphous pile of clay; gray, greasy-looking, dented, imprinted, slashed, and creased. Harry stared at it, searching for the form that might emerge.

"And God created man out of the earth, or words to that effect." Caz approached and looked over his shoulder. "Here, he said, nudging him as a horse might push with its head, and thrusting a chipped blue cup of steaming coffee in front of Harry's eyes. "Take a little rest, Harry, or you'll burn out a wire."

"You mean blow a fuse." He took the cup and brought it to his lips, facing Caz with weary frustration. "Do you ever get the feeling that you've used up every idea you'll ever have?"

"At least once a week."

"So what do you do?"

" Take a walk. Look at the sky, children crying or laughing, policeman giving citations, whatever is in front of me. Drink a *vin rouge* at a Cafe, listen to the chatter. Then come back and see what happens."

"Does it work?"

"I always start something new."

Harry dropped into the chair with a memory of a back, and put his cup down on the scored and bleached table, sweeping aside several tools with his left hand. His eye caught on an envelope imprinted with the circle of a coffee stain and in its center, the return address, Art Department, University of California, Berkeley California.

"What's this?" He held the envelope up by its corner and dangled it in Caz's direction, who lowered his thick eyebrows and squinted myopically before dismissing it with a shrug. "It's nothing."

"Mind if I look?"

"Go ahead. It might even interest you."

It was an offer of a one year visiting professorship in the art department. "This by you is nothing?"

"Ahh, too far away, too hot probably, and my English not good enough anyway. I forgot one thing," he added, striking himself in the chest with the flat of his massive hand. "Too old."

"Caz. You could use the change."

"Who would feed the cat?"

"I would."

"Tell you what, Harry, you go in my place."

"If they wanted me they would have written to me. Truth is they wouldn't know me from a bowl of corn flakes."

"How would it be if I write them and tell them you can go in my place, as my protégé? One who knows all that I know."

"Why not send the cat?"

"I'll send them your notices, some pictures of your work. What's the harm. Would you like that?"

"Like you say, Caz, at least it's a way of getting known."

"So you agree?"

"Sure, I'll even pay the postage."

February 23, 1954 – Winter

It took so long for the response that Harry put it out of his mind, not that he had taken it seriously in the first place. Why would the University of California at Berkeley want him in place of Caz? Not that he wasn't good, maybe as good as Caz, but there were hundreds of sculptors who would mean more to the reputation of the school and give more to the students.

He went on working. The sculpture he liked to call Caesarian after the hard conception, or perhaps for other more complex reasons, had been started, stopped in frustration, started again, and was finally, after six months, showing promise. It was metamorphic and amorphic at the same time, a shape not unlike like the lower torso of a woman in labor, but so different that not even a gynecologist, let alone a new mother, would be likely to see the emerging fetus. It was, like so much of his work, a study in evolving or dissolving form. He had already decided on a name, not the private one. It would be called "*Pieta,*" an homage to the sacrifice of woman to the feminine animating force of life.

He had come in out of a rotten day. Dark bilious clouds pressed the rooftops, the air was pungent with coal smoke and diesel, the rain flailed him like the tips of a scourge, wind passed through him like ice needles. He had forgotten to get new soles on his shoes and his left sock was soaked through, as was his worn G.I. raincoat. To make it worse, the stove that pretended to take the chill out of the cavernous studio was selfishly hoarding the heat. "Christ it's miserable out!" he said rubbing his hands over the top of the stove.

Caz was on his side, working the hem of a robe of an emaciated bishop. "You could have stayed here last night."

"I would have frozen solid overnight. I don't know how you stand it." The rain lashed and spattered the skylight, ran in gray streaks, and a bucket under the biggest leak sounded like a plucking harp.

"Makes you appreciate the spring," Caz said with a grunt as he worked the fluted hem. "It'll be the last one for you."

"The last what?"

"Parisian winter."

"Why."

"They want you to come."

"Who? I already told the Goya Foundation to stuff it." They had offered him a curatorial position and a studio.

"Madrid's nothing special in the winter either. I've heard tell Greece is nice."

Harry peeled off his dripping raincoat and hung it on a nail in the wall near the door. He lifted the wet cloth off of the clay form and confronted his new work hoping to see it after the absence of a day with a fresh eye. Yes, there was a suggestion of a Neolithic fertility goddess. Just a hint. He wanted that effect.

The semaphore conversation with Caz dropped through a hole in his mind and he began abusing and stroking the surface of the clay using wooden tools shaped like dull surgical instruments, concentrating to the extent that he no longer heard the military tattoo of the rain and no longer felt the wet sole of his foot. He was somewhere beyond feeling except for what came out of his dialogue with the changing mound of clay. Silence. No telephone and even the constant street sounds were muffled by the storm. Except for an occasional animal grunt of satisfaction or completion, Caz didn't speak. Harry might have been in a hut in the middle of a forest and if someone had tapped him on the shoulder and asked his name, he would have hesitated before answering.

It wasn't until the two of them sat at the table eating stale bread and *chevre* cheese that Harry again thought about the rain and his porous shoes. His mind shifted from the increasingly complex relations with Natale to the anticipation of a small party that night with the artist Jean Helion and writer Simone De Beauvoir. Both of them actually knew him by name, he recalled with self-deprecating pride.

"Have you got a pair of socks I can borrow?"

"Over there hanging on the line." Caz pointed to the clothesline that hung near the foundry. Caz poured some coffee for both of them out of the blue chipped pot he had bought in a flea market twenty years before. He went to the window box and opened it letting in a gusting spray of rain while he retrieved the milk bottle. Holding it at eye level admiring its form, he returned to the table.

"Listen, Harry, you ought to take a look at that letter."

"What letter?"

"The one I told you about this morning." Caz looked distracted as he decided where to set the milk bottle. Then he let his hand blindly browse a pile of envelopes, some unopened. "There."

Harry took the letter out of the envelope and read and reread it with increasing astonishment.

"Dear Mr. Czampolski: We regret your reluctance to accept our offer, but would welcome your protege, Harry Baer. Several of our faculty have heard of his work and we are confident that, having worked closely with you over the past four years, he will be able to share your unusual bronze casting techniques with our students, not to mention some of his own. The stipend for the year is $4,500 plus travel expenses and materials. We hope Mr. Baer can come and that you can convince him to give up Paris for a little while."

"What did you tell them, Caz?"

"Oh, I just built you up a little."

"I guess so. I can't teach anybody to cast like you."

"But you can teach them to cast like Harry Baer."

March 8, 1954 – Party

"And this is Germaine Richier." Natale presented the hostess with an outstretched palm. "Harry Baer." The artist, Harry thought, looked at him as she might have assessed the latest work of a rival. But there was more, he saw, or imagined he saw, a pallid ironic hint of a smile. As if to refute it, Natale added, "You recall his recent show in Milan."

"Yes, I was happy for you," she said, but the tone and look made Harry doubt the truth of it, for she looked to him like a distinctly unhappy person, moody and brooding. Her parchment skin, sharp nose, and tense wrinkles around the thin lipped mouth reminded him of one of Toulouse-Lautrec's portraits of a melancholy alcoholic.

"Natale, you look like May Day on Red Square," said Germaine referring to her tight-fitting red dress, pendant earrings looking much like drops of blood, and bright red nails.

"Appropriate dress for the occasion," Natale retorted with a steel edge in her voice.

Richier turned to another guest and Harry gazed around more at the appointments of the high ceilinged studio than the people, focussing on two large paintings by Jean Dubuffet: thick paint, children's stick and circle figures in subdued ashen colors. Natale was taken up by an acquaintance, someone whose name Harry had forgotten. He drifted away and wandered through the room.

"And the man literally starved to death, giving the little he had to his dog. Nearly blind, ancient and had at best another year to live," he overheard.

"You mean the man."

"No, the dog."

"A neighbor found him. The dog was howling with grief."

"No doubt the dog was his only friend."

Harry took this in, thought of an image, a hand and a dog's head, cast it aside. He poured himself a scotch—it was fashionable this year—and turned to admire the dark surface of one of Richier's sculptures, a head that resembled a water-washed rock broken at the top as if it had been crushed.

He felt Natale beside him and turned to see her troubled, questioning eyes. "Simone de Beauvoir isn't here," she said.

"Je suis désolé."

"She bought one of your etchings, you know."

He dropped his head to one side in acknowledgement.

"You're not seriously considering going to California?" It came out as a deprecating question.

"Why not?"

"There's no there there, like Gertrude Stein said. They only know how to make bombs and airplanes."

"There's the sun. Look what it did for Van Gogh and Renoir, and Matisse."

"Your work doesn't need sun. Besides, I've heard it's always foggy in San Francisco."

"I don't mind fog."

"You would give up all that we've built." She turned her head with a sweep suggesting that he was now a part of this room full of poets, artists and social activists of the left.

"Its only for a year. I'll come back."

"You won't ever come back. I know you." The words were salt and she punctuated them with a double click of her tongue.

"Come on Natale, is this the right place for this discussion?"

"Then why did you suddenly drop it on me halfway up the stairs as an after thought. By the way, I've decided to take my life."

"It's not that bad or that final."

"And what about your daughter, Therese? Will you just abandon her?"

"If Cybele can give her up, I'll take her with me."

"No you won't."

"There you are."

"And what about me?"

"Natale, you've made a career out of parting."

"*Salot!*" She turned away from him.

6

Harry, 1955-1975

April 3, 1955 – Berkeley

Nothing and everything Harry had seen in Europe prepared him for Berkeley. In France he had loved the fusion of patinaed stone, the look of proportioned buildings, worn and blackened, defined by an ordered Greco-Roman cultural heritage, or spiritual Medieval introspection. French countryside began outside the town walls, green rolling committed pasture, sharply ending where some hereditary forest began, each component of the tapestry existing in timeless equilibrium.

On the Berkeley campus, in Berkeley and in San Francisco, he recognized a collage of what he had left behind and admired: There was nature, not domesticated as it had been in Europe, rather showing vestiges, even in the urban center that clung to the long, bottlenecked bay, of the way it had been only a few hundred years ago. Indians had lived on its shores and the Europeans had sailed right by it, hidden as it was by the fog.

The campus itself was sylvan with a tamed Strawberry Creek meandering down from the wild hills, sheltered largely by tall columnar redwoods and crossed by paths and bridges that led to monumental free standing buildings of different styles and periods, often with tile cornices, stylized roman columns made of practical industrial concrete resembling stone, with long enlightening windows of steel, each module representing an area of study, Mining, Engineering, Fine Arts, autonomous but somehow connected by the paths, a common green botanic landscape, and an idealized vision.

The campus merged on three sides into a low profile of two story homes as diverse in their style as America, concealed by the crowns of trees and abutted an endless range of hills, canyons, and valleys, an undeveloped watershed where foxes still stalked rabbits and deer foraged without fear. At its heart was its own Campanile, a twin of the one he'd seen in Venice, and from its peak could be seen postcard vistas of the white city of San Francisco on its hills, the slender pewter bay, the metal arcing tracery of two bridges, and the Pacific Ocean, a horizon bound only by the encroaching fog and the imagination.

April 11, 1955 – Accidental Meeting

He found a studio apartment that opened through French doors into a garden in a Berkeley brown shingle house on Bienvenue Street. It was owned by an octogenarian retired professor of botany who spent her days propagating native plants and consulting for the U.C. Berkeley Botanical Garden in Strawberry Canyon behind the University. She was the author of the definitive guide to coastal California plants. Except for the late afternoon, when the falling sun worked its way under the overhang of the deck above, his studio was dark and cool. The single bed doubled as a couch with piled cushions covered in earthy Indian and Indonesian cloth. Three wicker chairs that crackled when you sat down served every other seating need. The Pullman kitchen was tiny, but complete, with a compact four burner stove and a six cubic foot refrigerator, small by American standards but luxurious compared to his Paris apartment. A stall shower, smaller than a telephone booth, which sounded like a gong when he banged an elbow against the wall, completed the amenities. He quickly removed the faded curling posters, lures for Guadalajara and Mexico City—sombreros, red lipped smiles and jacaranda— tacked to the wall by the former occupant, a graduate student who, he was told, had secured an associate professorship in chemical engineering at the University of Washington.

Olany Kormann, his landlady, "call me Ola " had the personality and look of late autumnal sun-pale, frail, yet giving off a welcome, if hazy, warmth. Dressed in baggy jeans and what might once have been her late husband's oxford cloth shirt; a large straw hat, which couldn't contain wisps of gray hair or conceal the dry humor in her eyes; she was, more often than not, seen on her knees bent over some ailing *consolida ambigua* or cutting dead heads off of the *coreopsis gigantea*.

That first week, before classes began, he found himself enjoying this garden, with its shady stone patio sheltered by the twisting extended arms of a live oak. Reclining in a chair made of woven grape vine prunings, Harry listened with half an ear to a curling strand of silver water falling from the mouth of a bamboo pipe into a stone basin, and read an underlined copy of Camus, *The Plague* that he had bought for twenty cents at Moe's used book store on Telegraph.

The former tenant had left behind a bicycle, with the note that whoever wanted it should send him whatever they thought it was worth. Having no car, Harry decided to try it out on an excursion to Telegraph to buy a few eggs, a tomato, a cucumber, a wedge of cheese—the selection wasn't very good—and some powdered soup. He was still shopping like a Parisian, taking no more than could be carried in a string bag and stopping for a cappuccino at the Cafe Med on the way back.

"The brakes are a bit iffy," Ola warned as he cautiously wheeled it toward the street. As a kid in the Bronx he had never owned a bike and had only learned to ride while visiting Aurora's parents. He was still a little shaky and tended to wobble the front wheel when he was going too slowly. He set off anticipating the fresh "French bread" from San Francisco, not like the ones in France, but at least they looked the same, forgetting that it was Monday when all, literally all, the bakeries in the Bay Area were closed.

Harry had lived in France for over seven years, long enough to form habits of taste, long enough, it seemed, to make him feel the outsider in California. He looked up at the sky, cloudless, the light unfiltered, seen through dry air, intense, clean, like the atmosphere of the south of France only broader, as if the unfathomable breadth of the American landscape and the endless ocean that enclosed it somehow added to its reach.

He had stopped in Cleveland for only a few days, long enough to feel uncomfortable, long enough to feel the differences of experience that now separated him from his sister's life. As for his mother, she was the same only older, a dead battery when it came to affection, her narrow view of perfection jaundiced by arthritis. Sitting there in the too-clean living room across from her, Harry had felt more like her cousin than her son. His mother sat stiffly, her smile painted on, faded and frayed like an old sun-bleached signboard. Her questions about his life were formal and her reaction to his successes were muted by veiled jealousy. He left her feeling like an empty unwashed milk bottle; stale, sour, and unfulfilled.

Cleveland had met him like an old high school friend. Harry knew that he had changed and he probed the familiar for signs that the town, its ring of forested parks, its shady suburbs, had changed as well. He was able to appreciate the unpretentious Midwestern energy leavened by a measure of Euro-centric culture. But it wasn't Paris. He couldn't get a decent cup of coffee let alone a fresh baguette.

Nell had given him comfort with her open warmth, enthusiasm, and sympathy. Her son, Bernie, did in fact look like their father and seeing him choked Harry up with recollections of the nurturing attention Pop had given him. From his father had come the belief that his painting would one day be recognized and the sense that, with perseverance, dreams could be made real. Nell was a bit more filled out now and more womanly. In spite of their sibling closeness, the visit made him aware how far he had traveled from her small-scale life with its horizon line no more distant than the flat rooftop and tar wrapped cornice across the narrow street. Going to California was, to her, like traveling to Rome. Separated from the support he derived from Natale and Caz and the occasional visits to Aurora's family to see Therese, Harry felt estranged even from his life in Paris, a stranger to Berkeley, and very much alone.

He got on the bicycle and pedaled shakily down the drive thinking about the bistro on the corner of his block in Paris, Chez Soulange, where the *pate maison*, a different soup every day, always complex in its flavors, and a carafe of Cote Ventoux could be had for the equivalent of a buck and a quarter. One burger and some french fries had been enough to incinerate his nostalgia for American food.

He reached the wide boulevard called Telegraph that narrowed to a bottleneck and finally spilled onto the campus at Sather Gate. He was riding between a brown high-sided United Parcel truck and a pea green VW bug when the cuff of his baggy French pants caught in the chain pulling his leg back. A light changed in front of him, he squeezed the brake handles and the calipers seized the front wheel, swinging the bike around and tossing him over the handlebars into the back of a slender man who, tripped by the side-slipping bike frame, dropped to his knees.

"Jesus, Mary!" The man picked himself up, looking with vitriolic scorn at Harry before bending to salvage the three books he'd been carrying that were splayed broken backed on the pavement.

"Sorry. The brakes gave out," said Harry picking up the bike and guiding it to the curb before the light changed. The man followed him.

"By the look of it, it's a danger to life and limb. Could've been ridden by Napoleon out of Russia."

"Sorry."

"No harm done," he said, dusting off his pant legs.

They looked at each other for the first time and Harry recognized him. "You're in the Art Department, right?"

"Sort of. The doctoral program—art history. And you are the wunderkind from Paris. I hope you know more about sculpture than you do about riding a bike. I thought they all rode bikes there."

"They do." He decided not to get into how he came to ride. "Harry Baer," he said, offering his hand and the man gave it a hard squeeze.

"Elgin Cooley. Walking toward campus? You'll want to stay off of that thing for now." Harry catalogued the man's features as they walked. He was slight, tightly built like a gymnast, a springy walk, pinched Irish face, eyes very close to mouth, button round blue eyes set deep in wrinkled sockets, boiled corned beef complexion, knobby nose, no bridge. His voice was sharp and piercing and there was a restless edge in it. He was wearing baggy wide-wale cords, scuffed loafers without socks, and a faded khaki GI tee shirt.

"War surplus?" Harry asked just to make conversation, pointing at the shirt. He hadn't seen one in years.

"Me or the shirt?"

"Both I suppose."

"Both. You too?

"Yep."

"What theater?"

Harry wanted to say Theater of the Absurd. "European."

"Pacific."

Both men left it at that and walked on in silence. Harry hadn't talked about the War in years, not since the last of his roommates had returned to the States at least.

"I sold mine in a flea market," Harry finally said.

"What?"

"Oh, the GI stuff. But I have a hard time getting rid of things. It's a problem with me I guess. I'm something of a collector."

"What do you collect?"

"Nothing of value. Junk, scraps, things I intend to use in my work."

"Sort of like Cornell?"

"I guess. Are you doing your research on a Twentieth Century artist."

"Yeah."

"Who?"

"Franz Marc, ever hear of him?"

"I know his work," said Harry thinking about his journal, still in his suitcase, wrapped in archival paper, unexamined since he'd arrived in Berkeley.

"You like it?"

"Yes. I do."

Cooley answered with an admiring little smile. "Not many people know that much about him over here. Kandinsky eclipsed him you could say. This is where I live," he said, pointing up at some bay windows above a used clothing store.

"See you around. Get that bike fixed."

Harry watched him pull the door open and disappear into the dusk of the stairway, thinking that, of all the people he'd met so far at Berkeley, this Vet comes closest to someone he might want to hang around with. He stopped there, not sure just what he might do, but wondering if he should see if, what was his name? Elgin Cooley, wanted to go out for a beer some-time soon and talk about Marc. In truth, Harry was feeling lonely.

Revelations

Friday night Harry and Elgin Cooley were both a little drunk. The sidewalk was crowded with young people just dis-gorged from the Telegraph Repertory Cinema. Fresh, musical voices struck Harry along with the scent of clove, sweat and marijuana. He turned to watch a girl, attracted by the swing-ing, round bottom divided by the seam of her jeans. He liked the diversity of the crowd on Telegraph. There were all sorts, mingling on the street, lolling against the walls, laughing and punching each other like puppies. Beatniks hunched over the dregs of a coffee cup, smoke from a forgotten cigarette curl-ing through their animated talk. Girls all in black, their eyes heavily lined, contrasted with scrubbed frat boys with crew cuts in starched chino pants and white bucks

"Just like Paris, huh?" said Cooley.

"Not exactly."

"You miss it?"

"Yeah."

"What?"

"Everything."

"You're pretty horny."

"You could say that."

"Don't worry, when classes get started they'll be taking numbers to climb into your sack."

"American girls?"

"Art students like to think of themselves as free from the middle class suburban conventions of their parents."

"I hope so."

"Ever hear of Jack Kerouac?"

"No. Is he a painter?"

"A writer, a Beat. I heard him read a couple of weeks ago in North Beach at City Lights. He takes it all on: capitalism, mechanization, mass culture, empty values."

"Sounds like an unhappy man. He needs a place in the country," said Harry, thinking of Monet's garden.

"Could be, but you've got to admit that there is something wrong, something basically wrong. This cold war shit, the bomb, missiles."

"I've got no beef with capitalism so long as it doesn't run amok. What we need is a big enough pie so that everybody can get their slice."

"What slice do you want?"

"Freedom to create. Recognition. Friends. A woman to love."

"Only one?"

"You can only sleep with one at a time." Aurora came back to him for a moment. "Feel like coming back to my place for a cognac?"

"You got some cognac at your place?"

"I brought it back from France. You like cognac?"

"To tell the truth, I've never had any. My ol' man drinks bourbon. I always thought it was out of my class. I drank a lot of *sake* though. One time on Okinawa we came on a cache of about 40 cases in one of those tunnels that you've read about."

"Good stuff?" Harry had never tried it.

"It gets you there, same as everything else of its kind."

They walked in silence. Harry read the shade and texture of light from the street lamps and moving cones of headlights on the pavement and shrubbery.

"This your place? Your own private entry and everything. What more could you ask in life."

Harry had made it his own, put up some posters, late Matisse, a De Kooning expressionistic woman, as well as a few of his own sketches—abstract, gestural, evoking demons left over from his war work—the latter tacked up at random. There was even a shoebox already brimming with objects

found on the street: bent nails, faded cigar wrappers, an envelope embossed with tire tread.

"Not bad for $45 a month."

Elgin sprawled on the bed and Harry poured two fingers
of cognac into a jam jar. "Hope you don't mind, the crystal's
at the cleaners."

"Hey, we got the same kind at home. So where's that stuff
you promised to show me."

In a loose moment while they were talking about Elgin's
work on Franz Marc, Harry had alluded to having something
of interest. Until that time the only other person who had
known about the Marc sketchbook was Aurora. He regretted
having said anything but his loneliness had impelled him to
share some confidence, perhaps, he supposed, to put a down
payment on Elgin's friendship. He fished under the bed,
opened his suitcase, took out the carefully wrapped package
and handed it to Elgin.

He accepted it with the solemnity of a bishop given a sacred reliquary housing the desiccated finger of a saint. The
crude Vet turned into the earnest scholar as he untied string
and opened layer after layer of paper with the care and delib-
eration of a curator. Harry saw the change in his expression,
curiosity become astonishment as, with a quick intake of
breath, he leafed through the journal studying the drawings.

"Do you realize what you have here?"

"Sure I do. Marc's last sketchbook."

"More than that. It's got studies for parts of several of his
important later paintings, even some of his thoughts.
Kandinsky knew about it, referred to it in a letter, but it disappeared. Some historians think that he had it with him in
the War. In any event when the Army shipped his stuff home,
it wasn't there. This is incredibly important, Harry. If I could
describe it in my dissertation, just that would put me on the
map." His face was a deeper shade of red and his pulse was
popping on the side of his head. "Where the fuck did you get
it?" Elgin's voice was edged with envy.

"Fortunes of war, Elgin. Some guys got a mouth full of
mud, you got your supply of Japanese booze and I got this.
Luck of the draw."

"Listen, I've got to be able to use this."

"Sorry. Nobody knows I've got it. It's kind of an icon to me. If you publish its whereabouts, some museum will say it was stolen or the estate or some foundation will claim it and I'll be right in the middle. Maybe I'd have to give it up, which I don't want to do."

"Well, it is stolen isn't it? You didn't just find it at the side of the road."

"In a manner of speaking, yes, I did. You could even say I saved it."

"Saved it?"

"The German's blew up the place where I found it soon after I got out. I saw it. Even got hit on the helmet with some of the debris. So I've got a right to it."

"Look, Harry, I'd give you anything to use it. What do you want, my sister?"

"Have you got a picture?"

"How about my immortal soul?"

"You haven't got one. Just forget you ever saw it, Elgin. I'm sorry I showed you. It was a mistake," Harry said with a hard look and Elgin turned his eyes away as he might from a glaring bulb. "Some more cognac?"

"Sure. Why not." Elgin sounded resigned.

There was no more talk of the sketchbook, but Harry saw a change in Elgin, A canny solicitude replaced the easy-buddy banter. Elgin had the look of someone who wanted something and might do anything to get it. Harry berated himself for the lapse. Since the War he'd been cautious, he'd learned to keep his helmet on and his head down. Now it was other, more diverse hazards, crazy drivers or people who might use or harm him. Caution was an organ of his being now. But he'd exposed himself to an acquaintance, someone he didn't yet and maybe couldn't trust.

September 12, 1955 – The Body Shop

Pauline Mudd reminded Harry of a Leger. She was oversized, heroic in proportion. A daughter of labor she was wearing a steel helmet which covered her face and brandishing in her gloved right hand a hissing wand. Its blue-white flickering stiletto point was raising a molten scar on the pipe like arm of a steel humanoid shape. High brick walls banded over by a concave hangar ceiling of wood beams that added an incongruous medieval aura bound the space in which she worked. Along the walls were rough work benches and the place was littered with metal scrap salvage ranging from old car fenders to the massive rusting organs of abandoned machinery: worn toothy gears, scored rods, handles for brakes, angry red lights, switches, and pulleys, all in a jumble. Leaning against the wall were old metal signs advertising chewing tobacco, identifying rail road or streetcar lines, or place names.

He watched her work and in his mind began to place the equipment for the foundry that was already stacked near the wide overhead garage door. She finished the weld, shut the gas off, and raised her helmet. Mopping her sweaty forehead with the back of her hand she took him in with a look of flinty curiosity. She was square jawed; narrow lipped and her eyes were deep set, round and steel gray and hostile. Her hair was short and curly, light brown and fine. Harry, with his crimson silk foulard, and black beret felt out of place.

"You must be Baer," she said with a voice that was surprisingly shrill.

"Call me Harry," he said and offered his hand. She took it and gave it a calloused squeeze.

"I'm Pauli. As you see there's plenty of room for the foundry since they moved the pottery studio over to the campus."

"It's a great space." He walked over and touched some of the industrial scrap. "Nice material."

"Ever work with junk? "

"No, not that I haven't thought about it. I like your work," he said, hoping to reach her with a compliment.

"It is what it is."

"Good art is never just what it is. It's always more."

"So what do you see in that?" she asked gesturing at a cage like form made of mutilated fragments of metal, splayed wire and mesh that housed the remains of the rear fender of a Chevy and a black and white sign bearing only the letter B.

"Waste, containment, emptiness, ugliness, alienation." He looked at her for confirmation, wondering whether he had missed the mark or whether he should elaborate. He was warming to the subject.

She vaguely nodded and looked like she was thinking about what he had said. "My father has a body shop in South City. I used to help hammer out the dents, cut off fenders too damaged to repair." He thought she was going to go on and talk about her work, but she stopped. "I've got to do a little bit more before my class. Nice meeting you." She was less hostile and there might have even been a smile starting on the scar of her mouth before she turned away and pulled the steel helmet down over her face.

Cire Perdue

The start of classes pulled Harry out of a funk. He slept better and his dreams were no longer troubled with the frustration of spoiled or ridiculed work. He fell easily into the theatrics of the cosmopolitan prodigy, making a grand entrance with the accoutrements of character, black fedora, black silk shirt, resembling in his own eyes at least, a modern day Faust, a stage magician, the impresario of a legitimate theatre. From the beginning he found that he loved teaching. All eyes and ears were his to captivate or dazzle with wit, anecdotes, but mostly the performance which came naturally to him, the act of creation. He never prepared for class, never knew what he would say until he said it, except that the syllabus dictated one or more subjects. The more outrageous his commentary, the more the students ate out of his hand. Without intending it, Harry became an icon of iconoclasm, appealing to the seething, anarchistic mood of the campus. For Harry was a master of ambiguity who tried as hard as he could to mesmerize with ideas that were as evanescent as the late evening fog that often drifted over the campus in rolling columns.

Beyond the class, the foundry became the focus of his life. Everything that he had absorbed working with Caz was coming to fruition. Intially he had put on a show of braggadocio that masked a real fear that he would blow it. He had learned a lot, but Caz had been the master of the technique while he, Harry, was little more than an apprentice. Even so, next to these fine artists and students who knew nothing of the lost wax technique of casting, he was the master. Just to be sure he spent hours reading relevant parts of Celini's autobiography and other texts and he put off the day when the foundry might be fired up and the bronze melted and poured for the first time.

He, and two other faculty members, both ceramic sculptors, Roger Marris and Sigmund Sielenbach, had each completed clay molds, no bigger than 24 inches. Harry's was knobby, attenuated, vaguely humanoid. They had coated the forms with wax and modeled the wax to approximate the desired outer surface, then encased it all in a thick block of perforated plaster.

Another costume, that of a modern day Vulcan, a long asbestos fiber coat and gloves that reached to the elbow, goggles deeply tinted against the sun like glare of the fire, the heavy egg shaped crucible lifted in its cradle from the furnace by pulley and jockeyed to the mold as the bronze seethed. It was a time of sweaty concentration and mystery, the captive molten bronze looking like a captive piece of the sun. Harry at one end of the cradle and Roger at the other gripped the double handles and slowly tilted it as the steaming yellow bronze poured into the orifice of the mold. They watched as the bronze melted and displaced the wax and waited, smoking a cigarette as the metal gradually cooled and solidified.

Although he joked casually with the others, Harry was nervous. The bronze could be deformed, crazed or cracked, different in critical ways from what had been intended and he sensed that, despite the comradery of the two other men, he was being judged like a new kid on the block. They would break the outer shell the next day. The three men parted having shut down the fire with a look of shared ritual expectation.

Harry got a little drunk that night with Elgin who continued to cossen, wheedle and threaten him about the Franz Marc journal.

Next day, the three carefully shattered the plaster until the bronze appeared like a butterfly emerging from a chrysalis. The surface was whole, except for a few nail head perforations and the patina was burned here and there and colored in a pleasing surprising way. They stood around it silently gazing at the fetal work: Marris, his thick skinned brow deeply creased, his finger picking at something between his teeth; Sielenbach, running his long fingered hand through thinning flaxen hair; and Harry, his dark eyes narrowly focused on the flawed surface.

"It worked," said Marris softly. "You did it, you smart assed s. o. b."

"You know what? I'm going to paint it," Harry said and the other two looked at him with bemused surprise. Harry's eyes shifted from the sculpture to his colleagues and he noted the effect of his pronouncement. "Thank you Caz," he muttered to himself and felt a stinging in his nose and tears in his eyes.

September 8, 1957 – Reception

"Think I'll get in?" said Elgin looking with anxious hope at the door to the gallery.

"You're with me," said Harry adjusting the collar of his black velvet jacket and, as an afterthought, dusting the tips of his patent leather pumps on the back of his pant leg as his father had done before launching into his career as a funny guy. The ghost of that night, as he had watched from the wings waiting for the first laugh, passed through him. The Japanese exchange student at the door recognized Harry with a respectful bow. He nodded, took Elgin by the elbow, guided him into the room and searched the crowd for familiar faces, noting several from the Art Department and the California Institute. Wine and cheese were being served at a table in the corner, and there was the usual crowd around it. He recognized David Park and Richard Diebenkorn talking to a woman in her early twenties. His first impulse was to join them, why not? But his interest in the art was more compelling and he let his eyes range around the four walls soaking up impressions. There was something of De Kooning and Roualt in the figuration.

All of the paintings were too literal for him. And yet the work was original and very appealing in the spontaneity and the dramatic and often fresh, passionate use of color. He could see why the curator, Mills, called it a "school." Seeing this body of work of so many artists, all of them working in and around Berkeley, made him feel that he had, without knowing it, landed in the right place at the right time. There was a coalescence of creative energy that, he knew, contributed to the work of each of them in the same way that the Impressionists had stimulated one another in France. Art history was full of such examples. Making art was solitary but also social. He walked over to a painting of what was both bright blocks of primary red white and blue color and a massive football play, the figures connected, massed, and also in motion. He recognized the work of Bill Brown, and saw him, his handsome cropped head nodding in agreement to a taller man. Harry turned to a moody and ambiguous painting of two nudes on a beach. Both sky and beach looked like a great fire might have been burning beyond the canvas, bleeding red orange, smoke and shadow. The landscape was austere, except for the color, and abstract, devoid of detail. Neither face could be seen, but there was some dialogue between them. The interpretation was up to the viewer. Was it confrontation, a shared intimacy, the communication of some revelation by the man to the woman? And why were they nude? Why was the perfectly composed image nude, or abstract? He moved closer and studied the brush strokes, observing the spontaneity and gestural freedom. It was the essence of abstract expression but confined to form.

To get a different perspective Harry took several steps back into a tray of cocktail wieners that overturned sending its slippery contents scurrying over the floor like legless mice. The tray struck the floor with a clang and did several noisy off center rolls before it settled. He turned, stepped on a wiener and looked up at a solid woman with her hands still outstretched, her face screwed into a hysterical stifled laugh.

She put her hand over her mouth, long thin fingers, covering her full, flaring lips and coughed a few times before she regained her composure, although the amusement never left her eyes. They were large, close-set, almond shaped eyes that showed white as pearl with an onyx iris. She had a round face; the flesh was soft and thick which made her cheeks full. Her nose was short, the nostrils were agreeably narrow, and her open white smile was dazzling against skin that was the shade of a good cup of English tea with a measure of cream

"I'm sorry," he finally said.

"I'm the one that should be sorry." Her voice was the sound of flowing honey. "I wasn't looking. I'm kind of new at this." She wanted him to know.

"You're not a waitress in real life?"

"Not even in my dreams."

"We'd better clean this up."

"No, you don't have to. I'll get something."

"I insist." He was already bending to turn over the tray and pick up the red puckered cocktail wieners.

"I'll be back," she said, and he looked up and watched her move with a long self-assured stride, observing the rhythm of her buttocks where they engaged the tight black skirt. She came back and bent down near him to mop the floor with a wet towel. He smelled the fresh herbal fragrance of her hair which was drawn back in a tight bun. Harry wondered about its texture and wanted to touch it.

"Pretty intimate down here, just you and me." he said.

A delayed response. "That your idea of flirting?"

"Give me credit for originality."

"You could've tried running me down in a cross walk."

"I'm Harry."

"I know."

"And you are?"

"Karine."

"Can I make amends by buying you a beer after you're done?"

"I've got someone picking me up. Besides, I don't drink beer."

"Too bad. For me I mean. Not for you."

"Thanks. Well, that ought to do it. I better go get some more wieners. The crowd looks pretty hungry. Nice meeting you Professor Baer."

"Call me Harry."

He got up and went to the men's room to wash his hands, possessed and wondering how best to approach this Karine. She was obviously connected in some way to the Art Department but he had never seen her. He had never been with a colored woman, not that he was prejudiced or inhibited. There was something exciting, enticing in the prospect.

David Park was in the men's room taking a pee. Harry dawdled at the sink, waiting for him. He had met him casually and wondered if Park would remember him. Harry was pleased to see recognition in his owl-like, serious eyes.

"Hello Baer," Park said as he washed his hands, "like the show?"

Harry didn't answer at first as he weighed the value of responding with a short affirmation, or a thoughtful critique. "It's bold and brave and accomplished, a successful rebuttal of Clement Greenberg and the New York doctrine that figurative painting has nowhere to go." Harry held the door for Park and they walked together back to the gallery.

"We've been told that we're backsliders. But out here we've always gone our own way, we're a little like the animals of Australia, cut off. After all there's nothing very "modern" about limiting yourself to abstraction because you want to be innovative. When it comes down to it, every square inch of a canvas is an abstraction. Look at Monet's application of paint."

"More than one way to skin a cat."

"You bet. See you around the men's room, Baer. Thanks for coming."

Harry looked around for Karine. He saw Elgin in the corner waiving his arms in some intense discussion with two graduate students and wondered whether he should join him. Sigmund and Pauli were speaking with several middle aged, stylishly dressed women that he took to be patrons or directors of the Museum. He could chat with them. Sigmund waved to him. As he walked toward the group his eyes still searched the gallery for Karine.

September 14, 1957 – Encounter

Harry had a capuchino in one hand and a copy of Le Figaro

under his arm. He was heading for a table against the wall not too far from the window when he saw Karine sitting alone, head bent over a paperback.

"What are you reading?"

She looked up at him with her big ivory and onyx eyes. There was no surprise in them, just recognition and a wisp of a smile as if she had expected him. "Durrell," she said in her slow honeyed voice, "*The Alexandria Quartet*. Backwards."

"I had an aunt who always read the last page of every mystery. May I sit down?"

"Plenty of room. I meant I'm reading *Justine* last."

"I understood. You come here often?"

"Before my afternoon seminars. The coffee keeps me alert."

"You drink a lot of coffee?"

"Doesn't every graduate student? Any more questions, professor?"

Harry took that as a rebuff, responded with an indulgent nod and opened his paper to the latest atrocities in the Algerian war and a speech by DeGaulle.

Karine went back to her book. After a time she looked up, took a sip of her coffee and said, "You always read the French paper?"

"Keeps my French from getting rusty."

"Did the beret come with the subscription?"

"Sort of. Are you poking fun?"

"Sort of."

Harry was pleased. She was interested in him. "How's your boy friend?"

She looked bemused but didn't answer at first. "Why do you ask?"

"Are you Jewish, Karine?"

"Why?"

"Because Jews always answer a question with a question."

"Why do they do that?" she asked, breaking into a wide, beguiling smile.

"To answer your first question with the obvious answer, because I would like to see you if you're available."

"Here I am." She straitened her back showing her wide shoulders and raised breasts behind the vermilion patterned blouse.

"If you're done clowning around."

"You want me to be serious, Mr. Baer?"

"Harry. As serious as I am."

"From what I've heard about you, that's not too serious."

"What have you heard, or should I ask?"

"That you're just a one night stand."

Harry felt the heat rise. Was she sticking pins in him? Did it hurt? Still, the very fact that she had talked about him with someone was another sign of interest.

"I admit I've got a wandering eye, but maybe it's because I'm always looking."

She grew suddenly serious, or so he thought. "What you looking for?" She had shifted to argot. She was like a fencer, always keeping him off balance.

"Intelligence, sensitivity, beauty, sensuality, wit."

"Is that all?" The smile again, but tainted with irony.

"So what's it to be? Do we have a future?" She had him going. He wanted to see her even more than before. Karine took a pen out of her purse and wrote something on it but didn't give it to him at first. As she got up and slung her book bag over her shoulder she let it fall to the table. "Gotta go."

He watched the scissor motion of her long legs, and felt himself grow hard. He looked down at the note on a paper napkin. "Karine Lawson LA 2547". A rush of anticipation came over him and a mind image of her flowing brown body moving toward him made him catch his breath.

September 19, 1957 – Getting To Know You

It wasn't what he had expected. How often was life what he had thought it would be, which was, like the process of making art, what made it so interesting. They went to a place near the Campus, well known for its chocolate mud pie, impenetrable bistro black interior, and thick smoky air. It was so dark he had to borrow a flashlight from the waiter, who was no more than a spectral head above a black turtleneck shirt. Across the flickering aura of candlelight, Karine laughed and joked that there was no danger he would be embarrassed about dating a colored woman in this place. The candlelight brought out the warm color of her skin and made her eyes and smile seem all the more brilliant.

She talked about her family over the Beef Stroganoff. Her father was a lawyer, her mother, a social worker. They lived in Detroit in a big old house. She had a brother who was an architect and another, an A.M.E. minister. She was the youngest and the only daughter. Her father, the president of the local chapter of the NAACP, had written an amicus brief in Brown v. Board, the Supreme Court case that had, a few years before, ordered the desegregation of public schools. She had taken her undergraduate degree at Barnard, as had her mother, and earned a Master's at University of Michigan before enrolling in the doctoral program in political science at Cal.

"So now you know all about me," she said, tilting her head toward him.

"I'm impressed." He should have said intimidated. "What, what are you doing your dissertation on?"

"W. E. B. DuBois and his influence on the NAACP. Ever heard of him?"

"Yeah," he said vaguely.

"Tell me what you know."

"Now you're embarrassing me."

"Tell me, it's a kind of a test."

"Well, he was a founder of the NAACP. . . ."

"You could of guessed that."

"And he was an advocate of political and educational rights for Negroes."

"You could of guessed that too."

"And his ideas contrasted with the idea of black separatism espoused by Marcus Garvey."

"Hey, now it's my turn to be impressed. How'd you know that?"

"I read a lot of stuff and it sticks. So did I pass the test, will you go to bed with me?"

"There's another test for that subject," and they both laughed and looked at each other for the first time with real warmth.

October 9, 1957 — The Nearness of You

Harry: "So what d'ya think?"

Karine: "It's nice."

"Nice? Is that all you can say?"

"Look, Harry, it's not exactly Telegraph Hill with a view of the Bay, is it?"

"And I'm not Cary Grant either."

"You think you are, admit it Harry, in your fantasies, and I'm sure you've got fantasies."

"Who doesn't. But I'm not Errol Flynn."

"So who would you like to be?"

"Just me, Harry Baer."

"But if you weren't you?"

"Don't you think we ought to get closer first?"

"What's your idea of getting closer, fucking?"

"That's a good start."

"That comes later in my book. Maybe that's a woman's point of view. Maybe fucking is all there is to a man and a woman for you."

"No, Karine, you fascinate me because of who you are, not what you look like, although. . . ."

"Although?"

"It was your looks that got my attention."

"So I noticed."

"Karine, believe me, my bones turn to butter when I look at you."

"Just the opposite with the other parts."

"You can be so fucking earthy."

"You know what they say about Negroes." She reached out suddenly and touched his cheek, tentatively, tenderly. His penis began to swell and his heart dropped an inch.

"Would you like some cognac?"

"Not really, Harry. Let's just get on with it. See how it goes. Or have you got some special seduction ritual that you go through?"

"Karine, the only ritual I have is to go right where my feelings take me."

"You the kind of guy that likes to undress women?"

"No. I like to watch."

"Ever play strip poker?"

"No."

"Wanna play?"

"Do you?"

"No." She reached up with both hands behind her head, the inside of her arms made triangles reminding him of a painting by Degas of a woman fixing her hair. She took the pins out of the bun at the top of her head and pulled it free, spreading it with her fingers. It fell like a shawl over her shoulders touching her cheeks. He ran his hands through it.

"It's so soft."

"What did you expect, brillo?"

"No but I thought—"

"Tell me the truth Harry. Am I the first Negro woman you've slept with?"

"Why, is there something I should know?"

"Just answer me straight."

"Yes."

"I thought so."

November 3, 1957 – Karine-A letter

Dear Paula:

Yes, it's finally happened. I'm in love right up to my gold hoops. It's sort of like the flu. It's strange how in a short time it went from curiosity, to interest, attraction, infatuation, fixation, and finally obsession. First off I should tell you that he's from a working class Jewish background. You know the "yu hu Missus Golboig" type. Not even the shabby intellectual type that go to lectures on Kierkegard on Friday night and string quartets playing Prokofief (did I spell those right?) on Saturday afternoon. Not even the soul searching, breast-beating liberal/radicals who want to wash the feet of the tired and hungry huddled masses, like your folks. Just Plain Bernie and his wife whoever, (he never mentions his mother's name).

Don't get me wrong, Paula, he ain't no slouch, no long haired grungy beatnik, not Harry. It's not a question of rejection of my family and their bourgeois values. I've got no problem with being comfortable, never have, never will. He's brilliant and brash enough to have gotten himself an associate professorship in the Art Department without a college degree! He didn't even drop out. But I have to say; he's not very nice. Oh, he can charm the skin off a snake when he feels like it. He's, I have to admit it, a bit of a prick: self-centered, but generous; seductive as hell; funny; a kick when he gets going. And he is in love with me, so it's mutual and isn't that refreshing?

So why, all of a sudden, do I go for this guy? He's even used: he's been married and has a daughter in France. So why this guy, you say; why not a latter day George Washington Carver or Harry Belafonte? Don't think I haven't thought about it. And I've come to the conclusion that Harry ain't white. He's blacker than me. Of course, he kind of looks, well, Jewish, with big dark soulful eyes, a hawk's nose. But it's his being that is metaphorically black. The outsider who both wants inside and doesn't; who wants to be accepted, but who wants to stay different; who is incapable of just blending in: the cherry in the fruitcake.

So here I am, in the middle of my dissertation and addled and bothered by this passionate, wildly sexual guy. I never thought it would be, or could be, like this, Paula. We dissolve into each other. We take each other to another dimension. And when we come down, Harry is, or can be, just another Tom Cat. Paula, you're the only one I can tell. I'm addicted to Harry, dependent on his attention, his love. I never imagined that I could be this way. I was too strong, too self-sufficient. It scares me. I suspect that one day he'll turn into an overgrown rat and I'll be cured. Until then, it's the roller coaster. Sweet Jesus what an obsession is love!

Anyhow, that's the weather report. Stormy weather with occasional bright sunshine. Let me hear from you. Have you gotten a job yet? What about you and Karl? Write soon.
Your roomie, Karine.

November 8, 1957 – Harry Writes Caz

Dear Caz:

I know I should be writing to you more often. But you are even worse than me with letters. I just have to tell you first off how much you are in my work. Not that what I do looks imitative. No. It's the technique and the care and the ruthless abandonment of anything that compromises the vision. I hope you get some pleasure out of the fact that even when I am dazzling students, I see myself as your apprentice. Enough praise, I know it embarrasses you. But I have to acknowledge my debt. On a related subject, Natale sent me the reviews of your retrospective. How did it feel to be compared favorably to Rodin?

Enough about art. I have to tell you something, and don't tell Natale. After Aurora I never expected to have any more than shallow, transient contact with women. For one thing I was afraid of another loss. It was too painful. Call it a phobia. Not that I haven't had plenty of company along the way. That has changed. I am in love again. And not just physically, although she is stunning. Her body is like burnished bronze, and there are no angles, only curves, endless curves. Picture a Maillol nude brought to life. She moves with the fluidity of a dancer. Even more, she is clever, independent, and self-possessed. She is very talkative and well read. We have long provocative conversations. She doesn't let me get away with anything, and yet she lets me be who I am. Sometimes, I confess, she intimidates me. Her name is Karine.

Enough of me. Natale said that you have been ill. I hope it's nothing serious. Your studio is so cold it's a wonder you haven't succumbed to pneumonia. I suspect that you are as tough as bronze by now. Buy yourself a good space heater. Better yet make a visit to Berkeley and dry your lungs. The Department would love to have you come and speak, I'm sure. And I would welcome a critique of my new work, photos of which are enclosed.
Fondest regards,
Harry

Caz Writes Back
(A post card with a view of Sacre Coeur)

Dear Harry:
　　Early or late Maillol? I like your new work. You are no longer an apprentice. It is too late for me to come to America. I will take your advice and buy a space heater. The winters seem colder.
Caz

May 13, 1958 – Betrayal

Elgin and Harry were fishing, sitting on the edge of the old pier that pointed a finger at the white profile of San Francisco. It had once extended the streetcar's reach from Berkeley, shortening the ferry ride before the construction of the Bay Bridge in the 30s. Now old men and idlers spent sunny mornings perched on up ended buckets waiting for a bite.

The day was blue to white. Clouds, vague and undefined, covered the sky. The afternoon winds had roughed up the water's surface. Here and there white-hulled sailboats, their triangle sails arched and driving, gracefully defied the water.

Fishing was new to Harry. When he was a boy, fishing had seemed to be a pastime for the *goyim*. At least once each summer his family would pack a wicker basket, folding chairs, and the Sunday paper, and stake out a few square feet of sand on a wide beach at Cedar Point, wedged between four lumpish squabbling families, like checkers on a board. Once installed, they alternately, dozed, ate salami sandwiches with new dills, drank iced tea, sweated, baked, played chess or argued lethargically about the events of the week as reviewed in the Plain Dealer. They cooled off with a dip in the lake or perhaps tossed a beach ball and kicked sand in the face of a cab driver or had it kicked in their face by a screeching toddler. Exhausted, arms burning, following the waning sun, they went back to the sand-covered hotel room. Harry would suck the dried French's mustard under his fingernails and finger a shell lodged in his pocket. Before bed sand would spill out of his cuffs onto the worn wood floor of his room as he undressed. This all came back to him with the smell of San Francisco Bay.

At first Harry had been a little squeamish about impaling a slithery worm on a spiked hook and Elgin had done it for him. It was all Elgin's father's gear: the bait bucket, the line to string the fish, the collection of hooks in the tackle box, the lead sinkers. He was bored. It was just something different, something other people did, like lawn bowling, and he was curious. By the third time he began to appreciate the pace of it. He was normally as tense as the spring of a wind-up toy, his mind always in motion. After only an hour out on the pier, the air moving brisk and unimpeded over the water, his lungs felt refreshed and his mind at peace.

There was nothing to do but watch the wheeling, diving gulls, listen to their screeching cry, observe the plodding progress of a bulk carrier into the Bay and wonder about the sailors on board, or catalogue the changing nuance of color on the water's choppy surface. Occasionally there was the excitement of hooking and reeling in a fish, a feeling not unlike winning third prize in a raffle. Between times there were the six bottles of Schlitz. Elgin wouldn't leave until they were gone, whether or not they had caught any fish.

Tired of sitting, Harry walked down the pier to talk to several of the regulars, earthy, gregarious people with a different, sometimes fresh if eccentric view of life. He saw Tony, an artisan who made gutters and downspouts and always wore a dirty seaman's hat. Tony told him his dog had been hit by a car but wasn't hurt too bad, his wife had won $50 at the church bingo night and bought herself a coat made of rabbit fur that looked just like mink, "You couldn't tell the difference". He went on to say that adding fluoride into the water system would increase the incidence of cancer but "now the Russian's got that Sputnik we'll all be dead within five years anyway."

As evil as the Russian leadership might be, they wouldn't push the button and end the world, Harry told him. But even as he said it, the worm of doubt nibbled at his optimism. The piles of clothing, the crematory ovens, the mass graves still scarred his vision. Just the other day, Sigie Sielenbach had been talking about a new novel, *On The Beach*, survival in

Australia after the nuclear war before radiation sickness killed them all. It wasn't science fiction. It could happen. There were even people building bomb shelters in their back yards.

He drifted back to Elgin, stooping to pick up a rusty nail on the way, and sat down on the folding canvas stool.

"Any bites?"

"Naw."

Harry began to work out in his head the compositional problems of an etching.

"Heard from the committee?" Elgin was sweating out the approval of his dissertation.

"Yeah. They approved it."

"That's great! Congratulations."

Elgin pried the cap off of a bottle of beer and swilled it down. "Want one?"

"No thanks."

"They loved my commentary on the lost sketch book."

An alarm went off in Harry's head. "What gave you the right to make reference to it? I told you I didn't want anybody to know about it."

"Academic freedom. It exists. You showed it to me. It would have been dishonest to ignore it."

"You couldn't have been very academic about something that you saw for fifteen minutes or so." Harry curbed his anger. There was nothing to be gained from a tantrum. The cat was out of the bag and, in a way, he was glad.

"Didn't your landlady tell you?"

"Tell me what?"

"She let me into your apartment. I knew where you kept it."

"You didn't take it?"

"No, nothing like that. I just took some pictures and put it back. No harm done."

"You brazen bastard!" Harry grabbed both fishing rods and threw them into the Bay.

"That's my father's stuff!" Elgin piped.

"Too fucking bad!"

Harry strode down the pier toward the shore feeling the anger and humiliation of betrayal and abusing himself for having told Elgin about it in the first place. He imagined a letter from some foundation demanding its return. By the time he reached the shore, the edge of his indignation was blunted by amusement and grudging respect for Elgin. What a rogue. The break-in went too far but otherwise it was a scholar's right to mention the work once he knew about it. After all hadn't he, Harry, liberated it from a trunk in the first place? Who knows, the notoriety might even do him some good, he told himself.

July 8, 1958 – New Digs

He was always moving it seemed, always leaving a place that had grown comfortable and familiar, he thought, recalling the place he and Aurora had shared and the thought of it made him tearful. He had grown fond of the garden, fond of his landlady, but it was just too small. He needed space to work, diffuse light and high walls to catch and hold it. Not that he intended to paint. That was in fact the only media that daunted him. And as with so much in his life he had stumbled on a studio, an old garage on Gilman Street, not unlike the Body Shop but smaller, with high brick walls, sky lights, and a cross beamed open roof. The workbenches were still in place against the walls. He and Jonah Robb, a carpenter he had befriended in a bar, had thrown up some partitions in the back which gave him a bedroom, and in the same space, a large claw foot bath tub with exposed pipes. The Salvation Army, Goodwill, and several used furniture stores had provided the furnishings: chrome kitchen chairs with gaudy yellow torn plastic seats; a rag-tag band of oak steam boat carpenter chairs with broken spindles and split seats, no two alike; a massive oak table with a surface that had weathered many winters in the sun and rain; an ancient wheel chair; a dentist's chair that swiveled and reclined with round red leather cushions; a weathered wood Corinthian column that had once supported the roof of a porch—nails driven into it were hung with clothes—whatever caught his fancy with a $15 limit on any item.

Karine had made giant pillows with deep natural colors.

There was even a twelve-inch Zenith TV with a neurological tic. An old Columbia 360 record player gave music, although his collection of records consisted of four LPs; The Modern Jazz Quartet, Louis Armstrong, Pete Seeger and Arthur Rubenstein. An ancient GE refrigerator with a round compressor on top that he called the cyclotron was half full of beer. A large basket on the table held a cornucopia of fruit: red dry skinned pomegranates with their seven pointed crowns; bananas, golden and black smeared; oranges and lemons.

It was the most space he had ever had to himself and he reveled in it, sometimes running and dancing in circles. Wherever he went there was something no one wanted that he saw a use for. He had even written his aunt and sent her a money order to pay for the shipment of the mud and other stuff he had brought home from the War. It was stacked in the corner, in labeled boxes. He would feel its essence when he tuned into it, just as everything he came in contact with had a breath and even a voice that told him something.

Karine was sitting at the table cutting Swiss and Ementhaler cheese and stale French bread into cubes for cheese fondue. The plum colored tunic contrasted amiably with the warm tea tone of her skin. Harry turned to watch the movement of her arms and the softly glowing light on their surfaces, each line, so polished, so pliant, so modeled, not sharp, not even where the collar bone raised concavities, or the tendons rose from her shoulders. She was so well proportioned, so like a cat in its perfection that he wished for a moment he could sculpt her as Phidias might have. He hitched the collar of his black velvet smoking jacket, bent down and kissed her on the back of the neck. She turned and gave him a grateful smile.

Jonah Robb was sprawled on the floor, his back propped against a pillow, his silky blond hair splayed behind his head, a bottle of beer in one hand, a cigarette in the other, watching Steve Allen interviewing Audrey Hepburn on the TV.

Pauli and Roger, two of the three of his colleagues at the Body Shop, were at the other end of the table playing checkers, their heads bent over the board. Elgin Cooley was watching the game over Roger's shoulder, a bottle of Schlitz held like a microphone. A gray tiger-striped cat, Mr. Katz, was curled on a purple cushion, sleeping, its head cradled on one paw. The cat had adopted Harry. It had shown up at the door looking hungry, hopeful, and insistent.

Harry felt a warm bath of contentment. He had just completed another etching, a rendering of the prodigal son bending before his father. A sculpture of a collapsed mailbox was out of the kiln waiting for a patina. Perhaps he would paint it. His classes at the University were going well. Students followed him around like sheep. Some had talent, and he enjoyed helping them develop it each in their own way.

He went over to the roll top desk that had been abandoned by the former proprietors of the garage and rummaged through a pile of unopened mail. He had an aversion to mail. It represented to him bills that he didn't like to pay, unsolicited requests that he contribute to something that made him feel guilty when he didn't respond, and bad news. He fanned out the envelopes, saw the stripes of a foreign air mail letter and opened it. From Natale. A picture of Therese, his daughter, looking more and more like Aurora, sitting on a stoop, a wide grin, a crucifix dangling from a chain around her neck, her chubby fingers on the flat head of a seated black and white spaniel with a lolling tongue.

He opened the thin paper and read, "My dear nephew-in-law:" very droll of Natale, to open that way, he thought. "As you can see by the enclosed photo, your daughter, Therese, is happy and well, thriving on the fresh air and healthy fruits and vegetables of the Champagne. She's a good little French girl, loves the local cheeses. She is especially fond of the stuffed rabbit you sent for her birthday and sleeps with it. I hope that you will soon come to visit her. On the subject of people left behind, Caz was in the hospital recently. A gall bladder attack. He had an operation and he is recovering, you will be glad to know. I went to see him. He looked terrible, gaunt and hollow-cheeked, all eyes, but defiant. He appreciated your postcard.

"I sold several of your etchings and have deposited the money in your Bank of Paris account. Now that you are in

America, it's not as easy to sell your work. You are no longer the expatriate. You have become a provincial, if we can call California a province. Well, a province of some place, perhaps New York. And on that subject I have a New York gallery interested in showing your work. How is that for dedication? The dealer's name is Hans Springle, a Swiss, from Zurich originally, who acquired a fine collection of German Expressionists along the way and represented Hans Hoffman, a fellow Californian. I sent him photos of your work and he has heard of you. By the way, he mentioned something in his last letter about your having a lost sketchbook of Franz Marc. Where in God's name did you get it? A flea market perhaps, and why didn't I know about it, given that you met Aurora in front of one of his works in my gallery, you may recall. In any event, Hanzl is a dear man, rather cherubic, which masks his razor-sharp business mind. He loves your etchings and wants to give you a show of your latest work.

"Well, that's probably all you care about. Paris is again under siege owing to the Algerian war. Police everywhere with machine guns and lead weighted capes. Reminds me of the War except, of course, that these police are ours. My life has been somewhat dreary since you left, I must confess. Despite the fact that you are a sewer rat, you somehow added spice to my daily soup—not the aromatic herbs of the Provence, more like Hungarian paprika. Even so, you aren't the first moth to gnaw holes in my life. That's a confession of sorts.

"Please write and thank me and above all don't stop creating. You have, above everything, a gift, a promise of greatness."

He looked at the picture again, decided he must get a frame for it, and showed it to Karine.

"My daughter."

"Doesn't look much like you, except maybe a little in the eyes." She looked from the photo to his face for confirmation.

Elgin looked over his shoulder, "Cute as a button." He had been contrite since Harry's display of pique on the pier, appearing a few days later unannounced with a bottle of Remy Martin as a peace offering. In fact, Harry had by then concluded that there was no harm in acknowledging the sketchbook, having decided that it would get him some attention. After all, it wasn't some lost masterpiece by Michealangelo. Even so, it had been prudent to keep quiet about it while he was in France. And he would never part with it. Like most inanimate objects the sketchbook was like a touchstone, giving off creative energy only to him, he fancied. He thought of Natale's letter. Yes, he had a gift, but more as a medium to express the creative energy that was lodged in everything. He was like a radio, an instrument to pick up the energy and translate it into something palpable. That was his gift.

He was still standing over Karine's head, ostensibly watching her cutting the cheese, actually musing over this notion. Roger had spoken to him, he realized, but Harry was listening to his own inner voice and he hadn't heard him.

December 3, 1958 – Faculty Party

"Well, Karine, It's good of you to come."

Norbert Dawe, was taking her measure with mental calipers and, seeing his ranging eye, she was glad that she had worn a loose fitting dress. It was enough that she was the only non-Caucasian at the party. Norbert's wife, Sally, had welcomed her at the door, with studied sincerity. She looked away from him and took in the room, the Scandinavian teak furniture, the wall of windows looking across the Bay at the incoming fog, the redwood walls and obligatory floor to ceiling book shelves, with the requisite quantity of what, in her house, would have been coffee table books.

"Can I make you a drink?"

"Just a coke would be fine." She wasn't sure what to call the Chairman of the Art Department, not that his thinning gray hair entitled him to any respect. But she had been raised polite, and anyone her senior was Mister or Mrs. She was still smarting from Harry's casual invitation. He had known about the party for weeks and never mentioned it until she was almost out the door on her way to an N.A.A.C.P. Board meeting. Then he had made a scene, as if she were violating a sacred duty by not changing her plans at the last instant.

"Shall I pour it for you?"

"No, I like the fizz."

"It is a matter of taste. I can't take the stuff myself," he said, swirling ice in his scotch on the rocks. "Not since I found out that you can clean the rust off of chrome bumpers with it."

That's a party for you, random small talk, stream of consciousness, she thought, then she added something about Coke that came to mind, just to keep it going. "It started out as a feel better tonic, laced with cocaine, you know."

"Really!" he said with a wide gap toothed smile looking as if she had revealed to him that her mother was a Nobel Prize laureate.

That was the end of Coke. She took a sip and felt it sand her throat. What next? Dawe drank off half of his scotch and looked like he knew that this was her time of the month.

"Harry told me you work for the NAACP, is that right?"

"Yes, that's right." Karine braced herself for the next question.

"Must be an exciting place to work."

"It is. Are you a member?"

"I thought—"

"No. You don't have to be colored."

"Pardon my ignorance. I'm not very political. One of these guys that turns right to the sports page, I'm afraid."

Here comes Harry to the rescue.

"This guy bothering you?" said Harry.

"No, officer," she retorted.

"You just call me if he does," he said as he drifted across the room and rejoined his gaggle of admiring graduate students.

Dawe watched Harry walk away then turned to Karine with an avuncular look and said, "Harry's lucky you came into his life, Karine."

"I'm not sure I would describe our relationship in those terms, Mr. Dawe, but I appreciate the compliment all the same."

"All I meant to say was, he's sort of a boat without a rudder."

"If you think that I provide him with any direction, you

are mistaken."

"No, not that. But maybe some stability. Someone to come home to."

"French toast Sunday morning, folded underwear, is that what you mean? Wrong again."

"I guess what I was trying to say, is," he swallowed the rest of his scotch, "If I were Harry, and had you to come home to, I wouldn't hang around in bars much with Elgin Cooley and Sig."

"Maybe I got involved with the wrong professor."

"I guess Harry can't help being himself. He's kind of a tumbleweed. Have you ever seen one?"

"Can't say that I have. But let me say before you jump to any more conclusions, that I don't sit around waiting for Harry to come home. I have a life, very much my own. And it doesn't depend on Harry. Maybe that's why he finds me interesting."

Dawe looked at her with respect and seemed to back away. If she had intimidated him, she thought, so be it. She hadn't come to the party to be Harry's good-will ambassador.

"I'm sure that's not the only reason, Karine." And with that sober pronouncement, he excused himself to perform his "hostly" duties.

May 12, 1959 – NAACP

"Get ready, Harry, or we'll be late."

Harry was bent over a copper plate, burin in hand, tracing the lines of a drawing. He turned toward her with a wan look of apology. "Sorry, honey. I can't stop what I'm doing."

"Why not?"

"If I leave it now I'll lose it. I feel this incredible concentration."

"You'll get it back. You always do."

"But it'll be different. Why don't you go without me. It's not my thing."

"Come on, Harry. You promised me you'd come."

"I'd just be a fifth wheel."

"It's important to me that you come. How many student and faculty events have I come to with you."

"But you enjoy it."

"But you don't enjoy a reception for a bunch of civil rights activists."

"As a matter of fact, I don't particularly."

"Because you're not the center of attention."

"They have nothing to say to me. I'm just there because I'm with you."

"Harry, has it ever struck you that in a mutual caring relationship, that's a good enough reason?"

"No, not really." Harry tried to be blithe.

"Sorry, I interrupted you." Karine's look was hard as stone and her tone was glacial. She wanted to tell him that he was the most selfish person she had ever met but it would have shattered her equanimity and provoked a defensive and belligerent response. Besides he was, in a way, right. He was no fun when people around him didn't recognize his brilliance. He could be morose, sarcastic, or even say something embarrassing, insulting, or outrageous, just to get attention.

"No problem. Enjoy yourself," he said moving toward her to give her a kiss.

"Save it, Harry." And she turned and left.

July 18, 1961 – Telegraph Hill

It could only have been in San Francisco. No other city in the world could boast the urbanity of a Bauhaus modern apartment perched on a rock cliff fretted by wooden steps around which tumbled a romantic wild garden running to the stoops of humble salt box cottages, a pleasant walk from the office buildings of the financial district. From the windows could be seen covered piers, anchored freighters, the rippled changing waters of an urban bay enclosed by distant undulant hills and the diadem of art deco towers and graceful arching wires of the bridge spanning the Golden Gate. Looming over the apartment was a phallic tower—the legacy of an eccentric woman infatuated with firemen.

Elgin and Harry stood at the door marveling at the interior furnished to match the building: Breuer and Miller, brushed aluminum, dark leather and thick glass, and on the walls, here a Jasper Johns, there a Rauschenberg, a Diebenkorn from his Berkeley period. The thirty or so guests hardly filled the room, which was large enough to be a studio.

The man who let them in had the tanned and weathered look of someone who spent a lot of time on the Bay and the tennis court. His thinning gray hair was tightly plastered to his fine Celtic head and contrasted with heavy dark eyebrows. His too even smile might have had some help from a dentist, Harry mused, looking beyond him at the assortment of leggy women, mostly in tight basic black dresses, some with spaghetti straps some without, and spidery leering or posturing men.

Elgin had gotten the invitation to the party through his connections with the Fine Arts Museum. He introduced Harry, who was chagrined to see not even a mote of admiration or recognition in the host's watery gray eyes. Something might at least have come from Harry's outfit, appropriately theatrical and eccentric, a black silk Russian style shirt and black straight pipe pants—not seen since the thirties and rescued from a back rack of his favorite vintage clothing store—not to mention the red silk bandanna. As for Elgin, he was in his uniform: faded jeans, faded work shirt, wide belt with silver buckle commemorating his father's light middleweight something or other.

Harry advanced toward the center of the room met by the strong sharp scent of hashish. From the languid looks and slow movement, the sudden ecstatic bursts of laughter, it was obvious that many, if not most, of them were stoned.

The bar was self-serve, only the best names, Chivas and Black Turkey, and so was the buffet. The food was heartier than he had expected: sliced ham, turkey, unevenly cut. Egalitarian, Harry judged. The host must be a liberal, probably a big contributor to the ACLU and the ADA. He poured himself a scotch and watched Elgin migrate toward some guy who was wearing a bronze tinted rug and had to be one of the Museum Board members. Elgin never wasted words at shindigs like this, not even when he was on the hunt. A man passed him a joint and looked at him with interest that Harry took to be a sexual appraisal. Harry passed on the joint, not that he didn't feel like it, but you never knew where that mouth had been recently. He preferred taking a toke from women. Sharing a joint was the beginning of intimacy, a sort of breaking down the wall of clothing and a lack of shared experience, part of the mystery that kept him incessantly looking and pursuing any woman who stirred a ripple of desire or curiosity in him. He looked around disappointed that there was no one who he even remotely recognized. Harry scanned the crowed for an appealing woman—one that looked approachable. He finished the scotch, felt his scalp go soft, and walked toward the windows, his attention caught by the contrast between the molten indigo of the Bay and the black opacity of the hills beyond.

"Don't I know you?" He turned toward a shrill, strangled soprano voice to face a woman in her mid-thirties, about his height, thin-skinned, with wide spaced amber eyes, wide pointed cheeks, and a loose lipped bemused smile. Her hair was short, casual, brown with auburn highlights. Harry could tell a lot about women's hair, it was more revealing than handwriting. She had a glass of scotch in one and a cigarette in the other and her head was cocked to one side in a way that reminded him of a dog trying to make sense of strange words. She was interesting.

"Let me help you," he said.

"With what?" she asked her voice trailing into snuffling laughter.

"Whatever. You name it. I'm easy."

"You might be getting in over your head," she said, a whimsical challenge in her eyes.

"I'm used to deep water, I thrive in it."

"Oh, I'm not deep. Don't worry about that."

"Everyone is deep in places, even if they are shallow on others."

"Metaphorically speaking?" She mocked him but it was friendly mockery.

Harry looked at her with attentive self-possession, hoping to find out how she might react to silence. It was another one of his analytical tests.

"You must be the entertainment," she said, looking at his

shirt.

"I've been accused of that."

She swayed on her heels just enough to tell him she'd already had too much to drink. "You're not going to give me that lecture? I can tell by your face."

"What lecture?"

"You've had too much to drink, Christine. I can hear my husband saying that."

"Is he here?"

"Who?"

"Your husband."

"Oh, him." She dismissed the thought with a frown. "No. He's long gone."

"Sorry."

"I'm not. I've got the better part of the deal. Listen—"

"Harry."

"Yes, Harry. Don't go away. Nature calls. Promise me you'll—"

"Promise."

"Stay?"

"Sure you can drive a Maserati, Harry?

"I can drive anything with a steering wheel, Chris."

"You are a helluva guy, Harry. I'm dying to see your paintings."

"Sculpture."

"Whatever. Just don't take it over the redline, Harry."

"The redline," Harry said, dropping into the low bucket seat and fishing for the ignition. What did she mean by that?

"That has to be the world's biggest bed." The indirect light was rose tinted. Music from four hi fi speakers mounted on the wall surrounded them with mellow blues, Ella Fitzgerald alternating with Marian McPartland, good for 45 minutes. Christine dissolved into the black satin sheets, her skirt midway up her thighs.

"This is nice, Harry. What would you call it, an environment?"

"That's the idea. Someplace to relax."

"It's very sensual." He sat down and the bed began to roll.

"God, I hope I don't get seasick."

"Want some Dramamine?"

"Very funny. Harry, undress me. And I'll undress you."

"You got a deal, Chris."

"What's this Harry?" Karine was standing at the door of the bedroom. Something pink, lacy, and gossamer was dangling from her thumb and forefinger.

Harry was bent over his worktable, gazing at an unfinished collage, rummaging among a pile of found objects, wrinkled cellophane, bits of string, remnants of cloth, decals of butterflies, leaves, bubble gum wrappers. He turned toward her, annoyed that she had broken his concentration.

"Looks like a pair of panties."

"I found them in the bed when I was changing the sheets."

"You must have forgotten them."

She glowered, her breathing audible. "You screwed a woman in there while I was in Chicago."

"So?" He was bracing himself; he could feel the barometer falling, feel the static electricity. He turned to face her, head her off if she tried to break something. "That was our deal. I told you when we got together that I would play around."

"Play around! You've made a career of it."

"What do you expect, Karine? You're gone more than you're here. And that's your deal. Your work is important, to you and to your people. I respect it. We're both free, both committed to what we do." He turned back to his work, aware that she was approaching him, feeling his heart quicken with the uncertainty of what she would say.

Karine stopped just behind him and said to his back, "Sleeping around is one thing. An occasional admiring student, a ripe apple pulled off the tree. Even a tart picked up in a bar. I can live with that, given what you are. And you're right. I'm on the road a lot. But bringing them home to our bed is something else."

"Don't get technical on me. She wanted to see my studio. Besides she was too drunk to drive herself and I wasn't about to take her to Hillsborough." He turned to face her wide, angry, hurt eyes.

"Hillsborough!" It came out like an indictment. "Did she commission something for the garden? A little business maybe?"

"Cut the anti-Semitic allusions, Karine. It's beneath you."

She dropped her head forward and answered with a malignant smile. "Promise me one thing, Harry. Don't bring them home, if you want me to stay in your life."

"OK, OK. If that will make you happy. I want you to stay in my life." Harry reached out and tentatively touched her shoulder. She shrugged his hand off but he persisted, touching her chin. "Look, I'm sorry. I can be a jerk. But when you signed on you got the whole package. And you know that you're the only one that matters." His voice was tender, gentle. "You know it."

She looked at him, nodded ruefully. "I wanted it to be so nice. I was going to make lasagna, buy a bottle of Chianti. I've got so much to tell you."

"We still can."

She nodded and gave him an acknowledging smile.

"Are you going shopping?" he asked.

"Yes, soon. What do we need? "

"We're out of Half and Half."

She tossed the panties on to his worktable and turned away. He had already bent over his collage. He swept the panties into the pile of found detritus thinking that parts of them might be useful.

March 27, 1963, 11:30 P.M – The Wall

Hans: Is that you, Harry?

Harry: Yes.

Hans: It's Hans.

Harry: I know. What's up, Hans?

Hans: I thought you would like to know how the opening went.

Harry: To tell the truth, Hans, I wasn't giving it much thought. I'm in the middle of something, and you know how that is.

Hans: Yes, of course I do. But even so I thought you'd like a report.

Harry: Did anything sell?

Hans: Four sculptures and two more on hold.

Harry: Which ones.

Hans: I don't have the list handy. I can get it for you. I'm at home you see.

Harry: It doesn't matter. Was there much of a crowd?

Hans: I rounded up the usual suspects. A very good crowd. And a lot of compliments. They liked the structural elements, the verticles, the worked surfaces, the flat surfaces, the suggestive abstract forms mixed with the identifiable ones, the bottles and key holes and the like.

Harry: I'm glad. Any reviewers?

Hans: Yes, as a matter of fact, Winston from the *Times* was there. Non committal as always, but taking notes, a lot of notes.

Harry: Maybe he's writing a food and wine column.

Hans: No, (chuckling) I think he'll write about you this time. I've been working on him, even took him to lunch.

Harry: Service above and beyond the call of duty, Hans.

Hans: Not at all. I don't dislike him. He's amiable and knowledgeable. It's just that he has his tastes.

Harry: Yes, pistachio or nothing.

Hans: You are being too hard on him, Harry.

Harry: Let's hope he doesn't reciprocate. Hans, thanks for calling but I've got to get back to the clay.

Hans: What are you working on?

Harry: A wall.

Hans: A wall?

Harry: You'll see. I'll send you a picture. Gotta go.

He debated taking the phone off of the hook but got distracted. This work had been haunting him for weeks, teasing him with its amorphous forms suddenly showing themselves then disappearing into the miasma of his mind as a stripper might show a little flesh. He had worked his way through all the symptoms, waking suddenly in the night trying to remember a fragment of a dream that, he knew, held an original image, a connection between form and event that was new and fresh yet gone like the nocturnal fragrance of an unseen flower. He had borne the anxious pacing, the agitation, the interrupted concentration, the starting and stopping before something would finally show itself in a confluence of lines on paper. And finally the release of energy as the sketches took shape and related to each other. In the end they were familiar to him, the demons that had haunted some of his etchings, humanoid but abstracted, dissolved, misshapen, recognizable, alien. Insects, they could be, or men without human feelings believing themselves to be insects.

He was building the form, two feet wide at the base and a vertical wall, ten feet wide and six feet high. He had pulverized some of the mud brought home from Auschwitz eighteen years before and never used, and mixed it into the clay to give the work a soul. He was bound to the work now, obsessed.

March 28, 1963 6:25 A.M.

Nell: Harry? It's Nell. Did I get you up?

Harry: No.

Nell: You sound sleepy and hoarse. Do you have a cold?

Harry: No, It's just that I've been working all night.

Nell: Why? Harry, you'll take 20 years off your life that way.

Harry: The coffee and the cigarettes keep me going.

Nell: Even worse.

Harry: Nell, it's good to hear your voice. So tell me, how are the kids and everything?

N: Never mind the kids. They're ok. It's you I'm worried about.

H: Is that why you called, to tell me to get my sleep and eat an apple a day and take vitamin c?

N: Well, you need somebody.

H: I've got Karine.

N: Karine. So what's she doing?

H: She's away at a conference. SNCC.

N: What's that?

H: Student Non-Violent Coordinating Committee. Where've you been, Nell, on the moon?

N: Between work and the kids I fall asleep in front of Edward R. Murrow.

H: So, Nell, what's on your mind?

N: I called to wish you a happy birthday. It's your 38th birthday.

H: Thanks for reminding me.

N: And I wanted to tell you how much I enjoyed the work. I actually got Ben to go to the opening.

H: Did you buy one? I can get you a good price.

N: No. But I loved the box with the artist's stuff inside.

H: If it didn't sell, I'll make you a present.

N: No. Don't be silly.

H: I mean it. I haven't given you anything of my work in 10 years or so. I'll call Hans in a few days and tell him.

N: I call to wish you a happy birthday and you give me a present?

H: Why not. But listen, Nell. I'm in the middle of something and I just can't talk now.

N: I'm sorry, Harry. Better get some sleep. And take care of yourself. (the moist sound of a kiss) Love you.

H: I love you too. You take care, now.

Except for the section he was working on, the wall was draped with moist cloth to keep the clay pliant. He stopped to make a fresh pot of coffee and wash his hands and face with cold water. Hunger gnawed at his stomach. He took a crackling bite out of an apple, then sat down and looked at the figure, a succubus, emerging from the wall.

He dozed off for a moment, perhaps longer, and didn't hear the door. Startled awake, he saw Karine standing over him, looking tired and sullen. He struggled out of the chair, his limbs stiff, his mouth dry and tasting foul.

"You're back. I didn't expect you until tomorrow."

"It is tomorrow."

"What day is it?"

"Thursday."

"Jesus, I lost a day, I've been working constantly." He gestured toward the wall.

She glanced at it and turned back to him.

"What do you think?"

"I'm pissed off at you for not picking me up at the airport. I spent fifteen dollars on a cab."

"I'm sorry, Karine. You know how it is when I'm in the middle of something."

"Yes, I know. You might as well be dead."

"How can I make it up to you?"

"You can't, Harry. What's done is done. There's no restitution for a wrong."

"You're talking like a lawyer or a minister."

"There were plenty of both at the conference."

"Anything happen?" He said trying to show some interest in her work and dilute her anger.

She looked at him with hardly concealed disdain. "Lots. But I don't want to talk about it now. I need some sleep. I've been up two nights in a row."

"Doing what?"

"Not screwing if that's what's running through your mind."

"Come on, Karine. What's with you?"

"I'm just tired, and high in a way."

"What did they do, make you the grand dragon?"

"That's not funny."

"Sorry."

"You're not sorry, Harry, you're never sorry. You think all this stuff is—"

"Is what?"

"You're sympathetic, but you don't share the burden of it. It's not your fight."

"Why? Because I'm not colored? Plenty of whites are getting beaten up down there too."

"Not as many as before. It's becoming more our struggle now."

"Is that what came out of the meeting?" He took a few steps toward the wall. Something disturbed him about the head and he pinched at a knob that might have been a nose.

"Go back to your work. I'll get some sleep. We'll talk later."

Sensing something new and ominous in her mood and tone, he turned toward her. "Something happened. Tell me what."

She didn't answer at first. When she spoke he voice was measured. "They want me to head an office in Meridian, Mississippi. Voter registration."

"You're not going?"

Again she delayed and he thought he saw conflict and uncertainty but her features hardened and she said quietly, "I am going."

"For how long?"

"Until it's over."

"What about your work here, what about us?"

"You answer that one, Harry."

"What do you mean?"

"We've gone as far as we can, you and me." She looked at him as if across a void, a sad, helpless look, and he saw her already far away as through the wrong end of a telescope. She picked up her suitcase and walked toward the bedroom.

He went suddenly cold as if his heart had stopped. The chill yielded to a rush of indignation and disbelief. She couldn't just walk away from him. The words exploded out of him before he could check them. "Yeah, maybe you're right. We should have just fucked. That's all we had in common." He looked at her with bruised contempt.

"You can be so mean when you want to be." She said it calmly but with bitterness and her eyes were so distant and detached she might have been looking at a dead moth.

"Me! What about you? I don't pick you up at the Airport because I'm obsessed with what might be the best thing I've ever done, working around the clock, and you tell me you're on your way to Mississippi and we're finished. Do you know what it is to loose your awareness of everything but the thing in front of you?" He stopped, realizing that he was shouting. "To help it take shape from inside you and become something you can feel and respond to, something that will speak to strangers with a voice I've given it."

"Must feel like God." Her voice was detached.

"How do you think that makes me feel?"

"Right, that's all you can think about, how you feel."

"Save it for later."

"There's nothing to save."

"What's happened to you?" Harry's shoulder's contracted; his voice was rising and strident, yet pleading.

"I guess once I was out from under your long, deep shadow I realized I didn't want to be there anymore." She said this without feeling as though she were reporting the weather.

He looked across the room and saw a manikin of Karine. His exhaustion, the sense that she had poisoned the satisfaction with his work with her insensitivity to his needs, her willingness to abandon him, her distance, all combusted. "Then just go! To Mississippi! To hell! I don't really give a shit!" he shouted.

Karine looked over her shoulder at him, an injured, closed look. She opened her lips as if to say something, murmured, "You bastard," and turned away.

He watched her close the bedroom door, regretting his words, already feeling the void of loss, wondering if he should follow, touch her, make love to her. But he had nothing to give at that moment and no desire to reach out to her. Let her leave. She didn't understand him, didn't appreciate him.

He went back to the soft and pliant clay, and his own feeling for anything but this, his work, hardened and cracked.

December 20, 1964 – Letter from Karine

Dear Harry:

The work here in this strange and sometimes frightening place literally takes up 14 hours of the day, seven days a week. The hostility of the white establishment, the harassment, official and unofficial, creates an atmosphere of constant stress but it brings us all together. We feel so close, so good about what we are doing. The black people who live on their side of the town or on little farms in two room unpainted houses are even more scared than we are but they are nice, gentle, patient, and caring, and certainly appreciative. They've been cowed by the whippings, the church burnings, the hangings, the beatings, but their faith keeps them hoping and going forward and, little by little, the timid get courage at the church meetings and, one by one, they register to vote believing that one day they will be counted. I've never felt better about myself. So much for my work.

I missed you a lot in the beginning even though we had a hard parting. I know in retrospect that one of the reasons I took this on was to put some distance between us. Despite the fact that our lives were different, it was hard for me to be just me when you were in my life. You are such a big presence that the people around you can't do much more than stand in your shadow.

Sure, we had a great sex life, but beyond that I don't think that you really gave a damn about what I really thought about anything, or about who I was or wanted to be. You're just too wrapped up in yourself, in your work. Oh I don't fault you for that. Your work is everything to you. Don't get me wrong. You're a lot of fun. But it left me with an empty sack much of the time. And this isn't just sour grapes because you never once talked about marriage and kids. I don't doubt your love for me, but I know you could never bring yourself to marry a "colored" girl, not even one with a classy pedigree. It's just a matter of where you came from, that lower middle class neighborhood insulated by the Irish on the one side and the Italians on the other side from the "Shvartzas." So I guess in a way that's also why I'm down here, hoping that maybe someday kids, American kids, won't be put off by race or religion when they fall in love.

Yes, you fell in love with me, you wanted me, you pursued me, and I gave of myself for years before I realized that there was an invisible wall that would always keep us apart, a color wall, not much more. That's what that wall you were working on came to symbolize that day I came home from the SNCC meeting. Not that it isn't great art. But I tell you I wanted to knock it over.

I guess when you didn't stop screwing around with other women, I should have taken the hint. But I thought, well that's just Harry, the free spirit, ain't nobody gonna keep him down, not even me. In a way I gave you credit for that freedom, I knew they never meant anything to you. It wasn't about me. But maybe it was.

I'm crying as I write this letter on this cold for Mississippi night, crying with rage and longing. I still love you, and haven't been able to be with anyone else since I've been down here. You're still inside me.

March 12, 1966 – Harry Writes Karine

Dear Karine:

It has taken me a long time to answer your letter. I know and I apologize, not that it makes it any better. You've got my number. I do put everything behind my work. It's the only thing that makes me feel whole. As for your accusations, they hurt, but they are probably true, at least in part. I did love you, I love you now. I fancy myself a person who soars above the petty conventions, but I guess I'm like a kite, way up there on the wind, looking down on the world, but tied to it by a string. I wish it could have been different, but I never wanted to confront it. We had each other and that was enough, or so I imagined. I took your cynicism, your sardonic jabs as just who you were. I never took them personally. Oblivious me.

I would have written sooner, but I had to go to Paris for a room installation, an interior sculpture. I call it, "Behind The Face." I spent two days with my daughter Therese. She's charming, just beginning to bud, and still looks so much like her mother. She was very affectionate, put her arms around me, kissed me on the cheek. We went for walks together, places I had gone before she was born. It was very poignant at times. . . .

April 7, 1966 – Sacrifice

Harry was bent over a sheet of Lucite under a bright light, sculpting what might have been a bas-relief, except that he had another use in mind. Like a dentist, he was chipping, scraping with hand tools and brushing and sanding with an electric rotor. Beside him was a loose sketch of the subject and the outlines of the images could also be seen drawn on the glassy plane of the Lucite except where they had been chiseled away. The central figure was clear, the shape of its elliptical muscles raised out of the channels that defined the shapes in much the way that stained glass pieces were separated by black, opaque lead. The figure was, in fact, reminiscent of those he'd seen in stained glass windows in France. The image as a whole was full of disparate shapes and figures connected by theme. The kneeling figure was wrapped in the loins of a woman whose torso was not visible. Bent soldiers clutched upstanding swords by the blades; a naked figure was suspended in the air by a rope. The sky was seamed and textured and there were whorls that resembled flowers or eggs; a beam that might be a cross.

The theme of the work was sacrifice, sacrifice of the innocents and it was his homage to the subject, one link of an endless disparate, yet connected, chain of etchings dealing with dimensions of death and transcendence. Where it led, he didn't know. It was a journey that he took now and then when he felt impelled to: intuitive, visceral, dreamlike, disconnected, an attempt to translate themes and feelings, fears, inevitabilities, randomness, into visual images that were as equivocal and complex and subjective as life.

He had been working outside time. He might have missed a class for all he knew; it might have been day or night. He had stopped only for coffee, cigarettes, and to relieve himself. Each motion with a tool was an unburdening of inner weight, a creative exorcism, for he hoped, on completion, to feel lighter, free of the moving ephemeral nagging shapes and shadows that had become this hard, shallow sculpted image of death and suffering and, perhaps—even he wasn't sure—birth.

At times like this he felt himself possessed in the sense that there was no room in his conscious being for anything other than the creation of some compulsive vision by an endless series of inner directed, yet sure, movements of the hand or arm. Sometimes he worked continually, only stopping to stare at the unfinished piece, waiting until he could go on with certainty.

October 24, 1967 — Darah

His car, a '57 pearl gray Chevy wagon with 86,000 miles on it, wouldn't start. Harry turned the key in the ignition and nothing happened, not even a whine. It was after two in the morning. The Med had closed. He was parked on a side street and there were no people around. A light but soaking rain was falling, the first of the season. It wasn't the battery; he had just replaced it. Beyond that, he had no feel for the electrical system of a car. What was under the hood had always been a greasy tangle, just as the boiler room of the apartment had been out of bounds, the realm of a sweaty, hairy, custodian who sucked on snuff to cover his boozy breath. He pulled out his wallet, fished out his auto club card and confirmed that it had expired. He was resigned to finding a telephone booth on Telegraph and calling a cab when a black Karman Ghia convertible pulled up beside him.

The window rolled down and he heard a woman's voice. "Are you leaving?"

"I would if I could."

"What's wrong?"

"It won't start."

Without a word she pulled forward, turned off the engine and got out. She was short, narrow hipped, and dressed in tight jeans and a man's worn brown leather bomber jacket. Her hair was straight blond and cut short in a pageboy style parted at the center so that a strand fell loose across her cheek. She had a square Slavic face, narrow eyes, and flaring lips. All of this he noted as she approached the car.

"Release the hood," she said.

"You a mechanic?"

"I know something about cars." She nodded several times as if to convince him.

He obeyed. She raised the hood and bent over the engine. Harry got out to watch.

"You can wait in the car. No need for both of us to get wet."

"You might need some help. Besides, it doesn't seem right."

"A matter of scruples," she said as she snapped the clips

off of the distributor cap.

"Not exactly." No one had ever accused Harry of being scrupulous, not that he could recall.

She went back to her car, returned in a few moments with a nail file. Opening the points she ran the file across them and replaced the distributor cap. "Try it now."

He got into the car, turned the key and the engine started. "You're fantastic. How did you do that?"

"Just luck."

"Listen, I want to pay you back in some way. Can I buy you a beer or a glass of wine?" Harry was lonely and she was pretty.

"You don't have to. All I want is your parking place. I live in there." She said, pointing toward a small red gabled house.

"No, I would like to get to know you. I . . . I'm looking for a good mechanic."

"Well, that's not my line of work."

"What do you do?"

"I'm a baker. You know Madeline's? On Shattuck? Near Walnut?"

"Do I know it? It's incredible." They had the closest he had found to a real French baguette.

"You'd better go before something else happens."

"Not before I get your name."

She didn't hesitate. "Darah Keswick."

"Mine's Harry Baer."

"I know who you are," she said returning to her car.

November 6, 1967 – Closed Room

Darah walked around the studio gaping in wonder at everything she saw, and as her guide, Harry was both flattered and in a way dismissive of her open acceptance without reserve, of everything he had recently done, even the incomplete work. She gazed at the vertical latex wall panel, not flat but raised and dented in a way that, with the light and shadow playing on its surface, gave it the illusion of drapery or a polished landscape. "Wonderful!" she said.

"What do you like about it?"

She looked at him, her narrow slate green eyes showing

perplexity, as if she hadn't expected the question. "I can't put it in words."

"Why not?"

"I think it's trivial to try to describe art. I'd rather just take it in at an emotional level."

He nodded and she looked up at him expecting a comment.

"So?" she said.

"I'm responding in kind with silence. Let's eat."

Harry had made pasta with a marinara sauce. He seldom cooked but had a few simple presentable favorites to provide when there was no one living with him. A bottle of Heitz Martha's Vineyard Cabernet was airing, and there were two loaves of bread—a baguette with a golden crust and Italian country raisin bread—which Darah had brought. The yeasty smell of the bread mingled with the olive oil and tomato and starch smell of the spaghettini. Harry poured a glass of wine and held it out to her.

"Sure you won't have some?"

She hesitated then took it. They touched glasses and drank.

"I thought you didn't drink," Harry asked her.

"I'm easy."

And she was. Easy to be with. He broke the bread, observed the flaking crust, the chewy texture. "I haven't had bread like this since I left France."

"Can you describe it?"

"Touché," he said, then added, "On second thought, it's like mother love," knowing that he wasn't much of an expert on that subject, but it sounded right.

He was interested in her, less than she in him, he could see. She kept her eyes on him with the same open childlike innocence that she had given to his work. He liked being with her, liked the silken feel of her hair, her smooth pale skin, even the patchouli and herbal fragrance that surrounded her. In the short time he had been with her, he could see that she made no demands on him other than that he be exactly what he was at any given moment. She was like the bread she baked, solid, substantial, good, elemental: the building block of a life.

This was only the second time he had seen her. He had gone to the bakery where she worked with some daffodils to thank her for helping him out, only to find that she wasn't there. He left the flowers with a card and his phone number. She called the same night and they met for coffee and talked about bread and art, especially ceramic art, both shaped by hand and baked.

He asked and she told him how she had become a baker. After two years at Antioch College, a choice that neither parent had approved of, she took a junior year at the University of Paris in French literature. She came back, fluent in French, but having worked six of the nine months as an apprentice in one of Paris' famous boulangeries, one Harry remembered. Darah had met one of the bakers in a cafe and had an affair with him. So much for French literature. Reading was more enjoyable than teaching or writing about it. Rather than go back to Antioch just to get a degree she had no use for, she came west, spent a year in a commune in Mendocino County raising organic fruits and vegetables and perfecting her bread baking, followed by six months in Tassajarra, the Zen retreat. There she mixed Zen meditation with baking. Finally, she came to Berkeley intending to open a bakery. Her older sister loaned her the money, her parents looked down on the idea and refused to support it. That was a year ago. It was hard work, seven days a week, but she liked it and had already gotten a write-up in the food section of the *Chronicle*.

"What does your father do for a living?" he asked. "Mine was a would-be comedian," he volunteered.

"Guess."

"Stop me when I get it right," and he rattled off twenty jobs ranging from proctologist to window dresser.

"A United States Congressman."

"Hey, fantastic. The closest I've come to a public figure is one time the Mayor of Cleveland shook my hand and gave me an art award."

"When was that?"

"High school. So what's it like to have a celebrity father?"

"Sometimes you feel like one of his constituents, and not one of the heavy contributors." He poured more wine for both of them and she began to talk, at first hesitantly, then in an associative stream. She was animated, moving her head and hands as she spoke, sometimes frowning a little or wrinkling her brow. Words coming in quick images she sketched a mural of an almost unbelievably ideal life in suburban Michigan: private school, Tudor house with three bathrooms, tennis lessons at the club, older sister a prom queen, younger brother a competitive swimmer, her mother's bridge and golf trophies in a case in the rec. room, Chippendale in the dining room, French provincial in the living room, Pendleton in the closet, all the celebrations, the birthdays, Christmas with the grandparents—a Norman Rockwell painting—her father, everybody's nice guy, but always too busy making something of himself. She told him, with pain in her voice, about the times he had apologized for not being able to be with her; a piano recital, even high school graduation—he had been held up in Washington for an important vote. As for her mother, she had been too involved with herself to give more than a sense of how to behave properly, when to write a thank you note.

"Sounds just like my mother," said Harry and he felt connected to her by a common thread and saw the same in her eyes.

They finished dinner, washed the dishes together. Like an old married couple, he mused. He turned on KJAZ, pulled her toward him and they danced, slowly. He liked the way she felt, firm but her flesh was soft as well and they fit together, even where his cheek touched her hair. She yielded into him, wrapped him like a blanket about her, and he felt her gentleness where they touched. The music gave way to talk. They stopped, looked at each other as if asking something. She took her hand away from his then touched his palm lightly with her nails.

"What's that over in the corner?" she asked, pointing at an object that looked like a shiny black ribbed tent. He led her to it. It had an opening, a tube like the entrance to an igloo.

"Want to go inside?"

"Sure."

They got down on hands and knees and crawled through the opening. Inside was ink black. The floor was furry and there were objects placed at random, abstract forms, neither organic nor geometric, shapes to be felt.

"What is it?"

"It's a kind of sculpture. But one you feel rather than see, one that encloses you. Have you ever wanted to get inside of a sculpture?"

"Can't say that I have."

"Well I have. Just be still and listen to it. What do you hear?"

"Billy Holliday."

"I mean inside your head."

"Give me a clue."

"I can't. It's different for everyone. Do you see something in your head I mean?"

"No. Not really."

"Touch things and let your mind wonder about them."

They were silent, listening, touching, first the objects then each other.

December 2, 1967 – Darah's Bread Book

Darah kept a loose-leaf recipe book. The cover was hand-tooled leather worked by a friend at the commune. In it she kept her recipes for bread with personal comments about the character of the dough and her observations on consistency, flavor, and ingredient variations. Between the recipes were observations about the men she had slept with, how she had met them, what impressed her about them, random notes, as telegraphic as the recipes. She wasn't a writer, in fact a poor speller and grammarian. The two subjects, sex and bread, belonged together in Darah's life. They were the two activities she most cared about. Making bread and making sex were both physical acts, nurturing, primary, and sensually gratifying. She had slept with many men before Harry. She was generous, guileless, and lacking in surface inhibition. If she liked a man, not just physically but his character, his spirit, she let things happen. Not that she ever thrust herself on any man, she simply let it be known to him by the way she looked at him or touched him tenderly that she was open to his advances. If he didn't respond that was no tragedy. Darah was pretty and comely. People liked her. If one man passed out of her life, so be it. Another would come along who she might find even more interesting. Harry fit the type of man that attracted her. His assertiveness fit her open passivity as a key might fit a lock. His work was physical, metamorphic, and he loved sex as much as she did. She soon filled up a page about Harry just behind her recipe for Holiday Raisin Challah.

She didn't know where it would go or how it would end. She tried to take every day as it came and make it as fresh as the bread she baked. She made no demands on him. She was there when he wanted to see her. Darah didn't mind that Harry saw other women. He was free to do what he liked as long as he respected her when they were together. She understood him intuitively, understood the sensitivity under the effusive braggadocio. Knew that he was struggling to express ideas and feelings that were timeless and transcendent and that he would only expose his true core in his ambiguous works. And that true core, she believed, was pure and innocent, as pure as the life force that bound everything together. All the baggage he carried, his egocentricity, his occasional rudeness or insensitivity, his dark moods, like the interior of his sculpture was just a protective crust. The real Harry was what radiated from his art.

12/14/67 – Inter-office Memos

To: Harry Baer
From: Norbert Dawe, Acting Chairman, Art Department

As I mentioned yesterday, Harry, several members of the faculty thought we should give you a formal reminder of expected deportment at faculty meetings. True to our nature, we try to be less formal that other departments, considering the demands of personal studio work and the like. Of course we recognize that, as much as any of us, you maintain an arduous and successful program as a creative selling artist and that the recognition you have achieved as an innovator brings honor to our department and even attracts students.

Still, there are others who possibly resent that you assume less than you should or might of the collegial burdens of the faculty. If I may be frank, your attendance at faculty meetings and committee meetings is sporadic. If there is any constant in your performance it is that you arrive late and, more often than not, leave early. At least that is my perception. I'm sure you feel that you have good reasons for doing so. The fact that you never take off your hat, be it your Greek captain's cap, your beret, or your Borsellino, makes some people feel that no sooner have you arrived than you are poised to leave. The fact that your students give you high marks does not relieve you of the humdrum duties of committee work that we all must share equally.

Harry, I must ask you to please try to be more conscientious. Doing so might help motivate others to support the idea of a modest, though thorough, retrospective of your work.

To: Norbert Dawe, Acting Chairman, Visual Art Department
From: Harry Baer
Subj: your 12/14 memo
Dear Norbie:

I got a good laugh out of your memo. I might even put it into a collage, as yet unnamed, dedicated to Brobdinagian humbug. You know damned well that these criticisms don't have anything to do with my merits as a member of the faculty. I see my role satisfied if I teach and inspire students to develop their skills, talents, and vision as artists and to bring some credit to the Department with my own work in the way that some faculty members publish text and footnotes. As for any colleague who criticizes my lack of interest in faculty softball or the like, he is just plain envious. I, for one, gave up masturbation when I took up with women, but masturbation is the name of the game in so much of the faculty goings-on that I had to distance myself in order to feel good about the Department. So let our nameless colleagues who enjoy jerking off the Chancellor

and sitting on scholarship committees do so, if that keeps their tin foil egos intact, and let me just teach and paint. That way we'll cover all the bases. As for my hats, some Jews just like to keep their hat on. Maybe it's regression. Merry Christmas and Happy Easter if I don't talk to you before then.
As always,
Harry

Harry:
You forgot to put gas in the car again. I ran out of gas and was late for work. We need to take the time to get the gas gauge fixed. It's no fun running out of gas at four a. m. If I hadn't bought that can and filled it last week, I'd still be sitting there.
Darah

March 3, 1968 – Letter to Karine

Dear Karine:
Darah and I have rented a place on Bodega Bay, little more than a fisherman's shack, a real fixer-upper. That's an oblique way of saying that I'm involved with another woman, a baker of great bread, steady, calm, childlike in a way, nothing like me and a good influence. She likes to fish and hike. She gets me away from my work. No, she is not Jewish. Yes, she is WASP. A real goy with a capital G—she wouldn't know a blintz from a knish. It's a strange thing, Karine, as much as I live for my work, I can't work without a woman in my life. You figure it out.
Stay well and safe. Don't get in trouble with those racist rednecks. Some advice, as if you'd listen. Truly, I think about you, miss you, know that some way we will again meet. Until then, I remain, your dedicated, cowardly lover,
Harry.

June 3, 1968 – Bolinas

They had taken a picnic and walked the bluff north as far

as they could, Harry, Darah, and Therese. A warm spring day, the sky, pale blue fading to a milky haze on the horizon where the fog still lay, held off by the sun, but waiting to advance and cover the land within the ocean's reach. They ambled along, dipping into or jumping over the deeply notched stream beds still flowing secretively toward the ocean from sources in the hills. The meadows were already fading, it had been more than a month since the last rain, but the flowers were still in bloom.

It was only the second day of Therese's visit. Harry had picked her up at the San Francisco Airport and driven right out to Bolinas with a stop at the studio—she wanted to see it. Therese was still a little shy and formal, testing her English which was simple and rough. For the most part they spoke French.

"What shall I call you?" she asked Harry, "It can't be papa, you know, I call my grandfather by that."

"Just Harry will do."

"I couldn't do that."

"Why not."

"It would be disrespectful."

"It's OK. This is California."

"Are the customs very different here?"

"Very."

"What is different, can you say?"

"Darah, what's different?" She was lolling a little behind looking dreamy and swinging the wicker picnic basket.

"You can't take dogs into restaurants, unless you are blind. And students don't stand up when a teacher comes into the classroom," she answered.

"Oh *mon dieu*," Therese said, laughing at the response and she ran ahead, pigtails dancing, her long legs spindly in the loose dark blue shorts. She stopped suddenly, her eye caught by a white iris. "Harry!" She tested the name. "Look at this! I've never seen one this color before. There are so many."

"They grow wild here."

"What's that flower called over there?"

"A Sticky Monkey Flower, I think. That right Darah?"

"Yes. Mimulus."

"Darah's the expert on flowers."

"Sure I am."

"What a funny name,"said Therese.

"Look closely. Doesn't it look like a monkey?"

"No, not very."

"Good try, Harry," said Darah.

They spread a blanket near the edge of the cliff and Darah unpacked the lunch, foods selected to make Therese feel at home; a pate maison from a new shop run by her friend Gisette who made her own pate and sausages, her own baguette, a Boursan cheese from the Cheese Board Collective, cherries, and a surprise desert that she refused to disclose. Harry supplied a Mondavi fume blanc.

The afternoon breeze off the ocean brought the iodine smell up the cliff to merge with the pollen and grass fragrance of the meadow. Gulls glided on the wind, dove, landed. The water lapped and eddied around the dark glistening rocks. Creamy spindrift and sea plants swayed. Harry saw the luminous contentment on his daughter's face and knew that he had been right to come here first. She was, after all, a child of the countryside and he knew from Natale's letters that Therese loved plants. It was a strange feeling to see this young girl, so polite, animated and bright, to be with her after so many years of knowing her only through a snapshot or from letters, watching only the progress of her handwriting and expression. Again he marveled at her resemblance to the adult Aurora. So much time had passed that the evocation of Aurora in his mind did no more than fill him with a transient nostalgia. As for Therese, he felt kindly toward her but not paternal. At this point in her life there wasn't much that he could identify with other than to be satisfied that she was sound. If having been raised by loving grandparents scarred her, it wasn't apparent. Harry took comfort in the fact that they had given her more love and security than he could or would have. But looking at her made him regret not having been with her as she grew. A child was the ultimate work of art, after all. And now it was too late, he would never have another.

"Is this the first time you have been to the sea, Therese?"

Darah asked, handing her half a ham sandwich.

"I went to Bordeaux once with my class. But it was nothing like this."

"What was different."

"More houses, more people."

"You like the solitude?"

"Yes, very much." She fingered the gold crucifix that dangled on a chain and looked thoughtfully toward the horizon. "Japan is there?" She pointed toward the horizon.

"More or less," said Harry.

"How long would it take to get there?"

"By boat, ten maybe twenty days."

"That's a long way. England takes only a few hours from St. Malo."

After they had eaten, Therese was ecstatic when Darah dramatically unwrapped the *pain au chocolat*. "I baked them specially for you."

"How did you know? They are my favorite!"

"I just guessed." Harry looked at Darah and nodded with approval. He hadn't planned it this way, but he couldn't have found anyone better than Darah to make Therese feel comfortable.

"You'd make a great mom, Darah," he told her later that night after Therese had gone to sleep. They were sitting in front of the grate of the wood stove watching the fire dance, a bottle of cognac between them. The house belonged to a fisherman he had met in a bar: an unpainted board interior, a shed-like kitchen appended to the back and a light filled sun porch with mullioned windows on two sides that faced the Pacific.

"I'm glad you think so, Harry." there was something in the way she said it that put him on alert but he let it pass.

"You are great with kids."

"My mom was a good teacher, by negative example as I've told you before." He rubbed her back, stroked her hair, he liked the silky feel of it. She purred. He stopped. "More," she said. He started again.

"I like this dump a lot," he said after a time. "Even if it is falling apart. We could fix it up; it's got potential. I could even build a studio, a little one."

"You're not thinking of buying it?"

"Why not? I'm forty-three, got the bags under my eyes and the little bit of gray hair to prove it. I'm tenured. The Metropolitan Museum of Art bought one of my pieces last year. Isn't it about time I did something for myself?"

"You? When did you do otherwise? Excuse me, I couldn't resist."

"You sound like Karine. She was always sticking it to me."

"You deserve it, Harry. But it's OK. I love you anyway." She kissed him on the cheek and ran her fingers through his hair. You think Cesar Mendes would sell it to you? It's been in the family so long."

"I think so. I asked him. He can use the money. He'll take $11,000 cash. I think I'll do it." He'd been thinking about it for a year. It would anchor him to a small piece of the land, a hundred feet of bluff that held off the Ocean, a kind of metaphor. He had grown to love the solitude. He looked at Darah. Without her he would never even have considered buying the place. She had somehow made him want to do it without ever saying so. Darah was anything but conventional, but to Harry she represented the closest he would get to a button-down life. Beneath her counter-culture veneer was the dress pattern of a midwestern suburbanite. The practical way she approached the business of baking bread was proof. She was reliable, organized. She had become more than a companion and a lover, she was something of a mate, in the way that Aurora had shared his life, comfortably, with accommodation to his needs.

"You're really going to buy it? That's just great!" She picked up her glass and they touched glasses and drank off the cognac.

"There's a hitch though."

"What? You haven't got the money? Don't look at me, Harry."

"This is a community property state, you know."

"What's that supposed to mean?"

"Married people own everything together."

"What's that to us? We're not married."

"We could be."

"Sure we could be. What are you trying to say, Harry?"

"Just a minute. I'm not sure myself what I'm trying to say." He poured himself another drink and downed it. "This takes courage. Think you could put up with me for the long haul?"

"I do put up with you."

"Listen, I have to tell you. I can guarantee you I'll screw around. Maybe not as much as I used to."

"Lucky for you I spent some time on a commune where the nights were long and there was no TV." He gave her a long agonized look. "Are you proposing or what, Harry? If you are you don't need to. I'm happy just the way we are."

"I think so. Yes. Yes. I am." Harry sounded and looked surprised as if he hadn't expected this. "Will you be Mrs. Baer?"

"No. But I'll be your wife. I like my own name. Unless you want to be Mr. Keswick."

"C'mon!" He put down his glass and rolled on top of her.

August 8, 1968 – In Memoriam

Dear Nell:

Death, even one that has been expected for a long time comes with a shock—especially the death of a parent. I have to confess that many times in my life I wished that Pop had not died so early. And if one of them had to die you know which I would have preferred. And now I confront mother's death, and the remembrance of her cold love, with cold sorrow. I must admit that she prodded me to do the best I could in everything, and that I may owe my obsessive work habits to her. But her guidance had all the nurturing of a Dickensian headmaster. I would have hoped for an easier death for her, than to be knotted and twisted with arthritis. I can see her, twirling on the dance floor, skirt billowing, or carefully putting on makeup in the mirror. What an awful change.

Now that she's dead I regret that she couldn't have shared more of the pleasure that my work has given me. Her reactions seemed so pallid as if she were continually surprised at my good reviews and my sales. I'm glad that I was able to help with the nursing home costs. She seemed to appreciate the money I sent her more than anything. I certainly don't wish for longevity if it comes with a blurred consciousness, constant pain and weakness. I'd rather cash in my chips while I'm ahead in the game. I trust that you and the family are well.

Harry

September 20, 1968 – From Shira's Journal

So there he was all of a sudden, wearing this beret tilted over his brow and a black velvet jacket, a little too big like he'd gotten it from some theatrical costume store and a white shirt with thin pin stripes like a high class pimp, or somebody he wasn't or wanted to be, and with a nod and an imperious smile—no not imperious, charming, no, seductive, in a way but diffident too—he takes the enrollment cards of all twelve of us and announcing the next meeting of the class, away he goes out the door down the hall. Shit! Who does he think he is? I heard about these big universities where the full professor, full of you know what, goes about his business of getting more famous, while some pipsqueak sycophant TA deludes the class, or tries to. Well sometimes they're ok, I would be, I know that.

So I wait just a few seconds, then grab my book bag and head out after him and he's moving quickly so I run to catch up to him shouting as I go, "Hey Mr. Baer, wait a minute," and he hears me and turns and gives me this imperious stare, this time it really is imperious as if to say, who the fuck are you, since maybe he doesn't recognize me from class which is right since he never saw me before in his life, and I say to him, "I thought we had a class scheduled, so where you going?" and with a grin he says, "Right in here," and in he goes to take a pee or something leaving me outside the swinging door like a body guard. At least he's trapped, I think, I can still catch him when he comes out, but he doesn't come out for so long that I figure he's constipated or maybe he's the kind of guy that sits there and dreams up new work on the

can or maybe he forgot his notes for the class which is drain-
ing away or maybe he got away through the window or another door, so I go in where I've never been in my life since
maybe I was a little girl at the Yankee's game with my dad and
it didn't matter. So I stand there gawking at these long porcelain things that go right down to the floor and think, that
sure wouldn't work in the ladies room, when out he comes
from a stall zipping up his fly and he sees me and and he kind
of shakes his head with disgust and says "What are you a
transvestite or something?" "No I'm a girl." "So get the hell
out of here." But of course I don't leave until he does because I still haven't talked to him and he owes me that at
least if he's copping out of the first class. So out in the hall
he heads for the stairs and I follow him right out to his car,
while all the while he's trying to pretend I'm not there but I
am dogging his every step, so close once I even step on his
heel, sorry about that. So finally in front of this ratty white
Chevy he turns, glares at me and says "what do you want from
me?" and I tell him, I came out from New York having passed
up a chance to go to Pratt on a scholarship because I'm very
smart and talented for my age which is 18 last month and
here I am paying $520 of my old man's bundle that I've got to
give him back—after all what does a barber in the Bronx
make—and he interrupts me with, "So my father was a presser,
you know what he made?" and I say, I don't give a fuck what
your father made, and he rolls his eyes and tells me, something like 85 cents an hour, and I say that's not the issue and
he says what is the issue, laughing a little for the first time at
the absurdity of this conversation. He's got his hand on the
door of this ratty Chevy and I say, I can't believe you'd drive a
car like that, you a world famous artist, and he says a little
calmer now, clearly interested, what should I drive? and I tell
him, at least a TR-3, British racing green or something like
that and he laughs again and says, on a professor's pay? so
what do you spend your money on and he gets a little pissed
and says that's none of your fucking business and for that
matter where did you get those wacky glasses with the points
and the fake diamonds, you look like an emaciated Mae West,
so I say, well at least you took some notice.

So with that we both shut up and I see he's looking at me with different eyes, maybe he thinks I'm interesting because of my quick wit and confrontational manner, I had just read Saul Alinsky. Then he pats me on the head and says, So tune in tomorrow and I figure I've said enough and I let him get into his crappy car which doesn't start right away and farts a lot of smoke in my face when it finally goes and I watch him thinking I've been had. But later I changed my mind.

December 20, 1968 – Alida

He sat in the waiting room thinking how different it was from the last time. He had been in the studio working when Darah's water broke. She was washing dishes. The suitcase with her things was all packed. It took 20 minutes to get to Kaiser Hospital, running two stop signs. She was having irregular contractions, but she was in good spirits, not afraid, even joking about how good it would be to lose all that weight, to have sex again, to not have to run to the bathroom because the baby was standing on her bladder, to stop drinking all of that water because her kidneys were a little strained and she had swollen ankles. She wasn't worried; the women in her family never had complications, although Harry had heard that once before.

He smoked another cigarette. The waiting room was saturated with smoke. There were two other fathers waiting, both much younger than he; a black man wearing a tee shirt and tight jeans and an Asian with a nervous tic on the side of his cheek. How many fathers had smoked how many cigarettes wondering about the child's sex and if it would be a healthy baby or if they would have to cut it out of her or use the forceps and make a dent in the kid's head, and who it would look like? Harry was forty-three, almost too old for this. But it would keep him young. Darah would stay home for at least six months. She had two younger bakers working with her. She could go in while the baby was sleeping or even take him or her along. Harry was looking forward to it in a way. He would have the experience that he had not had with Therese. He thought of the song from the musical, *Carousel*. Darah wanted a girl. He didn't care, but was hoping for a boy. He looked at the clock. It had been three hours now. Harry went to the coffee machine, put a dime in and got a paper cup full of sludge. He sat down and began to sketch the other would-be fathers. The black man noticed and complimented the work. He gave them each a sketch, signed and dated, and they began to talk about their families, how long they had been married, how many children they had, what kind of work they did. Learning that he was an artist the two men promised to frame the sketches.

"Are you famous?" asked the Asian.

"Depends on what you mean by fame."

"Like the painter who went to Tahiti."

"'Fraid not."

"Mr. Baer?" he flinched with momentary anxiety until he saw the smile. "You've got a healthy girl, congratulations. Come with me."

With a tweaking in his nose and tears coming to his eyes he got up and grinned at the two other men. The man in the tee shirt gave him the thumbs up sign.

"Whom do you want to see first?" the nurse asked turning to look at him.

"Surprise me."

He followed her to a window. Inside the room a nurse, wearing a surgical mask, pointed to his daughter: a round, red face with loose folded flesh wrinkled into a frown, the right hand bunched into a fist. Harry blinked back the tears, blew his nose and tried to make light of his reaction. He knew the feeling. Not so much love as pride and wonder at the outcome of creation. He had felt much the same, stepping back to take in a just completed sculpture.

Darah looked weary but self-satisfied. Her face was ruddy, her eyes puffy, her hair damp with sweat. She gave his hand a squeeze and he bent over and kissed her on the lips.

"Don't start up," she managed to joke.

"I'll wait till you get home."

"So, what do you think?"

"Looks like an advanced alcoholic sleeping it off, or maybe my high school English teacher."

"Not the one you did the cartoon of?"

"Just kidding. What shall we call her?" They hadn't gotten around to talking about names. Darah was superstitious. Harry had assigned her a catalogue number, 68-13.

She looked at him tentatively. "I like Alida. It was my grandmother's name."

"Alida." he repeated. "It fits."

April 20, 1969 – A Dog Named Franz

On his way to the Med after class, Harry detoured to witness the "liberation" of the square block off Telegraph Avenue that the impromptu coalition of runaways, drug users, back to the land proponents, and on-and-off campus radicals had begun to call People's Park. Intended for student housing, bulldozed clean of its houses, the derelict field abutting the back end of Telegraph Avenue shops had become a hang out for drug addicts and a laissez fair parking lot. Somebody, Harry didn't know who, had gotten the idea that it should be turned into a public park with grass, trees, and playground equipment. The idea had caught on and was being implemented with contributions of equipment and plants, by a latter day Coxey's Army, with shovels and picks.

Fifty or so people were chopping at the soil in one corner. Another group was rolling out sod. Others were sitting cross-legged in a circle having a discussion. Rock music was blaring from a portable radio. He looked toward an area where four picnic benches had been installed, saw Jonah Robb and strolled over to speak with him. His long blond hair was tied back in a ponytail, he was sprawled back against the tabletop, wearing faded jeans and a work shirt embroidered with Navaho abstractions in red white and yellow. A thick sandwich of seven grain bread, cheese and sprouts was in one hand like a harmonica and the remains of a joint on the end of a paper clip was suspended delicately between thumb and forefinger of the other.

"Hey, Harry, grab a shovel."

"No, I just came over to say hello. I haven't seen you in a while."

Jonah acknowledged with a blink, covering his tired blood-shot blue eyes, and he processed the words before answering in his drawling way. "Yeah, I got myself involved in this. It's kind of a turn on to see what people can do to change things."

"People power. Isn't that the slogan?"

A man walked up to them. He wore a long untrimmed beard that came to a point on his bib overalls. Harry assumed he was a back to the land type down from Humboldt County to sell his crop of marijuana. He was carrying a squirming black white and brown longhaired, long nosed puppy in his arms.

"Excuse me, but I've got a puppy I want to get rid of, pure bred Collie."

"Harry, you could use a dog. Keep your kid happy."

Harry looked at the dog, petted him or tried to. The dog kept nipping and licking his hand. He had never had a dog, certainly not growing up in an apartment, but he had always wanted one. Now that they had the place in the country a dog would be fun to have. He could take it for long walks on the bluffs, and it would be a good companion for Alida, even at home. Darah liked dogs. He took the puppy, cradled it in his arms, it stretched up and licked him across the lips.

"Affectionate."

"The mother's real gentle, good with kids."

"What do you want for him or her?"

"Him. Nothing. Just a good home. I'm on my way back to Sebastopol. We've got more dogs than we can feed."

"No that wouldn't be right," Harry said and he fished into his pocket and pulled out five dollars."

The man took it with a grateful smile. "The dog'll need shots."

"Hey, how about that, Harry. Go with the flow."

Harry nodded, stroked the squirming puppy, feeling a wet spot on his silk shirt. "You could say that. Well, I better get this mutt home."

"See you around, Harry."

He walked away looking down at the dog who was trying to lick his chin. The slippery wet caress sent a strangely sensual current through him. What are we going to call you? I hope you don't have fleas. He recalled a sketch Franz Marc had done—one of the last one's in the book—of a sad collie standing with its head down on what might have been a battle-field.

"We'll call you Franz," he said and the dog seemed to like that, for he nuzzled the palm of Harry's hand with his cold wet nose.

May 14, 1969 – People's Park

Harry had stopped at the Med for a cappuccino an hour before class. Spontaneity in the process of creation, was the topic shown in the course syllabus. Better practiced than preached, he thought, penciling that phrase along with associated random thoughts on a napkin. After a few minutes, having noted ten or so comments that had come to mind, he left off.

The Med was high-ceilinged and had a buttery yellow smoky atmosphere from the walls and overhead lights. Harry was sitting against the wall a few tables back with a hazy view of Telegraph. Outside were more than a few police loitering in pairs, looking for something or talking. Someone had told him that the University had erected a wire mesh fence around People's Park.

He had just bought a used treatise on chemistry at Moe's— he loved to browse in the upper floors, often buying used books on any subject that aroused his interest. He was hoping to find some process that might be useful in casting and shaping sculpture. He found a section on pigmentation and iridescence. The feathers of a peacock came to mind, and he began to speculate on how internal iridescence could be created in a sculpture. Another chapter dealt with polymers, atoms of oxygen and silicon. Harry looked up for a moment, distracted by a growing clamor on the street, then returned to his reading. Halide of organic silicon compounds could be made in many forms, even rubber like substances, he read. He gazed out the window at a passing crowd, not really seeing it, his mind still glowing with the possibility of using soft silicon in sculpture.

"The Blue Meanies," he heard someone say, and he looked

up again, now registering the flood of people filling Telegraph's two lanes and sidewalk. He could see heads, bare and covered, and signs on sticks bobbing overhead. It came to him that he could synthesize the two processes he'd been reading about, make sculpture out of silicon, soft and hard, and impregnate it with luminous, even iridescent, color. So far as he knew, he would be the first to do it and a ripple of anticipation went through him. For the first time he looked at his watch and realized that he had about five minutes to get to his seminar.

The cacophony of voices congealed into a rhythmic chant, "Take back the park, take back the park, take back the park!" He remembered the planned rally on campus and chastised himself for going to Telegraph at all until he considered his luck in finding the chemistry book.

He got up and went to the window. The crowd had stopped moving, blocked by a shoulder to shoulder line of Alameda County Sheriffs in blue jump suits and white helmets, carrying shot guns or long wooden clubs. The chant pulsed on like the drone of a bagpipe. Harry wondered how he could transpose the essence of it into visual or tactile form. How could he abstract anger, frustration, and rebellion? He began to focus on individuals in the crowd: excited and determined students fresh from the rally on the campus dressed in khaki and plaid, some just enjoying the experience, long hairs, short beards, sun glasses, some weathered faces, a man carrying a child about two on his shoulders. All this fuss over a parking lot. War images, his war, flashed in his head like a fast run newsreel: machine gun bullets patterning the stucco of a house, screaming bombs falling from diving black Stukas, the menace of the long barrel of a gun on the turret of a Tiger tank slowly rotating toward him, and small gray-green figures silently advancing across the frozen stubble of a field. Now there was this confrontation so stupid and unnecessary when contrasted with the tidal wave of altruistic commitment that had swept up everyone he knew in that remote time of his life. Yes, there was another War now, but getting your head beaten in over a liberated parking lot seemed to be an absurd way to oppose it. Maybe he was just out of touch, too wrapped up in his own life. If he were nineteen again would he be out there on the street? he wondered.

He looked at his watch again. If he didn't leave now his students wouldn't even wait, not that he was Mister-On-Time. He put his new book into his book bag, and left through the back door, turning over the exciting notion that sculpture molded with silicon gel might be made to look and feel like living flesh.

Creativity

Harry took off his Greek captain's cap and put it on the table bottom up. His notes for the class were inside, not a lecture, not even sentences. Just the phrases he had jotted down and a few references he wanted to quote from memory.

"Creativity," he pronounced, looking meaningfully at the eight students seated around the table, noting the range of attitudes from indifference to obsessive attentiveness. "Can anyone define it?"

"Change, affirmative change as opposed to degradation," said Enid Marks, nodding her curly head in affirmation.

"But can't degradation be creative? Can't even garbage be creative?"

"Depends on how you arrange it," said Pete Stickney, the class smart-ass.

"Coincidentally, Pete that's on the mark. About the only element that applies to all creation is change. Who can impose any judgement on it, although of course we all do, all the time, observers, participants, artists, critics, as a society, as an era. All it means in Latin—you expected me to say from Hebrew?"

"Not me, Harry, I'm Catholic," said Pete.

"All it means is to make. You take dirt, you heat it, you make a pot or something out of metal. So, is self-expression essential to creativity? Anybody."

"Sure, from the standpoint of the artist it's the essence of it." said Nikki Rush.

"How about spontaneity?"

"Depends on what you want to get out of the work."

"Is there any such thing as spontaneity? Or is the design

built into the soul of the artist, not before birth, but over the artist's life time?" Harry was having a good time and so was the group—he could see it. He was just warming up and he had no idea where the discussion would lead. Occasionally they would all end up at a studio and he would put himself into high gear and do something, a drawing, a clay sculpture in a matter of minutes. Then they would analyze it on the spot.

The door opened and Shira came in, a red swollen bruise on her temple, her black hair tangled, her long sleeved black blouse torn at the shoulder. She slumped into a chair and looked at him with a mixture of pain and indignation.

"What happened to you?" he asked.

"A fucking police riot, is all. The demonstration over the fencing of People's Park turned into a march and smacked right into a wall of the Blue Meanies. They were blocking Telegraph with clubs and shotguns, just waiting. Some insults, a few rocks and beer bottles were tossed at the fuzz." She stopped speaking and he saw the memory of it written on her face. The students all were watching her. No one spoke. Harry could feel the attention.

Shira shook her head in negation of some thought then she began again, looking only at Harry. "The cops fired their shot guns right into the crowd, like a Coney Island shooting gallery, only we were the ducks." Her voice grew shrill. "People were falling, screaming, there was blood, people stepping on each other to get out of there and the cops chasing after people, beating them to the ground with their clubs, even when they were just lying there, and dragging them away." She turned her palms up and shrugged her shoulders. "What had we done? I got slammed with a club, which stunned me but pissed me off, so I turned on the son of a bitch and kneed him in the balls. You should have seen his face; it was the one laugh of the hour. He kind of seized up and groaned like the pig he was, then reached for me and got my shirtsleeve. I ran like a halfback and he lost me or beat somebody else instead, I didn't look back. Sorry I'm late for class, Harry." She looked up at him, tears of rage streaming from her eyes.

"Listen, maybe you should go to the infirmary, Shira. You

might have a concussion or something."

"No, just a little head ache. He didn't get me square and I didn't pass out. I wasn't even dizzy—not much—or I wouldn't have been able to get back at him."

Everyone started talking, congratulating her, asking her questions, berating the administration, the Governor, the sheriff, the crypto-fascists, the rise of the police state.

Harry went around the table, touched the swelling on her forehead. She winced but pulled away from him angrily, "Get away, it's nothing!"

"I'll get you a couple of aspirin and some water, at least."

"A joint would be better."

"Anybody got a joint?" he asked the class.

"In here?" said Rhonda Wells.

"Seems like the fuzz have got their bird brains fixated on something else right now," said another.

Rhonda pulled a tin box out of her book bag and rolled a joint. She lit it and passed it across the table to Shira, who took a long pull, held her breath then let the smoke slowly out of her nostrils. She passed it around and they each had a hit. The anger and tension dissolved in the smoke and became sullen indifference.

They looked at Harry, expecting him to say something that would define the moment. "We need to put what happened out there on the street, what happened to Shira, away and use it. In fact, I'm going to give an assignment. Next week I want each of you to bring something with you that relates to what the police have done. And I want you to limit the time you take to finish it to 15, maybe 20 minutes, tops. And I want not more than five sentences written about it. I'll do the same. As for Shira, she's excused. She's already completed the assignment."

"What? What did I do?"

"You kicked the cop in the balls." His voice disappeared in the roaring pulsing stutter of a helicopter flying low over the campus.

"What next? Napalm?" said Steve Wells.

"Come on, Shira, I'll drive you home," said Harry and she looked up at him through the armor of her anger and he thought he saw a hurt child grateful for his concern.

Wake Up Call

Harry had just moved the studio to a warehouse on the Oakland estuary. It was a much bigger space and a lot cheaper than the one in Berkeley. Rents for commercial space had been going up. The studio was still chaotic and probably always would be, given Harry's propensity to collect any object, large or small, which interested him. The place was spooky at night; the manufacturers that had once occupied the area were gone. Darah hadn't been very enthusiastic over the location. But Harry was there most of the time and Franz, when sufficiently aroused, had a loud and menacing bark. On the plus side there were always boats to look at—sailboats and freighters from all over the world, not to mention the planes always taking off and landing at the Naval Air Station on Alameda Island.

He came through the door and Franz scrambled to his feet, rushed toward him, and repeatedly jumped and climbed up his leg, tongue extended, trying to lick his face. He bent down and rubbed his ears, turning away as the smooth wet tongue caught his lips and nose. "Hi ya, Franzie,"

Darah was in the kitchen, a long and thin space just outfitted with a six burner restaurant stove, double stainless steel commercial sink, and lively Mexican tile set by Jonah Robb. The smell of veal stew came to meet him. He gave Darah a kiss and a hug, looked around for an open bottle of zinfandel and poured them each a glass, using the new heavy blue Mexican goblets.

"You know what happened on the campus today?"

"I saw it on the tube. It's awful. Jonah Robb was shot in the leg. He called. He's at Alta Bates. He's not the only one. One guy might die."

"Does he need anything?"

"He'll probably need somebody to pay the bill."

"We can do that if we have to. How's Ali."

"Fine. Seems to like the play pen."

"What next."

They went out the back and sat on the edge of the water in the twilight. The fog was tinted a rare blue and contrasted with the pewter indigo shade of the channel. Harry made a mental note of the hues. Up the estuary on the Alameda side a high-sided ship was loading cargo. Trucks and jeeps were being driven up a ramp into its center. A deck crane was swinging brown containers from the pier to the hold. Yellow floodlights were growing stronger as the sky darkened making the activity around the ship look like a stage set.

"You know, Darah, when I came home from Europe after the War, I thought, naively, it would be the last time I saw men in khaki going off to be killed. I guess I didn't have much vision. I thought what I had seen was so awful that no country would repeat it. Then we had Korea and before that Greece, and then the Bomb. And now we've got Viet Nam and the National Guard in Berkeley. Have you ever read Bergson?"

"No."

"He's a philosopher who says things generally get better if you take the long view."

"They might," Darah said, sounding unsure and watching the loading ship, a somber look on her face.

"Yeah. Maybe."

"You want to do something tonight? We could go to a movie and take Ali along."

"You know what I want to do?" asked Harry putting his arm around her waist

"What?"

"Eat dinner, finish this bottle of wine and get in bed with you."

"I like that."

April 20, 1970 – Seduction of Sorts

Shira: "Why not?"

Harry: "Just because."

S: "Tell me why. There has to be a reason."

H: "I don't have to tell you anything. I just won't!"

S: "Harry you would fuck a dog in heat, so what's wrong with me?"

H: "Nothing's wrong with you. You're great. You're brilliant. You've got talent. You're probably terrific in bed. But I'm not the one."

S: "Why?"

H: "I'm married."

S: "That never stopped you before."

H: "I'm older now. I'm a father. "

S: "I like older men."

H: "The home for the aged is in Oakland, Shira. Shira, get off my back! We have a nice relationship, you and me. I enjoy your company, you're funny, creative, original, stimulating. What are you doing? Don't touch me that way."

S: "Harry, just try me. I'm good."

H: "Look, Shira, maybe I'm old fashioned but I'm not used to being propositioned, except by a whore."

S: "So? You're an innovator. You can change."

H: "I enjoyed the chase, Shira. Even if I wanted you, you've taken all the thrill out of it. I probably wouldn't even get a hard on."

S: "You don't know me, Harry."

H: "Anyhow, I'm not supposed to sleep with my students. If you turned on me they'd kick me off the faculty. Stop laughing. I'm serious."

S: "So what are we going to do?"

H: "I know what I'm going to do. Put your skirt down! I know you've got great legs. I'm going home to Darah and Alida. And you, go find yourself an undergraduate, some hunk, or some potential summa cum whatever. And in the meantime, get on with my curriculum *raisone* for which you are handsomely paid in my gratitude."

S: "Harry, you are full of shit."

H: "So are we all. It's the human condition. See you tomorrow."

July 9 1974 – Tide Pooling

"I'm taking Ali down to the water, Darah. We'll be back for lunch. She's been noodging me for an hour." Harry was sitting near the front window of the Bolinas house in a bleached and seamed rocking chair he had rescued from disintegration at an Alameda flea market. He was going over the long list of pieces prepared by Shira that were being considered for the retrospective of his work. "Did you check the tide chart?"

"Low tide was about two hours ago. We'll be fine. Come on Ali, have you got your sneakers on?"

"Yep, I have." He looked down at her and saw his own large brown eyes, honest, direct, eager, set in a pudgy version of Darah's face, fair skin and fine cornsilk hair trailing over the rounded forehead. She was wearing apple red denim shorts and a tee shirt emblazoned with the self-confident head of Mickey Mouse and showing signs of the strawberry jam she'd smeared on her toast. She would be a beauty some day, he thought, and a real heartbreaker.

Franz watched him prepare to leave, looking hopeful, his pointed ears forward. He rose with a scratching of claws on the floor and went to the door. A full -sized collie with a tan saddle, Franz was very calm and gentle with Alida. Harry picked up the clipboard with the catalogue of pieces. The idea of the retrospective sent a thrill down his back. He recalled the bitter disappointment he'd felt at the hands of critics who had, often as not, ignored, misunderstood, dismissed, or trashed his work. But a retrospective was above criticism. It was a level of recognition that couldn't ever be taken away— the high water mark of his career, so far at least. Beginning in San Francisco, it would travel to Los Angeles, Youngstown, Minneapolis, and Syracuse, finishing at the Whitney Museum of American Art. About 100 of his works from every period would be included: prints, bronze sculptures, one of the ceramic walls, an interior, the vacuform sculptures, even the newest work, the silicon sculpture.

Elgin Cooley's persistence had made it happen. Abrams had published his book on the art of Franz Marc. Two drawings from the sketchbook were included. Insured for $100,000, the sketchbook was Harry's little nest egg. In pushing the retrospective, Elgin was, in a way, paying a debt. The notebook reference in his dissertation had, as much as anything, been a catalyst in Elgin's career, a key to its publication. As Chairman of the Art History Department at San Francisco State University and a member of the Board of the Oakland Museum, he had some influence and he had used it. Elgin was in fact at work on the monograph for the catalogue. Harry thought back on the time he had literally run into Elgin in the cross walk and later tossed Elgin's father's fishing rod into the Bay. Serendipity. Symbiosis. Give and take. An artist works alone, but not in a vacuum.

He took Ali's hand. It was like the touch of a loving woman only different. It evoked in him the bond of blood, the complex sense of duty and protection of a parent and the trust that she returned. She believed in him, never doubted him, unless what he wanted didn't suit her at the moment.

"Got your bucket?"

"Yes."

"Remember your job. What are you going to look for?"

"Sand dollars and little rocks with pretty colors."

"Good."

Franz hurled out the door, barked impatiently, and began to circle and herd them through the dry grass toward the cliff edge, looking up with vigilance and sniffing the wind.

"Can I ride on Franz?"

"No, Franz is too busy now."

Darah came to the door and shouted, "Don't forget lunch."

The path down the cliff was buttressed in the steepest places with weathered boards held upright with lengths of steel pipe or rusted rebar driven into the soft sandstone. It led to a small cove, no more than a crescent of blue-gray water-washed pebbles wedged in a dent in the cliff, protected on one side by a scored finger of basalt. Dark, shiny, pocked, and bearded with a stubble of red and pale green plants, the rocks and the stone beach were under water at high tide. At low tide the ridges in the rocks became pools teeming with plant and animal life. At its edge, waves crested, exploded in a spray, and were sucked back in a perpetual noisy stand off, the water assaulting the battered buttress of rock. Below these rocks, among the undulating gray-green-red leafed water garden, Harry sometimes caught snapper or sea bass.

He carefully descended the path behind Franz keeping a tight grip on Ali's shoulder. She was very independent and insisted on going down on her own, even though some of the steps were half her size and she had to sit down and ease herself onto the next one.

The sky was covered by a high mucous gray overcast and the

surface of the water was opaque and milky. Except where it broke and curled against the rocks, the ocean's skin was serrated like rows of saw teeth. He listened to the steady hiss and sigh of the water. "Maybe we'll see a seal today, Ali, would you like that?"

"Yesss!"

They reached the bottom, he dropped the clipboard on the pebbles where the air had dried them, and they went slowly over the weathered and pocked slab of rock toward the largest tide pool. Open at both ends but deep in the center, the trough surged with water that kept strands of sea grass dancing. They stood watching a pale pink star fish inch forward, tiny red crabs, the spikes of the inky blue black urchins, and the pale green almost iridescent flower of the sea anemones. Ali bent over and touched one with her finger and gave a cry of delight as it closed. Harry fished out a hermit crab which retreated into the shell that it carried and lived in. Franz studied the water's movement, lost interest and went ranging over the rock surface sniffing at everything in his path.

After a time, they went back to the beach and Harry, his back propped against a bleached log, began to review the list, occasionally crossing off pieces. Ali scavenged the beach for interesting shapes of driftwood, shells and pebbles, each of which she brought back to him for inspection and approval. Franz ran around, found a piece of drift wood that was too big to handle, dropped it in favor of one that fit his mouth and brought it to Harry. He dropped it at Harry's feet and waited, tongue lolling, eyes on the stick, until Harry found the time to toss it toward the water. Fetching sticks and balls was the first thing Harry had taught him, possibly the only thing. Harry thought that it was demeaning to an animal to teach it tricks. Franz was not much good at catching a stick. He was better with a tennis ball, and having been hit on the head a couple of times, he let it drop before grasping it in his long jaws, manipulating it to get a good purchase, and prancing back for another round. Eventually, Franz got bored, left the stick where it lay, stretched Sphinx-like, his head on his forepaws and went to sleep.

After twelve, the sun began to melt its way through the overcast, a pale limpid sphere, drawing blue and green out of the depths of the ocean which was by now sneaking up the crescent of beach for another assault on the cliff.

Time for lunch. Darah would be impatient. Harry got up, feeling heavy, and walked toward the path. Ali gave him her hand. Hearing the clatter of rocks, Franz roused himself and followed. Ali went first so that he could catch her if she slipped. She moved slowly, putting her bucket half full of pebbles and shells on the shelf, then scrambling over the step. Half way up, the bucket turned over and most of the rocks spilled down the edge and rolled to the bottom.

"My stones and shells!" she wailed.

"It's OK, Ali, I'll help you up to the top then I'll go back and get the ones I can find."

She looked at him with a pout. "Find the red one and the round black one and the sand dollar, Dad," she ordered.

He helped her to the top, watched as she skipped across the bluff toward the house and went down again. Franz looked from one to the other, not sure who to follow before deciding to stay with Harry. It must have been ten minutes of bending, studying the pebbles before he saw one the color of blood and near by, a perfect sand dollar. As he stood up he felt dizzy and short of breath but assumed it was from bending over.

He started up the steps. His legs felt like lead. He began to sweat. He sat down on the edge of one of the steps thinking that he must be catching the flu. He got up, climbed two more steps and was out of breath again. His lungs felt as if they were being squeezed in a vice. His chest had turned to stone and a sharp, shrill pain cut through it, as though some muscle had ripped. His heart was beating fast, fluttering like a bird caught in someone's hand. Don't panic. He stopped again, afraid to breathe or even move. No better. He had to get to the top of the cliff and get help, but the effort was like lifting a boulder. He had to go slowly, conserve the little strength he had. He began to pull himself up but his reserve of strength left him and he collapsed, straddling the path, gasping for air. Franz got ahead of him, looked down and nudged Harry's cheek with his wet nose.

"Go get Darah, Franz," he said and he gestured with his arm up the cliff, "Fetch Darah." The dog looked at him, watched the direction of his arm and followed it. Harry looked at him pleading with his eyes and mind. "Fetch Darah," he said again. Franz seemed to understand. He scrambled up the path and disappeared over the edge. Harry went limp, tried to breathe slowly, and began to climb up on all fours resting after each motion. He was nearly at the top when Darah came rushing down to him.

"What's wrong? Did you fall?" She bent over him, took him by the shoulders and began to pull him up.

"It's my heart." He hardly had the strength to speak.

"Does it hurt?"

"Yes. Listen, just go and call the Fire Department or somebody."

"I can't just leave you here!"

"You've got to." She hesitated, torn between running for help and doing what she could for him. "Go on!"

He watched her scramble up the steps and tried to remain still. Breathe as little as possible, look up at the wide wings of a hawk soaring above him and isolate the pain, he told himself. But the pain, sharp, pulsing, searing, wouldn't let him forget it. It traveled through him, cut through the muscles of his back, filled his consciousness like red dye poured into water. Nausea rose up in him and he turned his head aside and vomited.

Darah came back. He opened his eyes and saw her bending over him touching his forehead. "They're on the way," she said.

"Daddy!" Ali took his hand as if to comfort him and looked at him wide-eyed and afraid.

"It's going to be OK, Ali," he managed to say. "I found your red pebble."

Notes From Harry's Chart

Angina, Myocardial infarction, coronary insufficiency, intermittent fibrillation, semi vertical heart, EKG T wave inversion, abnormal. 128/82, Pulse 82, Demerol, Atromids. Feld.

July 15, 1974 – Recovery

Harry was propped up in the hospital bed feeling lousy.

His limbs were lead and they had given him something that made him sleep a lot of the time. The first time he had seen himself in a mirror he'd turned away. He looked older, gaunt, pale as skim milk, puffy dark circles under his eyes, skid-row stubble on his hollow cheeks. And more gray hair? Even so, he was lucky to be looking at himself at all. The bullet had missed this time. He should have been happy, and he made light of it to Darah, played the clown to Ali, flirted with the nurses. But at night before he slept, foreboding pressed a heavy hand against his chest, a sense that most of his life was behind him and what lay ahead could be as flavorless as a hospital meal. At times he was angry. He was at the peak of his creativity and just now beginning to enjoy the fruits of recognition. He would challenge it, defy it, live his life without compromise even if it left him with no more than a few years. He would try to escape the moods by drawing them out. He'd been drawing since he could sit up, depicting uncertainty, fear, steps that led nowhere; delicate abstractions, transient as a plucked wild-flower. It was restorative, better than any medicine. He thought of Franz Marc, drawing his sketches in some hole in the ground and compared his own work to the familiar drawings in the sketchbook.

The bad news was that his heart muscle was badly damaged. Circulation would never be fully restored. He would have to take care of himself, Doctor Feld, the "heart man" told him. No coffee, no cigarettes, and exercise to strengthen the good part of his heart. It had happened once and it could happen again, worse than the first time, even fatal. The good news was that it was a warning to him to mend his ways, take better care of himself, sleep regular hours, eat the right foods. And if he treated himself right he could live a long complete life. Doctor Feld didn't look too healthy himself, Harry thought, with his pasty, folded fleshy face, thin dry hair, and tired, kindly eyes.

He was drawing on an envelope—something, he wasn't sure what. Shira burst in the door and hovered over him looking like a sister, or a guard dog, concerned, protective, bossy. She had come every day, even the first days when he didn't feel like talking and had little more than a pallid smile and a reassuring squeeze of the hand for everyone.

"I brought you an iris, Harry, something to inspire you. And here are the pens you wanted from your studio at school," Shira fished everything out of her deep Guatemalan book bag, threw her faded blue jeans jacket across the foot of his bed, and sat down.

"How about a coloring book."

"Fuck you, Harry."

"I thought we'd been through that."

A wolfish grin spread her deep red lips.

Dr. Feld, came in. He acknowledged Shira without looking at her, took Harry's pulse, listened to his heart with his stethoscope, nodded. She crossed her long legs, longer looking in their tight jeans, and gazed up at Dr. Feld, theatrical seduction flashing out of her lined eyes. He nodded, a benign acknowledgement on his pale face, patted Harry on the shoulder, and muttered, "Better, better." With that pronouncement, he removed his stethoscope and turned to go.

"Wait, Doctor Feld. When do I get paroled?"

"Soon," he said, already half out the door.

"Listen, Shira, you want to really do something for me? You're from New York, you'll understand."

"What?"

"I crave a corned beef sandwich on rye with a new pickle, which is weird because I hardly ever eat it. What is it regression brought on by illness?"

"Sorry, Harry. You just can't get it out here. What should I do, call my father and have him ship it out?"

"At least Darah has been bringing me fresh baguette."

"You're on the mend, I can tell. You've got some color on your cheeks. That first day you looked like a stiff."

"You say the nicest things."

"And those silk pajamas. Makes me want to crawl in beside you." She smirked.

"Shira, what's going on with the catalogue?"

"I'm not supposed to bother you with that. Everything's copasetic. Elgin's almost done with the first draft of his monograph and the committee's selecting the work,"

"Wait a minute!"

"You'll have a final say so, but remember this is a curated exhibit."

"Yeah, but I don't want them to treat me like I'm not around."

"Nobody could do that. Isn't there somebody to put this flower in water?" She picked it up, brandished it, then put it back down on his bed table scanning all the items around it, the paper cups, the carafe of water, the stack of paper backs. She picked up *Angle of Repose*, riffled the pages. "Have you read this?" She didn't wait for an answer. "So what have you got there, you pack rat," she added, looking at his little collection of gauze, Band-Aids and a suture, "What next, an enema bag, or an appendix? Well, they go with your silicon pieces."

"I've been doing little sketches, just to pass the time."

"Harry, take a break. You work all the time."

"Thanks for the good thoughts, Shira, really. But I can't stop, not as long as I can hold a pen. It defines me."

"But you need to rest."

"Don't worry they won't let me on the track."

She looked at her watch, swept her jacket off the bed, slung it over her shoulder. "Gotta go. What more can I do for you?"

"If the corned beef is out, how about a pack of Camels?"

"Somebody else can be your executioner. It's not my job."

"So go, go, don't let me keep you. But, Shira,"

"Yeah?" She looked over her shoulder.

"Thanks for caring."

"Don't get sentimental on me, Harry."

August 10, 1974 – The myth of Narcissus retold

"Are you going to die, Daddy?" Her eyes were solemn and she had that earnest mature expression that was both incongruous and painful when seen on a child's face.

"What makes you ask that?"

"Mommy thought you were dead on the beach."

"Well she was wrong. But everybody dies sometime."

"Then do they come back like you did?" she asked as if convincing herself.

"Not as themselves, they don't."

"As what?, Dad."

"Remember I told that story about the handsome young boy named Narcissus. Remember the first time you saw the flower and asked what it was called?"

"Tell me again."

"The boy was so beautiful to everyone and in his own eyes that he couldn't love anyone else. All the love he had he turned on himself. So a goddess named Echo—"

"Echo?"

"Yes, Echo. She got mad because he wouldn't love her. So she turned him into a flower. One that was as beautiful as he was."

"Which one?"

"One with six petals, like a star and in the center what looks like a little horn. It's sort of a small version of a daffo-dil. And he comes back over and over again every spring"

"You won't turn into something when you die, Dad."

"I don't have to. I've already become something else."

"What!" She had a gleam of excitement in her eyes like a child about to open a present.

"Well for one thing, you."

"Me!" she exclaimed.

"I'm a part of you. And I'm also a part of every piece of art I've ever made. So when you look at something I've shaped out of clay, or silicon, and turned into something else, it was my thoughts and my energy that went into it. And what I put into it stays there forever."

Her eyes widened as if she had seen something for the first time, something wondrous, like the first daffodil that opens out of its green sheath and stretches its limbs and looks up at the sun.

"Alida, why don't you draw me a picture of that little flower from your memory."

"OK." She gave him a lugubrious kiss on the lips and went off on her mission.

Harry sunk back into his pillow. He was feeling rotten, too damned weak. It was hard to pick up a glass of water. He didn't know when he would die but at the moment it seemed like it would be sooner rather than later. He thought of Narcissus, of the concept of metamorphosis, the exchange and transformation of energy from one form to another. Wood combusts with hydrogen and oxygen and turns into evanescent heat and light or by way of a less spectacular transformation is broken down and eaten by microscopic creatures until it turns into soil, a nursery for a seed that ultimately becomes wood if it isn't eaten by a deer before it grows up. Between the two he would rather be the comforting heat and changing dancing light and smoke. Short and spectacular. Something to talk about, admire, an immediate if transient comfort.

He picked up a block of soft silica, the color of amber. Trapped within it were other pieces, one of which might have been a bruised heart behind a veil with a plume of red flowing out of it, diffuse as blood spilled in water. Within the ambiguous, organic form, a luminescence, like the reflection of a candle viewed through a stained glass window, or a life. Harry turned it this way and that and admired the effect. Somehow, it managed to absorb light and send it back changed. He didn't know how or why. It was one of those accidents that occurred as part of the process, like some unexpected patina that appears on cast bronze, unplanned and unique.

December 8, 1974 – Support

Harry met Elgin for a beer at Larry Blake's on the way home from the Campus. One had stretched to two then three. Elgin wouldn't shut up about the catalogue notes he was writing for a John Singer Sergeant retrospective. Harry had filled up on pretzels and chips and the time had gotten away from him. It was a stinging cold night, with an Arctic high-pressure front that had settled over Northern California, bringing the day time temperatures down to 40.

He found Darah at the table with Ali, who was just finishing her supper.

"Where were you? I called your office. I thought something might have happened to you." Her voice had the sound of someone who had just been in an accident and she had the hand wringing look of barely held back grief. Harry brushed it off as concern for his health combined with irritation because he hadn't called to say he'd be late, something he avoided in any event because it made him feel like she had him on a leash. She was always telling him to cut out the cigarettes, annoyingly so. He'd been out of the hospital now for five months, long enough to have fallen back into the patterns of a lifetime, though not completely so. Hidden from everyone, even from Darah, was a monitor on excess, the voice of an uncle telling him to take it easy. He had made a bargain with himself, a few cigarettes, not too many, a few drinks, and more sleep.

"I had a beer with Elgin and couldn't get away from him. You know how he is when he gets going."

"I needed to talk to you."

"What's wrong?"

"My father. . . ." She couldn't get the words out.

"Did something happen to him?"

"Grampa died," Ali said in the matter of fact way of the very young for whom death is still an abstraction. Franz got up and walked toward him. Harry let his hand drop onto the narrow head.

"How did it happen?"

"Coming into O'Hare in bad weather."

He went toward her, put his arm around her shoulder, and stroked her hair, going through the motions of consolation. In fact he felt nothing except the burden of sadness that came with every death, the ones seen on television: the victims of war, of car accidents, the serial murders, every death was an outrage. He hardly knew the man, had met him twice and found him friendly in a distant way. As for Darah, he'd always been too busy to be a real father to her. He had treated her like a major contributor to his campaign, except for the family photo opportunities. She couldn't feel that much now, he imagined, except guilt for not feeling more.

"Mommy's going to Chicago to be with Gramma because she's so sad," Ali announced.

"When are you going?"

"Tonight. I called Nina. She will stay with Ali."

"Good."

"I'll probably stay two weeks. Mom will need a lot of help. She's never been . . . Dad always handled everything."

"You'll come for a few days with Ali, for the funeral." It was more than a request.

"Don't ask me to do that." He reacted even before he could weigh the effect of his words, not even thinking that it might hurt her.

"Harry," she said her tone both a plea and a reproof.

He went to the stove, poured some coffee and sat down with her, realizing that he had hurt her and wanting to assuage it. "I hate funerals. I'd be no good to you. I'd just be in the way."

"You're my husband, Harry. I want you beside me on this."

"I didn't even know your father. He didn't even recognize me that last time we met."

"It's not for him. It's for me."

"It would make your mother uncomfortable. She doesn't like me."

"Maybe she would like you if she saw you giving me some support when I need it."

"You can't say you really care. You never liked him. You were never close."

"It's for my mother." Her voice trembled. "It's to close the book. You don't understand that do you? It's beyond you, beyond the bounds of your cosmic compassion. Never mind." She got up, not looking at him, her face closed. "I'd better pack."

"I'll drive you to the airport."

"Don't trouble yourself." She walked into the bedroom and closed the door.

Ali looked at him. "You hurt mommy's feelings, daddy. You better go say you're sorry."

"You really think so, Ali? Yeah, I think I did."

Harry went with Darah to the funeral.

May 2, 1975 – Opening

With its unfinished concrete walls and high windows, the

Berkeley Museum was the interior of a cubistic sculpture. Its open galleries ascended in stepped tiers around the perimeter of a central space to a concrete beamed ceiling.

"This space could have been built for my work," Harry said, looking around him.

"So what does it feel like, to see your life's work arrayed in a museum?" Elgin asked, swirling champagne in the glass and watching it fizz. There was ten minutes to go, the gallery was nearly empty, except for a few curatorial types and the caterers, the former doing a last minute review to make sure the descriptions matched the hung and positioned work, the latter opening wine bottles and arranging glasses on a red table cloth.

"A stratospheric high. An endless orgasm."

"I bet it does."

"There's another side of it, of course."

"What?"

"The end of expectation, anti-climax. What next. Is this the high point? Is it down hill from here? Anxiety that they won't come, that the critics will trash me."

"Or even worse, ignore you."

Darah came up to him, looking well put together; a tight fitting black dress, with a v-neck, lipstick, black heels. She gave him a kiss. "You OK?"

"Aside from the nausea and the shakes, I'm a rock."

"I wanna kiss you too daddy," said Ali looking up at him, her hair just combed, her new sky blue dress still unstained. He bent down; she wrapped her arms around his neck and gave him a wet kiss on the cheek. "Daddy is all this yours?"

"'Fraid so."

"That's a lot."

People began to drift in, some stopping to look at the work, others making for the bar, some seeking out Harry with congratulations. For the next hour he was surrounded by people who either struggled to get his attention to compliment his work or share some observation on a given piece.

In a lull, several of his colleagues, the "bootblacks" he called them, came up to him. He waited, not sure what they would say. Buckner spoke first, "Seeing it all stacked up, Harry, gives me new respect for your work." New respect my ass, Harry thought.

Leavis delivered his judgement next, "Too bad some of your best work isn't here. Well, congratulations. It's a tour de force in any event."

He looked at each of them with appropriate solemnity, intending to mask a mocking irony and said, "Thanks guys for all your help and support."

And Leavis, who had undercut him for years in every snide way, had the brass to say, "You deserved it, Harry." With that they drifted off, leaving him strangely triumphant and sour.

He looked around at the clusters of people, friends, collectors, museum staff, teachers, artists, several hundred in all, drinking boutique chardonnay, eating rumake and smoked salmon canapés circulated by the catering staff wearing short red jackets. Many guests were actually studying the work. Here he was, surrounded by the output of his life, the center of attention and adulation, whether or not sincere or transient. It was better than a bar mitzvah, and the 1938 Rolls Royce sent to bring him from his studio to the Museum had been a real surprise. Other similar triumphant moments came to him: the Cleveland mayor giving him the art award, his father showing one of the drawings he'd done in the sixth grade to all the relatives one Passover, the first piece anybody had bought at the first show in Paris.

He was suddenly alone and his eyes wandered around the room renewing his acquaintance with images and sculpture he hadn't seen for years. Each piece was speaking its own language to him, reading its own memory trail: pain, spontaneous combustion, anguish. Each one had its own biography, its own tie to him. He was pleased overall, but there were some that were not included and he recalled his petulance over the selection. He had fought with the committee to include his largest interior sculpture, but the budget had its limits. He had wanted them to fill the first upper gallery as well. It was only a sample. Even so, how many artists his age had gained this kind of attention? Caz would have been proud. Had he lived, Harry would have flown him over. He saw to it that Elgin had included his influence in the catalogue text.

Caz, more than anyone, had shown him the significance of the dialogue between the artist and the material. Harry sipped his champagne and wondered where he would have been now, if Caz hadn't gotten the offer to come to Berkeley. Serendipity. The roads not taken. He suddenly felt like a stranger at a show given for another artist.

Across the room, Elgin was holding court surrounded by his own retinue. Elgin's ego investment in the project was large. He had assumed almost a proprietary role and had given Harry's reputation the biggest single boost of his life. Well let him bask in it, Harry thought. The retrospective would never have happened if Elgin hadn't pushed it for years. And he couldn't have done it if the work wasn't consistently original.

He waived to his barber who acknowledged with a thumbs up salute. A museum trustee was steaming his way, her oversized body precariously perched on tiny spiked strapped heels. He adjusted the upper frog of his black velveteen jacket, hand tailored for the occasion, and turned to face one of his most recent soft silicon sculptures hoping she would pass him by. It had been long enough since he had finished it that he could look at it with a more or less fresh eye. It was flesh colored and glossy except where it was perforated by an eruption of what might have been dirt, the soil of People's Park. It called to mind a wound or a bullet hole.

"Pardon me, Mr. Baer."

He turned toward the voice relieved to see, not the trustee but a comely undergraduate with a doe's sensitive brown eyes, a lush gold silken head of hair, flaring lips and an open smile revealing even teeth with a slight overbite. She was dressed in a trim beige shirt dress that showed off her small waist and rounded hips. "I'm Nora Artimus from the *Daily Cal.*" she gave him a firm handshake.

"Nice to meet you Nora Artimus," he said returning her gaze. "I like your name, and you have beautiful eyes."

"Thank you," she looked alternately flattered and flustered by his attention. "Is this a good time to ask a few questions?" she asked with an earnest, hopeful look.

"As good as any." They began a stroll through the gallery,

picking up a train of people who followed and eavesdropped.

"Is there a common theme in your work?"

"Life and death in all of its disguises, anxiety, the fears that won't let go of us, evanescence, ambiguity."

She muttered, "hmm," in her deep appealing voice and dutifully wrote down everything on a green stenographer's pad with a yellow number 8 pencil.

"You have a remarkable facility with materials, those well, plastic looking sculptures for example."

"Cast epoxy, butyrate and Plexiglas."

"What made you want to work with them?"

"Curiosity. Just to see what happens when you do this or that. Experimentation. Fun. The same reason a good cook makes up a recipe."

John Salmonson approached him head on, ignoring the reporter. He was tall, thin, and was wearing an elegant Saville Row suit. John had the most successful gallery in San Francisco but had passed over Harry. "Very impressive, Harry."

"Thank you, John."

"Will you call me next week? I'd like to include some of your most recent work, the silicon pieces and the hand made paper sculptures, in a group show."

"With pleasure. Do you know Nora Artimus? She's a stringer for the *New York Times*."

"Really?" he said and without even acknowledging the introduction, looked beyond her and nodded to Derick Haus, one of the *Chronicle* art critics. "Excuse me," he said shearing off toward Derick and trading his empty wine glass for a full one mid-stride.

"He's the spitting image of a Macy's window dummy I once met in a bar. With one important difference. The dummy had a sense of humor," Harry said, and Nora exploded with laughter. A woman cut in front of them; Harry stopped abruptly and felt something bump into his back. He turned and looked into the eyes of Karine.

He wrapped his arms around her but she drew away. "My God, it's you," he exclaimed.

"It better be me or you're gonna feel pretty foolish kissing a total stranger."

"It's you alright. Same sardonic wit." Harry couldn't stop looking at her. She was still beautiful, sensual and ripe, an Indian deity. A little more flesh in the arms and below the waist and some fine lines around the eyes, he saw.

"Somebody's trying to get your attention, Harry." He looked away and remembered Nora.

"Can I call you and finish this tomorrow?"

"Sure, sure, any time," Harry said dismissing her with a momentary smile. "What are you doing in Berkeley?" he asked, feeling his heart pumping air. She looked the same, he thought, only a little more substance. The same close-set eyes, narrow nose contrasting with the full lips, and her skin hadn't aged at all.

"I'm back." She kept her eyes on his like radar locking on a target. She looked guarded, composed, watchful, like a wild animal ready to bolt if he made the wrong move.

"A visit."

"No. I'm the West Coast development director of the United Negro College Fund."

"That's a little tame for you isn't it?"

"Had enough excitement, thank you."

Elgin approached with a diminutive woman in her mid fifties. "Harry, Rosanna Birge would like to meet you."

He recognized the name. She was a wealthy Tiburon collector. He turned to her with a flash smile, took her frail hand and touched his lips to it. "Charmed, Mrs. Birge. I hope you're enjoying the opening." Without waiting for her response, indifferent to the respect in her eyes, he said, "You'll pardon me but I have just encountered an old friend and I don't want her to get away." He took Karine by the arm and steered her through the crowd. Passing a curious Darah he beckoned to Karine to follow him down the stairs to the lobby of the Pacific Film Archive. He stopped in front of a Marcel Pagnol poster.

"Same ol' Harry," she said.

"Different ol' Harry. Before you left you claimed my art was everything. Now you see I can walk out of my retrospective opening just to show you how important you are."

"Film it and hang it on the wall."

"You haven't lost your sting."

She softened and said, "I saw your wife and kid. Both lovely."

"Yeah, they are great."

"Your show is wonderful, Harry. You are the man of the hour."

"Thanks." She could still turn his bones to butter, after all this time. "It's incredible that you should turn up. Remember the first time we met, another opening, and I knocked over the cocktail wieners?"

"Yes, I remember. Listen, I'm flattered for the special attention, but you better get back up there. It's your big moment. May never come again."

"You never know, Karine." He turned to go then asked tentatively, "Can I call you?"

"I promise to answer the phone."

"Can we get together for coffee or something?"

"Depends on the something. I didn't come back to be a spoiler, Harry."

"Don't worry."

"No need to." She took a step away from him.

"Karine, you look great," he said wanting to touch her.

"Thanks. You look a little peaked, yourself."

May 14, 1975 – Conflict

They were sitting over the remains of dinner, Harry and Darah, just finishing the buttery crust of a still hot apricot tart.

"How did you like it?" Darah asked. Wearing faded jeans patched at the knees and a faded blue U. C. Berkeley sweatshirt, her hair cropped, she might have been a teen-ager. She picked up the gray stoneware mug and took a draught of coffee, watching Harry over the rim.

"Liked what?" He had been eating but his mind was rolling over the best method of impregnating pigment into hand made paper.

"The crust. It's a new recipe."

"I hadn't realized." He looked from the empty plate toward her.

"Are you kidding? It's totally different in texture and flavor."

"I liked it fine. It was great. What do you want, the Prix Gastronomique?"

"You don't have to be rude about it. Your opinion is important to me. You could at least show some interest in something that doesn't have the mark of your bottomless creativity. I know what I do is prosaic to you."

Since the opening, he'd been walking around in a fog. It wasn't the usual funk which came on him when the reviewers failed to understand what he had done or even worse when they made no mention of him at all. They had all been nice, this time, and not condescending, as if they were beginning to understand the importance and depth of his work. Suddenly with the shock of a photoflash she realized what was eating him. How dumb of her not to have seen it. He was mooning over Karine, mooning like a sixteen year old, which was giving him credit for too much maturity.

"Come off it, Darah. It's just that I take it for granted that you're a wonderful baker."

"You take me for granted."

"No I don't."

"You do. Lately you're like a sleep walker around me, except when you're talking about your work."

"Come on, Darah." His voice softened and he covered his pique with an uneasy smile. "What am I going to say to you about it. Do you like it? Is it nice? Is it pretty?"

"You don't give me any credit for understanding it."

"I give you plenty of credit. You're a great person: kind, humane, loving. But you're not my art mentor. Would you ask me how to make Tuscan bread?"

She answered with a wry shake of the head. "You've always got an answer and you really don't give a shit about my feelings." Darah got up and began to decisively clear the dishes with a lot of percussion.

"Want some help?" Contrite.

"Go back to your work." Rebuke.

Harry poured the last of the zinfandel into his French cafe glass and drank it off.

Out of the blue from behind her back she said, "Have you been seeing Karine since she got back?"

He looked up. "A couple of times, as you would expect."

"I would expect." She turned and faced him, her eyes level, earnest, and searching. "Have you slept with her?"

"No."

"Why not?"

"She doesn't want to be a home wrecker."

"That's a good one." She turned to the sink and began scraping a pot with a brush.

"You'll wear it out," he said looking at her rigid back.

" Did you tell her it was OK?"

"No."

"Don't."

"We just had some coffee! We talked. . . ." His voice rose. He was losing his patience. Darah had no right to dictate the terms of his social life. He was about to react but held back.

She turned to him, her face flush, a tear running down her cheek like a line of lacquer. "When we married it wasn't to tie you down or take away your freedom. I just wanted to be a part of your life. But things have changed, Harry. We've got Ali. We're a family."

"And we'll stay a family, whatever happens with Karine."

"No we won't." Her tone was hushed but heavy.

"What do you mean? I would never leave either of you."

"If you take up with her, Harry, I'll take Ali and walk." She said this tentatively, as though she were trying on something new to see if it fit. Once it was out of her mouth, she lowered her head and fixed him with a gaze that was both tentative and hard. It was something new and he felt like he had been shoved off balance. Harry offered a weak smile. He turned up his right hand in supplication.

The gestures brought a flush to Darah's cheeks. "I mean it Harry! Don't think you can laugh it off."

"I'm not."

"This isn't some swooning sophomore. Take up with her again and it will split you down the middle."

"Ok, ok, I get the picture, Darah. Calm down." He got up, went to her, wiped away a tear with his finger, kissed her softly on the lips, and she looked up at him with injured eyes.

"Darah, I have to admit to you. When she came back, it was not the way it was when she left. It felt like the first time I saw her."

She drew away from him. "I understand. Which makes it all the harder for you and for me. Can you accept that?"

"You are the greatest human being, Darah."

She answered with a look of bruising scorn and turned back to the sink.

May 18, 1975 – Karine Again

Harry was waiting on the edge of the parking lot in front of the Legion of Honor. He was leaning on the edge of the balustrade looking through the frame of dark shaggy Cyprus across the rolling brighter deep green of the golf course toward the City, observing in the sharp blue tinted light the twin white towers of the church in North Beach. His eye swept across the undulating white and gray mosaic of buildings and roofs bordered by a green ridge on the right and the negative space of the Bay and the misted Oakland hills beyond.

He looked at his watch. Karine was twenty minutes late. Maybe she had changed her mind. Impatience was turning to anger. He wanted her to come, if only to spend an hour or two near her. A tour bus stopped in front of the wide walk leading up to the Museum's white marble Roman facade. By the look of the solid occupants dressed in forest colors, brown and moss or loden greens, they were Germans. He turned away from the afternoon breeze that was coming through the Golden Gate and lit a cigarette. He would only smoke part of it.

After she left for Mississippi, he had put Karine behind him, in the way he parted with a loved sculpture shipped off to the dealer and sold to a stranger. It surprised, disquieted, and finally pleased him that the sight of her, her scent, and the touch of his palm on her back had awakened the desire to be with her. In some way she had become an unexpected part of the retrospective, another dimension of his life's work, one of the sources of his creativity. Since her return, he had

thought about her often, even when he and Darah were together in bed.

He smoked another cigarette, lighting it with the stub of
the last one. He shouldn't smoke. It wasn't good for his heart.
But he was fine, healthy again, working as hard as before with
a renewed intensity. The heart attack and months of recovery
had both defined the limit of his power and given him a new,
more intimate, view of death.

"Smokin'll be the death of you, Harry." he turned with an
instant smile as he heard her familiar dusty voice.

"You snuck up on me."

"You didn't see me drive up. I saw you leaning on the balustrade, in your beret. Is that the same beret?" her voice spun
up with the question a little flat, as the black dialect did and
probably had in Africa in some other tongue.

"You picked up an accent down south."

"Just for the effect, Harry. Same ol' me inside. A few extra
pounds from the southern cookin'."

"I noticed, but it looks good." She was wearing a dress
with a grape and chocolate brown swirling pattern that he
took to be African and her hair was tight on her scalp and
tied in a bun. "I don't like your hair that way."

"I didn't ask for a critique, not that my opinion ever stopped
you." He saw a burst of reproof in her eyes and he wondered
if it was too late to start up again. Did she despise him? Had
she come to the opening just to taunt him?

"Do you want to go inside?"

"We've come this far." Her smile was wry, ambiguous, but
she took his arm, adding to his confusion.

They walked through the colonnade into the open court,
passed the Rodin Thinker and entered the Museum. They
strolled one of the galleries, walking slowly, gripped in a self-
conscious awkward silence, stopping momentarily to look, but
not see, the paintings.

"A museum's a good place to revisit an old love," Harry
finally said.

Karine didn't acknowledge the quip. "You know, Harry, I've
never been much for art before the impressionists."

"Funny, you never told me that."

"You never asked me. You weren't much interested in what I thought. I was supposed to come along, be a backboard for your judgements and opinions."

"I'm asking you now."

"Tintoretto and Rafael weren't part of my cultural heritage."

"My father used to take me to the Art Museum. He loved it. Maybe that's what got me started."

They sat down on one of the benches in the gallery facing a Monet of lilies that covered most of a wall. The pond was layered with color, dense, and abstract from close up.

"Karine, I. . . ."

"Yes."

"I'm having a hard time beginning."

"Not you, Harry, the speechless humble routine won't win you any points."

"I wanted to say that seeing you made me feel like the first time I saw you." She looked like she didn't believe him. "Normally it's easy for me to walk away. Maybe its a flaw." She nodded slightly.

"Whatever there was between us, Harry, it wasn't strong enough to overcome your inhibitions about race." She had dropped the dialect. The words were coming from the upper class educated Karine who had spent her summers on Martha's Vineyard and had attended the Symphony with her parents since she was eleven.

"I wonder if it was more the fact that your parents both had graduate degrees that inhibited me,"

She shook her head and faced him with a flat look of disbelief.

"But whatever it was, you're right. I held back."

Her lips were tight and her breathing short and intense with unspoken angry words. "You didn't hold back. You spread it around. A little to the bimbos, a little to the student sycophants who spread their legs under their pleated kilts."

"You were too much for me, Karine. I couldn't handle you like I've handled everybody else in my life."

"Now that's an insight. Have you been seeing a shrink?"

"No, but I read a lot of do-it-yourself books."

"That's you all over. Do it yourself." Silence again as they stared at the deep opaque moving surface of the painting.

"Why did you come to the opening?" Karine had stepped on Harry's expectations. His voice was subdued and he was preparing to close the door on his hope.

"To celebrate your achievement."

"Wasn't there more? You wanted to see me didn't you?"

"No, not really. It took me long enough to get clean of you. I never have, if you want to know the truth. I've been with men but . . ."

"So you wanted to get together."

"Whatever I want or don't want doesn't matter. You've got a wife and a kid."

"We can still see each other."

"The museum, coffee? How are you? I'm fine? We've done that. No thanks."

"Karine. I had a heart attack last year. I almost died."

"I heard. How am I supposed to react to that? Pity?"

"I only meant to say that it's given me an urgency and an intensity about my work, life, everything. A clarity of sight as to what's important."

"What's important?" Her tone was mocking, skeptical.

"My work."

"Nothin' new about that."

"And sharing with people I love."

"Harry, you're maudlin. You ought to write a soap opera."

Her hostility was like ice water poured down his back. He stood up, walked closer to the painting. It had been a mistake. She was simply punishing him for the past. He began to doubt his own feelings for her. They were an illusion, a trick of the mind to restore something that was gone. He began to immerse himself in a study of the multi-layered surface of the painting.

He felt her beside him. "Harry," she said, her voice tender, contrite. "I'm sorry. I'm just bitter. All those lost years."

He turned toward her and said with exquisite sincerity, "You have every reason to be."

May 20, 1975 – Domesticity

"How many colors are there, dad?" Ali was sitting on the

floor, leaning forward over a large sheet of newsprint, a shoe box full of crayons of various sizes within reach, and twenty or thirty nubs of pastel sticks scattered on the floor in random pattern. Her blond hair hung loose and framed her face. She was wearing patched jeans and a tie-dyed T-shirt with a yellow sun burst surrounded by vermillion and blue streaks. She was concentrating on the drawing, moving the crayons with an intensity and spontaneity. Harry was nearby, bent over a wide table in a pool of white light, sketching, producing color patches and assembling detritus for a soft silicon gel sculpture. Responding to her question, he broke from his own work and turned to watch her.

"The colors in your crayon box?"

"No, in the whole world."

"As many as the stars in the Universe."

"How many is that?" She looked at him as though the question might decide the fate of a nation. Ali was intense about everything. Franz got up from a nap, stretched his body to twice its size and walked toward them. He looked closely at her drawing then, one large paw extending across it, dropped to the floor.

"See, that's you, Franzy," she said pointing with a crayon at a four-legged animal with a long pointed nose and jagged teeth.

"Millions. Every shade is unique."

"What's unique mean?"

"Different. Just like you are different from your friends in many ways." He picked up a dry maple leaf, handed it to her. "Now look very closely and you'll see all the many shades in the red and yellow."

She nodded soberly, studied the leaf, put it down and went back to her drawing. When it was finished, she pulled at Harry's sleeve to get his attention and they studied it together: a large happy sun, a dog sleeping at the feet of a child.

"Is it done?" She nodded. "Then let's put it up." They carried it to a wall and stuck it on with scotch tape along with half a dozen of her paintings and drawings, defined by a hand lettered sign that said, "Ali's Gallery".

7

Harry and Franz

May 27, 1975 – Final Stroke

She looked surprised to see him standing in the rhomboid of light from the half open door, Franz looking up at her, his feathery tail wagging hopefully.

"I was on the way home and just thought I'd stop to see if you were here."

"It's after eleven on a work night," Karine said with a guarded look. She was wearing only a brown cotton robe tied at the waist. Her hair was loose and hanging about her shoulders. "I was just about to take a bath," she added responding to his wandering gaze.

"Can I join you?"

"Same old Harry." Her full lips parted in an arch smile, less than inviting, he saw, but open to his hopes. "Who's your friend? Was he on the way by too?"

"Franz, a dog. Listen you'll catch cold if you don't close that door soon."

"Take your foot out of it and I will." Harry and Franz both looked at her with silent plea. "Come on in."

"Cute place."

"The owner says it used to be a goat shed." Looking pleased, Karine half turned and surveyed the place and Harry took his own rapid inventory: large mullioned bay with a window seat piled with mauve, grape and chocolate colored cushions, studio kitchen in what might have been a closet, even a small cast iron stove wedged in a corner. The furniture was casual, a cut above Goodwill except for the original Jacob

Lawrence painting over the maple table at the far end of the
room, a family scene with kids and old people.

"Where'd you get that?"

"I didn't sleep with him if that's what you mean."

"Don't be defensive."

"A present from my dad."

He looked around the other walls for the prints he had
given her. "Your prints are in the bedroom," she said as if she
had read his thoughts.

"Just where they ought to be."

Harry took off his jacket and dropped it on a maple chair.
Franz circled the room sniffing and collapsed on a hooked
rug in front of the stove.

"Can I get you something? Some brandy? Sorry I haven't
got any biscuits for the dog. I wasn't expecting him. Or you
for that matter."

"You knew I'd show up." She didn't respond as she went
to the kitchen cabinets, old dark redwood with leaded glass
fronts. She brought out two brandy snifters and poured two
fingers for each of them.

Harry took the glass, clinked it with hers, "To Life," and
drank half of it. Karine sat down on the sofa half facing him.
He lit a cigarette and looked at her through the fluting smoke.

She reached out, took the cigarette from his hand and put
it out. "Don't smoke, Harry." Her tone was soft, even tender.
She let her hands drop to her thighs and looked at him. "Tell
me what you are working on."

"Those soft silicon sculptures. You saw a couple of them
at the retrospective. They've got phosphorescent pigment so
that in the dark they glow with purple and other colors like
some tropical fish. And they are soft like flesh."

"Sounds like you're trying to make them live."

"You could say that. Mind if I take some more brandy?"

"Help yourself. If you're allowed to drink it."

"You sound like Darah." He poured himself two fingers,
added some more with a defiant grin, took another gulp and
sighed. "That's better. I'm tired, I've been working since early
morning." He felt the hot trail of liquor and a relaxed rush of
heat in his head and he let himself settle back into the cushions.

"At the studio?"

"Yes."

"Then you weren't on the way home."

"I ran out of cigarettes."

"So you came six miles out of the way for cigarettes."

"I came to see you."

"What did you tell Darah?"

"She's up at the Bolinas house."

"I think I get it now."

"I thought you got it at the Museum." He reached up and touched her hair, let his hand alight on her shoulder, brought it back to his lap.

"What do you want from me, Harry?"

Her gaze was earnest, searching. He had finally breached her defenses and was looking into her tender core now, the part of her that was faithful and true to whatever she believed in. Once she had believed in him, believed in the constancy of his love in spite of all the conflicts, the distractions, the peccadilloes. Now he wanted her to know that the core of his feelings were as pure they had been then. At the moment he was convinced that they were. In spite of his love for Darah, what he felt for Karine was of a different pallet. "Just what we had."

"It's gone. Those years have gone, those hours, those times, those two people are gone."

"No they aren't. They are glowing inside of each of us, just like that phosphorescent stuff inside the Souls that I make. All they need is light to bring them out."

"What do we need?"

"Only touch." He reached out and gently drew her towards him and she yielded. Their lips met, she let her cheek touch his. It radiated through him and opened like a white camellia. His heart began to race, he felt lightheaded, and her breath became a deep audible sigh like wind stirring winter branches. They clung together gently, and gradually he let his fingers get to know again the mounds and swales of her, and she felt his touch deep inside her.

Karine had tried to put him off out of true deference to his family. She had been too many times the victim of his wandering to inflict the same pain on another woman, no matter how much she wanted to be with him again, at least once. She had never stopped wanting Harry. His image had lurked behind every man she had been with. Now his touch, his scent, his aura, steadily washed away her defenses as a wave might melt a sand castle. Let it be so.

She took him by the hand and led him into the bedroom. They fell together on the patchwork quilt that covered the bed and slowly she undressed him while he caressed her. Franz followed them and sat down at the foot of the bed his ears cocked, eyes fixed on them.

Where she touched him he was sanctified, transformed from flesh and bone to ether, to music echoing through him. He rose to her and she took him in with great arcing sighs. They met and merged, and for once in his life except for his dreams, he lost all sense of himself. There was only the coursing thrill, the splashing images. Random fleeting flashes of root quickly extending through opaque soil, granite surfaces grinding against each other like mill stones, lines etching into a plate. Half-formed creatures dissolved into each other like salt in a tide pool, became defined viscous tracks, ebbing and flowing with the motion of an unseen force then disappearing.

He heard a sigh that might have been a last breath, a bark that could have been an explosion, and he saw what might have been the mute tableau of a battle field: puffs of smoke, endless pocked mud, pits half full of murky water, men in strange gray uniforms holding rifles. He saw a man he thought he knew collapse and roll into a crater, his lifeless feet resting in the black water, his hand clawing the gray mud. The field was suddenly empty and dark, except for a dog, a collie, looking down at the man or at him, prodding him with his cold wet nose, barking silently, his mouth opening and closing.

From within that vacuum forming from the vapors rising from the crater emerged a fan of horizontal late sun and within it, a meadow bordered by a white fence, and within the pale, three horses grazing, black and white, all of which he had seen before. Outside the fence, ahead on a path drawn between tall grasses, he saw a girl, her light brown hair soft and billowing like a cloud. She turned and he saw her familiar face, soft flaring lips, smiling open showing even teeth, her eyes beckoning, smiling too, narrow eyes of jade, with brows like gull's wings. She spoke, his name perhaps, and beckoned with her hand, and then she turned and walked on. Some part of him, a residue of passion, trembling light rising from and falling after the memory of the now set sun, some part of him followed. . . .

Shards

June 3, 1975 – San Francisco Chronicle

NOTED ARTIST DIES

"Harry Baer, well known artist and sculptor, died suddenly of a heart attack while visiting a friend. He is survived by his wife, Darah, and two daughters, Alida and Therese. Baer was a member of the studio art faculty at the University of California at Berkeley. His work is in major museum collections including the New York Museum of Modern Art, the Cleveland Museum of Art and the Guggenheim Museum. A major retrospective of his work will travel the country next year and finish at the Whitney Museum of American Art. He was born in Cleveland, Ohio served in World War II in the European theater and lived and studied in France. At the memorial service held on the Berkeley Campus, Professor Bear was extolled for his continual innovation and his dedication to his students. . . ."

Darah and Karine

"I'm very sorry, Darah. Very sorry."
"It wasn't your fault."
"I really tried to keep my distance."
"Nothing could keep Harry from getting what he wanted. Besides, I know that he loved you."
"In his way."

"I told him I'd leave him if he took up with you again, I have to tell you that. But Harry always had the last word. Instead he left me." Darah began to laugh. She couldn't stop herself. It quickly turned to weeping.

Karine took her in her arms and held her feeling the convulsive sobbing and the tears and the void.

New York Times

FRANZ MARC SKETCHBOOK BRINGS $125,000 AT AUCTION

A sketchbook authoritatively attributed to Franz Marc, co-founder with Vasily Kandinsky of the Blaue Reiter movement, brought $125,000 last night at the Sotheby auction of Twentieth Century Art. It was purchased by an unknown bidder. Believed to have been largely the product of Marc's war time experience, the sketch book included drawings and notes in the artist's handwriting. It was sold by the estate of California artist, Harry Baer. It had been in the artist's possession since his stay in France after World War II. He is said to have acquired it at a Paris flea market for the equivalent of two dollars.

Darah and Ali

Ali had a lump of Harry's clay and was kneading it. Having shaped it into a crude ball she took the end of a paintbrush and punched two holes for eyes and cut a deep line for a mouth. Finally she pinched the clay and formed a nose.

"What are you making Ali?"

"It's Daddy. We can bake it just like he did, and when it's done I'll put it on the table next to my bed. You think it's done? "

"Not quite." Darah left for a time and returned with an eighth of a cup of gray-black ashes. She spilled the contents of the cup on to a piece of waxed paper, spread them like powdered sugar and rolled the soft clay sculpture around in them until the clay was impregnated and thoroughly coated. Ali watched. She knew and understood. They baked it at 475 degrees for one hour.

Some of Harry's ashes they scattered off of a rock on the beach in front of their house. It mingled with the spume and rode the outgoing tide. A few days later in the afternoon, with a strong wind gusting off the ocean, they took handfuls, tossed them into the wind and let them fly. Once free, they unwound like a gray silk scarf and soared aloft, the ghost of a gull in pursuit of the infinite.

Acknowledgements

The help of the following people is gratefully acknowledged: Mary Mackey, novelist; Ira Wood and John Taylor-Convery, editors; Laurie Dolphin, designer; Paula Shuster, publicist. Others who contributed to the process are Judy and Talia Greene, Debby Paris, Joseph Goldyne, Connie Wirtz, Peter Selz, Ruth Braunstein, Tony Henning, University Art Museum, University of California at Berkeley, and of course Franz Marc and Harold Paris. Images on the cover are derived from catalogues published by the University of California, the Berkeley Art Museum and are reproduced with their consent. The painting fragment is from *Animals in a Landscape (Painting with Bulls II)* the original of which is in the collection of the Detroit Institute of Arts.

About the Author

Sheldon Greene is the author of *Lost & Found* (Random House). He lives in Berkeley where he is an avid art collector and sings bass with the Oakland Symphony Chorus.